MARCHING THROUGH
PEACHTREE

MARCHING THROUGH PEACHTREE

HARRY TURTLEDOVE

MARCHING THROUGH PEACHTREE

This is a work of fiction. All the characters and events portrayed in this book are fictional, and any resemblance to real people or incidents is purely coincidental.

A Baen Books Original

Baen Publishing Enterprises
P.O. Box 1403
Riverdale, NY 10471
www.baen.com

ISBN: 0-671-31843-8

Cover art by David Mattingly

First printing, November 2001

Library of Congress Cataloging-in-Publication Data

Turtledove, Harry.
    Marching through Peachtree / by Harry Turtledove.
      p. cm.
    "A Baen Books original"—T.p. verso.
    ISBN 0-671-31843-8
    1. Civil war—Fiction. 2. Serfdom—Fiction. I. Title.

PS3570.U76 M37 2001
813'.54—dc21   2001037898

Distributed by Simon & Schuster
1230 Avenue of the Americas
New York, NY 10020

Production by Windhaven Press, Auburn, NH
Printed in the United States of America

10   9   8   7   6   5   4   3   2   1

MARCHING THROUGH
PEACHTREE

I

Count Joseph, called the Gamecock, was not a happy man. Joseph was seldom a happy man; he would have been of more service to King Geoffrey had he been. But then, he most cordially loathed his sovereign, a feeling that was mutual. Still and all, when Avram, the new King of Detina, had made it plain he intended to free the blond serfs in the northern provinces, Joseph couldn't stomach that, either. Sooner than accepting it, he and the rest of the north had followed Avram's cousin, Grand Duke— now King—Geoffrey, into rebellion.

A sour expression on his face, Joseph—a dapper, erect little man with neat graying chin whiskers on his long, thin, clever face—left his pavilion and stared south toward the province of Franklin, from which the foe would come . . . probably before too long. The air of southern Peachtree Province was warm and moist with spring. It would have been sweet with spring, too, but for the presence of Joseph's army and its encampment by the little town of Borders. Not even the sweetest spring air could outdo thousands of slit trenches and tens of thousands of unwashed soldiers.

One of Joseph's wing commanders came up to him. Some

said Roast-Beef William had got his nickname from his red, red face, others from his favorite dish. Saluting, he said, "Good morning, your Grace."

"Is it?" Joseph the Gamecock asked sardonically.

"Well, yes, sir, I think it is," William replied. Unlike a lot of officers who followed King Geoffrey, he was not a man of breeding. He *was* a skilled tactician, and had written the tactical manual both Geoffrey's soldiers and the southrons used. Also unlike a lot of Geoffrey's officers, Joseph emphatically included, he was not a prickly man, always sensitive of his honor. He'd even got on pretty well—as well as anyone could—with Joseph's luckless predecessor in command of the Army of Franklin, Count Thraxton the Braggart.

"By the Lion God's mane, what makes you think so?" Joseph inquired with real if dyspeptic curiosity. He pointed south. "Every southron in the world—well, every southron east of the Green Ridge Mountains—who can carry a crossbow or a pike is gathering there with nothing on his mind but stomping us into the mud. Gods damn me to the seven hells if I'm sure we can stop them, either."

"Things could be worse, sir," Roast-Beef William said stolidly. "Things bloody well *were* worse when the southrons chased us up here last fall after they drove us off Sentry Peak and Proselytizers' Rise. I was afraid this whole army would just up and fall to pieces then, Thunderer smite me if I wasn't."

"I know precisely how bad things were then, Lieutenant General," Joseph the Gamecock said. "Precisely." He pronounced the word with acerbic gusto.

"How could you, sir?" William inquired, confusion on his face. "You weren't here then."

"How could I? I'll tell you how. Things were so bad, King Geoffrey felt compelled to lift me from the shelf where he stowed me, dust me off, and put me back in the service of his kingdom. Things had to be pretty desperate, wouldn't you say, for his bad-tempered Majesty to chew his cud of pride and judge a soldier only by his soldierly virtues and not by whose hindquarters he kisses?"

Earnest and honest, Roast-Beef William coughed and

looked embarrassed. "Sir, I wouldn't know anything about that."

"Lucky you." Joseph's scorn was withering as drought in high summer. "Three years of war now, and I've been on the king's shelf for half that time, near enough."

"You were wounded, sir," William reminded him.

"Well, what if I was? I shed my blood for this kingdom in Parthenia Province, protecting Geoffrey in Nonesuch, and what thanks did I get? I was shoved aside, given an impossible assignment by the Great River, blamed when it turned out I couldn't do the impossible, and put out to pasture till Thraxton so totally buggered up this campaign, even Geoffrey couldn't help but notice."

"Er, yes, sir." Roast-Beef William nervously coughed a couple of times, then asked, "Sir, when the southrons move on Marthasville, can we hold them out of it?"

"We have to," Joseph said. "It's the biggest glideway junction we have left. If we lose it, how do we move men and goods between Parthenia and the east? So we have to make the best fight we can, Lieutenant General. That's all there is to it. We have to hold the foe away from Marthasville." He brightened as much as a man of his temperament could. "And here comes a man who will help us do it. Good day to you, Lieutenant General Bell!" He bowed to the approaching wing commander.

"Good day, sir." Bell's voice was deep and slow. His approach was even slower. He stayed upright only with the aid of two crutches and endless determination. He'd lost a leg leading soldiers forward in the fight by the River of Death, and he'd had his left arm crippled in the northern invasion of the south only a couple of months before that. Using the crutches was torment, but staying flat on his back was worse for him.

"How are you feeling today, Lieutenant General?" Joseph asked solicitously.

"It hurts," Bell replied. "Everything hurts."

Joseph the Gamecock nodded. He recalled Bell from the days before he'd got hurt, when the dashing young officer had made girls sigh all through the north. Some called Bell the Lion God come to earth. With his long, full, dark beard and his fiercely handsome features, he'd lived up to the name. He'd also lived up to it with his style of fighting. He'd thrown himself and his men at the southrons and broken them time and again.

Now he'd broken himself doing it. His features still showed traces of their old good looks, but ravaged by pain and blurred by the heroic doses of laudanum he guzzled to try to dull it. "Does the medicine do you any good?" Joseph inquired.

Bell shrugged with his right shoulder only; his left arm would not answer. "Some," he said. "Without it, I should be quite mad. As things are, I think I am only . . . somewhat mad." His chuckle was wintry. "I have to take ever more of it to win some small relief. But my mind is clear."

"I am glad to hear it," Joseph said. He didn't fully believe it. Laudanum blurred thought as well as pain. But it did so more in some men than in others. Though he carried scars of his own, he didn't like to think about what Lieutenant General Bell had become. To hide his own unease, he went on, "Roast-Beef William and I were just talking about our chances of holding the southrons away from Marthasville this campaigning season."

"We had better do it," Bell said in his dragging tones. Laudanum was probably to blame for that, too, but he'd reached the right answer here. Joseph was in no doubt of it whatsoever. His wing commander continued, "The southrons humiliated us at Sentry Peak and Proselytizers' Rise. We have to keep them out of Marthasville or we become a laughingstock."

That wasn't the reason Joseph the Gamecock wanted to keep General Hesmucet's army out of Marthasville, or Roast-Beef William, either, but Bell wasn't necessarily wrong. Joseph said, "By what I hear, we humiliated ourselves at Proselytizers' Rise."

"I wouldn't know, sir, not firsthand," Bell replied. "I was, ah, trying to get used to being lopsided, you might say." Joseph nodded, trying not to stare at the pinned-up leg of Bell's blue pantaloons.

"I believe you're correct, sir," Roast-Beef William said. "Count Thraxton's spell did not work as he'd hoped it might."

"No, eh?" Joseph the Gamecock's voice dripped sarcasm. "I never would have noticed. Why, I thought we'd be moving from Rising Rock on to Ramblerton next week. That *is* our plan, isn't it?"

"Sir?" Lieutenant General Bell said, face blank from more than laudanum. He wouldn't have recognized irony had it pierced him like iron.

"All right, sir," Roast-Beef William said—he, at least, got the point Joseph was making. "Count Thraxton's magic flat-out failed. It beat us. Without it, why would our men have run from the top of Proselytizers' Rise when they could have held off every southron in the world if only they'd stood their ground?"

"Still no excuse for that skedaddle," Bell said. "No excuse at all. You go forward and you fight like a man. That's what the gods love."

You go forward and you fight like a man. Bell had lived by that, and he'd nearly died by it, too. *Now I'm in command here, and we'll try things my way,* Joseph thought. *If we can make the southrons pay and pay and pay for every foot of ground they take, maybe all their mechanics and artisans and farmers will get sick of fighting us and let us have our own kingdom. It's the best hope we have, anyhow—we're not going to drive them away by force of arms.*

"I intend to make the enemy come forward and fight like men," he said. "I intend to make them die like men, too, in the largest numbers I can arrange. Let's see if they go on backing Avram's plan to crush us into the dust and free all our blonds from the land after they've spent a while bleeding."

"Not chivalrous," Bell said.

"I don't care," Joseph the Gamecock replied. That brought shock to Lieutenant General Bell's face despite the laudanum he poured down. Joseph repeated it: "I don't care—and by all the gods, my friends, that is the truth. I am here to keep the southrons from snuffing out this kingdom. Whether I do that or not matters. How I do it . . . Who cares?"

"Don't you want the bards singing songs about you hundreds of years after you're dead?" Bell asked. "Don't you want them treating you the same way they treated the heroes of the first conquest, the men who crossed the Western Ocean and threw down the blonds' kingdoms?"

"I couldn't care less," Joseph said, and shocked Bell all over again. "King Geoffrey gave me this job to do. He thought I was the right man for it, and I aim to show him he was right." *I aim to show him he was a perfect jackass for not giving me more to do a long time ago.*

Roast-Beef William said, "A defensive campaign on our part will be the most expensive for the southrons and the least expensive for us. Since General Hesmucet has far more men than we do, we need every advantage we can find."

"Where is the valor in letting the enemy dictate the terms of the campaign?" Bell asked.

"Where is the sense in attacking the enemy when you are weaker than he?" Joseph the Gamecock returned.

"We attacked the southrons at the River of Death and prevailed," Bell said.

"Yes, and you outnumbered them when you did it, too," Joseph pointed out. "King Geoffrey detached James of Broadpath's force—and you with it, Lieutenant General—from Duke Edward of Arlington's Army of Southern Parthenia and sent it here by glideway to add its weight to the fight. Without it, Count Thraxton would have been badly outnumbered, and wouldn't have attacked."

Slowly, Bell shook his head. "You make war most coldbloodedly, your Grace."

"King Geoffrey says the same thing," Joseph replied. "As you may have gathered, the king and I have a good many differing opinions. My opinion is that one makes war for the purpose of defeating the enemy by whatever means are available. If that involves wearing him out to the point where he chooses not to fight any more, so be it. I see no better hope. Do you?" He looked from Bell to Roast-Beef William.

"No, your Grace, though I wish I did," William said.

"My own view is that the purpose of war is to fight, to smash the foe," Lieutenant General Bell said.

"If we could do that, nothing would make me happier," Joseph the Gamecock said. "Do you see us doing it against

General Hesmucet and the host he has assembled by Rising Rock?"

Had Bell nodded to that, Joseph would have lost his temper. But the cripple who still wanted to be a soldier shook his big, leonine head. "It is as my comrade says," he answered. "I wish I did, but I do not."

"All right, then," Joseph told him. "We are in accord." He had his doubts about that, but, for once, did not state them. He made more allowances for Bell than for most men—certainly more than he made for King Geoffrey. "That being so, I intend to make my fight in the way I mentioned. I have sent orders to the north and west to have estate-holders get their serfs out to start building fieldworks for us."

"Already, sir? So soon?" Roast-Beef William asked in surprise.

"Already. So soon," Joseph the Gamecock said grimly. "You're our master tactician, Lieutenant General, so think tactically here. If we are going to make this kind of fight, shouldn't we get ready for it ahead of time? Otherwise, our soldiers would have to do the digging themselves, as the southrons do."

"Here I agree with you completely," Bell said. "Not fitting for Detinans to do such labor when we can call on the subjected blonds."

"Just so," Joseph said; he was, for once, as well pleased to have escaped argument. "Unless this campaign very much surprises me, we shall need those works."

"If Hesmucet thinks he and the southrons can storm straight through us, he had better think again," Bell said. "I have to be strapped onto a unicorn to stay aboard, but I expect I may have one last charge left in me."

Joseph the Gamecock was an irascible man, yes, but also a courtly one. He did not care to think about twice-mangled Lieutenant General Bell going at the foe like that, but bowed from respect for his courage. Bell would do it; he didn't doubt that in the least. Bell would, in fact, surely do it with a song on his lips. That didn't mean Joseph didn't reckon him somewhere close to mad for even thinking of such a thing.

But Joseph didn't say that, either. What he did say was, "Let us hope, gentlemen, that we never have the need for such desperate measures." For a wonder, neither Roast-Beef William nor Lieutenant General Bell disagreed with him.

From his unicorn, General Hesmucet looked west to Proselytizers' Rise, then north to Sentry Peak, the stony knob that towered above the town of Rising Rock. The autumn before, blue-clad men who called Grand Duke Geoffrey the rightful King of Detina had held both strongpoints. The traitors' flag, red dragon on gold, had flown above them. Even Hesmucet, as grimly aggressive a warrior as any who followed King Avram against the traitors, marveled that the northerners had been driven from those heights, but now Avram's banner, the proper royal banner, gold dragon on red, waved over the high ground.

Hesmucet scratched at his chin. He wore a close-cropped, almost stubbly black beard, just beginning to be streaked with gray as he edged into his forties. He was not very tall and not very thick through the shoulders, but had a lithe sort of wrestler's strength that made him much more dangerous in a mêlée than he looked. He also had a driving energy that was, at the moment, aimed northwest.

Beside him, mounted on a unicorn finer than his own, sat Lieutenant General George, his second-in-command. Turning to him, Hesmucet said, "We're going to smash right through the traitors, by all the gods."

"May it be so, sir," George replied, "but I have my doubts."

"Of course you do," Hesmucet answered. "Why else would they call you Doubting George?" They also called George the Rock in the River of Death; if it hadn't been for the stand his soldiers had made the autumn before, Thraxton the Braggart's men wouldn't just have beaten southron General Guildenstern's army—they would have annihilated it. George had earned all the credit he'd got for himself that day.

Hesmucet contemplated General Guildenstern's fate. These days, that worthy was chasing blond savages on the trackless steppes of the east. He was lucky to have been allowed to remain in King Avram's service: if going off to the steppes to harry savages counted as luck, at any rate.

That could happen to me if I bungle this campaign, General Hesmucet thought. Unusually for a Detinan, he was named after a blond himself: the chieftain who'd given the kingdom so much trouble in the War of 1218. That did nothing to improve his opinion of blonds, and especially of unsubdued blonds. As far as he was concerned, the only good one was a dead one.

He brought himself back to the business at hand. "I had a message by scryer this morning from Marshal Bart in the west," he told Doubting George.

"Did you indeed?" George said, as if that were a great surprise to him. "And what did the marshal say?"

"That he is moving north today against Duke Edward of Arlington and the Army of Southern Parthenia," Hesmucet answered.

"Thunderer and Lion God bring him all success," George said. Hesmucet wondered exactly what the lieutenant general was thinking. Like Duke Edward, Doubting George was a Parthenian. Also like Edward, he was a serfholding noble. Unlike Edward, though, he'd stayed loyal to Avram and the idea of a united Detina rather than going into revolt and treason with his province and false King Geoffrey.

Did George ever stop to count the cost? He'd paid one: Geoffrey had confiscated his lands (as Avram had confiscated Duke Edward's estate, which lay just across the river from the royal capital at Georgetown). Had George chosen to shout, "Provincial prerogative forever!" he could have kept his holdings—and the north would have gained a dangerous fighting man.

George looked north and west, too. "If Marshal Bart is setting off to tangle with Duke Edward and the Army of Southern Parthenia, don't you suppose it's time we paid a social call on Joseph the Gamecock and the Army of Franklin?"

"Ah," Hesmucet said. "That must be what this little assemblage here is all about."

Again, Doubting George spoke as if in surprise: "Well, who would ever have thought of such a thing?"

This time, Hesmucet looked back over his shoulder. The entire might of his force was mustered there: unicorn-riders aboard mounts whose horns were shod with polished iron; pikemen whose spearheads gleamed in the bright spring sun; endless regiments of crossbowmen with shortswords on their hips to give them something with which to fight in case they shot their bolts and missed; mages riding asses. The soldiers' tunics and pantaloons and the mages' robes were all of one shade of gray or another. Hundreds of color-bearers carried the red dragon on gold. Great columns of ass-drawn supply wagons and siege engines on wheeled carriages completed the immense warlike host.

"Are we ready?" Hesmucet asked George.

"You're the general commanding, sir," Doubting George replied. Hesmucet cocked his head to one side, studying the reply. George wished Marshal Bart had named him, not Hesmucet, commander over all of King Avram's armies east of the Green Ridge Mountains. He made no bones about that. But was he so jealous and resentful as to be unable to serve as Hesmucet's chief subordinate?

He'd better not be, Hesmucet thought. *If he is, I'll find somebody else, and I won't waste a heartbeat before I do.* For now, he gave George the benefit of the doubt. "That's right," he said. "I am. Let's go, then."

He waved to the mounted trumpeters just behind him. Their polished bugles gleamed like gold under the strong spring sun as they raised them to their lips. The first thrilling notes of the Detinan royal hymn blared forth. A moment later, a great cheer from the long column of gray-clad soldiers drowned out the hymn.

"Forward!" Hesmucet shouted, trying to make himself heard above the din. "Forward against the traitors!" Those of his men who did hear him cheered louder than ever.

In the manner of a northern noble, Doubting George made his unicorn rear and paw the air with its forelegs. That, too, wrung a cheer from the soldiers. Hesmucet, who was only an ordinary rider himself, found the stunt showy and artificial. Again, he wondered whether George was trying to show him up. Again, he gave his second-in-command the benefit of the doubt.

I wonder if Joseph the Gamecock has these worries, he thought as he began to ride north. *I know Thraxton the Braggart did. But then, Thraxton worried about every officer under his command. He did everything he could to make every officer under his command hate him, too. Just as well for the rightful king's cause that Thraxton never came close to realizing it.*

Thraxton, these days, was back in Nonesuch, giving King Geoffrey advice. The two of them got on well, however much trouble both of them had getting along with anybody else. *They deserve each other*, Hesmucet thought.

"You're not dividing up the force," Lieutenant General George remarked.

"No, I'm not," Hesmucet agreed. "I don't know where in the seven hells we'll end up having to fight. Wherever it is, I want to strike as hard a blow as I can with my men."

"Good," Doubting George said. "When Guildenstern marched north from Rising Rock last fall, he split his army into three parts. We're lucky Count Thraxton didn't destroy us in detail. Losing the battle by the River of Death was bad, but that would have been even worse."

"I've got a whole swarm of scouts out ahead of us," Hesmucet said. "If Joseph wants to try to ambush me, I wish him joy of it."

"He won't have an easy time of it," George agreed. "But he has his own scouts, too, you know."

Hesmucet nodded sourly. "Every single gods-damned northerner who sees us is a scout for Joseph the gods-damned Gamecock," he said, and waved in the direction of a woman planting crops in a field. "Her husband's probably fighting for Geoffrey, and she probably has ways of getting news to his commanders."

"Too true," George said. "The other thing you'll notice in country where we've been around for a while is that you'll see almost no blonds in the fields. They will all have abandoned their lands and their liege lords and run off to us."

"I know," Hesmucet replied. "And gods damn me to the hells if I know whether that's a good thing or not,

Lieutenant General. I have no great use for blonds. I never have, and I probably never will. I don't know what the devils we're going to do with all these northern blonds if they aren't going to be serfs any more. And if anybody, including King Avram himself, has any clearer notion, it would come as a great surprise to me."

Doubting George chuckled. "You sound more like a northern aristocrat than many a northern aristocrat I've heard. If you feel that way, why didn't you side with Grand Duke Geoffrey against King Avram? Some few southrons did."

"And they're all traitors, too, and they all deserve to be crucified for treason right along with Geoffrey," Hesmucet ground out. "It's very simple, as far as I'm concerned. There is only one Kingdom of Detina. One, mind you, not two or three or twelve or twenty-seven. And there's no doubt whatsoever that Avram is the rightful King of Detina. As far as I can see, that settles that. I'm a simple man. I don't much believe in or care about complicated arguments."

"Any man who calls himself simple opens himself to suspicion, in my view," George said. "If someone else calls him simple, simple he may be. If he calls himself simple, simple he is not, for if he were, he would not see that there was any other possibility."

"Hmm." After thinking about it for a little while, Hesmucet took off his gray felt hat and scratched his head. "That's a little too . . . unsimple for me."

"Is it? You'll forgive me, sir, but I have my doubts about that," Doubting George said. He hadn't got his nickname by accident; from everything Hesmucet could see, he had his doubts about everything. After a moment, he went on, "And things generally aren't quite so clear as you make them out to be, if you'll be kind enough to forgive me that as well."

"No, eh?" Now Hesmucet bristled. He didn't care to be told he was, or even might be, mistaken about anything. "How not?"

"Well, sir, if you reckon blonds worthless for anything but serfdom, how is it that you have some thousands of them serving in the various regiments of your army?"

"They aren't all good soldiers, by any means." Having

taken a position, Hesmucet was not a man to retreat from it even in the face of long odds.

"No doubt you're right, sir." For a moment, Lieutenant General George sounded like the northern noble he was: most dangerous when most polite. "But then, would you say all the ordinary Detinans fighting for King Avram are good soldiers?"

"Only a fool would say all of them are, and I hope I'm not that particular kind of fool," Hesmucet replied. "I will say, though, that more Detinans make good soldiers than is true for the blonds. We're warriors in the blood, and they're not." He stuck out his chin and defied Doubting George to disagree with him.

And Doubting George didn't—not, at least, in so many words. He did murmur, "Surely the chieftain for whom you're named would have some remarks on that subject." Hesmucet's ears grew hot; Hesmucet the blond had been as fierce a warrior as any ever born, whether of his kind or among the swarthy Detinans. George added, "These northern blonds, you must recall, have been raised as serfs. If you untie a man who's been tightly bound, do you not expect to see the marks of the rope on his flesh for a time?"

"Well, well," Hesmucet said. "I didn't think you were a blond-lover, sir."

He wondered if he'd gone too far. In a different tone of voice, that could have been a deadly insult. As things were, George only shrugged and remarked, "Some of them, I assure you, are quite lovable." He took his hands from the reins for a moment to shape an hourglass in the air.

Hesmucet laughed. "Well, maybe so. I have heard stories along those lines. I suspect you would know better than I, though." How *had* Doubting George amused himself on his estate in Parthenia? Did he use the labor of any young serfs who looked like him?

George didn't answer any of that. Instead, he counterattacked: "You had your chances, too, sir, didn't you? Don't I remember that you were teaching in a military collegium near Old Capet when Grand Duke Geoffrey took the northern provinces out of Detina?"

"I was indeed," Hesmucet replied. "But what you also

need to remember is that I had my wife along with me while I was there."

"I see," George said. "Yes, that could matter. It would make more difference to some than to others, I suppose."

Which sort are you? lingered behind his words. "I'm not General Guildenstern, if that's what you're wondering," Hesmucet said.

"Few men are," Doubting George replied. "I know of at least one pretty little blond girl in Rising Rock whom Marshal Bart—he was only General Bart then, of course— turned down flat. Not that she was so flat herself, you understand, and not that Guildenstern had turned her down before, either."

"I'm not surprised Bart turned her down," Hesmucet said. "He really is enamored of his wife."

"She—the blond girl—was quite miffed," George said. "Marshal Bart's wife would have been, had things gone otherwise. 'Turned me down flat,' the maid kept saying."

"Let's see if we can turn the traitors down flat," Hesmucet said, and his second-in-command nodded agreement. Hesmucet wondered if George had tried to soothe the blond girl's wounded feelings. Bold as he was, he lacked the nerve to ask.

Captain Gremio was still getting used to wearing epaulets on both shoulders. He'd spent the first two and a half years of the war as Captain Ormerod's lieutenant in this company of crossbowmen recruited from in and around Karlsburg, the capital and chief town of Palmetto Province. But Ormerod had stopped a crossbow quarrel trying to stem the northerners' rout at Proselytizers' Rise, and so the company had been in Gremio's hands ever since. He'd finally even got the rank that went with company command.

Not all the other officers in Colonel Florizel's regiment approved of Gremio's promotion. His lip curled. He had a long, thin, intelligent face—and a gift for making his lip curl and assuming other expressions at need: he was a reasonably successful barrister in Karlsburg.

His success in his chosen field kept his brother officers from making their sneers too open. But it also guaranteed that the sneers would be there. Almost all those putative brothers were noblemen, liege lords, owners of broad estates and overlords of serfs sometimes by the dozen, sometimes by the thousand. They looked down their noses at him because he made his living by his own wits and not from the sweat of blond brows.

He looked down his nose at them because they were, for the most part, blockheads of the purest ray serene. He also envied them because, in the society of the north, acquiring an estate full of hard-working serfs was the be-all and end-all. He was a hard-working curiosity. The nobles, in their opinion and his as well, were the salt of the earth.

"Good morning, Colonel Florizel," he called, tipping his hat as the regimental commander limped by.

"And a good day to you as well, Captain." Florizel, though a belted earl, did treat Gremio as if he were of noble blood himself. Gremio couldn't find fault with the regimental commander over that, and Gremio was a man who, before the war began, had made his living by finding fault.

"How's your leg, your Excellency?" he asked now.

"Well, it'll never be what it was," Earl Florizel replied. He'd been wounded in the battle by the River of Death the autumn before, and hadn't been able to get about for some time afterwards. Even now, he looked as if he would be more comfortable leaning on a stick. But he went on, "If Lieutenant General Bell can lead a wing without a leg, I suppose I can try to lead a regiment with a sore one."

"Bell's courage is an example to us all," Gremio agreed. He had a lower opinion of Lieutenant General Bell's brains, but kept that to himself. It didn't change the point Colonel Florizel was trying to make.

Florizel snapped his fingers. "Speaking of wing commanders, that reminds me. You'll be pleased to hear that Leonidas the Priest has returned to command a wing of the Army of Franklin."

"I will?" Captain Gremio said in real surprise. "Why?"

Colonel Florizel had big bushy eyebrows. They fluttered now, like moths trying to escape from his forehead. "Why? I'll tell you why, Captain. Because having a hierophant of the Lion God leading our soldiers will surely lead the god to support us with claws and fangs."

"Surely," Gremio said. Being a barrister, he had practice disguising his tone, and Florizel would think he had agreement, not sarcasm, in mind. "Indeed, sir, Leonidas the Priest is a very holy and pious man."

"He certainly is," Florizel said. "And any man dismissed from his command by Thraxton the Braggart has to have more going for him than meets the eye."

"Hmm. I hadn't thought of that. You've got a point, your Excellency, no doubt about it," Gremio said. That he meant. But it remained one of the all too few points in Leonidas' favor, as far as he was concerned. The hierophant of the Lion God *was* a holy and pious man. As far as Gremio could see, though, neither holiness nor piety was an essential soldierly virtue. Of those virtues, Leonidas had displayed very few.

"Thraxton was a disaster for this army—a disaster, I tell you," Florizel said. "I do hope Count Joseph will be able to pick up the pieces and shape us into a decent fighting force once more."

"So do I," Gremio said. "He'd better. If he doesn't, this whole eastern land is lost to King Geoffrey, and I don't see how he can hope to hold off King Avram without it."

"Avram is a tyrant. The gods hate him," Florizel growled. Gremio nodded; he certainly agreed with that, and knew hardly anyone from Palmetto Province who didn't. His home province had been the first to renounce allegiance to Avram and fall in behind Geoffrey's banner. After a ruminative pause, Colonel Florizel continued, "But, as you say, Captain, Geoffrey does need land of which to be the king. We shall have to do everything in our power to hold back General Hesmucet, then."

"He'll have more men than we do," Gremio said gloomily. "The southrons always have more men than we do—except at the River of Death, and Count Thraxton frittered away what we won there."

"They may have more men, but we have better mages," Florizel said. "We have to have strong sorcery at our disposal, for we need it to keep the serfs subdued. The southrons are a land of shopkeepers and peddlers. What need have they for the true practice of magecraft?"

"The true practice of magecraft is a very fine and important thing," Gremio said. "What we've had . . . Everyone denies it, but everyone knows we lost at Proselytizers' Rise because Thraxton bungled his spells. One of them was supposed to come down on the southrons' heads but landed on our poor men instead, and sent them running off to be shot down like partridges."

"I have heard that," Florizel said. "I was not close by at the time of the battle, so I can't testify as to its truth."

Gremio smiled. "Spoken like a barrister, sir."

"From you, Captain, I will take that for a compliment," the regimental commander replied with a smile of his own. "There are other men, you will understand, who would use it intending something else."

"Yes, sir," Gremio said resignedly. He knew people sneered at men who practiced law. He never had quite understood why. Without barristers and solicitors, how would men who disagreed solve their problems? *By going to war with one another, that's how,* he thought. Some wars were necessary— this one, for example, since King Avram insisted on trampling down long-established law and custom in the northern provinces. But most arguments were, or could be, settled more readily than that.

Colonel Florizel tipped his hat and took his leave, still favoring that leg. In an odd sort of way, the wound he'd taken by the River of Death might have saved his life. Major Thersites, who'd taken over the regiment while Florizel couldn't fight, had died on the forward slopes of Sentry Peak, vainly trying to hold back Fighting Joseph's southrons. Florizel was a brave man. He might easily have perished there himself.

Gremio missed Thersites even less than he missed Captain Ormerod. The major had been a swamp-country baron. He'd claimed he was a baron, at any rate, and he was a good enough man of his hands that no one ever challenged him on it. But all he'd done, besides aping and envying his betters, was criticize and carp at them. A little of that was bracing. A lot of it was like drinking vinegar all the time. Gremio wondered in which of the seven hells the unlamented Thersites' soul currently resided.

"Leonidas the Priest in charge of a wing again!" Gremio said—even easier and more enjoyable to resent a live man than a dead one, for a live man might yet offend afresh, where a dead man's affronts were fixed, immutable.

After a moment, though, Gremio shrugged. The Army of Franklin hadn't performed noticeably better without Leonidas than it had with him. Presumably, that meant his return wouldn't hurt the army much.

Someone coughed behind Gremio, as if tired of waiting to be noticed. Gremio turned. "Oh. Sergeant Thisbe," he said. "What is it?"

The company's first sergeant was a lean young man who, unusually for a Detinan, kept his cheeks and chin shaved smooth. Gremio approved of him; he did his job competently and without any fuss. "I was just wondering, sir," he said now, "if the colonel had any word on when we'd be moving out of winter quarters. The sooner I can prepare the men, the better."

"Quite right, quite right," Gremio said approvingly. "But no, Joseph the Gamecock has yet to issue any orders along those lines."

"All right, sir," Thisbe said. "I expect we'll know when General Hesmucet starts moving north against us."

"I should hope so," Gremio exclaimed. "This is our country, after all. When the enemy moves through it, the people always let us hear what he's up to."

"Yes, sir," the sergeant said. "Same as the blonds do for the foe with us."

"Er—yes," Gremio said. It wasn't so much that Thisbe was wrong. The sergeant, in fact, made a real and important point. "Good of you to think of that." Here in the north, Detinans were so used to thinking of their serfs as hewers of wood and drawers of water, they too readily forgot blonds were men like any others, with eyes to see, wits to think, and tongues to speak.

"I hear we've got serfs digging trenches and making earthworks for us from here all the way up to Marthasville," Sergeant Thisbe said. "Do you really suppose, sir, that some of them won't tell the southrons as much of what we're up to as they can figure out?"

"No, I don't suppose anything of the sort." Even had Gremio supposed anything of the sort, he wouldn't have admitted it. A barrister never admitted anything he didn't have to. He went on, "We do try to keep as many blonds from escaping as we can, you know. I'm sure the general commanding is doing his best to make sure no really important information gets to Hesmucet."

"I hope so." Thisbe's light tenor could be remarkably expressive. Here, the sergeant packed a world of doubt into three words. Gremio wouldn't have wanted to go to court against a barrister with such dangerous skills.

Before he could say so—he would have meant it as nothing but praise—horns blared, summoning the regiment to assembly. No, not just the regiment: the whole brigade, maybe even the whole army. Those horns were blaring all over the encampment in and around Borders.

"We can talk about this more another time, Sergeant," Gremio said. "For now, we've got to round up the men." He spoke of them as if they were so many sheep. He sometimes thought of them that way, too, though he was careful not to let them know it. He had to keep their respect, after all.

"Yes, sir." Thisbe saluted. The sergeant went about the job with quiet but unhurried competence. Gremio wondered what he'd done in or around Karlsburg before taking service with King Geoffrey's army. He didn't know; unlike most of his men, Thisbe didn't talk much about what he'd done or what he hoped to do. He just did whatever needed doing, and did it well.

Thanks in no small part to him, Gremio's company was among the first in Colonel Florizel's regiment to assemble. Small farmers, tradesmen, shopkeepers—by now, after three years of war, telling at a glance what a soldier had been was a hopeless, unwinnable game. Despite individual differences, all the men looked very much alike: lean, sunbrowned, poorly groomed, dirty, wearing blue uniforms in no better shape than they were. Some of those blue tunics and pantaloons had started life as gray tunics and pantaloons, and been taken from southrons who didn't need them any more and then dyed. Some few gray pantaloons hadn't been dyed at all. That went against orders, but happened nonetheless.

A nasty, frowzy crew, would have been the first thought of anyone seeing Gremio's company—or, very likely, any company in the Army of Franklin. But a second thought would have followed hard on its heels: *these men can fight*.

Florizel limped out in front of the regiment. He carried a folded sheet of paper, and ostentatiously unfolded it to draw the men's attention. *A nice bit of business*, Gremio thought, resolving to use it in the courtroom one day.

"Men of Palmetto Province!" Florizel boomed. "We were first in our rejection of that gods-damned maniac who calls himself King Avram and sits in the Black Palace in Georgetown like a hovering vulture, waiting for the north to die so he may feast on our dead flesh and crack our bones. Now once more his wicked armies advance on us, and we must be among the first to throw them back."

They raised a cheer. Gremio found himself cheering, too. He wondered why. They'd all had countless chances to be maimed or killed. Now Florizel was telling them they were about to get more. And, instead of cursing him, they cheered. If they weren't utterly mad, Gremio had never heard of anyone who was.

"Men of Detina! Brave men! Patriots!" Florizel went on. "There are two gaps through which the cursed southrons might attack us. We shall beat them back from both. We shall not let them ravage Peachtree Province. We shall not let them steal from us the great city of Marthasville. The gods love King Geoffrey. Our cause is just. Provincial prerogative forever!"

"Provincial prerogative forever!" the men shouted. Gremio's voice was loud among them. The Army of Franklin was in good spirits, if nothing else. However much that would help in the fight against Hesmucet, Joseph the Gamecock had it working in his favor.

Lieutenant General Bell reached for his crutches. Getting out of a chair was a struggle for a man with one leg and one good arm, but he managed. The trick was to lunge forward and upward, gain momentary balance, get one crutch under his good arm for a second point of support, and then get the other crutch under his bad arm, under the worthless piece of flesh and bone that hung from his shoulder but would never be good for anything again.

Oh, it's good for something, he thought as he swung himself forward and ducked his way out of his pavilion. *It's good for causing me pain.* The shattered shoulder still felt as if it had melted led poured into the joint. It hurt even worse than the stump of his leg, and the festering in his thigh had almost taken his life, there after the fight by the River of Death. He remembered the stink of the pus after they'd drained it. The chirurgeons assured him that was all over now.

They assured him of that, yes. But why did he still hurt, then?

Why, in the end, didn't matter so much. That he still hurt . . . that mattered. He paused, steadied himself on his crutches, and used his good hand to extract the bottle of laudanum he always carried with him. Bringing the bottle up to his mouth, he extracted the cork with his teeth. He swigged. Laudanum wasn't made to be swigged; it was made to be taken by the drop. Bell didn't care. Drops didn't come close to making his torment retreat.

Spirits and distilled poppy juice: fire and night going down his throat together. After a little while, he grunted softly and said, "Ahhh!" The pain didn't disappear; it never disappeared. But it receded, or, more accurately, he floated away from it. The laudanum didn't make him sleepy, as it did with many men. If anything, it left him more awake than ever. But it did make him slow, so that he often had to grope for a word or an idea.

All around him, the Army of Franklin's encampment bubbled like a pot left unwatched on a cookfire. A squadron of unicorns trotted off toward the south. A column of men tramped away, heading southeast. Joseph the Gamecock was doing everything he could to hold back General Hesmucet's bigger army.

Everything he could to hold it back, yes. Lieutenant

General Bell muttered something his bushy beard and mustaches fortunately swallowed. He'd never been one for hanging back. He wanted to go at the enemy, not try to keep him away from a city. What kind of war was that?

Joseph's kind of war: he answered his own question. He muttered again, rather louder. A sentry gave him an odd look. He glowered back. The man dropped his eyes.

His aide-de-camp, a dour major named Zibeon, came up to him and asked, "What do you need, sir?"

Now there was a question with a multitude of possible answers. *A new leg* was the first that sprang to Bell's mind. *An arm that works* followed almost at once. Not far behind ran *a way to banish pain without slowing my wits to a crawl.* And, outdistanced by those three but still galloping hard, came *a command due my station.*

But Zibeon couldn't give him any of those things. The first two would have taken a miracle from the gods, and the gods doled out miracles in niggardly wise these days. The third would have taken a miracle among the healers—more likely, but not much. As for the fourth, that lay in King Geoffrey's hands. Lieutenant General Bell found himself not altogether without hope there.

"Fetch me my unicorn," Bell said. That Major Zibeon could do.

That Major Zibeon plainly did not want to do. "Sir, wouldn't you be more comfortable in a buggy?" he asked.

"No," Bell snapped. So far as it went, that was true. Bell would not be comfortable in a buggy. He wouldn't be comfortable anywhere, probably not till they laid him on his funeral pyre. He might perhaps be less uncomfortable in a buggy, but he had no intention of admitting that to his aide-de-camp. "My unicorn is what I asked for, Major, and my unicorn is what I require."

Zibeon's long, sad face got longer and sadder. "Sir, if you were to fall off the beast, the result would be unfortunate for you. It would also be unfortunate for the kingdom, if I may take the liberty of saying so."

"Fall off?" Bell echoed in tones of disbelief. "Fall off? How in the seven hells can I fall off the gods-damned beast?" He gestured toward his pinned-up pantaloon leg. "You've got to tie me aboard the miserable animal to get me to stay on at all. Does a lashed-on sack of beans fall off an ass' back? My name isn't George, Major, but I doubt it."

The laudanum took the edge off his temper, as it took the edge off his torment. It would have left most men as insensitive as they were insensible. Bell, now, Bell reached for his swordhilt, although, considering his mobility, he would have had a better chance trying to brain any foe with a crutch.

With a sigh, Major Zibeon yielded. "Let it be exactly as you say, Lieutenant General." He raised his voice, shouting for a serf.

The blond groom fetched the unicorn in short order. Bell clambered aboard the splendid white beast, disdaining help from either the blond or his aide-de-camp. He wasn't weak, even now. Certain parts were missing, sure enough, or didn't work as the gods intended, but what remained in working order still worked well. He tolerated the straps that did indeed make him feel like a sack of beans. Without them, he could not sit the unicorn.

Another general who'd served in the Army of Southern Parthenia was known as Peg-Leg Dick these days. But he'd lost his leg below the knee, and had enough left to grip a unicorn's barrel as he rode, even if the peg stuck out at an odd angle and made him instantly recognizable. Bell's leg was off only a few inches below the hip. He would never have a peg. He would never be able to stay on a unicorn without help, either.

But, once helped, he could ride. He set spurs—well, spur— to the beast. It bounded away, leaving Zibeon and the serf groom behind. For a moment, Bell felt almost like the man he'd been before the fights at Essoville and the River of Death. For a moment, he felt free and strong and able. Maybe the laudanum let him forget his wounds a little longer than he would have without it.

When he reached the house where Count Joseph made his headquarters, he had to untie himself from the saddle, hand his crutches down to a waiting soldier, and then descend from the unicorn and reclaim the crutches. The process was slow, laborious, and painful. Almost everything

Lieutenant General Bell did since his maiming—no, since his maimings—involved long, slow, painful processes.

Joseph the Gamecock came out of the house while Bell dismounted. Courteous as a cat, the general commanding the Army of Franklin waited for his wing commander to gather himself before bowing. "Good day, Lieutenant General," Joseph said. "What can I do for you this lovely afternoon?"

"Is it?" Bell hadn't noticed. He attacked conversations as directly as he attacked enemies: "The southrons are moving."

"Indeed they are," Joseph agreed. "Both hereabouts and in Parthenia, I am given to understand."

Bell ignored that, too. Parthenia was, at the moment, outside his purview. "Where do we strike them?" he demanded.

"We don't." Joseph the Gamecock was every bit as blunt. "We have been over this ground before, you know."

"Yes, I do know, and the more I think about it, the more it pains me," Bell replied. "Some pains, sir, laudanum does not touch."

With a sigh, Joseph the Gamecock condescended to explain: "Consider, Lieutenant General. We have to the south of us the rough country of Rockface Rise. There are only two gaps in the rise, two places where the southrons can come at us. By all the gods, I hope they try smashing through the Vulture's Nest or the Dog's Path. If they do, we'll still be killing them there this fall. I intend to send your wing to hold the Vulture's Nest. That will give you enough bloodshed, I vow, to satisfy the most sanguinary man ever born."

"Killing southrons is all very well," Bell said stiffly. "Indeed, it is better than very well."

"I should hope so—it's what we're here for," Joseph the Gamecock said. "And when your wing takes its position, you will find that the serfs I've set to work have fortified the gap so that not even a mouse could sneak through without paying with its life—not even a mouse, I tell you."

"That is good, in its way," Bell said, "but only in its way. I do not care to fight in the open field as if I were besieged in a castle."

"Our whole kingdom is besieged," Joseph said, "and we needs must keep the enemy from entering into it."

"We can drive them back," Lieutenant General Bell insisted. "We can beat them in the open field."

"You may perhaps be right," Joseph said. "If the Army of Franklin were yours to command, you might venture the experiment. But, since King Geoffrey has seen fit to entrust it to me, I have to do what I believe to be in its best interest, and in the best interest of the kingdom. Do you understand me? Have I made myself clear enough, or shall I scratch pictures in the dirt for you with the point of my sword?"

Bell glared at him. "Is that an insult, sir?"

"Only if you choose to take it as one," Joseph the Gamecock retorted. His temper was, if anything, even shorter than Bell's, and he had not the excuse of pain from his wounds, for he'd been hurt almost two years before and was fully healed. His own eyes snapping, he went on, "I reckon it an insult that you challenge the orders of your commanding officer in this unseemly fashion."

"You are welcome to challenge me, sir," Bell said. "Unfortunately, as my rank is lower than yours, I am forbidden by King Geoffrey's regulations from challenging you. But I assure you, sir, I will endeavor to give satisfaction."

"I don't want to challenge you, you young idiot," Joseph said testily. "I want to use you. I want to use you to kill the southrons in great whacking lots as they come north. In my view, that remains our best hope of winning this war: to make the enemy too sick of the fight to go on. If every other household in New Eborac and Loveton and Horatii is in mourning, the people will make King Avram give up the fight and let the north go our own way."

"Gods grant it be so," Lieutenant General Bell replied. "A surer way, I think, is to defeat the invader on the battlefield in open combat."

"That would be easier if we had twice the men he did rather than the other way round," Joseph the Gamecock said. "I ask you straight out: will you defend the Vulture's Nest for me, or shall I give the job to Roast-Beef William or to Leonidas the Priest?"

"I will defend it," Bell said. "I fail in no obedience, sir. But I am a free Detinan no less than you. I do intend to state my mind."

"Really?" One of Joseph's expressive eyebrows quirked. "I never would have noticed. Very well, Lieutenant General. You are dismissed, and I shall rely upon your formidable skills. I know you serve the kingdom with a whole heart, regardless of how you chance to feel about me."

"Yes, sir. That is true," Bell agreed. Because of his crutches, he didn't have to salute the commanding general. He hitched away, struggled aboard his unicorn after stowing his crutches, waited for the attendant to tie him on, and rode back to his own headquarters.

Once there, he sat down inside his pavilion, inked a pen, and began a letter to a man with whom he'd been corresponding ever since becoming one of Joseph the Gamecock's wing commanders. *Your Majesty*, he wrote, *I have just come from yet another conversation with the general commanding, this one no more satisfactory than any of those I have previously held with him. As I have said in my earlier letters, my opinion continues to be that the Army of Franklin is in better condition and more capable of offensive operations than Count Joseph believes. How can any man doubt the fire inherent in the hearts of our brave northern soldiers, and their innate superiority to the southron foe? We could, and we should, go forth against the enemy instead of waiting for him to come to us.*

He inked the pen again, paused for thought, and then continued, *As proof of the straits to which the southrons are reduced, I need do no more than note that, in the army now moving against us, General Hesmucet has, mixed promiscuously through its ranks, several brigades' worth of blonds. If the fighting spirit of the southrons were not all but extinct, would they resort to such a desperate expedient? Surely not, your Majesty; surely not. In the hope that the gods grant you the good fortune and victory you deserve, I have the honor to remain your most humble and obedient servant. . . .*

After signing the letter, he sealed it with his personal signet, addressed it, and called for a runner. "See that this gets into the post to Nonesuch without delay," he told the man. "Its existence is, of course, completely confidential."

"Of course, sir," the courier replied.

Rollant was glad to be marching north, marching against the Detinan noblemen, the Detinan liege lords, who would have left the kingdom when Avram proposed freeing their serfs from the land they tilled. He sang the Detinan royal hymn with particular fervor as he tramped along. It meant, he thought, more to him than to many of his comrades.

"You can't sing worth a lick," Smitty told him. The two crossbowmen had fought side by side ever since the regiment formed a year or so before. Smitty came off a farm outside the great city of New Eborac. He was a typical enough Detinan: on the stocky side, swarthy, with black hair and eyes and a shaggy black beard.

"I don't care," Rollant answered. "I have fun trying."

"Nobody who listens to you has any fun," Smitty assured him.

"Don't listen, then," Rollant said. "Sing."

Sing he did himself, loudly, enthusiastically, and probably not very well. He lived in New Eborac, with his wife and little boy. He made a good enough living as a carpenter, or had in peacetime. Thus far, he seemed a typical enough Detinan himself.

Thus far—and no further. He wore gray tunic and pantaloons like Smitty, like everyone else around him. There their resemblance ended. Rollant was fair-skinned and blue-eyed, with hair and beard yellow as butter. He'd grown up on a feudal estate in Palmetto Province, not far outside Karlsburg—and had fled the land to which he was legally bound, fled south to New Eborac, where serfdom had long been extinct, about ten years before. His wife was born in the south, and had never known a liege lord's exactions. Thanks to Norina, Rollant had his letters.

Smitty said, "Suppose I tell you to shut the hells up or I'll pop you one."

"Talk is cheap," Rollant answered. "You want to try and do something about it after march today, you come right ahead and see what kind of welcome you get."

Smitty was his friend, or as close to a friend as a blond could have among Detinans. They'd fought shoulder to shoulder. They'd saved each other a couple of times. But Rollant didn't dare take a challenge like that lightly, and he wasn't sure whether or how much Smitty was joking.

I have to be twice as good, twice as tough, as an ordinary Detinan to get myself reckoned half as good, half as tough. Rollant had had that thought so many times, it hardly sparked resentment in him any more. It was part of what being a blond in a black-haired land meant.

A lot of Detinans thought blonds couldn't, wouldn't, fight for beans. The Detinans' ancestors had crossed the Western Ocean centuries before, and promptly subjected the kingdoms full of blonds they found in the north of this new land—and the more scattered hunters and farmers who lived farther south. The campaigns were monotonously one-sided, from which the Detinans inferred that blonds were and always would be a pack of spineless cowards.

They had iron weapons. We had bronze. They rode unicorns. We'd never seen them before—we had ass-drawn chariots. They knew how to make fancy siege engines. We didn't. Their mages were stronger than ours. Their gods were stronger than ours. No wonder we went down like barley under the scythe.

Like almost all blonds in the Kingdom of Detina these days, Rollant reverenced the Thunderer and the Lion God and the rest of the Detinan pantheon. He knew the names of the gods his own ancestors had worshipped—or of some of them, anyhow. He still believed in those gods. He believed in them, but he didn't reverence them. What point to that? The blonds' gods had been as thoroughly beaten as their former votaries.

"Never mind," Smitty said, and started blatting out the royal hymn himself.

Rollant howled like a wolf. "You're worse than I am—to the seven hells with me if you're not."

"To the seven hells with you anyway," Smitty said cheerfully. He kept on singing.

Sergeant Joram winced. "Lion God's hairy ears, Smitty, stuff a sock in it. You couldn't carry a tune in a knapsack."

"Sergeant!" Smitty said reproachfully, but he did quiet down.

"*I* told you you couldn't sing, too," Rollant said. "Would you listen to me?"

"I wouldn't listen to Joram if he weren't my sergeant," Smitty answered. "That's what being a free Detinan is all about: the only person you have to listen to is yourself, most of the time."

"By the gods, I know *that*," Rollant said. "Why do you think I ran away from my liege lord's estate? I got sick of having somebody else tell me what to do all the time. Wouldn't you?"

Before Smitty could answer, Joram went on, "And you, Rollant, you sound like a cat just after its tail got stepped on."

"Thank you, Sergeant," Rollant said sweetly. Under his breath, he said something else, something less polite. Smitty guffawed. Sergeant Joram sent them both suspicious looks, then went off to harass somebody else.

Smitty said, "I'll tell you something. Back before the war, I didn't have any idea what being a serf was like. We haven't had anybody tied to the land since before my pa was born, not in New Eborac we haven't. But this whole business of soldiering, of having somebody telling you what to do just on account of he's got himself a higher rank than yours—it sticks in the craw, it surely does."

Rollant didn't particularly like taking orders, either, not when he'd run away from Baron Ormerod to escape them. By the mad fortune of war, Ormerod had almost killed him in the skirmishing before the battle by the River of Death, and he *had* killed his former liege lord not long after gaining the top of Proselytizers' Rise. He couldn't think of many things of which he was more proud.

Still, Smitty needed an answer. Rollant did his best to give him one: "It's not the same. There are rules here. Liege lords, the only rules they have are the ones they make up. If you lose a trowel and your liege lord decides to flay the hide off your back with a whip for it, who's to say he can't? Nobody. If you give him a sour look afterwards and he whips you again, who'll stop him? Nobody. He'll say he reckoned you were plotting an uprising, and he doesn't have to say anything past that. Or if he thinks your sister is pretty, or your wife . . ."

"They really do that?" Smitty said.

"Of course they really do that," Rollant said. "Baron Ormerod, he was a regular tomcat amongst the serf huts. Why not? If your mother was a serf, you're a serf, too, even if you do look like your liege lord."

"That's a pretty filthy business, all right," Smitty said.

With a shrug, Rollant answered, "Whoever's on top is going to give it to whoever's on the bottom." He used a gesture that showed exactly what he meant by *give it to*. Smitty clucked in delicious horror. Rollant went on, "If we'd licked you Detinans a long time ago, you'd've ended up slaving for us. But that's not what the gods had in mind, and so it didn't happen."

Smitty grunted. He plainly didn't like thinking about might-have-beens. But then he wagged a finger at Rollant. "You've got no business talking about 'you Detinans.' If you're not one yourself, then what's King Avram been fussing and fuming about all this time? If you're not one yourself, what are you?"

"What am I?" Rollant echoed. It was a good question. He spoke Detinan. He followed Detinan gods. Avram *did* want to free his people from their ties to the land and make the law look at them the same way it looked at every other Detinan. And yet, the question had a dreadfully obvious answer. "What am I? Just a gods-damned blond, that's all. And there's plenty of southrons who'd say it along with the traitors in the north."

He wondered if Smitty had ever said such a thing. Probably. By everything he'd seen and heard, there weren't a whole lot of Detinans—ordinary, gods-fearing Detinans, they would surely call themselves—who didn't say such things in places where they didn't think blonds could hear. But Smitty didn't mock blonds when Rollant could hear him, which put him up on a lot of his countrymen.

What Smitty said now was, "You aren't the only blond in King Avram's army, Rollant. When we get done licking the northerners with them helping, folks'll have a lot harder time saying blonds can't fight. And if a man can do a proper job of fighting, he's on his way to being a real Detinan."

If a man can stand up to a Detinan was part of what he meant. The Detinans had spent centuries forcing blonds down, and then wondered that they didn't leap to their feet at once when no longer held down by laws. Rollant said, "Well, there's Hagen, or there was."

"Gods damn Hagen, and I daresay they're doing it," Smitty said. "On account of Hagen, we've got Lieutenant Griff in charge of this company instead of Captain Cephas, and Griff isn't half the man the captain was."

"Captain Cephas turned out to be too much of a man for his own good," Rollant said. "If he hadn't messed around with Hagen's wife—"

"Corliss didn't need much messing with," Smitty said.

Rollant couldn't argue that. It hadn't been a rape, or anything of the sort. He felt a certain amount of responsibility for what had happened, because he'd found the two blonds and their children near Rising Rock after they'd fled their liege lord. Hagen had cooked and cut wood and fetched and carried for the company, getting paid for his labor for the first time in his life. Corliss had got paid for doing laundry, too. She hadn't got paid for warming Cephas' cot, not so far as Rollant knew. She'd just wanted the company commander, as he'd wanted her. And, right after the battle of Proselytizers' Rise, she'd gone into his tent—and Hagen had followed her with a butcher knife. Now all three of them were dead; Cephas had managed to use his sword before falling.

"You can't say Hagen didn't act the way any outraged Detinan husband would have," Rollant remarked.

"Well, no. So you can't," Smitty admitted. "But I wish to the gods he hadn't done it. Griff *squeaks* when he talks, gods damn it." His voice went into falsetto for a moment to imitate the young lieutenant.

They tramped on. They'd come this way before, on the way to what turned out to be the fight by the River of Death. They had a bigger army now, and it was all together, not scattered into several detachments. They also had General

Hesmucet leading them now, not hard-drinking General Guildenstern—surely a gain. Even so, Rollant made sure his crossbow and quiver of bolts were where he could grab them in a hurry.

A cheer started somewhere behind him. He looked back over his shoulder, trying to see what was going on, and almost tripped over the feet of the man in front of him. That put his mind back on what really needed doing. But he'd seen enough, and started cheering, too.

"What's going on?" Smitty asked.

"Doubting George is coming up," Rollant answered in his normal voice. Then he shouted some more: "Huzzah! Huzzah! Huzzah for the Rock in the River of Death!" Smitty cheered, too, and waved his hat.

Lieutenant General George rode up alongside the marching men on a fine unicorn. He smiled at them and called, "Hello, boys! When we finally get our hands on those stinking northerners, are we going to whip 'em right out of their boots?"

"Hells, yes!" "You bet we will, Lieutenant General!" "Nobody can stop us, long as you're along for the ride!" The men yelled lots of things like that. Rollant wasn't behindhand in shouting George's praises, either. Nobody who'd been through the fight by the River of Death, who'd watched Doubting George's defense of Merkle's Hill after the rest of the army was routed, would ever greet him with anything less than heartfelt praise.

George tipped his hat to the soldiers. "We'll win because we've got the best fighters in the world," he said, and rode on, more cheers echoing behind him.

"You know what the funny thing is?" Smitty said.

"You mean, besides you?" Rollant returned.

Smitty made a face at him, but refused to be distracted: "What's funny is, Doubting George talks like a stinking northerner himself." He did his best to put on a northern twang as he spoke. His best was none too good.

Rollant considered. "He just talks," he said at last; George's Parthenian accent wasn't that much different from the one he had himself. "You think I sound like a stinking northerner?"

"Sometimes," Smitty said. "But anybody can see why you got the devils out of there. George, he's a nobleman. He had estates with serfs on 'em himself. But he didn't turn traitor along with Geoffrey and the rest."

"He's loyal to Detina." Rollant raised an eyebrow. "Why should that be so hard for a Detinan to understand?"

Smitty gave him a dirty look. "You like to try and twist everything I say, don't you?"

"Of course," Rollant said gravely. "If I didn't, what would you have to complain about?"

"Huh," Smitty said. "You ought to be a sergeant, the way you think."

"Me?" Rollant's voice squeaked in surprise. There were a few blond corporals and sergeants in King Avram's army, but only a few. Detinans—ordinary Detinans—didn't take kindly to the idea of obeying orders from blonds.

But Smitty answered, "Stranger things have happened."

"Maybe." Rollant didn't sound convinced. But he did like the idea, now that he thought about it. "Maybe," he repeated, in an altogether different tone of voice.

II

Doubting George had seen a good many strong positions in his day. The one Joseph the Gamecock held here in southeastern Peachtree Province looked as formidable as any, and more so than most. "We'll have a demon of a time breaking in," he told General Hesmucet. "That ridge line shelters the enemy almost as well as Proselytizers' Rise did, and I know Joseph. He'll have fortified the gaps till a flea couldn't get through them, let alone an army."

"I know Joseph, too," Hesmucet replied, "and I've got no doubt that you're right. If we put our head into one of those gaps, we'll be asking the terrible jaws of death to close on it."

"You have a gift for the picturesque phrase, sir," George replied, wondering if Hesmucet also had a gift for hard fighting. Marshal Bart must have thought so, or he wouldn't have left Hesmucet in command here in the east when he was summoned to Georgetown to oppose Duke Edward of Arlington and the Army of Southern Parthenia. *No, he would have left me,* George thought—not with a great deal of bitterness, but some seemed inescapable.

General Hesmucet didn't look unduly worried. "Joseph the Gamecock is strong here, but I think we can shift him," he said.

"I hope you're right, sir." Lieutenant General George looked at the forbidding terrain ahead. "I have to say, though, I have my doubts. If we try to go straight at them, they'll give us lumps."

"Who said anything about going straight at them?" Hesmucet replied. "Joseph the Gamecock is strong here—what better reason not to hit him *here?*"

"Ah." Doubting George heard the enthusiasm return to his voice. "What have you got in mind, then, sir?"

"Up about twenty miles northeast of here is a valley called Viper River Gap," the general commanding answered. "If we can push a force through there, we'll march right into Caesar, square in Joseph's rear. He'll have to retreat, we'll smash him up, this part of the war will be won, and we'll all be heroes."

"As simple as that," George said dryly.

"As simple as that," Hesmucet agreed. "As simple as that, provided the Gamecock doesn't make it more complicated. He may. I'd be a liar if I said anything else. But it's the best chance I can see of getting Joseph out of the position he's taken."

"Not a bad notion at all, sir," George said. He'd proposed something not too different back in the middle of winter. Nothing had come of that—*he* wasn't the general commanding. But he still thought the plan good, no matter who ended up with the credit for it. "Only one thing: how do we fix Joseph *here* while we shift part of our army toward the gap and Caesar?"

Hesmucet looked faintly embarrassed, an unusual expression for him. "Some large part of our army will have to stay here by Borders while the rest slides north."

"Some large part of our army, eh?" George said. "Why do I think I have a pretty fair notion of which large part of the army you have in mind?"

"You've proved you know how to make a convincing demonstration against strong enemy positions," Hesmucet said.

"Is *that* what I've proved?" Doubting George wondered. "I thought it was just a knack for banging my head against a stone wall." *And also a knack for being ordered to bang my head against a stone wall,* he added to himself.

"Your men were the ones who broke through at Proselytizers' Rise," Hesmucet said. "Who knows? Maybe they'll do it again, and steal the glory from Brigadier James."

"You'll send James the Bird's Eye on the flanking move?" George said.

"I will indeed." General Hesmucet grinned. "Who better to see the opportunity if it be there?" James had got his nickname at the military collegium at Annasville because of his extraordinarily keen eyesight.

"He's an able officer," George allowed. "Why not use him to make the demonstration here and send the larger force up onto Joseph's flank?"

"I thought about that," Hesmucet replied. "It seems to me that, were I to do so, Joseph would realize what I had done and shift footsoldiers north to block the move before it could have any hope of success."

Doubting George considered. He wasn't sure General Hesmucet was right about that, but he wasn't sure Hesmucet was wrong, either. "Very well, sir," he said. "I shall, of course, do whatever you require of me."

"I knew you would," Hesmucet said, in tones suggesting he'd known no such thing. "I intend to get James the Bird's Eye moving this afternoon. Your men will, I hope, keep Joseph the Gamecock too busy to use his own eyes."

"We'll do our best, sir," George said, that being the only thing he could say. No, almost the only thing, for he couldn't help adding, "I do wish my men would sometimes get the command to do themselves rather than to help their comrades do somewhere else."

"That day is coming, Lieutenant General," Hesmucet said. "You may rely on it: that day *is* coming. It's a hundred miles, more or less, from here to Marthasville. Only the gods know how many battles we'll fight before we get there. I'm no god. I'm just a man. But I can tell you we'll fight a lot of them, and I can tell you your men will have their chance to do great things. They can hardly help it, wouldn't you agree?"

"Put that way, I don't see how I can do anything but agree." Doubting George plucked at his long, thick beard, which was just beginning to be frosted with gray. "You plan an ambitious campaign."

"Marshal Bart aims at the traitor realm's head in his move against Nonesuch," Hesmucet replied. "Me, I intend to tear out its heart. A kingdom can't live without a head, and no more can it live without a heart. If we take both of them away from false King Geoffrey, what has he got left? Wind and air, Lieutenant General, wind and air and nothing else but. And not even a windbag like Geoffrey can make a kingdom from wind and air alone."

"I do not for a moment disagree with you, sir. It's only that . . ." Doubting George had to pause and marshal his thoughts before he could continue. "It's only that, the first three summers of this war, we were fighting battles. One of our armies would collide with an enemy force, we'd fight, and then we would see what happened next. Here"—he paused to think again—"here the battles are just incidents, parts of something bigger that you and Marshal Bart have in mind."

"And King Avram," Hesmucet said. "Never forget King Avram."

"I wouldn't dream of it," George said. "If it weren't for King Avram, we wouldn't have a war right now."

"Not right now," Hesmucet said. "But we would have fought a war over serfdom sooner or later. We almost did ten years ago, till Daniel the Weaver, Henry Feet of Clay, and John the Typhoon worked out the compromise that satisfied King Zachary and the northern nobles both. But it didn't satisfy anyone for long. This fight was coming. Now that it's here, we have to win it."

"Fair enough," George said.

He went off to confer with his own subordinates. His wing commander, Brigadier Absalom the Bear, wore a long face. "We can do what you want, sir," he rumbled in the bass growl that helped give him his sobriquet. "We can do it, sure enough, but we won't get through and we will get mangled."

"We have to try it," George replied, "for the sake of the

army as a whole." He turned to Brigadier Brannan, who commanded all his siege engines and dart throwers. "What can you do to make our job easier?"

"Easier? Not fornicating much, sir." Brannan was a man who spoke his mind. "Absalom has it right: we're going to get mangled. The most I can hope to do is mangle a few more traitors than we would otherwise."

"All right. Do that," Doubting George said. "We commence this afternoon. Give us the best chance you can."

At the appointed hour, horns blared. All of Brigadier Brannan's engines, brought forward to bear on the trenches protecting the northerners, began to shoot at once. Stones and firepots flew through the air. So did streams of darts from repeating crossbows. Columns of smoke marked where firepots struck home. George's wizards, in long gray robes to match the southron soldiers' uniform tunics and pantaloons, sent bolts of lightning down from a clear sky onto the enemy's heads.

Had Joseph the Gamecock's troopers just taken their positions, the bombardment and the sorcerous assault might have driven them off. But they'd had days—weeks—in which to ready themselves for the assault they must have thought likely. Darts and firepots and levinbolts no doubt slew some of the northerners, but had not a prayer of dislodging them from their field fortifications.

Doubting George sighed. He'd expected nothing different. General Hesmucet had expected nothing different, either. If he was going to keep Joseph the Gamecock from looking north and west toward James the Bird's Eye's column advancing on Caesar, he would have to make a convincing assault on the Vulture's Nest and the Dog's Path. A convincing assault would also be an expensive assault.

With another sigh, Lieutenant General George nodded to the trumpeters standing close by him. "Forward," he said. Their martial music blared out. Obedient to his will, the southrons hurled themselves at the two gaps in Rockface Rise.

"King Avram!" the soldiers shouted, and, "Freedom!" and, "One Detina, now and forever!" Doubting George believed in all those things, especially the last. If he hadn't believed

in a united Detina with all his soul, he would have gone
with King Geoffrey, gone with the province of Parthenia.
Instead . . .

*Instead, in the name of a united Detina, I'm sending
hundreds, thousands, of young men forward in an attack I
know and they probably also know has no chance of getting through,* he thought. *I had better be right, that's all.*

Regardless of whether he was right about the cause he
served, he rapidly proved right about the attack's chances.
Joseph and his wing commanders and brigadiers were every
bit as capable as the southrons facing them. *Exactly as
capable,* Doubting George thought. *How could it be otherwise, when we all studied side by side together at the
military collegium?*

The men who wore blue and had followed King Geoffrey
away from Detina struck back, and struck back hard, as
soon as George's soldiers came into range at the Vulture's
Nest, where he watched the assault. Neither bombardment
nor sorcerous assault had silenced the northerners' catapults
and repeating crossbows. They scythed through the southrons'
ranks, as did the quarrels from the crossbowmen in the
trenches across the mouth of the Vulture's Nest.

Absalom the Bear came back to him in something of a
temper. "Sir, may I withdraw the men now? If I keep sending them forward for long enough, the traitors will kill every
last one of them, and then where will we be?"

"In the front rank, I assume," George said mildly. His wing
commander gaped at him. He went on, "No, you may not
withdraw them, Brigadier. As you know, their purpose is not
to break through but to distract."

"It had better not be to break through." Absalom's voice
was hot. "We haven't a prayer of breaking through, any
more than we did at—" He hesitated.

"At Proselytizers' Rise, you were going to say?" Doubting George smiled.

Absalom the Bear didn't. He looked positively bedeviled
by bees. "That was Thraxton the Braggart's magic going
wrong. Otherwise, we'd have been battered there, too."

As if to prove him right, northern wizards struck at the men
in gray trying to get into the Vulture's Nest. Their lightnings—

most of their spells—were more potent than those of the southrons. Their magecraft been honed in keeping their blond serfs afraid and subjected. In the south, spells went into manufactories, and weren't so readily adaptable to war.

Runners brought back reports of how the fight was going at the Dog's Path. As far as Doubting George was concerned, they hardly needed to have come: the southrons had no more luck breaking through Joseph the Gamecock's defenses there than at the Vulture's Nest. He hadn't expected better news, but he had hoped for it. Not all hopes were realized.

Wounded men came back past him in a steady stream. Some were walking, clutching wounded arms or roughly bandaged about the head. Others lay on litters: some still and silent, others writhing and screaming out their torment to the world at large. The hot iron stink of blood grew stronger as the day wore on, so that the battlefield took on the reek of a vast outdoor butcher's shop—which, in a manner of speaking, it was.

The setting sun shone red as blood, too. When at last it touched the western horizon, George spoke again to the trumpeters: "Sound the recall. We've done everything we can do today." As the notes that surely must have relieved his army rang out, he called for a messenger. When the runner trotted up to him, he said, "Go ask General Hesmucet if what we've done here today has been worth it." Saluting, the young man dashed off.

He returned half an hour later, with twilight deepening. Saluting again, he said, "The commanding general's compliments, sir, and he says this attack did just what it was supposed to do."

"Good," Doubting George said. "Considering what we paid, I'd hate to see it wasted."

Joseph the Gamecock was about as happy as a man of his dour temperament could be. "We held them," he said to anyone who would listen, as twilight deepened around him. "By all the gods, we held them!" He was as bubbly as if he'd been drinking sparkling wine.

His good mood even survived the arrival of a runner who said, "Sir, the scryers need to see you right away."

"I'm coming," Joseph replied. "The way I feel right now, I'd come even if it were King Geoffrey looking at me out of the crystal ball." Geoffrey was his sovereign. He gave the king all due obedience. That didn't keep him from thinking his Majesty had not a clue concealed anywhere about his person when it came to running a war.

But it wasn't Geoffrey's face in the crystal ball. It was one of Roast-Beef William's brigadiers, an officer called Husham Forkbeard, who had charge of the northern garrison up in Caesar. Even in an outstandingly shaggy army, Husham's whiskers were exceptional. At the moment, so was his alarmed expression. "Sir, you've got to help me!" he exclaimed the moment he saw Joseph the Gamecock.

"What's wrong?" demanded the commander of the Army of Franklin.

"I'll tell you what's wrong, sir," Husham replied. "What's wrong is, we've got a whole great swarm of southrons pouring through Viper River Gap and coming straight for Caesar, that's what."

"I am an idiot," Joseph said softly.

"Sir?" Husham Forkbeard asked.

"Never mind," Joseph told him, which did not stop the commanding general from bitterly reproaching himself. *Of course* General Hesmucet wasn't so stupid as to think he could break through at the Vulture's Nest or by the Dog's Path. He'd made a big, noisy demonstration there to keep the Army of Franklin in its position, and then swung part of his own enormous force north on a flanking maneuver—and it was liable to work. "You have to hold him," Joseph said urgently. "You have to. If he takes Caesar, he's got the glideway line between us and Marthasville. We can't afford that."

The understatement there would do till somebody came up with a bigger one. Joseph the Gamecock suspected that would take a while. If he couldn't get supplies up from Marthasville, the only question was whether the Army of Franklin ran out of crossbow bolts before or after it started starving. Joseph didn't care to make the experiment.

He didn't intend to make the experiment, either. Husham Forkbeard asked, "What am I going to do, sir?"

All at once, everything became glassy clear for Joseph. "You are going to hold on till the end of tomorrow afternoon," he replied. "You are going to hold on at any cost and at any hazard, but you are going to hold on. Do you understand me, Brigadier?"

"Yes, sir. I understand you fine," Husham replied. "The only thing is, I don't know if we can do it."

"You *will* do it," Joseph said coldly. "It is not a matter of choice. It is obligatory. If you run short of firepots and quarrels, you will receive the enemy with pikes and shortswords. Whatever happens, however, you will not retreat from Caesar and you will not yield the glideway line. You are to fight to the last man. If your soldiers are all slain, their ghosts are to continue the struggle."

"Heh," Husham said nervously. Then he saw that Joseph the Gamecock was not laughing—was, in fact, deadly serious. Husham nodded. "Yes, sir."

"Stout fellow," Joseph said. "I will get reinforcements to you directly. You hang on till they arrive, that's all." He made it sound simple. He wished it were simple. He knew the problems involved in holding off a substantially larger force. He'd had to do it in Parthenia, defending Nonesuch against the massive southron attack up the Henry River.

And if I hadn't been wounded there, the Army of Southern Parthenia would still be mine, and no one, very possibly, would ever have heard anything much of Duke Edward of Arlington. Joseph the Gamecock shrugged. He couldn't do anything about that, not now. No one could do anything about that now, not even the gods. Dealing with the southron attack at Caesar was going to be trouble enough, and that was within the theoretical range of things possible.

"Hang on," he told Husham Forkbeard once more. Then he nodded to his scryer. The fellow broke the mystical connection between his crystal ball and the one up in Caesar. Husham's shaggy face vanished. Joseph the Gamecock hurried out of the tent, shouting for runners.

He sent one man off to order two brigades north right away. The others summoned his wing commanders to him as fast as they could get there. Roast-Beef William arrived first, and in a jubilant mood. "The way the men fought today goes a long way towards redeeming their sorry performance at Proselytizers' Rise," he said.

Leonidas the Priest came next. "The Lion God favored our arms with victory today," he declared.

"I presume he told you afterwards that he'd done it?" Joseph murmured. The hierophant of the Lion God gave him a wounded look, but did not reply.

Lieutenant General Bell got there last—not surprising, given his wounds. But he was, as always, full of fight. "Now we've shown the southrons they can't come in," he said. "When the sun rises tomorrow, we ought to charge out through the gaps and drive them away."

"No," Joseph the Gamecock said.

"I beg your pardon, sir?" Bell said, eyebrows rising at Joseph's bluntness.

Count Joseph had never been one to suffer fools, or even disagreement, gladly. "That is a technical term, Lieutenant General, meaning, in essence, *no*."

Bell had a temper of his own. "Why the devils not, sir?" he demanded, waving his good arm. "We can go forth and conquer."

"Or we can go forth and be beaten," Joseph the Gamecock said. "Since General Hesmucet has close to twice as many men as we do, which do you reckon more likely? We can't afford a beating like that, not when we have Marthasville to protect. If we beat Hesmucet, what happens? He falls back to Rising Rock, at the most. That does us very little good I can see."

"But, sir—" Bell tried again.

"No," Joseph repeated, and took no small pleasure at interrupting his insubordinate subordinate. "And I will give you one more reason, Lieutenant General: a column of southrons is pushing through Viper River Gap toward Caesar, twenty miles north of here. Don't you feel we ought to think just a little about that, perhaps even do something about it?"

"Viper River Gap? Caesar?" Bell brooded for a moment—although, after his pair of dreadful wounds, his expression was always brooding. At last, he said, "Oh. That alters the situation."

"Just a bit." Joseph the Gamecock could no more resist

being waspish than Lieutenant General Bell could resist charging forward regardless of whether the situation called for it.

Roast-Beef William said, "I wouldn't be surprised if Hesmucet didn't attack so hard here to keep us busy while he sent that column up to the north."

"Exactly what I was thinking," Joseph replied, as benignly as he could. Even he had a hard time barking at someone who agreed with him.

"Very clever," Leonidas the Priest said, by which he no doubt meant he would never have thought of it himself.

"Very clever indeed," Bell said. "Sneaky. Perfidious. Underhanded." By that he no doubt meant he not only would never have thought of it himself, but also reckoned less than chivalrous the enemy who had.

"The only rule you can't break in war is that you must win," Joseph said. Bell looked ready to argue, but Joseph overrode him: "Husham Forkbeard is up at Caesar all by his lonesome. The first thing I have to do is reinforce him, so the southrons can't seize the glideway. Leonidas!"

"Sir?" the hierophant of the Lion God replied.

He wasn't a great soldier. He never would be. But he was willing, he was brave, and, even more to the point, he led the soldiers farthest north in the main body of the Army of Franklin. Joseph said, "Get your men on the road at once. I want them to reach Caesar as fast as humanly possible, and to give Husham all the help he needs to hold the place."

"Yes, sir," Leonidas said. "Ah . . . What do I do if I reach Caesar and find it fallen to the southrons?"

That was a better question than Joseph the Gamecock would have expected from him. After a moment's thought, the commanding general answered, "Counterattack. The southrons can't have enormous numbers there. But I hope— I pray, if you like, holy sir—Husham will hold the town. He's a solid fighting man, a warrior of the old school."

"All right, sir." Leonidas the Priest saluted. "I just wanted to know what you required of me." He saluted and strode away, his blood-red vestments bright even in the deepening twilight.

"What of the rest of the army, sir?" Roast-Beef William asked.

"We'll leave enough men behind at the gaps for a little while to make sure the southrons don't swarm through," Joseph answered. "As for the rest, we'll all get down to Caesar as quick as we can. Unless I'm altogether mad, that's where General Hesmucet is going. If he brings his whole army down there, we ought to give him a proper reception, don't you think?"

"*I* think we ought to attack," Lieutenant General Bell said.

Joseph the Gamecock shook his head. "If you ever command this army, you may lead it as you please. While I command, you will obey me. We have trenches waiting all around Caesar. Our men are going into them."

Stubbornly, Bell said, "Entrenchments weaken the fighting spirit of the men. They would be bolder, fighting out in the open."

"They would take more losses, fighting out in the open," Joseph said. "We cannot afford to take more losses. Why won't you listen to me? The idea is to make the southrons take losses, to make them take so many that they get sick of the war, give it up, and leave us alone. Have you got that?"

"The idea of fighting a war, sir, is to win it." Bell had no more give in him than did his superior.

"Go on," Joseph the Gamecock growled. "Just go on. I promise you, there will be plenty of fighting for everyone before this campaign is through. As for now . . . just go." He didn't quite scream, *Get out of my sight!* That he didn't he reckoned a sign of nearly godlike restraint on his part.

If the southrons break into Caesar, if Husham Forkbeard can't hold them away from the glideway, we'll all have more fighting than we want, but not for very long, he thought. The Army of Franklin would break up, and that would be the end of King Geoffrey's cause here in the east.

Riding a unicorn toward Caesar was a torment for Joseph, not because he was saddle sore but because he was in an agony of suspense. Finally, he couldn't stand it any more. He rode off into a field and motioned for a scryer to come to him. The man did his best, but said, "I can't bring

Husham Forkbeard's scryer onto the crystal ball, sir. I'm sorry."

"Gods damn it, how am I supposed to know what's going on if no one will tell me?" Joseph ground out. The likeliest reason Husham's scryer wouldn't or couldn't talk was that the man was busy fighting for his life. Joseph knew that only too well. However well he knew it, though, he didn't care to think about it.

At last, when Joseph was within three or four miles of Caesar and about to boot his unicorn up into a gallop so he could find out how things were going there, the scryer said, "Sir, here's Brigadier Husham."

"Well, gods be praised!" Joseph the Gamecock snatched the crystal out of the scryer's hands and rode along with it in his lap. "Husham! Tell me at once, are we holding there?"

"Yes, sir." Husham Forkbeard's fierce features blazed with pride. They also showed a sword cut he hadn't had before. "They came at Caesar. We gave 'em a nice warm northern hello with massed crossbow volleys and all the engines, and they fell back. Right now, they're digging in across the mouth of Viper River Gap."

"Let 'em," Joseph said. "We're not trying to break out, no matter what Lieutenant General Bell says." He breathed a sigh of relief—two sighs of relief, in fact, one for holding and the other . . . "Seems to me General Hesmucet doesn't quite know what to do with his great big army yet. Good."

"Maybe that's it," Husham allowed. "I tell you for true, though, sir, if they'd hit me with everything they had, gods only know how I would've held 'em. Now I've got that brigade from Leonidas the Priest, so I'm good for a while longer, anyways. And I hear tell you're bringing more men up towards Caesar."

"I'm bringing the whole army, Brigadier," Joseph answered. "And I'll tell you something else, too: I don't think I'm the only one."

In a tent just east of Viper River Gap, General Hesmucet looked daggers at Brigadier John the Bird's Eye. "You had them," Hesmucet growled. "Gods damn it, you had them, and you let them get away. The sort of chance a soldier only gets once in a lifetime. You could have strolled right into Caesar—"

"Begging your pardon, sir," the younger man broke in, "but that isn't true at all. I tried to break into Caesar, and I took some hundreds of men killed and wounded for my trouble, and I did not succeed."

"One understrength brigade holding the town," Hesmucet grumbled. "You outnumbered the traitors three or four to one. You could have had your way with them, could have seized Caesar, could have cut Joseph the Gamecock off from Marthasville, which is the one thing in all the world—the one and only thing, mind you—he knows must not happen to his army."

"Sir," James the Bird's Eye said stiffly, "my orders were to attack the glideway line to see how it was defended, and then to dig in at the mouth of Viper River Gap and to have my men ready to pursue the northerners if they took flight. I followed them exactly as you gave them to me. If you blame me for that, sir . . ." He didn't go on, not with words, but the tip of his curly black beard quivered in indignation.

And Hesmucet, contemplating the orders he had indeed given, let out a long, rueful sigh. "Very well, Brigadier. You have a point, and you made it well. I can still wish you might have done more, but you were perfectly justified in doing as you did on the basis of what I told you."

"Thank you, sir," Brigadier James replied, his tone still aggrieved.

I meant every word of what I told you, though, Hesmucet thought. *You had the sort of chance you may never see again, and you didn't take it. The northerners were strong enough to stop your first tap, and you didn't tap twice. If you had, you'd be a hero today and probably an earl tomorrow.*

"May I make an observation, sir?" Joseph the Bird's Eye asked.

"Go ahead," Hesmucet said, though most men would have quailed at speaking too frankly by the way he said it.

Young James had nerve, even if he hadn't done everything

Hesmucet would have wanted of him. He said, "Sir, if this was supposed to be your striking force and the one attacking the gaps farther south your holding force, you might have done better to let me assail the Vulture's Nest and the Dog's Path and to have sent Lieutenant General George up here with his much bigger army to strike at Caesar."

Hesmucet pondered that. He was not a sweet-tempered man, but he was, on the whole, a just one. However much he wanted to scorch Brigadier James for his presumption, he discovered he couldn't. "Well, gods damn it, you're right," he said.

James the Bird's Eye blinked. "Sir?" Evidently, that wasn't what he'd expected to hear from the general commanding.

"You're right," Hesmucet repeated. "I wish you weren't, but you are. I sent a boy to do a man's job, and I had a man ready to hand. That was a mistake. I hope I won't make the same one again. A good general makes mistakes once. A bad general keeps doing the same stupid gods-damned thing over and over."

"That's . . . probably something worth remembering," James said.

"So it is—for you and me both," Hesmucet said. "All right, Brigadier—you may go. It would have been nice if we could have just swarmed into Caesar and ruined Joseph the Gamecock right at the start of this campaign, but if we can't, we can't. We'll try something else, that's all."

Saluting, James the Bird's Eye ducked his way out of the pavilion. Hesmucet paused, thinking how the war had changed since its early days. Doubting George had had it right. Back then, armies on both sides had largely marched where they would. When they happened to collide with an opposing army, they would fight. Now both Marshal Bart and Hesmucet himself had clear goals in mind: Bart to hammer the Army of Southern Parthenia till it could stand no more hammering, Hesmucet to do the same to the Army of Franklin. No one in the first two years of the war could even have imagined such efforts. These truly were campaigns, perhaps the first such that had ever been fought in the Kingdom of Detina.

"What that means is, I'd better not bungle this one any

more," Hesmucet muttered. He stepped out of the pavilion and called for a couple of runners. When the men came up, he said, "My compliments to Doubting George and Fighting Joseph, and ask them to attend me here at their earliest convenience."

"Yes, sir," the runners chorused. They put their heads together for a moment, no doubt deciding who would go to which general. Then they loped away.

Lieutenant General George got to Hesmucet's tent first. The commanding general would have been surprised had it been the other way round. *George might not love me, but he does love the kingdom,* Hesmucet thought. *Fighting Joseph loves Fighting Joseph, and nobody and nothing else.*

"Your flanking move didn't quite work, sir," George remarked.

"No, not quite," Hesmucet agreed. "I probably should have used James the Bird's Eye to demonstrate against the two gaps farther south and sent your bigger army through Viper River Gap against Caesar."

"I rather thought so at the time, sir, but I doubted whether I should press the point," George said. "I know you're keeping that kind of eye on me."

"Well . . . yes." Hesmucet wasn't easily nonplused, but Doubting George had done the job. "We will manage to work together, though, one way or another, I think. And I'm still figuring out what I can do with all the soldiers I've got here. This is a large command. Next time, I'll manage my moves better."

"Fair enough, sir," George said. "I don't doubt that in the slightest."

Fighting Joseph rode up just then, a procession of one. Hesmucet, an indifferent rider, had an indifferent unicorn. Doubting George, a good rider, had a fine unicorn. And Fighting Joseph, a splendid rider, had the most glorious unicorn Hesmucet had ever seen: whiter than snow, horn shod with polished silver rather than workaday iron, coat and mane and tail all combed to magnificent perfection.

Fighting Joseph looked moderately magnificent himself. He was a handsome, ruddy man whose hair had gone silver, not mere gray. He looked as if he ought to be a king, not so lowly a creature as a general. Many people—King Avram not least among them—believed he thought he ought to be king, too. Avram had given him command in the west anyhow the year before, willing to gamble victories against the chance of a usurpation after them.

He hadn't got the victories. Duke Edward of Arlington not only beat but embarrassed Fighting Joseph at Viziersville. Now Joseph commanded a wing here in the distant east, not an army in the vital west. But he still thought well of himself.

"Good morning, gentlemen," he said as he dismounted and tied his unicorn to a tree branch. He saluted with a certain reluctance, as if unhappy about acknowledging any man his superior, even if only in a formal sense. "Now that we didn t break through here, what are we going to try next?"

"Breaking through again, obviously," Hesmucet said. Fighting Joseph had nerve, throwing his failure in his face like that. But then, Fighting Joseph *did* have nerve and to spare. What he didn't quite have was the soldierly talent to go with it.

"Just as you say, sir," Fighting Joseph replied. "I did it on the slopes of Sentry Peak, and George here did it at Proselytizers' Rise—with a little help from Thraxton the Braggart, of course." He chuckled. "I expect we can manage something along those lines for you again."

Hesmucet glared at him. He'd led troops himself in that fight, but he hadn't taken Funnel Hill south of Proselytizers' Rise—the defenses there turned out to be stronger than he and Marshal Bart had believed. To be reminded that his subordinates had done what he hadn't stung. If he showed the sting, though, he gave Fighting Joseph what he wanted.

And so he said, "I'm sure you'll do your best." He pointed westward. "Going through the Army of Franklin won't be so neat or so cheap as stealing a march on it would have been, but we do what we have to do, not always what we want to do." *I have to put up with you, for instance, not least so King Avram doesn't have to do it on the other side of the Green Ridge Mountains.*

Fighting Joseph peered west, too. So did Doubting George.

Fighting Joseph coughed once or twice before remarking, "Those are formidable works the traitors have there."

"I know," Hesmucet said. "They set their serfs to digging like moles. If we can force them out of their trenches, though, the advantage swings to us. You and Lieutenant General George will try tomorrow at sunrise."

Faced with a direct order, Fighting Joseph said the only thing a soldier faced with a direct order could say: "Yes, sir."

When Hesmucet glanced toward Doubting George, his second-in-command nodded and also said, "Yes, sir." He added, "I hope we'll have as much magecraft as possible supporting the attack."

"You will," Hesmucet promised. "Now go ready your men." The two generals saluted again and rode off toward their own encampments. Hesmucet called for two more runners. "Fetch me Colonel Phineas and Major Alva," he said.

The mages arrived together, both of them aboard asses; for some reason Hesmucet had never been able to fathom, wizards made shockingly bad unicorn-riders. "Good day, sir," Phineas said. He was round-faced and plump and bald as a turnip. He'd been senior mage in the army since General Guildenstern commanded it. He was excellent at keeping track of things, but, like a lot of southron sorcerers, only moderately good at actual conjuration.

"Good day, Colonel," Hesmucet returned, every bit as formally. Getting the most out of Phineas involved taking him seriously, or at least seeming to.

"What can we do for you, sir?" That was Major Alva, his young voice cracking with eagerness. He was tall and skinny, with a beard still patchy in spots and with a shock of panther-black hair that wouldn't lie flat no matter how he greased and combed it, but that stuck out in all directions like the springs from a skinned sofa. He'd been Lieutenant Alva till a few months before, but he was the most potent southron mage Hesmucet had ever found. Phineas kept track of things. Alva *did* things, and liked doing them.

"We are going to have another try at Viper River Gap tomorrow," Hesmucet told him. "We want to take Caesar away from the traitors. Anything you can do in the sorcerous line would be appreciated."

Colonel Phineas coughed a couple of loud, formal coughs. "If you could have given us more notice, General, we might well have been able to offer you assistance of a more comprehensive nature."

"No doubt you're right, Colonel," Hesmucet said. "But you will, I trust, understand that war is not a business where we know everything ahead of time. If James the Bird's Eye had broken into Caesar a couple of days ago, I wouldn't be worrying about attacking the place now, would I?"

"Most disorderly," Phineas said disapprovingly. Phineas was good at disapproving of things, less good at approving of them.

Alva said, "Don't worry, sir. I expect I can come up with something." He ignored the existence of every other mage in Hesmucet's army. Considering his strength as compared to that of the other mages, Hesmucet didn't blame him. Leaning toward the commanding general, he asked, "What have you got in mind, sir? Shall we try scaring the northerners out of their shoes, the way we did at Funnel Hill, or doing something to help our men move forward?"

"Let's see what we can do to help our side, Major," Hesmucet answered. "Fine as your spells were at Funnel Hill, they didn't shift the enemy so much as I would have liked. The northerners are traitors, but they're Detinans, too, same as we are. They don't scare easily."

"Right you are, sir." Alva was an easygoing fellow, if he deigned to notice you at all. Hesmucet took a certain amount of pride in being able to draw the wizard's attention. Alva turned to Phineas. "That variation of the befoggery we were talking about the other day . . ."

"On that scale?" Phineas looked dubious. He often did. The way his face settled into the expression like a fat man sinking into a soft, comfortable hassock proved as much. Shaking his head, he went on, "It's too much for any one man, yourself included, I'm afraid."

"Oh, don't be afraid, sir," Alva said, which made Phineas splutter and turn red. Alva blithely pushed ahead: "I can set it up and leave parts of it for squadrons of mages to put into operation."

He casually assumed himself to be worth whole squadrons. By the way Phineas grunted, he assumed Alva was worth them, too, but he didn't like the idea. "*Can* you set it up in that fashion?"

"Of course I can." Now Alva sounded certain, infuriatingly certain. "Same principles of division of labor that go into a well-run manufactory. I create, the others duplicate. Should be easy." Phineas looked appalled at that. Alva didn't seem to notice. He turned to Hesmucet. "Do you want to know what we're talking about, sir?"

"No," Hesmucet told him. "I want to know what you'll do, and when. How is your business." Alva beamed at him. He chuckled, a bit self-consciously. More than half by accident, he'd said the right thing.

Rollant had several extra sheaves of crossbow quarrels clipped to his belt. He was far from the only man in Lieutenant Griff's company to take such a precaution. Despite that, he wasn't unduly astonished when Griff singled him out: "Don't you know that's contrary to regulations, soldier?"

You wouldn't pick on me if my hair were black, the escaped serf thought. Aloud, he said, "Yes, sir." He made no move to divest himself of the extra crossbow bolts. Lieutenant Griff didn't ask him to, either. The company commander had got it out of his system by complaining. Rollant sighed. Sure enough, he was a lodestone for such gripes.

Trumpets blared. "Come on!" Griff yelled. "Form up! Nobody's going to say this company doesn't pull its weight in the regiment."

So far as Rollant knew, no one had ever said any such thing. Griff always needed something to be unhappy about.

Colonel Nahath, the regimental commander, surveyed his men. "We're going to break into Caesar, boys. There aren't enough traitors in front of us to stop us. There aren't enough traitors in the whole wide world to stop us. We're good New Eborac men, and there isn't anything at all in the whole wide world that can stop us."

The soldiers raised a cheer. Lieutenant Griff added, "Remember, men, we got to the top of Proselytizers' Rise. If we can do that, may the Thunderer smite me if we can't do anything."

Beside Rollant, Smitty murmured, "Oh, he's right, no doubt about it. All we need is for the northerners to botch another spell, and we'll just walk into this Caesar place."

"We can lick the traitors," Rollant said. That was why he'd taken King Avram's silver: to hit back at the liege lords who'd held him down just as men with dark hair had held down his ancestors since their ancestors came ashore on the beaches of the Western Ocean.

"Of course we can," Smitty agreed. "We wouldn't be up here in Peachtree Province if we couldn't. But saying the enemy is going to make another mistake and make things easy for us is just a piece of gods-damned foolishness."

"Quiet in the ranks," Sergeant Joram growled. He knew what his job was, and he did it.

Nahath spoke again: "We're going to advance a little slower than usual, because the mages have something special in mind to help us."

"Gods help us," Rollant muttered, and Smitty nodded. The northerners were stronger mages than the southrons. Even the botch from Thraxton the Braggart that had panicked his own men on Proselytizers' Rise was a botch on a scale the southrons wouldn't have tried to imitate.

More horns screeched. Along with countless other men from Doubting George's army, Rollant and his comrades advanced on the traitors' trenches in front of Caesar. Those trenches looked like formidable works—and so, no doubt, they were. *Why shouldn't they be?* Rollant thought. *Plenty of serfs have spent plenty of sweat on them. Liege lords won't dig when they've got blonds to do it for them.*

Men in blue caps and tunics peered out of the trenches at the advancing southrons. Rollant waited for shouts of alarm to ring out. He also waited for firepots and stones to start flying from engines, and for repeating crossbows to start hosing the southrons' ranks with death.

As he tramped forward, he yanked the bowstring on his crossbow back to the locked position and set a bolt in the groove. All he had to do now was raise the weapon to his shoulder and pull the trigger. Loading without orders went against regulations, too. He didn't care. Neither did most of the other veterans. Sergeant Joram stalked by. He had a quarrel in the groove of his crossbow, too.

Closer and closer to the enemy lines came the southrons. "Why aren't they shooting at us?" Smitty demanded. "We're in range, gods know."

"Maybe they don't see us," Rollant said. "Maybe . . . maybe our magic really is working."

Smitty shook his head. "There's got to be some kind of explanation that makes better sense than *that.*"

But the northerners kept right on not shooting even after the southrons' crossbow bolts started landing among them, even after men started falling and crying out in pain from wounds. "What the hells is going on?" Rollant heard a man in blue yell, nothing but confusion in his voice.

And then, either because some traitor mage defeated the southrons' spell or because the two armies drew too close together for it to hold any more, the northern men in the trenches realized there were indeed foes in front of them. They cried out again, this time in rage and fear. Those whose crossbows were loaded started shooting, but they weren't so ready as they might have been.

A northerner stuck his head up above the rampart in front of the trench so he could see to aim. Before the enemy soldier could shoot, Rollant did. He missed; his quarrel dug into the rampart and kicked up dirt into the traitor's face. He came close enough to killing the fellow, though, to make him duck down in a hurry instead of doing any shooting of his own.

Frantically reloading, Rollant yanked back the bowstring and set a new bolt in the groove. All around him, other southrons were doing the same. Somebody right in front of him dropped a quarrel in his haste to reload. Instead of snatching another one from the sheaf, the soldier stopped and stooped to pick up the one he'd dropped. "Clumsy fool!" Rollant shouted, doing his best not to trample the man.

"Futter you, blondie," the soldier said.

Rage ripped through Rollant. Worst of it was that he couldn't fall on the fellow and give—or try to give—him the thrashing he deserved. Maybe after the battle was over, if they both came out alive, they would have something more to say to each other, with words or with fists. Now . . . now the northerners were awake to their peril. The real fight was with them, not with the man who also fought for King Avram.

But how are they and he different? Rollant wondered.

One obvious answer was that the trooper in a gray uniform like his own wasn't trying to kill him at the moment, and the traitors were. A southron only a couple of feet from Rollant went down with a groan, clutching at the quarrel that had sprouted in his belly. "Litter!" Rollant shouted. "Litter over here!" He doubted if the healers would be able to save the man; wounds that pierced the gut usually killed by fever if they didn't kill by bleeding.

He had no more time to think about that than he did about the southron who didn't love blonds. He shot at the northerners again, reloaded, and shot once more. He didn't know if any of the quarrels struck home. What he did know was that his comrades were scrambling over the rampart and starting to drop down into the trenches Joseph the Gamecock's soldiers manned. He slung his crossbow, yanked out his shortsword, and swarmed over the ramparts himself.

He'd fought in the trenches before. The only good thing he could say about it was that he could hit back at the foe. Charging the enemy when he was entrenched . . . that was worse. But this was quite bad enough. Men screamed and groaned and slashed at one another and shot one another and swung clubbed crossbows and wrestled and punched and kicked and bit.

Reinforcements in blue came rushing up from the direction of Caesar to try to hold the southrons back. But more men in gray from Doubting George's army dropped down into the trenches. A crossbow bolt scored a bleeding line across the back of Rollant's hand. Half an inch lower and it might have left the hand crippled forever.

"Forward!" Lieutenant Griff shouted shrilly.

Forward they went—for a little while. After that, the enemy got as many reinforcements as they did. That made the fighting even more desperate than it had been. Rollant was no great swordsman. He'd never used a sword before the war: only a woodworker's tools. And the shortsword was a clumsy weapon anyhow. But his blade soon had blood on it.

"King Geoffrey!" the traitors shouted, and "Provincial prerogative forever!" and "To the seven hells with King Avram!" and "To the seven hells with the blonds!" Here and there, when they surged east again in a counterattack, they would capture some of Avram's soldiers and manhandle them back to the rear. They had camps for southron prisoners, just as there were camps for northern prisoners in the south. But they didn't manhandle any blonds back to the rear. Ex-serfs who'd taken service against their liege lords almost always ended up dead on the field when things went wrong for their side.

I can't be captured. Rollant knew that. In the early days of the fighting, a few blonds had been forcibly returned to serfdom. That didn't happen any more. The northerners hadn't needed long to realize a man who'd taken up arms against them once was liable, even likely, to do it again as soon as he saw the chance.

Some time in the middle of the day, a lull fell over the field, with both sides equally exhausted. Rollant had a moment to snatch a few breaths and look around. He discovered Smitty only a few feet away, also panting and looking around to see what the attack had gained.

"Well, this isn't like going at that Vulture's Nest place," Rollant said. "We could've kept fighting there till the last war of the gods and never broken through."

"We've got a chance here, sure enough," Smitty agreed. "More room to wiggle here. That other gap, we almost had to go in there single file to get at the fornicating traitors."

Rollant pointed ahead. "You think we'll take that Caesar?"

"We'd better," his comrade answered. "If we don't, Doubting George'll eat every one of us, and without salt, too."

"You're right," Rollant said, and forced a smile. The Detinans dimly recalled the days when their ancestors had been maneaters. Those days were long gone now, and had been for centuries even before the dark-haired men crossed the Western Ocean and set foot in this land, but the memory lingered in jokes like that. So far as Rollant knew, none of his own forebears had ever done anything so barbaric.

Other small things reminded Rollant he wasn't quite an ordinary Detinan, even if he fought alongside thousands of them. Pointing ahead again, he said, "Who or what's a Caesar?" He had no idea.

To his surprise, Smitty only shrugged. "Beats me. Probably just a made-up name."

"Suppose you're right." Rollant seized the moment to plunge his sword into the nearly blood-red dirt of southeastern Peachtree Province—very different from the black mud he'd grown up with in the swamp country of Palmetto Province—to clean it. He said, "Our magecraft did work, at least pretty much."

"So it did." Smitty nodded. "That's something. I bet the traitors are mad enough to spit nails like a repeating crossbow, too."

"Probably." Rollant cocked his own hand-held crossbow, fit a bolt to the groove, and took a shot at motion in the trenches the northerners still held. As often happened, he couldn't tell whether he hit or missed.

That one shot seemed to be a signal to resume the fight. A thirty-pound stone ball from a northern catapult thudded down only a few paces away. Some of that blood-red dirt splashed up and hit Rollant in the face. A southron soldier the stone struck screamed, but not for long. More southrons started shooting at the enemy. Before long, the battle blazed at full fury once more.

And at full fury it remained for the rest of the day. Try as they would, the southrons didn't manage to break into Caesar. But Rollant was sure the enemy spent men like coppers holding them out. "They can't go on doing that," he said as the sun sank behind the town. "They won't have an army left if they do."

"That's always been one thing we could do," Smitty said. "If all else fails, we can grind the bastards down till they've got nothing left. Only trouble with that is, it grinds down an awful lot of us, too."

"I know," Rollant said dolefully. "But it's pretty plain we aren't any smarter than they are, even with General Hesmucet in charge instead of General Guildenstern. So we'd better be tougher, wouldn't you say?"

"We'd better be something, anyhow," Smitty answered. "The something I am right now is gods-damned tired." He took his blanket from his knapsack, cocooned himself in it, and started to snore.

Rollant stayed awake a good deal longer. Maybe that meant he'd had more sleep the night before. Maybe—and more likely—it just meant he was too keyed up after the day's hard fighting to wind down in a hurry.

The traitors seemed very much awake, too. Their campfires burned brightly all the way back to Caesar. Every once in a while, a bolt or a stone or a firepot would land among the southrons. By all the signs, they needed to be ready to fight again in the morning, or perhaps in the middle of the night.

Rollant had just dozed off when Sergeant Joram shook him awake for sentry-go. Rubbing sleep out of his eyes, he stared off to the west. "What's going on there?" he asked, pointing to two new blazes beyond the profusion of northern campfires.

"Gods damn me if I know," Joram answered. "Maybe they're burning what they can't use."

But what Joseph the Gamecock's men were burning, dawn revealed, was the pair of wooden bridges over the Rubicon, the river that ran west of Caesar. They'd kept campfires going close to the southrons, but they'd had only a handful of men around them. Now their whole army had crossed the Rubicon, and was retreating toward Marthasville as fast as it could go.

Lieutenant General Bell could not have been more revolted if he'd faced the prospect of losing his other leg and having his other arm crippled. His men tramped glumly north, along with the rest of the Army of Franklin. The only man in the whole army who seemed satisfied with what they'd done at Viper River Gap was Joseph the Gamecock.

"We hurt them," he said when Bell, strapped onto his unicorn, rode up to remonstrate. "We hurt them badly."

"But they hold the field . . . sir," Bell growled.

"But the field is not important," Joseph answered. "No field this side of Marthasville is important. We'll find another miserable little place to defend in a few days and let them squander more lives attacking it."

"When do we attack them?" Bell asked.

"If we see a chance, we can do that," Joseph said. "More likely, though, we'll go on defending."

That made Bell take a swig from his jar of laudanum. But not even the potent drug eased the turmoil in his mind. As soon as the army stopped for the evening, he began a new letter to King Geoffrey. *May it please your Majesty*, he began with malice aforethought, knowing that what he had to say would not please the king at all, *I have just witnessed and been compelled by circumstances to take part in the most disgraceful and disgusting withdrawal ever recorded in the annals of warfare.*

"Is that too strong?" Bell wondered aloud. He shook his big, leonine head. It wasn't. He would have taken oath to any and all gods that it wasn't.

Joseph the Gamecock ordered this army out of its works and into retreat, abandoning all parts of Peachtree Province from Caesar northward to the provincial border to the foe. The Army of Franklin—the Thunderer grant that it see once more the province for which it was named—was not defeated in the fieldworks it was trying to defend. Caesar was not on the point of falling when the general commanding abandoned it to an evil fate.

He paused to ink his pen once more and to look up at the ceiling of his pavilion, seeking inspiration from the gods or wherever he might find it. A moment later, the pen was racing across the paper again. *However well the Army of Franklin fought in the fieldworks, I have seen no sign that it can fight outside of them. Entrenching does indeed kill soldiers' spirits. The sorcery is slow and exceedingly subtle, but no less sure for that.*

"What to do?" he muttered. "What to do?"

So long as the general commanding has and is known

to have your confidence, your Majesty, we can but obey his orders and hope they will serve, however unlikely that may seem. But it would be disastrous and unfortunate to see this campaign come to an ignominious conclusion when you have officers who would gladly serve you for the sake of the glory they might win in the said service.

I have, sir, the honor to remain your most humble and obedient servant. . . . Bell signed his name, sanded the letter dry, sealed it, and sent it out in the same clandestine way he had with his earlier missive. He didn't know what results that one had had—none he could see yet. He hoped this one would do more.

"Cowardice," he muttered. "If it's not cowardice, it must be treason. They are there. How can we drive them away without hitting them?"

It all seemed obvious to him. It seemed so obvious, he started to hitch his painful way over to Joseph the Gamecock's pavilion and confront him. After heaving himself to his feet—*no, to my foot,* he thought—he checked himself. Even he could see that that would do him no good.

He took the bottle of laudanum from his pocket, pulled the cork with his teeth, and swigged. As always, it tasted vile. As always, he didn't care. "Ahhh," he said, the soft, sated sigh of a man returning to the bosom of his beloved. He waited for the potent mix of spirits and poppy juice to work its will on him. He had not long to wait.

Calm flowed through him. He no longer wanted to do anything dreadful to Joseph the Gamecock. He recognized that that would not be a good idea: if without leave he assailed the general commanding, had he any hope of afterwards ascending to the command? No. Surely it would go to a plodder like Roast-Beef William. Best to wait, then, and let his letters work . . . if they would.

As the laudanum took its soft, sure grip on his soul, he floated away from some, at least, of the pain tormenting him. And as the pain receded, so did some of his anger at Joseph the Gamecock. With enough laudanum in him, Bell could look at things more disinterestedly. James was assuredly loyal to the kingdom if not to the king. He was doing what he thought best, what he thought right.

"That doesn't mean it *is* right, though," Bell rumbled. Laudanum might ease his mind, but didn't change it.

He grabbed his crutches, heaved himself upright, and went out into the hot, muggy, firefly-punctuated night. "Good evening, sir," Major Zibeon said smoothly, materializing at his side.

"And what, by the gods, is so good about it?" Bell demanded. "Did you see one chance, one single, solitary chance, where we might have struck the enemy today?"

"No, sir," his aide-de-camp answered. "And I was looking for such a chance, too."

"So was I," Bell said. "I didn't see one, either. If I had, I would have hurled my men against the gods-damned southrons in the open field, and to the seven hells with what Joseph the Gamecock had to say about it."

"I have no doubt you would have, sir." Zibeon did not sound approving.

"We've got to hit the southrons a blow," Bell insisted, as he'd been insisting since before the campaign began. "How far north will we go before we dare turn and face them again? All the way to Marthasville?"

"Not so far as that, sir," Major Zibeon said, sounding as much like a good servant as a soldier. "From what I hear, the general commanding intends to halt at the fieldworks outside Fat Mama."

"Hells of a name for a town," Bell muttered; that one penetrated even laudanum. Then, more slowly than he would have done before he was maimed and had to drug himself to hold anguish at bay, he called up a map in his mind. "Fat Mama? That's bad enough—it's halfway to Marthasville, by the Lion God's fangs."

"Not quite, sir," his aide-de-camp replied. "And the position is quite strong. With any luck at all, we should be able to hold them there for some time."

"I doubt it," Bell said, unconsciously imitating Lieutenant General George. "Joseph will decide we're too fornicating outnumbered, and he'll find an excuse to skedaddle again."

"As Hesmucet comes farther up into Peachtree Province, the glideway path on which he depends for food and crossbow bolts and firepots and such grows longer and longer,"

Zibeon said. "He needs more and more men to guard it, which leaves him with fewer and fewer men to put in in the field against us."

Bell fixed him with a stare so cold and fierce, it might indeed have come from the Lion God. Campfirelight only gave his eyes a cold glitter that made his aide-de-camp involuntarily give back a step. "So what?" Bell said. "Joseph won't care. You mark my words. He doesn't want to fight, is what's wrong with him."

"I think you're mistaken in that, sir," Major Zibeon said, gathering himself. "And Joseph is looking for ways to get Ned of the Forest to attack Hesmucet's supply line. When Ned strikes a glideway track, you may be sure it is properly struck. Ned plays the game for keeps."

"It is not a game," Bell insisted. "It is a war for the safety of our kingdom, one we must not lose. But if such as Joseph remain in charge over us, the war will be lost before it is well begun, for we shall do no fighting in it."

"Joseph believes the war is already lost, if it be a matter of man against man, for the southrons have too many more men than we do," Major Zibeon said. "To him, our best hope is to make the southrons weary of spending their lives to subdue us."

"I have heard Joseph upon this subject more times than I care to. He would, I am certain, make a most excellent bookkeeper," Bell said, acid in his voice. "Up until this time, I was unaware that casting accounts had become a cardinal military virtue."

Zibeon was an imperturbable sort of man, but he winced. "Your outspokenness may land you in difficulty, sir," he remarked.

"So what?" Bell said with a laugh. "What can my friends do to me that my foes haven't done already?" He made certain the crutch under his right armpit was secure before gesturing at his ruined body.

Did Major Zibeon flush? In the firelight, Bell couldn't be sure. His aide-de-camp said, "If you offend those set above you badly enough, they can remove you from your command."

"Only Joseph the Gamecock is set above me in all the Army of Franklin," Bell said. "Should he dare to have the nerve to seek my removal, you may rest assured I would appeal to the king."

"Would Geoffrey hearken to such an appeal?"

He'd better, Bell thought. But not even Major Zibeon knew of the letters he was writing to the king in Nonesuch. And so Bell stuck to what everyone in the northern provinces— and probably half the southrons, too—knew: "King Geoffrey and Count Joseph have been known to disagree in the past. Anyone who disagrees with Joseph may have Geoffrey on his side."

"*May*, I believe, is the critical word," Zibeon said. "Remember, sir, that we left Detina over the question of who was and who should be at the top of the hierarchy. Geoffrey's natural instinct is to support those who are higher against those who are lower. That means Joseph, not you."

"*My* natural instinct is to go out and smash the enemy," Bell retorted, "and Joseph the Gamecock has done a good, thorough job of stifling it. *I* am no bookkeeper on the battlefield, regardless of what he may be."

"When we get to Fat Mama—"

"No." Bell cut off his aide-de-camp with a toss of the head. "I told you once, and I tell you again, he'll find some excuse to run away from there, too. You mark my words and wait and see."

"Yes, sir," Major Zibeon said tonelessly. "If you will excuse me, sir . . ." He strode off into the night.

Lieutenant General Bell grunted. He didn't think he'd convinced Zibeon. On the other hand, he didn't worry about it very much. His aide-de-camp had gone on and on about hierarchies. In the hierarchy of the northern army, Bell ranked far above Zibeon. He didn't have to worry about what the major thought unless he chose to do so.

Unfortunately, the same did not apply to Joseph the Gamecock's opinions. Joseph could do as he pleased here— could and would, unless King Geoffrey reined him in. "Fat Mama," Bell said contemptuously. He turned around and stumped back into his pavilion.

When he lay down, he couldn't sleep. He took another slug of laudanum. The doses he poured down would have felled a man not used to the drug: would have knocked him out and might have stopped his heart. But the laudanum didn't even make Bell sleepy. If anything, it energized him, so that he lay on his cot with thoughts whirling like comets through his brain. Not all of them would be the best thoughts; he knew that. He would have to look at them in the morning, or whenever he turned out to be less drugged.

When I'm drugged all the time, though, how do I choose between the good ideas and those that aren't so good? he wondered. He shrugged, then wished he hadn't; even with the unicorn-stunning dose of laudanum in him, pain shot through his ruined left shoulder.

He did eventually fall asleep, whether in spite of the laudanum or because of it he could not have said. And as he slept, he dreamt. In his dream, he was whole. He had two legs. His arm did everything an arm should do. And, indeed, he did more than a mortal man might expect to do, for he found himself flying up to the mountain beyond the sky where the gods dwelt.

"What is your wish?" the Lion God asked him. The god had a lion's head on a hero's body, though his hands and feet were clawed and a tail lashed from the base of his spine.

Even facing the gods, Bell did not hesitate. "Lord, let me lead this host!" he said fervently.

"What will you do with it if you lead it?" the Thunderer asked.

"Go forth and fight the foe wherever I find him," Bell answered.

The two martial gods looked at each other. "So shall it be," they said together.

Lieutenant General Bell woke up then, with the sound of the gods' voices ringing in his ears, ringing in his soul. He knew he remained a cripple. For a moment, for one precious moment, it didn't matter. "The Army of Franklin *shall* be mine," he whispered. He hadn't asked the gods how well he would do with the army if he got it. He didn't worry about it now that he was awake, either.

III

"So this is how we're going to play the game, eh?" Doubting George said to Hesmucet as the southron army tramped north towards a hamlet with the unlovely name of Fat Mama.

"That's how it looks to me," General Hesmucet answered. "We'll fight somewhere, Joseph the Gamecock will pull back, and then we'll have to fight again."

"He's not been making things easy for us," George observed. "Of course, that's not his job, is it?"

"He won't stake everything on one throw of the dice, gods damn him," Hesmucet said. "We flanked him out of Borders, we beat him out of Caesar, but his army's still intact, and he's still got it between us and Marthasville."

"And as he falls back, he concentrates his force. And we have to thin ours out to protect our supply line," Doubting George said. "That's not good. If Ned of the Forest got athwart the glideway . . ."

"I'm doing my best to make sure that doesn't happen," Hesmucet said. "I've sent a good-sized force of unicorn-riders out from Luxor on the Great River against him. With luck,

Sam the Sturgeon will whip Ned. Even without luck, he'll keep him too busy to bother our supplies."

"May it be so." Lieutenant General George pointed ahead. "What are those men doing?"

"They're digging trenches, that's what they're doing," Hesmucet said.

George had already seen that for himself. "Yes, sir," he said. "What I should have asked was, why are they doing it? We're supposed to be on the march, not so? Did you give any order for us to entrench?"

"Lion God claw me if I did," Hesmucet answered.

"Well, then," George said, and rode toward the soldiers who were digging in. "What are you men playing at?" he demanded in his most formal tones.

"Making us some trenches, sir, just in case," one of the southrons replied.

"I see that. What I don't see is any traitors close by," George said. "In case of what, then? Since there aren't any traitors close by, why do you think you need the earthworks?"

"Just in case, sir, like I said," the soldier answered. He flipped another spadeful of red Peachtree dirt up onto what would be the parapet of the growing trench. "Somebody saw that the northerners had been digging a couple of fields over, so we thought we'd better have some trenches of our own."

"What kind of preposterous excuse are they giving?" General Hesmucet demanded as he rode up.

"As a matter of fact, sir, it doesn't sound so preposterous to me," Doubting George replied, and then explained.

"Gods damn entrenchments!" Hesmucet burst out. "Gods damn them to the seven hells. They take the offensive spirit away from our soldiers altogether."

"No, sir. I wouldn't say that." George shook his head. "The Detinan soldier fights his war the same way he runs his farm or his shop. If he invests in fighting, he expects that investment to pay."

"Well, these fellows are a pack of idiots for entrenching when there aren't any traitors in sight," Hesmucet said, and George couldn't very well disagree with that. The general commanding raised his voice: "You boys had better get moving and keep moving, or I'm going to have to find out who in the hells you are."

"Uh, yes, sir," the soldiers said in a ragged chorus. They abandoned their half-dug trenches and hurried away.

"Disgraceful," Hesmucet said.

"I still don't think so, sir," Doubting George replied. "They fight hard whenever we send them at the foe. Think of that fight by Caesar a few days ago. You can't ask for more than those men gave."

"You can always ask for more," Hesmucet said in a steely voice. That grim determination was thought-provoking. Hesmucet repeated, "You can always ask for more," and then added, "Sometimes asking for it makes the men give it to you."

"A point," George said. "A distinct point."

"What I want to know is, will we ever get to this Fat Mama place?" Hesmucet grumbled. "In this country, the gods would have to work a miracle for us to get anywhere at all. I rode through it twenty years ago, and it hasn't changed since—certainly not for the better in any way."

That was a distinct point, too. Swamps and pine woods and stands of shrubs and thorn bushes and saplings that had sprung up where the pines were cut down dominated the landscape. The roads, when there were roads, were narrow and seemed to wander at random rather than actually going anywhere. Without the sun in the sky, George would have had no idea where north lay.

With cries of alarm, a whole company of soldiers a hundred yards ahead started running away as fast as they could go. "*Now* what?" Hesmucet growled.

Before long, one of those cries of alarm developed words, or at least *a* word: "Hornets!"

"If you'll excuse me, sir," Doubting George said, and rode away from trouble as fast as he could. He was not unduly surprised to discover General Hesmucet also retreating as fast as he could persuade his unicorn to go.

"By the power vested in me as commanding general, I hereby declare those wasps traitors against King Avram," Hesmucet declared.

"That sounds good to me, sir," George said. "Shall I order

the men to arrest them and take them back to Georgetown for trial?" Before Hesmucet could reply, he went on, "Or do you suppose they're enough of a trial right here?"

Somebody yelled as he was stung. More soldiers broke ranks to escape the hornets. Ruefully, Hesmucet said, "They're doing more to slow us down than Joseph the Gamecock has so far."

"You were the one who said it, sir: as long as he holds Marthasville and keeps his army in the field, he's doing everything false King Geoffrey could ask of him. He's not the same sort of fighter as Duke Edward, but he knows his business."

"I can't argue with you there, much as I wish I could," Hesmucet answered. "He pulled out of Caesar just as slick as you please—didn't leave so much as a wagon or an ass that wasn't too lame for us to use."

Before too long, the front of the line of march sorted itself out again. But the hornets caused a traffic jam all out of proportion to the amount of harm they could have done and to the number of men they actually stung. When a handful of people stopped and flabbled because of the wasps, everybody else behind them had to stop and wait while the chaos subsided. Delay went through the whole long column of marching southrons, as one could watch a devoured pig going through a big snake.

And then, just when things finally seemed to have got back to normal, the roads opened out on a little northern town—one that wouldn't have existed if it weren't for a crossroads—called Dareton. Joseph the Gamecock had left a brigade of men behind there to skirmish with the southrons.

Colonel Andy, Doubting George's adjutant, was indignant. "What can he hope to accomplish with that?" he demanded rhetorically. "He can't possibly hope to hold us back."

"To hold us? No, not when his whole army couldn't at Borders or Caesar," Doubting George said. "To delay us? To give him more time to settle in at Fat Mama farther north and make it tougher to crack? That's what he's got in mind, sure as I'm looking at those works ahead."

"Not chivalrous," Andy sniffed. "Not sporting, either."

Peering at the fieldworks in front of Dareton, Lieutenant General George was inclined to agree. Red earth ramparts sheltered soldiers and made catapults and repeating crossbows harder for the southrons' engines to reach. "He'll try to do us as much harm as he can and then pull back," George predicted.

"Let's just mask his position and then go on," Andy said.

But it wouldn't be that easy or that cheap. By the way Joseph the Gamecock's artificers had sited their wards, they'd made sure the southrons couldn't pass on the open ground between Dareton and the forest to the east without coming in range of their weapons.

"Do you know what I am going to do?" Doubting George said, a certain bleak amusement in his voice.

"No, sir." Andy didn't sound amused at all. He sounded thoroughly indignant at Joseph the Gamecock.

"I am going to get rid of a cockroach by dropping an anvil on it."

"Sir?" Andy didn't get it. When the gods were passing out imagination, he'd been in line for a second helping of diligence. That made him an excellent adjutant, and would surely have made him a disaster as a commander.

"Never mind, Colonel," George said soothingly. "I'll show you." He began giving orders.

The southrons' siege engines rumbled forward on their wheeled carts. They started heaving stones and darts and firepots at the entrenchments in front of Dareton. The catapults in the fieldworks answered back as best they could, but Doubting George had ordered far more engines into action than Joseph the Gamecock had left with the defenders.

And George threw more men at Dareton than Joseph had left behind to hold the place—many, many more. The whole Army of Franklin might have held his assaulting force out of the town. Then again, it might not have. A single lonely brigade, however feisty, had not a chance.

Its commander soon realized as much. He left one regiment in the field to hold up the southron army for as long as it could, but got the rest of his men out of the trenches and marching through Dareton and on to the north. Here and there along the line, columns of smoke rising into the sky marked burning siege engines the traitors couldn't take away with them.

All in all, it was a minor triumph of delay. Glum prisoners came trudging back through the southrons' lines. They cursed the men who'd caught them, they doubly cursed every blond they saw in a gray tunic, and they cursed Doubting George when they saw him.

"Freeze in the seven hells!" some shouted, at the same time as others were yelling, "Fry in the seven hells!"

George turned to Colonel Andy. "If half of me freezes while the other half fries, on average I ought to be pretty comfortable."

"Er, yes," his adjutant replied, and George stifled a sigh. He'd long since realized Andy had not a dram of whimsy concealed anywhere about his person. That being so, why was he disappointed now? *Because nobody likes to make a joke and have it fall flat,* he thought.

"Forward!" he shouted once more, and forward the soldiers went. But the stubborn defense at Dareton had cost them three hours of marching time, at the very least. Joseph the Gamecock's army was surely using that time to good advantage. George thought about marching his men into the night to make up for the time they'd lost.

He thought about that—and then dismissed the notion after one section of the army followed a looping country track through the woods that proved to double back on itself, so they took their comrades in flank. If they'd been northerners, his force would have been in trouble. As things were, straightening out the traffic jam and getting everybody on the right road took almost as long as smashing through the entrenchments in front of Dareton had.

Could we do this at night? George wondered. He shook his head. It struck him as unlikely. Weariness wasn't the only reason armies halted when darkness fell.

And so the army encamped at sunset well short of Fat Mama. Campfires sent savory smoke into the sky, smoke made more savory by the meat roasting above a good many of those fires. Some of the meat came from cattle the army had brought along. Some, George was sure, came from local beasts that had met an untimely demise thanks to southron foragers. That was against the rules of war King Avram had set forth. To the king, the northerners remained his subjects and were not to be despoiled. The reality was that the northerners hated Avram and his soldiers, and those soldiers returned the disfavor. If they were hungry, they would eat whatever they could get their hands on.

Some commanders discouraged them. Doubting George looked the other way. The harder the time the north had, the sooner the war would end—that was how he thought of things.

And, as always happened when southron armies penetrated into a new part of the north, blonds on the run from their liege lords started coming into camp. Some were men alone, others whole families together. The army had plenty of use for laborers and washerwomen, and the liege lords who had to do without the labor of their serfs would, with luck, contemplate the cost of rebellion against their rightful sovereign.

Taking in blonds also had costs, though. George remembered the one who'd murdered his wife and the officer who'd been trifling with her, though he'd also died, at the officer's hands. That had been a nasty business all the way around.

George grunted and shook his head. That was a nasty business on a small scale. The nasty business coming up would be much larger and much worse. One way or the other, this campaign and Marshal Bart's in Parthenia would say who won the war, and why. "It had better be us," George said, and rode on toward the north.

Captain Gremio found the little town of Fat Mama remarkable in no way but its name. It held a couple of thousand people, taking Detinans and blonds together, and had a main street full of shops, a few streets full of houses, the local baron's keep, and not much else. Lesser nobles' manor houses dominated the countryside, with the serfs' shacks usually close by.

Except for the glideway path that ran through Fat Mama and the low hills to the east and south of the town,

Joseph the Gamecock never would have stopped there. Gremio was sure of that. As things were, his company, along with the rest of Colonel Florizel's regiment, filed into trenches already waiting for them, trenches Joseph had had the local serfs dig ahead of time.

"I'm sick of earthworks," Florizel grumbled. "I'm sick to death of them, as a matter of fact."

"But, your Excellency, it's a lot easier to catch your death outside of earthworks," Gremio said.

In the Karlsburg circles he'd frequented before the war, such wordplay would have got the groan it deserved, whereupon everyone would have gone about his business. But Florizel gave Gremio a look straight out of a Five Lakes blizzard and then limped on down the trench. Gremio wondered what he'd done wrong. Figuring that out, unfortunately, took but a moment. *You just contradicted the regimental commander.*

He sighed. Back in Karlsburg, he wouldn't have been so foolish as to call a presiding judge a fool, even if he was one. He would have been especially careful not to do such a thing, in fact, if the presiding judge was a fool. But he was a free Detinan, and free Detinans had the privilege of saying what was on their minds. Now he saw that having such a privilege and using it weren't necessarily one and the same.

From behind him, someone said, "I thought you were funny, sir—and you told the truth."

He turned. "Thank you, Sergeant Thisbe," he replied. "Sometimes, though, the truth is the worst thing you can possibly tell."

Thisbe's eyebrows rose. "You say that, sir? You, a barrister? If there's no truth in the lawcourts, where can we hope to find it?"

"Lawcourts are for finding truth, sure enough," Gremio said. "That doesn't mean it's there to begin with. And there are ways to tell the truth and still not tell all of it, and to tell it in a way that makes you look good and the fellow you're at law against the greatest villain still unburned."

"That's . . . not the way it should be, sir." Thisbe was an

earnest young man, much given to thought about the way things should be.

Gremio shrugged. "It's the way things are in a lawcourt. And remember, the other fellow has a barrister trying to play all the same tricks you are." He waved toward the south. "King Geoffrey wouldn't need a big army if that abandoned fool of an Avram didn't have one, too."

Thisbe thought that over before finally nodding. "I suppose that's true, sir. Things have to balance out, don't they? But there aren't any judges in this fight, the way there are in a court."

"Of course there's a judge," Gremio said. Thisbe gave him a quizzical look. He explained: "The lawcourt of history will say who won. It's got to be either King Geoffrey or King Avram."

"Do you think we can still win this war?" Sergeant Thisbe asked.

"As long as we hold on to Marthasville, as long as we hurt the southrons every day, we can win," Gremio answered, and then, precise as a barrister, corrected himself: "We can make King Avram quit. We're not going to give up the fight, come what may. The only way the southrons can beat us is to knock us flat. But if they get sick of funeral pyres and of soldiers never coming home, then Geoffrey will be king in the north for a long time."

"Ah." Thisbe nodded again and rubbed his smooth chin. "That explains why Joseph the Gamecock is making the kind of fight he is. He's trying to get the southrons to sicken of the war."

"Yes, I think so," Gremio replied. "As long as we can stay in the field, as long as Marthasville stays in our hands, we've got a decent chance."

Before Thisbe could answer, a sentry sang out from the south: "The dust is stirring. I think the southron soldiers are coming."

Gremio muttered something under his breath. He hadn't expected General Hesmucet's men to get to Fat Mama quite so soon. The brigade down at Dareton should have held them up for quite a while. He wondered what had gone wrong. Something surely had, for the sentry was right: that rising cloud of dust could only come from the feet of thousands of marching men, the hooves of thousands of unicorns and asses, the wheels of thousands of supply wagons and engine-hauling carts. Even as he watched, the reddish cloud on the southern horizon grew taller and thicker.

Before too long, he started making out little flashes of light within the dust cloud. "Unicorns' iron-shod horns," he murmured.

He didn't realize he'd spoken aloud till Thisbe nodded once more and said, "Yes, and the heads on the spears the pikemen carry."

Watching the army General Hesmucet led come forward and deploy on the flat farmland east of the hills warding Fat Mama was awe-inspiring. Regiment after regiment of gray-clad unicorn-riders, pikemen, and crossbowmen seemed to fill every available inch of space.

"How can we hope to hold them back, let alone beat them?" Now Thisbe seemed to be talking to himself. "See how many men they have!"

"They're drawing themselves up like that on purpose, to try to intimidate us." Gremio would not admit, even to himself, that he *was* intimidated. "Their numbers are why the gods made field fortifications—and, even more to the point, why our serfs made them."

Thisbe said, "That's true. It's really amazing what a difference earthworks make in how many men get killed or wounded."

Gremio didn't want to think about getting killed or wounded. He knew such things were possible, but why dwell on them? He pointed toward the southern host, which had just about finished its evolutions. "When they're done trying to frighten us, then we'll see what they really have in mind."

"Nothing good," Sergeant Thisbe predicted.

"No doubt you're right," Gremio agreed. "If they had our good will in mind, they would leave us alone and let us run our affairs as we choose. That's the point of the war, after all. But it's not quite what I meant."

"What did you mean, sir?"

"Where they'll put their encampments and where they'll concentrate their men," Gremio replied. "That will tell us a good deal about how they plan to attack us or out-flank us."

"Oh. Yes. Of course," Thisbe said, which left the company commander somewhat deflated. He'd seen army commanders fail to pay enough attention to what the enemy was up to, but his sergeant took the notion for granted. Did that mean Sergeant Thisbe ought to be leading an army? Gremio had his doubts. But what did it say about the wits of some of the men who actually were in charge of armies and wings? Nothing good, he feared.

Tents sprang up like fairy rings of outsized toadstools. The southrons went about the business of setting up camp with the same matter-of-fact competence the men of the Army of Franklin displayed. Most of them were veterans. They'd encamped a great many times before. They knew how to do the job.

Thisbe said, "They must have a great plenty of men and money down in the south of Detina."

"They do," Gremio agreed. "More men and more money than we have, by far."

"How are we ever going to beat them, then?" the sergeant asked.

"We do have a couple of things going for us," Gremio answered. "For one, they're invaders here. This is *our* king-dom, and we know it, and we're fighting for it."

"That's so." Thisbe nodded yet again. "What else?"

"Why, the other thing we have going for us is that we're *right*, of course," Gremio replied.

Sergeant Thisbe smiled. "That's bound to gain us credit with the gods, sir. How much good will it do down here on earth?"

"Good question," Gremio said. "When I have a good answer, I'll let you know." He peered out toward the east. "No chance of hitting them tonight—that seems pretty plain. They've got everything well covered. They know as well as we do that we would hit them if they gave us half a chance." Gremio rubbed his chin. "Or I think we would. Ever since this campaign started, we've been letting them come to us. We haven't been looking for chances to go at them. That doesn't seem to be Joseph the Gamecock's style."

Thisbe pointed out toward the southron host with a grimy-nailed, callused hand. "Look at what we're facing. How can we possibly charge out against them? They'd chew us up and spit us out if we did, as many men as they have there."

"I think you're right," Gremio said. Most of the men he led, most of the officers over him, would have thought the sergeant was wrong. Most of them reckoned Lieutenant General Bell the perfect northern patriot, and admired him for the wounds he'd taken going straight at the foe. Of course, most of the officers over Captain Gremio were noblemen. He hoped he had a more practical way of looking at the world.

"Time to get *our* men bedded down for the night," Thisbe observed.

"See to it, Sergeant," Gremio said. Thisbe nodded. Gremio knew Thisbe would make sure everything was as it needed to be. He did give one additional order: "Put plenty of pickets well forward. After that spell the southrons used at Caesar, no telling what sort of sneaky things they might try. We haven't seen many night attacks, but I don't want to be taken by surprise."

"Yes, sir," Sergeant Thisbe said. "I'll see to it, sir." Off he went, brisk as if he'd just drunk four cups of tea.

Gremio wished he had that kind of energy himself. He yawned wide enough to split his head in two. Here and there in the trenches, men were getting cookfires going. The stews the cooks would serve weren't that good, but they did keep belly and backbone from gaining too intimate an acquaintance.

After patrolling the front his company had to cover, Captain Gremio lay down on his blanket and tried to go to sleep. The night was as muggy and almost as hot as the day had been, so he certainly needed no covers to hold the cold at bay. But mosquitoes buzzed in invisible but hungry clouds. They looked on Gremio the same way he looked on the cooks' stewpots. He ended up wrapping himself in the blanket just to keep himself from being devoured.

He slept through the night undisturbed. Because of the good luck the southrons had had with their sorcerously aided attack on Caesar, he'd wondered if they might try something similar here by Fat Mama. The confusion of night would, or could, have aided them, too. But everything stayed quiet.

When he woke, dawn was painting the eastern sky behind the southrons pink. Clouds floated through the air, looking thicker and darker off to the west. He wondered if it would rain. With all the moisture in the air, it seemed likely. The idea of staying in the trenches as they turned to mud didn't much appeal to him, but the idea of fighting outside them against that vast host of southrons seemed even less delightful. He'd heard Lieutenant General Bell was angry that Joseph the Gamecock wouldn't storm out to assail the enemy, but he couldn't see why. Joseph's plan made perfectly good sense to him.

Besides, he thought, *if it does rain, everyone's bowstring will be wet, and that will put a better damper on the fighting than anything this side of a peace treaty.* He snorted. As if Avram would grant terms the north could stand, or as if King Geoffrey could accept any the south was likely to offer. No, this fight would have to be settled on the field.

That thought had hardly crossed his mind before Sergeant Thisbe came over to him and said, "Sir, it looks like the southrons are doing something funny in their encampment."

"Funny how?" Gremio asked, his hand sliding of itself toward the hilt of his sword. "Are they deploying for an attack?" If they were, if Thisbe could see they were, then they weren't using the masking spell they'd tried in Caesar.

The sergeant shook his head. "I don't think so, sir. What it looks like is that some of them are going away."

"What?" Gremio said. "I'd better come have a look for myself."

But when he got to a good vantage point, he discovered that, as usual, Sergeant Thisbe had it right. A good many southrons did look to be breaking camp and heading north.

Excitement flowed through him. "They're trying to pull the same stunt they did down at Borders and Caesar," he breathed. "They'll leave some of their men behind to keep us busy here, while they use the rest to try to outflank us."

"I wonder if we can attack them, now that they've cut down the size of the host right in front of us," Thisbe said.

Attacking the whole southron army, Gremio was convinced, was madness. Attacking part of it . . . "So do I," he said. "It just might work."

Lieutenant General Bell liked very little about Fat Mama. He'd made his headquarters in a fancy manor house not far outside the town, and that proved a mistake. The baron who'd built the place had not only put in marble floors but also kept them polished to a brilliant gloss. They were so very slick, Bell's crutches didn't want to keep their grip. They kept trying to fly out from under him, in which case he would have gone flying, too.

If I break my neck along with wrecking an army and losing a leg, I won't be of much use to the kingdom or to myself, he thought after one such narrow escape. *A man does need a few working parts.*

The wing he commanded at Fat Mama was stationed farther north than any of the other soldiers in the Army of Franklin. Bell wondered whether Joseph the Gamecock had posted them there just to make him ride—and suffer—for an extra mile or two. He had no intention of asking Joseph, for the army commander was liable to tell him yes. They had enough trouble getting along without that.

Someone pounded on the door to the manor house. One of Major Zibeon's assistants went to see who it was. He came back to Bell and reported: "A messenger from Count Joseph, sir."

"I shall receive him, of course," Bell said, wondering what Joseph the Gamecock wanted to bother him about now.

When the messenger came in, he almost tripped on the smooth, smooth marble floor, and had to flail his arms wildly for balance. Oddly, that made Bell feel better. If a whole man could come close to breaking his neck here, he had no reason to know shame for having trouble getting around.

"What can I do for you?" he asked, more warmth than usual in his voice.

"Count Joseph's compliments, sir, and he requests the

boon of your company just as fast as you can get to him," the runner replied.

That meant travel, and travel meant more torment. Bell sipped from his little bottle of laudanum. "Why?" he asked, and warmth was only a memory.

"Sir, he says he is contemplating an attack, and desires your views along with those of his other wing commanders," the messenger told him.

"Contemplating . . . an attack?" Bell said, as if the young man before him had suddenly started speaking a foreign language. "Joseph the Gamecock is contemplating an *attack*? My ears must be tricking me." He dug a finger into one, as if to clear out whatever was blocking them.

All the runner said was, "Yes, sir. He is, sir. Truly."

"I can hardly believe it," Bell said. Curiosity was enough to outweigh pain, at least for the moment. "You may go back and tell him I shall attend him directly." The runner saluted and left.

Bell went to the commanding general's headquarters in a buggy, not on unicornback. It took him a little longer, but gave him time to think. He kept stroking his long, curly beard as the carriage bounced toward the home where Joseph the Gamecock had set up shop. What sort of ulterior motive did Joseph have for ordering an attack now, of all times? *Is he trying to discredit me?* Bell wondered. *Has someone let him know about my letters to King Geoffrey? That could be sticky.*

He had trouble getting very excited about it. Without the laudanum, he knew he would have been all in a swivet. Of course, without the laudanum, he would also have been in agony. As things were, he was merely in pain—and the drug laid a soft, muffling cloud over whatever else he might have felt.

When he got to Joseph's headquarters, he discovered Leonidas the Priest and Roast-Beef William there ahead of him. They both towered over Joseph the Gamecock, who was gesturing animatedly as they talked outside. Bell descended from the buggy and hitched his way over to the other generals.

"Good day," Joseph the Gamecock said with a courtly bow.

"Good day, sir," Bell answered. "What is this I hear of attack? Do we still recall the word?"

"We do indeed," Joseph said. "I have always said I would smite the stinking southrons if I saw the chance. Now I do believe. they are giving it to us, and I intend to use it."

"You had better tell me more, sir," Bell said, blinking. "This is extremely surprising." *This is nothing like what I've told King Geoffrey in my letters,* he thought. *What will he do if he hears of the Army of Franklin attacking? What will he do if he hears of it attacking successfully? Whatever it is, it will be nothing that works to* my *advantage.*

"I shall be delighted, Lieutenant General," Joseph the Gamecock said. "It appears that General Hesmucet is detaching some large part of his force for another move north around our flank. If we wait till that part has made its move, I think we can strike what's left with some hope of victory."

"Looks that way to me, too," Roast-Beef William said.

"I am dubious about the whole proposition," Leonidas the Priest declared. "I think it may be nothing but a trap, designed to lure us from our entrenchments so that the enemy may fall upon us."

Bell could have kissed the older man. Now he wouldn't be the only one speaking up against the whole idea. "I think Leonidas may have a point," he said. "I've had no reports of the southrons' moving north again come to my ears."

"You can ride out to the front line and see for yourself," Joseph the Gamecock said in some—more than some—exasperation. "Bell, you have been agitating for an attack ever since I took command of the Army of Franklin. How is it that, now that I propose one, you have not the stomach for it?"

"I want to attack with some hope of victory, sir," Bell replied. *I want to attack when it's my idea, not yours.* But he couldn't say that to the general commanding.

The general commanding, by his sniff, had no trouble figuring it out regardless of whether Bell actually said it. "You have a certain amount of trouble with subordination, don't you, Lieutenant General?"

"Duke Edward of Arlington never thought so, sir," Bell said stiffly.

"Duke Edward of Arlington gives men more leeway than most officers are in the habit of doing," Joseph retorted. "When I give you an order, I expect it to be obeyed. Have you got that?"

"Yes, sir," Bell said, holding in his rage. "I have failed in no obedience." And that was true, so far as the campaign itself went. Subordination, now, that was a different question—and Joseph the Gamecock didn't know *how* different an answer it had.

"All right, then," Joseph said. "I want all three of you to prepare your men for an attack tomorrow morning."

"Yes, sir," Roast-Beef William said. He asked no questions. He did as he was told. Joseph the Gamecock would never complain about his subordination.

Leonidas the Priest turned sorrowful eyes on the general commanding. "I fear the Lion God does not smile on this enterprise," the hierophant said. "The omens are not good. And without the gods' backing, where are we?"

"On our own in the world," Joseph the Gamecock said, fixing Leonidas with a glare like a flying crossbow quarrel. "I reverence the gods, holy sir—don't get me wrong about that. But until I hear them speak in my own ears, I have to make my choices about what to do. I have, and I am."

"May the Lion God not smite you for your arrogance, sir," Leonidas said. "I shall pray for his forbearance."

"Maybe we would do better to send out scouting forces come morning, to see if the southrons really did shift some large part of their host," Bell said.

Joseph threw his hands in the air. "By all the gods, gentlemen, how can I hope to attack when two of my three wing commanders think I'd be making a mistake to do so? And then King Geoffrey will blame *me* for not being aggressive enough."

You haven't been aggressive enough, Bell thought. *You may try to make up for it now, but you would have done better to strike at the southrons from the start.*

"I am an obedient man, sir," Leonidas the Priest said.

"If you order me to send my soldiers forward, I shall do so, regardless of my own personal feelings as to the wisdom of the order."

"No, no, no, no." Joseph the Gamecock shook his head. "If we attack, we should put all our force, all our spirit, into it. Otherwise, we might as well not do it at all." He swung his gaze back toward Bell. "Lieutenant General!"

"Yes, sir!" Bell said loudly.

"If you make this probing attack of yours and discover the enemy before you is weak, will you advance against him at all hazards?"

"Yes, sir. Of course, sir," Bell replied.

"All right, then," Joseph the Gamecock said. "Go ahead and do it. If the foe proves as weak as I expect, put everything you have into the blow."

"Yes, sir," Bell said for the third time. "If I may make so bold as to tell you, sir, you don't need to say that to me."

"All right," Joseph said, also repeating himself. "I know you strike hard when you strike. I hadn't thought getting you *to* strike would be so much trouble, though." He pointed to Roast-Beef William and Leonidas the Priest in turn. "Have your men ready to move, too. If Bell's attack shows the southrons to be as weak as I think they are, I'll want to hit them every which way at once."

"Yes, sir," Roast-Beef William said. He would obey without complaining and without making anyone feel he was doing him a favor.

"Yes, sir," Leonidas the Priest echoed. He wasn't happy about it, and he didn't care who knew he wasn't happy.

Bell just nodded and made his slow way back to the buggy. He felt Joseph the Gamecock's eyes boring into him every step of the way, but didn't turn around to look at the commanding general. When he returned to his own smooth-floored headquarters, he sent runners to the brigades under his command, ordering them to ready themselves for battle.

"What's going on, sir?" Major Zibeon asked.

Briefly, Bell explained. "This isn't the best time or place for the attack," he finished, "but I must obey."

Zibeon nodded. "It may not be so bad as you think, sir," he said, something like enthusiasm on his usually sour face. "If Hesmucet really has detached some large part of his force for a flanking attack, we can punish the rest before the detached portion is able to come to its rescue."

"That is also Joseph the Gamecock's theory," Bell said. "How it will turn out in practice remains to be seen."

"I know you've been eager to attack, sir," his aide-de-camp said. "Now Count Joseph is giving you your chance."

I don't want Joseph giving me anything, Bell thought. *I want to take for myself, and to do it with both hands.* But he couldn't explain that to Zibeon; he didn't know where the major's ultimate loyalty lay. "I intend to do everything I can," he said, and thought he was telling the truth. Some of it, anyhow.

As Joseph had ordered, he sent his men forward against the southrons at first light the next morning. He went forward, too, tied onto his unicorn. He'd never yet ordered soldiers to advance without advancing at their head. He had no intention of changing his ways because he was mutilated, either. Major Zibeon did ride at his side, and that was a change—before his wounds, no one would have presumed to do any such thing.

As they pushed toward the main body of the southrons, they overran a few pickets and sentries and scouts wearing gray. A few others escaped and fled toward their encampment. "So far, so good," Zibeon said.

"Yes, so far." Lieutenant General Bell sounded suspicious. "I only hope we're not moving forward into a trap."

"Not much to trap us with, sir." His aide-de-camp waved to show what he meant. "Nothing but flat land except for those trees off to our left, and there aren't enough of them to hide anything very big."

"May the Lion God prove you right," Bell said piously. "I still think the southrons could cause us trouble if—"

Before he could go on, southron unicorn-riders galloped forth to challenge his host, which had advanced about a mile. Some of them shot crossbows at Bell's men. The rest served a handful of catapults on wheeled carriages. They flung a few firepots and shot long darts. Northerners who were hit cried out in pain.

Bell's eyes kept going to those trees on the flank. "I think they've got more engines hidden away in there," he said nervously. "We'd better not go any farther, or the shots from the flank will tear us to pieces."

"Sir, I don't think you're right," Major Zibeon said, "and even if you are, we can send men over there to clear them out."

"No, my mind's made up," Bell said. "We're going back to camp. I think Hesmucet's just lying in wait for us, and to the seven hells with me if I'll give him a victory on the cheap." He shouted for his trumpeters and ordered a withdrawal. Joseph the Gamecock had ordered a probe, and he'd given Joseph that much. He had no intention of giving the commanding general anything more.

Colonel Andy eyed the retreating northerners in some perplexity. "Why are they falling back?" he asked Lieutenant General George. "They might have done us a lot of harm if they'd kept coming."

"If I knew, I would tell you," Doubting George answered. "I'll tell you this, though: you're not wrong. We just dodged a crossbow quarrel there."

"Yes, sir," his adjutant agreed. "They came forward bold as you please, and in some numbers, too. You wouldn't have thought they had that much zing left in 'em."

"It doesn't do to count the northerners as licked too soon," George said. "General Guildenstern did that, and look what it got him."

"A command out on the eastern steppe fighting the blond savages." Colonel Andy shuddered. "No, thanks. That isn't what I want to have happen to my career."

"That isn't what anybody wants to have happen to his career," George said. "It's all very well when it's the only game in town, when we're at peace everywhere else. But when there's a real war to be fought, you'd better do everything you can to fight it."

"Isn't that the truth!" Colonel Andy said fervently. He was a colonel because of the war. As soon as it ended, he would return to his permanent captain's rank—and, very likely, to a dusty fortress out on the steppe. Doubting George's own prospects were rather better; he was a permanent brigadier as well as a brevet lieutenant general. But the battle to get a decent post once the fight with King Geoffrey's men was over might well prove as fierce as any struggle in this conflict.

It could be worse, he thought. When the war was over and won—if it was to be won—the officers who'd abandoned Detina and King Avram for treason and Grand Duke Geoffrey would, George assumed, be out of the army for good. He also assumed a good many of them would go up on crosses for abandoning Detina, but that would be King Avram's decision, not his.

He called for a runner. When one of the young messengers came up, he said, "My compliments to General Hesmucet, and the northerners' attack appears to have fizzled out like a candle using up the last of its tallow. We can strike at the enemy here, if he likes, to keep Joseph the Gamecock from shifting forces to meet our latest flanking move. Repeat that back, if you'd be so kind."

"Yes, sir," the messenger said, and did. At Doubting George's nod, he hurried away.

Hesmucet himself came riding back to George before the messenger returned. The commanding general looked over the ground. "Do you know what, Lieutenant General?" he said.

"No, sir. Tell me what," George said gravely.

"I'll do just that," Hesmucet said. "Here's what: you're a lucky son of a bitch. We're all lucky sons of bitches. If the traitors had pressed that attack, you might've been in a peck of trouble."

"That thought did cross my mind, yes, sir," George said. "But Lieutenant General Bell started to come at us and then seemed as though he changed his mind with his move half begun. Peculiar."

"Bell?" Hesmucet said. "Are you sure it was Bell? He's not in the habit of pulling back from an attack once he starts one. That bastard will press ahead come hells or high water, and he hits hard when he hits, too."

"It was Bell—no doubt about it," Doubting George replied. "The handful of prisoners we took are from regiments he commands, and some of our riders saw him up on his own unicorn. With the short stump he's got on that one leg, he's not a man you can easily mistake for anyone else."

"I won't say you're wrong, on account of you're godsdamned well right," Hesmucet said. "Even so, I can hardly believe it. What made him pull back?"

"You'd have to ask him, sir, because I don't know," George replied. "All we had in front of him was the screen of Hard-Riding Jimmy's unicorn-riders. I wish I'd been able to put some men and engines in amongst the trees on his flank"—he pointed in the direction from which the northerners had come—"but I didn't have time to move any. To tell you the truth, I didn't expect the traitors to come out of their works."

"Well, now we know they will—or they may, anyhow," Hesmucet said. "We'll have to be more careful." He made a sour face. "That means more entrenching, gods damn it. I hate it, but I see no way to escape it."

"So long as we win, sir, I'm not fussy about how," George told him.

The commanding general nodded. "That is well said. It is full of the generous spirit I've looked for in you—and, I must say, I've found. We may not love each other, Lieutenant General, but we manage to work together."

"That same thing had crossed my mind a time or two, sir." George stuck out his hand. General Hesmucet clasped it. George went on, "And what do you require of me now that Bell's men have withdrawn to their trenches?"

"Be ready to pursue them and to attack if you see the opportunity when they pull out of those trenches again," Hesmucet replied. "I do not think they can hold their position long, not with another flanking maneuver even now aimed at getting into their rear."

"Just as you say, sir." Doubting George saluted.

"We're going to lick these bastards, is what we're going to do," Hesmucet said. "False King Geoffrey says he has a kingdom. He may even think he has a kingdom. What he has is a hollow shell, and, once we show that, this thing he thinks he rules will shrivel up like a pricked bladder."

"Duke Edward will have something to say about that, too," George said.

"Duke Edward is a lucky son of a bitch. I don't even think he knows what a lucky son of a bitch he is," General Hesmucet said. "All the battlefields over in southern Parthenia are cramped together. The land between Georgetown and Nonesuch works for him, because it keeps Marshal Bart—and whoever else commanded against the Army of Southern Parthenia—from using our advantage in numbers to outmaneuver Duke Edward, to hold him with part of our force and get around him with the rest."

"Fighting Joseph tried that," George remarked. "All he got for his trouble was embarrassed at Viziersville."

"I know, but that was Fighting Joseph." Hesmucet made a dismissive gesture. "A real general who tried it would have done a hells of a lot better."

Doubting George looked around to make sure Fighting Joseph was nowhere nearby. He might have failed against Duke Edward of Arlington, but he remained a proud and touchy man. He also remained nowhere in sight, for which George was duly grateful. George said, "Marshal Bart isn't trying to outmaneuver Duke Edward."

"It surely doesn't look that way," Hesmucet agreed. "He fought him in the Jungle, not far from Viziersville, and then again, and again. He's going to head for Nonesuch and to hammer Duke Edward flat if he stands in the way long enough. As I said, he hasn't got the room to maneuver that I do."

"All very interesting, and none of it quite what I expected when this spring's fighting began," Doubting George said. "I thought you would be the one who banged straight ahead."

"I might, if I were facing Duke Edward. He's fond of coming out and slugging," Hesmucet replied. "Joseph the Gamecock is different. He takes these defensive positions and invites you to bloody your nose on them. I'm not the only one shaping this campaign, and that's worth remembering."

"You're right, sir, and I hadn't thought it through." George nodded respectfully to Hesmucet. Sure enough, as with Bart, there was more to the man than met the eye. "You and Duke Edward would add up to something different from you and Joseph the Gamecock."

Hesmucet nodded. "That's right. That's just right. And Joseph and Bart would be different from what Duke Edward and Bart are turning into. The commanders on both sides make things what they are. As a matter of fact, I don't mind this game of maneuver so much as I thought I would."

"Really?" George raised an eyebrow. "Why's that, sir?"

The smile Hesmucet smiled was particularly nasty. "Because it lets me move through country that's never been fought over before. This far north, the barons and earls and counts supposed they were safe. They didn't think any southron army could ever come all the way up here. Now they're seeing they were wrong. There's no place in Geoffrey's so-called kingdom we can't reach. Let's see how much fight's left in the traitors once they start to realize that down in their guts."

As if to underscore the point he'd been making, a couple of dozen blonds—escaped serfs, every one of them, men, women, and children—came by, shepherded along by a couple of gray-uniformed southron soldiers. They were a couple of dozen people who wouldn't labor for their liege lords any more, and who would do useful work for King Avram's army. Doubting George nodded thoughtfully once more. He said, "You're fighting against Geoffrey's whole would-be kingdom, not just against Joseph the Gamecock, then."

"Well, of course," Hesmucet replied.

But it wasn't *of course,* not to George. It probably wouldn't have been *of course* to any general who'd fought before this war began, either. Wars usually aimed at defeating the enemy's army, not at smashing his whole kingdom flat. No, Hesmucet and Bart weren't playing by the old rules.

"Fighting won't be the same after this," Doubting George observed.

"I don't want there to be any more fighting in the Kingdom of Detina after this," Hesmucet said. "I want everybody to get the idea that it *is* one kingdom and it will *always be* one kingdom, and if I have to kill everybody who doesn't get that idea, or make him starve, or burn down his fancy manor and take away his serfs, I will do any of those things, and I won't lose a single, solitary minute's worth of sleep over any of it."

"You intend to be persuasive, you say." George's voice was dry.

"Gods-damn right I do," Hesmucet replied, taking his words at face value. "I want the traitors licked. I don't want them thinking, *Well, we almost won this time. Maybe we ought to try again.* If you get into a tavern fight with a man and you knock him down, you're always smart to kick him a couple of times afterwards. That way, he doesn't think the fight was close. He bloody well knows you licked him."

As a younger man, Doubting George had found himself in a few—perhaps more than a few—tavern fights of his own. The ones he'd won, he'd mostly followed Hesmucet's rule. The few he'd lost . . . Of itself, his hand rubbed his ribcage. Plenty of other tough young men thought the same way. He remembered boots thudding home, things he'd tried to keep out of his memory for years.

Hesmucet clapped him on the shoulder. "We *are* going to whip the northerners here, and I'll tell you why."

"I'm all ears," George said solemnly.

"Because Marthasville ties Joseph the Gamecock down, that's why," the general commanding said. "He has no choice: that's the place he's got to defend. If he doesn't, he might as well not be in the field. And that means, sooner or later, I'm going to flank him once too often. He'll either have to give me Marthasville or come out and fight. Either way, I'll have what I want."

"Gods grant it be so," George said.

"Don't talk that way around Major Alva," Hesmucet told him. "He'll give you plenty of reasons to think the gods don't much care one way or the other. Sort of makes you understand why they used to burn wizards every now and again." He walked off, whistling.

Doubting George had no intention of talking to Major Alva. Clever young mages were useful creatures. But, because they had a lot of the answers, they often thought and behaved as if they had them all. George was a profoundly conservative man. He'd been too conservative to leave Detina with his province and with Grand Duke Geoffrey: to his way of thinking, that there had always been one kingdom was the best argument that there should always be one kingdom. His belief in the gods and their potency was likewise deep and sincere. He didn't care to listen to a whippersnapper who would try to unsettle that belief.

If he were to try too hard, he would probably end up short a couple of teeth, George thought. *I'd kick him when he was down, too.* He didn't worry for a moment what a mage might do to him.

He called to Colonel Andy, who'd discreetly stepped out of earshot while he conferred with General Hesmucet. "Be ready to move forward at my orders or at the commanding general's," he said. "I don't think the traitors will trouble us much more with attacks of their own, not hereabouts."

"Yes, sir," his adjutant said.

"And move some of our engines forward, too," George added. "If we do have to assault the enemy's works, we'll want to make this, that, and the other thing come down on his head."

"Yes, sir," Andy repeated, rather more enthusiastically this time.

"Don't worry, Colonel," Doubting George said. "As long as we keep hammering at the enemy, we'll break him sooner or later."

"Yes, sir. That's what General Guildenstern said, too, sir, as you pointed out not so long ago."

Lieutenant General George winced. It wasn't quite what he'd pointed out, but it was pretty close. *I've been skewered,* he thought. *Which of us is supposed to be the one who doubts things? I was under the impression it was me, but I'll start wondering if Andy keeps that up.*

Joseph the Gamecock put his hands on his hips and glared from Lieutenant General Bell to Leonidas the Priest and back again. "Which of us," he asked Bell, "is supposed to be the one who wants to slug it out with the enemy, and which the one who would sooner fight positionally? Correct me if I'm wrong, but I had thought you owned the former role and I the latter. I will start wondering if you keep this up, though."

"I am sorry, sir," Bell said. "I truly am, but I do not see how we can hold our position east of Fat Mama if the southrons bring up their siege engines to bear on our works, as they are now in the process of doing."

"I must agree," Leonidas the Priest said, a lugubrious frown on his face.

"*Must* you?" Joseph snapped. Leonidas' nod was lugubrious, too. Joseph rounded on Roast-Beef William. "And what about you? Are you also of the opinion that we need to take flight?"

"No, sir," Roast-Beef William replied. "If the southrons come at us, I expect we can beat them back."

"Well, gods be praised!" Joseph exclaimed. He did a couple of mincing, mocking steps of a triumphal dance. "Someone who hasn't got his headquarters in his hindquarters, as that fool of a southron said he did a couple of years ago back in the province of Parthenia."

"Sir, I resent the imputation," Bell said.

Resent it? You don't even know what the hells it means, Joseph the Gamecock thought sourly. "You were all for attack before, Lieutenant General," he said. "You were *for* it when I was *against* it. It gave you something to complain about, in that I wasn't doing what you wanted. But when I asked you for an attack, what did I get? Excuses, nothing else but."

"Did you want me to send my brave men forward to be slaughtered?" Bell demanded. "The enemy's siege engines on our flank would have wrecked my entire wing. Anyone on the spot would have seen the same."

"By all I've heard, Lieutenant General, you were the only one who had even the slightest hint of the presence of these perhaps mythical catapults," Joseph said. "No matter what damage you may have feared, the actual damage you suffered from them was nil."

"I fear nothing," Bell rumbled. From most men, that would have been a brag or a lie. From him, Joseph the Gamecock believed it. It did not, however, necessarily make things better rather than worse.

"We've already yielded the southrons too much land," Roast-Beef William said. "If we have to leave Fat Mama, they hold most of the southern half of Peachtree Province."

"If we hold our ground here and are overwhelmed, what then?" Leonidas the Priest returned. "In that case, not only is the southern half of the province lost, but also the army that could defend the rest."

Joseph the Gamecock felt like tearing his thinning hair. "How, pray tell, is the enemy going to overwhelm us here?" he said. "These works are as strong as a swarm of serfs could make them."

"Not strong enough," Bell insisted. "If the southrons move forward and put their catapults on our flanks, they'll make us sorry we ever chose to fight here."

"We'll be sorrier if we leave," Joseph said. Roast-Beef William nodded, his ruddy face even redder than usual. But both Bell and Leonidas the Priest solemnly shook their heads. Joseph felt like kicking them. "What am I supposed to do?" he cried. "I want to stand my ground, but how can I possibly when two of my wing commanders think I would be courting disaster if I tried?"

"I was not the one who ordered us here to Fat Mama," Bell said.

"No, but you and this half-witted hierophant were also the ones who told me I didn't dare attack the southrons, and by all the signs you were wrong about that," Joseph the Gamecock growled.

"I am not half-witted!" Leonidas cried, turning almost as red as Roast-Beef William usually was.

"Quarter-witted, then," Joseph said with mock graciousness. Leonidas took it for the real thing for a moment, which went a long way toward proving Joseph's point. Then the hierophant of the Lion God bellowed in fresh outrage.

"Sir, you did not pick a good site to defend," Lieutenant General Bell said.

"You would have liked it a lot better had you picked it yourself," Joseph said.

Instead of answering, Bell drew from his pocket the little bottle of laudanum he always carried with him. He pulled the cork with his teeth, drank, and put the bottle away again. *That's where he gets his brains*, Joseph the Gamecock thought. At the start of the campaign, he'd admired Bell for his courage in staying in the field even with his dreadful wounds. Nowadays . . .

"If you feel the rigors of service in the Army of Franklin are excessive, Lieutenant General, you may be sure I would be of the opinion that your retirement would in no way affect your honor," he said in hopeful tones.

"I have not the slightest intention of retiring," Bell replied peevishly. "I aim to go forth and conquer the foe."

"Do you?" Joseph couldn't resist the gibe. "There he was, right in front of you, just waiting to be struck. You advanced a mile against no opposition, discovered catapults where no one else suspected them, and retired forthwith to your works. A less than heroic encounter, if I may say so."

"We *can* hold here," Roast-Beef William said, "providing we have the will to do so."

"Provided," Joseph corrected. William stiffened. Joseph realized he might have done better than to engage in literary criticism; William was on his side, even if imperfectly grammatical.

The wing commander had also accurately summed things up—if they had the will, they could hold their ground here. Joseph the Gamecock looked from one of his subordinates to another. Roast-Beef William had that will, or at least willingness. Leonidas the Priest? What was left of Bell? Joseph shook his head. Despair threatened to choke him.

"If we leave Fat Mama, where will we go?" he asked plaintively.

Bell glowered at him. "Where would you have gone, *sir*," —he turned the title of respect into one of reproach— "after the southrons flanked us out of here?"

Joseph the Gamecock glared back. It was, unfortunately, a sharp question. And, however much Joseph hated to admit it, it was a question with an answer, for he'd contemplated it himself. "We would have to move up to Whole Mackerel. With the hills around that place, it makes another good spot to try to slow the southrons and to hurt them."

"Well, then," Leonidas the Priest said, as if that settled everything.

It didn't, not so far as Joseph the Gamecock was concerned. "Don't you see?" he said, something that felt much too much like desperation in his voice. "By all the gods, don't you *see*? Shifting our position because the enemy forces us to do it is one thing. Shifting our position because some of our officers have a case of the collywobbles is something else again."

"Sound strategy dictates that we pull out of Fat Mama before disaster befalls us here," Leonidas intoned, as if chanting a prayer to the Lion God.

The god might have heard him with favor. He infuriated Joseph. "Sound strategy?" the general commanding the Army of Franklin exclaimed, his voice breaking like a youth's. "Sound strategy? What in the seven hells do you know about sound strategy, sirrah? You wouldn't recognize a sound strategy if it danced up and pissed on your boot."

That was the opinion of practically every officer who'd ever tried to command Leonidas the Priest. It was a matter on which Joseph the Gamecock and the now-departed Count Thraxton the Braggart actually agreed—one of the very few matters on which they actually agreed, as neither was much in the habit of agreeing with anyone else. Joseph was glad to have the men Leonidas had led into his army. He would have been even gladder to have them had they come without the general at their head.

"I shall pray to the Lion God for your enlightenment, sir," Leonidas said now. "Either he will give it or he will rend you for your presumption."

"I'm using my head, or trying to," Joseph snapped. He felt as if he were using it to pound it against a stone wall. "If thinking be impiety, it's no wonder you have a reputation as a pillar of the gods."

Leonidas bowed and strode off, his scarlet vestments flapping around his ankles. *I hope you trip and break your neck,* Joseph the Gamecock thought. But his prayer went unanswered. *Of course it goes unanswered. I'm impious. Leonidas just said so. That* must *make it true.*

Lieutenant General Bell said, "Stay in Fat Mama, sir. If you want to see your army destroyed without the slightest chance of striking back, by all means stay." And he hitched away, too.

"What can I do?" Joseph demanded of Roast-Beef William. "I think we can hold here. You think we can hold here."

"But we can't hold here if those two don't think we can," his remaining wing commander said, which was all too likely to be true. With a resigned shrug, Roast-Beef William went on, "Maybe they'll like things better up at Whole Mackerel."

"Not likely," Joseph the Gamecock said. But he tasted defeat. "My own wing commanders have beaten me worse than the southrons ever managed. Let it be as you say, William. We'll pack up shop and shift to Whole Mackerel. Maybe things will go better there." He didn't believe it, not for a moment.

And he hated drafting the orders that moved the Army of Franklin from as yet unchallenged works and sent it farther north yet. He hated even more watching the men in blue abandon those field fortifications. Some of them marched off to the north. Others boarded glideway carpets for the trip up to Whole Mackerel. Sorcerers had dreamt for ages of making carpets that would fly anywhere at the wave of a hand and a word of command. Glideways were as close as they'd come: carpets that would travel a few inches above the ground along very specific routes. They could carry men and goods as fast as a horse galloped, and they never tired.

Joseph wished he could say the same. He was very weary indeed as he rode out of Fat Mama for Whole Mackerel. It wasn't so much a weariness of the body as a weariness of the spirit. He'd done everything he knew how to do to keep the southrons from turning or overrunning his position at Fat Mama, and everything he'd done had gone for nothing.

And King Geoffrey will hear of this latest retreat, and whom will he blame? Me, of course, Joseph thought gloomily.

If there is ever any chance to blame me for anything, his Majesty is not the man to waste it.

He left behind a screen of unicorn-riders to destroy what the Army of Franklin couldn't take away with it and to hold off the southrons till his abandonment of Fat Mama was complete. Brigadier Spinner, who commanded the unicorn-riders, was competent but uninspired. He was plenty good enough for the task Joseph had set him. Even so, his presence on the field left Joseph unhappy.

I wish Ned of the Forest were here, instead of over by the Great River, Joseph thought unhappily. *I wish he were harrying Hesmucet's supply line. A glideway Ned attacks isn't any good to anyone for a long time to come.*

One of the reasons Ned was in virtual exile, Joseph had heard, was that he'd all but challenged Thraxton the Braggart to a duel after the battle by the River of Death. A good many northern men had felt like killing Thraxton at one time or another. Few of them found the nerve to come right out and say so. Ned of the Forest might not be a gentleman, but he'd never lacked for nerve.

Joseph the Gamecock looked back over his shoulder. Sure enough, there was the buggy carrying Lieutenant General Bell. Joseph muttered something uncomplimentary. Bell had come with the same reputation for vigorous fighting as Ned, even if no one ever claimed he made much of a tactician. But he wouldn't attack when Joseph really needed aggression from him. And he didn't think the Army of Franklin could have held Fat Mama. What did that say about him?

He's been wounded too many times, Joseph thought, as charitably as he could. *He takes too much laudanum. It clouds his judgment.* Of course, Leonidas the Priest hadn't thought the northern army could hold at Fat Mama, either. But what did that prove? Joseph the Gamecock let out a bitter snort of laughter. *Nothing much, and everyone knows it. If Leonidas thinks something can't be done, that usually proves it can.*

Too late now, though. Fat Mama lay behind the Army of Franklin, as did Caesar, as did Borders. Ahead, Whole Mackerel. After that, what? The Army of Franklin was tied to Marthasville, and Joseph knew it painfully well. Hesmucet could maneuver as he would. Joseph couldn't. He had to shield the town from the southron host. Hesmucet had to know that as well as he did, too.

He had to, but could he? *I don't know.* He was honest enough to admit as much to himself. However honest it was, the admission did nothing to reassure him. *Did King Geoffrey send me here to watch me fail?* he wondered. *Did he send me here in hope of finding an excuse to put me back on the shelf for good? To the hells with him. Gods damn me if I intend to give him one.*

IV

eneral Hesmucet eyed the pass leading through the hills northwest to Whole Mackerel. The pass would have been a nasty place to try to force a crossing even if the traitors and their serfs hadn't had weeks to fortify it. As things were . . . As things were, Hesmucet shook his head and spoke two words to his wing commanders: "No, thanks."

"Can't say I'm sorry, sir," Doubting George said. "Tackling that position would be as bad as going head-on at the Vulture's Nest and the Dog's Path. We could use up a lot of soldiers without getting much."

"Another flanking maneuver?" James the Bird's Eye asked eagerly. Of course the young brigadier was eager: if Hesmucet did try a flanking maneuver, he hoped his men would again be the ones to make it.

Fighting Joseph coughed a significant cough. "My warriors," he observed, "have not yet won their fair share of glory on this campaign."

"Haven't done their fair share of dying, do you mean?" George muttered. Hesmucet heard the gibe; he didn't think Fighting Joseph did.

He said, "Yes, I intend to flank the northerners out of this position. But I intend to use the whole army to do it." James the Bird's Eye's face fell. Hesmucet pretended not to notice. He went on, "Twenty years ago, when I was a subaltern, I rode from Karlsburg in Palmetto Province to Hiltonia here in Peachtree, and then on to Bellfoundry in the province of Dothan. As a young soldier is supposed to do, I noted the lay of the land hereabouts, and I think I still recollect it tolerably well. There is a place to the north of Whole Mackerel called Fort Worthless—"

"Cheerful name," Brigadier James said with a grin.

"Believe me, the place deserves it," Hesmucet answered. "They say the mosquitoes there spring from dragons on their mothers' side, and that they're big enough to carry off a man. I don't know about the second, but, having been bitten by more than a few of them, I would say the first is surely true. Now, if we can take this place, we interpose ourselves between Joseph the Gamecock and Marthasville. That is what I'm going to try to do."

"That's what you've been trying to do all along," Doubting George said.

"My own view is, we ought to just hammer the traitors," Fighting Joseph said.

"Nothing would please me better," Hesmucet said, "but Joseph the Gamecock declines to send his men out of their earthworks to be hammered. As long as he keeps his army intact and holds us away from Marthasville, he accomplishes his purpose. I don't aim to let him."

"How do we get to this Fort Worthless place, sir?" James the Bird's Eye asked. "How do we do it without going through Whole Mackerel, I mean?"

Hesmucet pointed not northwest but northeast. "Over there is a road junction called Konigsburg. I intend to move the army there first, and then shift west over Calabash Creek toward Fort Worthless. I have maps, which I can show you at your leisure, if you're so inclined."

"Thank you, sir," James replied. He *was* eager. In a war where so many had grown weary, that alone made him stand out. "I'd be pleased to see them."

"Next question is, how do we keep Joseph the

Gamecock from realizing what we're up to?" Doubting
George said.

His questions were always to the point, and all the more
so when most pointed. But Hesmucet said, "I have some
ideas about that, too." He set them forth.

"What's my part in all this?" Fighting Joseph asked when
he was through—a question altogether in keeping with his
temperament.

Lieutenant General George said, "None of that matters.
The plan matters. I think it's a good one."

James the Bird's Eye said, "I've started sending men down
some of these roads. I don't think the roads know where
they're going themselves."

Hesmucet nodded. "That's how I remember them. Even
the locals get lost half the time, seems like. But we've got
enough serfs coming in to us to keep us from getting too
badly confused. And most of the traitors won't have any
better notion of where the roads go than we do. Let's get
moving."

"You still haven't answered my question . . . sir," Fighting Joseph said. "What is my role in all this?"

"Whatever I order it to be," Hesmucet snapped, by now
out of temper. "Get your men moving along with everybody else's." Handsome face dark with anger, Fighting
Joseph stormed away. Hesmucet nodded to James and
George. Saluting, they left, too.

As they did so, Major Alva came up to Hesmucet. He
too saluted, sloppily—he was a soldier because he needed
to be in the chain of command, not through any innate
longing for the military life. In fact, Hesmucet doubted he'd
ever seen a *less* military man in all his life. "Can we go
on with it, sir?" Alva asked anxiously. "Can we? Please?"

He sounded as eager as a child with a new toy. In truth,
that was about what he was. One thing King Avram's army
did for him: it let him play with bigger, fancier toys than
he would ever have got his hands on in civilian life.

"Yes, we're going to try it," Hesmucet answered.
"Remember, the object is to make the traitors think we're
slamming our way through at Whole Mackerel."

"Of *course* I remember, sir." Alva sounded affronted that

Hesmucet could think he would forget anything. *And I probably am naive to think any such thing*, went through Hesmucet's mind. *Whatever else this puppy is, forgetful he isn't—especially when he does get to use his toys.* Alva went on, "Funny how, at Caesar, you wanted me to mask a real attack from the enemy, where now I'm going to be doing just the opposite."

"It's not funny—it's necessary," Hesmucet said. "If we do the same thing over and over, pretty soon it won't fool the northerners any more."

"Oh. Right. Isn't that interesting?" Alva blinked. He was a very clever young man. *He's certainly more clever than I am, at whatever he wants to turn his mind to*, Hesmucet thought. *But when he hasn't turned his mind to something, it just isn't there for him. He can see the magic, something I could never do in a thousand years, but he's never thought about whys and wherefores.*

He set his hand on Alva's shoulder, feeling downright grandfatherly even though he wasn't far past forty himself. "You tend to your business, son, and I'll tend to mine, and between us, with a little luck, we'll make Geoffrey's men mighty unhappy."

"I like that, sir," Alva said. "You know, people really shouldn't bind other people to the land. Who knows how many mages and artisans and such have sweated their lives away raising indigo and rice and sugar just because they happened to be born with blond hair?"

Hesmucet grunted. His own view of blonds was much less sanguine than Alva's. "Keeping Detina one kingdom counts for a good deal, too," he said dryly.

"Oh, yes, that, too, of course," Alva agreed, though to him it was plainly of secondary importance. "Tomorrow morning?"

"Tomorrow morning," Hesmucet agreed. "That will give the men a good start toward Konigsburg."

"All right, sir." Alva grinned a small-boy grin altogether unsuited to a major. "This should be fun!"

That evening, Hesmucet posted pickets well forward of his main line. He didn't want the northerners to have another chance to give him a nasty surprise, as they'd almost done at Fat Mama. If Lieutenant General Bell hadn't pulled back for no reason Hesmucet could see, he might have done a good deal of damage.

Here at Whole Mackerel, though, Joseph the Gamecock kept his men quiet inside their entrenchments. All things considered, Hesmucet didn't blame him. He was ensconced in a solid position, as solid as the one outside Borders. Head-on assault probably wouldn't take the place. If Hesmucet couldn't flank the traitors out of Whole Mackerel, they'd be there a long time.

Joseph, he knew, would pay him about as much money as false King Geoffrey had in his treasury to attack head-on. He lay down on his iron-framed cot with a smile on his face. Sometimes the best way to confound a man was to give him exactly what he thought he wanted.

When morning came, Hesmucet put most of his soldiers on the miserable roads north that led to Konigsburg. Colonel Phineas and almost all the rest of the army's mages had the job of masking that move from the northerners. Phineas wasn't much of a mage himself, but did have a knack for getting other mages to work together.

Major Alva, by contrast, had very little ability to work with anybody else. But he was a hells of a mage. Hesmucet had less ability to work with other officers than a lot of southrons, and was uneasily aware of the fact. But he was a good general himself, which made up for a multitude of flaws.

"Are you ready?" he asked Alva. A predawn mist still lingered over the field, a bit of luck he hadn't dared hope for.

"I sure am," Alva replied gaily. His eyes sparkled. He was indeed as ready as small boys were for a lark.

"Begin, then," Hesmucet said, "and let me know when I can play my part in this little show."

"Just as you say, sir," Alva replied, and he began to chant. He hadn't gone far before Hesmucet could feel power start to accrete around him, as layers of nacre accumulated around grit to make a pearl. That same sort of power had gathered around Thraxton the Braggart at Proselytizers' Rise, even if he'd botched his incantation in the end. Hesmucet had never seen any southron mage even try to control such forces.

Almost absently, Alva pointed to Hesmucet. If the commanding general hadn't been waiting for the signal, he might have missed it. Even as things were, he needed a moment to realize the gesture wasn't part of one of the passes Alva had been flinging around with what looked like reckless abandon.

Hesmucet turned to his trumpeters and made a peremptory gesture of his own. They blared out *Advance!* The handful of southron soldiers Hesmucet had kept behind outside of Whole Mackerel stormed toward the traitors' works, as if expecting to overrun them with ease.

Major Alva made one last pass, cried out, "Let it be accomplished!" and pointed toward the northerners' field fortifications. And suddenly, coming through that convenient mist toward the enemy were not a few soldiers but what seemed for all the world like General Hesmucet's entire army.

To Hesmucet, the sorcerous additions to the force looked ghostly, insubstantial. Alva had assured him that, from the front, they would be indistinguishable from real soldiers except for one unfortunate detail: they weren't actually there and couldn't actually fight. But they certainly could cause consternation, and that suited the commanding general just fine.

If we get very, very lucky, they might even make the traitors panic, and then the real soldiers whose numbers Alva is magnifying will drive the enemy out of his trenches, Hesmucet thought. He didn't really expect that to happen, but a general was entitled to hopes no less than any other man.

For a few heady moments, he thought those hopes would be realized. The northerners *were* filled with consternation when they saw what looked and sounded like an enormous army bearing down on them. The real soldiers and real catapults and repeating crossbows among the simulacra sent enough missiles toward the traitors' works to make the whole assault seem convincing, especially to startled soldiers not expecting any such thing.

Inside the northerners' fieldworks, horns blared and officers and sergeants shouted in alarm. A few men did flee; Hesmucet could see them scrambling out of the entrenchments and running back toward Whole Mackerel. More, though, sent an enormous storm of crossbow bolts and stones and firepots down on the heads of the advancing southron host.

The soldiers who weren't really there proved their worth against that vicious barrage. Since they didn't exist, they weren't likely to be killed by any merely material missiles. They kept right on advancing in the face of everything the traitors could do.

That apparent immortality might have brought even more fear to the foe. Instead, it ended up giving away the game. The northerners realized no mere human beings could possibly have gone through such a pounding without losing a man. And their mages were not to be despised; indeed, till Hesmucet came across Major Alva, northern mages had dominated the field.

"Counterspell!" Alva gasped. "Strong one!" He muttered charms and made desperate passes, but the northerners, once alerted to his magecraft, savagely tore at it. The advancing army of simulacra began to fade, to become one with the mist out of which they were advancing, and at last to disappear.

As soon as Hesmucet saw that begin to happen, he pulled back his real soldiers, lest the traitors swarm forth and overwhelm them. He set a hand—again, he felt grandfatherly—on Alva's shoulder. "Don't worry about it," he told the young mage. "You bought us a big chunk of the morning. That's as much as I was hoping for, and more than I expected."

"Gods damn it, I wanted everything to be *perfect*," Alva said.

Most southron mages would have been satisfied with coming close to what their commanders wanted. Hesmucet realized he had something very special in the line of sorcerer here. He patted Alva on the shoulder again. "Don't worry, son," he said. "Don't you worry at all. You did just fine."

✧　　✧　　✧

"Come on, men," Captain Gremio called as his company of northerners tramped almost single file along a narrow winding track somewhere north of Whole Mackerel.

"Another position abandoned," Colonel Florizel grumbled. The regimental commander rode his unicorn. The rest of the regiment, captains included, went on foot.

Gremio didn't contradict the colonel, not out loud. But he understood Joseph the Gamecock's reasons for pulling out of Whole Mackerel. Again, Hesmucet was playing the outflanking game.

This country was overgrown, almost jungly. It was full of bugs, all of which, in Gremio's biased opinion, seemed to be trying to bite him at once. He slapped and scratched and swore. His men were slapping and scratching and swearing, too, so maybe a few of the bugs did have extra time on their hands.

The soldiers splashed through a swampy stream. "Check for leeches," Sergeant Thisbe said—parasites of a sort Gremio hadn't thought of.

Coming up onto drier land, men did as the sergeant said. Some of them cursed and made disgusted noises when they found leeches clinging to their legs, too. "No, don't just tear them off," Gremio told a blue-clad trooper who was about to do just that. "The mouth stays behind when you do, and the wound will go bad."

"That's right, Catling," Thisbe agreed. "Touch a smoldering twig to the head end of the leech. Then it will really let go."

"It'll burn me, too," the soldier said.

"If you want to take a chance on going around with crutches like Lieutenant General Bell, do it your way," Gremio said. "If you want to do it right, do what Thisbe and I tell you to do."

"I'm a free Detinan, and my ideas are just as good as anybody else's, gods damn it." Catling yanked the leech off his leg. He poked at the wound. Sure enough, the leech's mouth remained locked to his flesh. He looked much less happy after that.

"Try a burning twig now," Sergeant Thisbe said. "Sometimes

the mouth will still let go even after you've ripped away the rest of the leech."

"He doesn't deserve to have the mouth come loose," Gremio said in considerable anger. "There are some people in this kingdom who think the greatest privilege the gods granted a free Detinan is the privilege of making a gods-damned fool of himself whenever it strikes his fancy. They do this—sometimes they do it over and over—and then, oftentimes, they expect the lawcourts to free them from their folly. To the seven hells with that, as far as I'm concerned. If you insist on being a fool, you bloody well ought to pay for your folly every now and again."

"Catling's a brave soldier," Thisbe said. "I'd rather have him hale so he can shoot at the southrons than laid up with a bad leg."

"You're too kind and gentle for your own good," Gremio said. Thisbe's clean-shaven cheeks made his flush easy to see. Gremio kicked at the mucky ground. Calling a sergeant gentle was bound to embarrass him before the men he was supposed to lead.

"Where in the seven hells are we?" somebody asked. Considering the weather and the landscape, the question seemed more than usually apt.

Precise as always, Gremio answered, "We're somewhere between Fort Worthless and Konigsburg. Fort Worthless is one of those places that live up to their names ninety-nine years and eleven months a century, but this is its month to shine. We've got to keep the stinking southrons from getting there till the army finishes pulling out of Whole Mackerel."

"When the southrons find themselves a real wizard, you know the war isn't what we expected when we started fighting it," Thisbe said.

"That's so," Gremio agreed, "but a real wizard isn't always just what you want. We had Thraxton the Braggart, for instance, but I'm just as well pleased he's gone off to None-such. He cost us the battle of Proselytizers' Rise."

"He cost us that battle a couple of different ways," Thisbe said. "It wasn't just that he botched the spell, though that was bad enough. But he sent James of Broadpath off to the southwest to attack Wesleyton while the southrons in Rising Rock were building up their strength. What sort of fool would do such a thing?"

"A sour one," Gremio answered. "He'd quarreled with James—he'd quarreled with everybody, I think—and so he sent him away. Thraxton's bad temper is why we haven't got Ned of the Forest leading our unicorn-riders, too. We'll end up paying a price for that along with everything else, I'd bet."

They splashed across another stream. Turtles and frogs sitting on rocks dove into the water and frantically swam away. One luckless frog jumped almost right into a water snake's mouth. The snake swam over and gulped. Gremio wondered uneasily if crocodiles lurked in the water, too. He hoped he and his men wouldn't find out the hard way.

"How far is it up to Calabash Creek, sir?" Thisbe asked.

"To the seven hells with me if I know, Sergeant," Gremio said. "I don't know how far we've come—I don't see how anybody could know how far we've come, considering how these roads all seem to bend back on themselves. And I don't know how far this creek is from where we encamped. For all I *do* know, that miserable little rill we just crossed was it, and we're heading straight for the southrons at Konigsburg."

"We'd better not be," Thisbe said.

"I don't know why not," Gremio said. "One thing I am sure of is that the southrons have to be as confused about all this as we are. If they're supposed to be at Konigsburg, they're probably somewhere else."

"But we're ordered to take our stand on the west bank of Calabash Creek and not let them advance on Fort Worthless." Sergeant Thisbe sounded worried. He took orders very seriously, which made him unusual among free Detinan men. *You can't tell me what to do* was one of the most common phrases in any Detinan's mouth.

"Don't worry about it," Gremio said. "Sooner or later, we'll find them, or they'll find us, and then we'll see what happens next."

What he expected would happen next was for both sides to entrench as best they could in this muddy ground and then shoot crossbow quarrels at each other. The landscape didn't offer room enough for big, sweeping charges. Not only that, both sides were less eager to make them than they had been earlier in the war. Big, sweeping charges left bodies strewn all over a battlefield, but rarely shifted the enemy if he'd already had time to dig in.

Colonel Florizel's regiment found the foe before finding Calabash Creek. Startled shouts rang out ahead of Gremio's company: "Southrons!" "Traitors!" Each side seemed equally appalled at stumbling on the other.

A crossbow bolt hissed past Gremio's head. He had no idea whether his own men or the southrons had shot it. "Forward!" he shouted. "We have to help our friends!" He was an officer, and bore a sword instead of a crossbow. When he drew it, he knew a certain feeling of unreality. As a barrister back in Karlsburg, he hadn't used a blade. Baron Ormerod, who'd led the company before him, had been a good man with his hands—which hadn't kept him from stopping a bolt with his chest trying to stem the northern rout behind Proselytizers' Rise.

"Forward!" Sergeant Thisbe's clear voice echoed his. Forward the soldiers went. They'd never been shy about fighting—only the southrons' numbers had kept them in their entrenchments through most of this campaign. Now they had, or might have, a good chance to meet the enemy on even terms. They rushed to take it.

The fight was even more confused than the woodland skirmishes before the battle by the River of Death. The overgrowth was thicker and lusher than it had been farther south; as soon as men took a few steps off the track, they had to navigate as much by ear as by eye. "Geoffrey!" the northerners cried. The southerners yelled, "Avram!" And both sides shouted, "Freedom!"—a good way to land anyone coming to what might be the rescue in trouble.

Gremio almost ran right into a southron. The man in gray shouted something a lot less complimentary than, "Avram!" and let fly with his crossbow. He couldn't have stood more than five feet from Gremio, but missed anyhow. Gremio had no time even to thank the gods for his good luck. He charged at the southron, expecting the man to flee.

Instead, the enemy soldier threw down the crossbow, drew his shortsword, and slashed at Gremio. With his own, longer, officer's weapon, Gremio had no trouble holding off the southron, but he couldn't finish him. Then a crossbow quarrel caught the southron in the thigh. As he howled and crumpled and clutched at himself, Gremio lunged forward and stabbed him. The southron's howl became a bubbling shriek. Gremio wasn't particularly proud of the victory, but a victory it was.

"Forward!" he yelled again. The southrons were storming forward themselves. On this overgrown battlefield, who had the most men close by was anyone's guess. Over in Parthenia, there'd been a fight in what people called the Jungle. Gremio had his doubts about what kind of place that really was, and whether it deserved its name. Here, though, here was jungle and no mistake.

Suddenly, without warning, gray-clad pikemen slammed into Colonel Florizel's regiment. In this overgrowth, where crossbow bolts were much less effective than in open country, the southrons with their long spears were a deadly menace.

"Avram!" one of them shouted, bearing down on Gremio. "Avram and freedom!"

"Geoffrey!" Gremio yelled in return. He chopped at the enemy's spearshaft just below the head, hoping to cut it off and leave the southron with nothing more than a pole. But a clever southron armorer had nailed a strip of iron to the spearshaft to keep a sword from doing any such thing. Gremio beat the spearshaft aside and kept himself from getting spitted, but that was all he could do.

Then, recklessly brave, Sergeant Thisbe grabbed the spearshaft. Gremio rushed at the southron. Unexpectedly deprived of the use of this weapon, he let go of it and ran away. "Are you all right?" Gremio asked Thisbe.

"Sure am," Thisbe answered. The sergeant reversed the spear, then shook his head. "I wasn't trained on one of these boarstickers. If I tried to use it, I'd get myself killed quick. You know what to do with it, Captain?"

Gremio shook his head. "Not me. Back before the war, if I wanted to kill a man, I'd use a writ, not a spear."

"That's funny." Thisbe grinned, then threw the pike on the ground. "Are we winning or losing?"

"Probably," Gremio answered, which jerked another grin from the sergeant. The company commander went on, "I wonder how many nasty little fights like this one are happening all over this part of Peachtree."

"Lots, I expect," Thisbe said. "The southrons and us, we're like a couple of blindfolded men groping for each other in a locked room."

Gremio nodded, appreciating the figure of speech, but he said, "Oh, it's even worse than that. Our left leg has bumped the other fellow, but our right arm doesn't know it yet."

He would have gone on with his own figure, but another pikeman burst out of the woods just in front of him. At close quarters, a pike was a demonically nasty weapon; just as Gremio's blade had more reach than a crossbowman's shortsword, so the pikeman could thrust at him without being vulnerable in return. As he had with the first attacker, Gremio managed to beat aside the spearhead, but he could do no more.

Then Thisbe picked up the dropped pike and rushed at the southron. When he turned to defend himself against this new assault, Gremio got inside his guard and slashed his arm to the bone. Howling and dripping blood, the soldier in gray tunic and pantaloons fled.

"Thank you kindly," Gremio said, tipping his forage cap to Thisbe. "Seems you know what to do with a spear after all, Sergeant. That took ballocks."

"Oh, I wouldn't say that," Thisbe answered.

"I would," Gremio said. "I'll repeat myself, in fact. Ballocks is what that took."

Sergeant Thisbe laughed. "All right, sir. If that's how you want to put it, I don't suppose I'd better argue with my superior officer." Gremio shook his head to show that Thisbe emphatically ought not to argue with him. The sergeant looked around, then said, "I don't see any more southrons, not on their feet, anyhow. Maybe we've driven them off."

"By the gods, I hope so." Gremio didn't see any more southrons, either. He plunged his sword into the soft red dirt several times to scour blood from the blade. "I hope so, but I don't really think so. They're pushing west again, and all we can do is try to hold them off." As if to prove his point, a racket of battle broke out somewhere not too far away. Gremio and Thisbe twisted their heads this way and that, trying to decide from which direction it was coming. Gremio scowled. "No way to tell whether we're going forward or falling back, even, not in this undergrowth."

"If the southrons turn up behind us, we've probably lost somewhere," Thisbe said.

"Yes, probably, but not necessarily." Gremio could still split hairs like a barrister, and still enjoyed doing it, too. "It could just mean they'd found a track through the bushes that we didn't happen to be guarding."

"You're right," Thisbe said after a brief pause for thought. "That wouldn't have occurred to me, I don't believe. But you, sir, seems like you think of everything." Admiration filled his light tenor.

Gremio's cheeks heated. "Thanks again, Sergeant. Praise from the praiseworthy is praise indeed. So people say, and I see it's true." More southrons broke from the woods just then, and the soldiers stayed too busy to talk for quite a while.

Rollant's hand strayed to the leg of his pantaloons as he sprawled on the ground during a break. Smitty saw the motion and shook his head. "Don't scratch," he said. "You'll be sorry if you scratch."

"I'm sorry now," Rollant said from between clenched teeth. "These gods-damned chiggers are itching me to death."

"I've got 'em, too," his comrade said mournfully. "They're worse after you scratch. I found out the hard way."

"I know it," the escaped serf said. "They have them in Palmetto Province, too. I didn't miss 'em a bit after I came up to New Eborac, I'll tell you that. But I itch so much now, I don't hardly care what happens later."

"You will," Smitty said. He was right, too; Rollant knew as much. In his head, he knew as much. But his leg still itched and his hands still wanted to scratch, and none of that seemed to have very much to do with his head.

Sergeant Joram came up. If chiggers dared afflict the exalted personage of an underofficer, he gave no sign of it. "Get moving, you lugs," he said. "We have to keep heading toward the Thunderer's shrine over there to the west." He pointed.

Smitty snickered loud enough for Rollant to hear, but not loud enough for his mirth to reach Joram's ears. He said, "That's south, Sergeant."

"It is not," Joram growled. But then he looked at the shadows tree branches were casting. He coughed a couple of times. "Well, it might be a little southwest."

Smitty didn't say anything. Neither did Rollant. For a couple of common soldiers, silence seemed the better course. The two men heaved themselves to their feet. *Harder to scratch if I'm marching,* Rollant thought. What he wanted to do was scratch and scratch till blood ran down his leg. Maybe then he would feel better.

Crows and vultures rose in flapping clouds from bodies already bloating under the hot northern sun. Rollant couldn't see whether the corpses wore Avram's uniform or Geoffrey's. They were just as dead either way.

"Just what's so important about this New Bolt Shrine?" Smitty grumbled as the men tramped along. "Why aren't the traitors welcome to the miserable place?"

"Crossroads, I suppose." Rollant wrinkled his nose, trying without much luck to clear the stench of death from his nostrils.

Sergeant Joram shook his head. "No, that's not what it is," he said. "Fort Worthless, now, Fort Worthless is a crossroads. We get our hands on that place, the northerners will have to go around three sides of a big square to get to any place they need to be. But New Bolt Shrine is different—I hear some runaway serfs told our officers about the place."

"Different how, Sergeant?" Smitty asked. Rollant was glad his companion had put the question to Joram. The sergeant wasn't out-and-out unjust to him very often because he was a blond, but Joram did talk to an ordinary Detinan more readily than he did to an ex-serf.

"It's supposed to be one of those places where the blonds

worked their magic back in the old days," Joram said. "It's an even stronger place for sorcery now that it's been reconsecrated to the Thunderer, of course."

"And our magecraft can use all the help it can get. Uh-*huh*." Smitty nodded. "All right, fair enough. That makes pretty good sense."

Sergeant Joram gave him a mocking bow. "Thank you so much, Marshal Smitty. I'm sure General Hesmucet'll be so glad you approve."

Rollant would have fumed under a taunt like that. Rollant, in fact, *had* fumed under a good many taunts like that. Smitty only bowed back. "Thank you so much, Sergeant. I do want the general to be aware of what's going on." Joram snorted and went off to bother a couple of other men in the squad.

"Nicely done," Rollant said.

"Thank you very much, Marshal Rollant," Smitty replied grandly. He *wouldn't* be serious, not when he had any other choice.

Heading toward a place of old magic made Rollant serious. He had no idea what the blonds in this part of Detina had done in the way of sorcery before the Detinans came conquering across the Western Ocean. The lands around Karlsburg, where he'd grown up, had been part of one little kingdom, this place here another. For all he knew, his ancestors and the local blonds had fought all the time.

He was sure Joram was right about one thing: since New Bolt Shrine had been reconsecrated to the Thunderer, the sorcerous focus there would be stronger now than it had been before. Iron weapons, unicorns, and more powerful wizardry—those were the keys to the Detinans' conquest of the blonds they'd tied to the land.

"I wonder if the traitors know what kind of a place this is," he said.

"It'd be nice if they didn't," Smitty answered. "Then we could just march right in and take the place away from 'em. I'm always in favor of getting what I want without having to fight for it, especially if the other bastards are likely to fight back."

"Right," Rollant said—half agreement, half irony.

But Geoffrey's men—Joseph the Gamecock's men—did know what they were defending. Rollant got a glimpse of the New Bolt Shrine, the Thunderer's lightning bolt done up in gold over the roof, but a glimpse was all he got. Strong northern forces lay between the southrons and the shrine, and they were not inclined to let themselves be dislodged.

General Hesmucet hurled his men at them again and again. The southrons ground forward, but paid a dreadful price for every yard they advanced. Rollant hoped the traitors paid even more, but knew he couldn't rely on that.

"How can we tell when we've won one of these fights?" Smitty asked. "We don't shift the bastards more than a couple of furlongs even when we do drive 'em out of their trenches. And when we do push 'em that far, they just find some other little knoll or overgrown patch and dig some more trenches, and then they're ready for us again."

"Half the time, they don't even need to dig," Rollant said. "Like as not, their officers have already got serfs digging trenches they can just move into. It's only when the traitors go someplace where there are no trenches that they have to do any digging of their own."

Not far away from them, their comrades were busy entrenching. And Sergeant Joram called out, "Come on, you lazy lugs. You know what to do with a pick and shovel as well as anybody else. Get busy and do it."

He had, at least, included Smitty in that *lazy* tag. A lot of Detinans reckoned all blonds lazy—an irony, considering how the nobles in the north piled work on their serfs. Rollant took his short-handled shovel out of his pack and made the dirt fly. Smitty did, too, but he was slower about it. Which of them was the lazy one, then? Rollant had his own opinion, but who cared what a blond thought?

Two days later, Colonel Nahath's regiment fought its way up to the very outskirts of the sacred precinct of which New Bolt Shrine formed the heart. In the face of stubborn northern resistance, their attack stalled there. In short order, the very reason for the attack became meaningless, for stones and firepots from southron siege engines reduced the shrine to smoking rubble.

That, of course, did not keep the southrons from attacking the place. They'd got their orders before New Bolt Shrine went up in flames, and the mere fact that it went up in flames didn't seem to register with the men who composed and gave those orders. They sent the regiment forward again and again.

Joseph the Gamecock's men defended wreckage just as stoutheartedly as they'd tried to hold the intact New Bolt Shrine, too. At last, though, a fierce assault cleared them from the precinct. Rollant strode over tumbled stones and burnt timbers. "This had better be worth something," he said, "on account of we sure paid a hells of a price for it."

"Maybe our wizards could make a gods-damned big magic and give us back some of the poor sons of bitches who died taking it," Smitty said.

"If they had that kind of magic, they could have found another battlefield to use it on," Rollant said.

Smitty gave him an impatient look. "I know that, you chowderhead. What I meant was, nothing they do here could be worth it, no matter what. *There.* Do I have to draw you a picture?"

Sergeant Joram spoke up: "Smitty, why don't I draw a picture of you going down and finding a creek and coming back with full canteens for everybody?"

"Have a heart, Sergeant!" Smitty moaned. Joram folded massive arms across a wide chest. Not only did he have rank on his side, he could have torn Smitty in two. Rollant held out his water bottle to Smitty. Cursing, the farmer's son took it.

A young fellow with a major's epaulets and a mage's badge prominently pinned to his tunic came up and prowled among the ruins as avidly as a hound looking for a buried bone. After a bit, his eye fell on Rollant. "You, there!" he said.

"Yes, sir?" Rollant came to attention.

"As you were, as you were." The mage gestured. "Can't stand that nonsense. Bunch of foolishness—and go ahead, call me a heretic. Where was I?"

"I don't know, sir," Rollant said truthfully.

"I know what it was," the young mage said. He looked frightfully clever, like a child too smart for its own good. "You'd be from around these parts, wouldn't you?"

"No, sir," Rollant answered.

"No?" Now he'd surprised the wizard. "Why not?"

Patiently, Rollant said, "Sir, I was born near Karlsburg, and I spent the last ten years before the war in New Eborac City. This is the first time I've ever been anywhere near this place. Not all blonds are the same, you know, any more than a Detinan from New Eborac is the same as one from Palmetto Province."

"Oh," the sorcerous major said. But then he nodded. "Yes, of course. That does make good sense, now that I think on it. I was going to ask you if you knew whether these ruins had any particular sorcerous focus."

"You're the wizard, sir, so you'd know better than I would," Rollant replied. "People have said there's one somewhere about, though. Otherwise, why would we have fought so hard over it?"

"Because, as often as not, people are a pack of gods-damned fools," the major answered. Rollant's jaw fell. The youngster laughed. "Never underestimate that as a possible reason. People *are* a pack of gods-damned fools a lot of the time. If the northerners weren't gods-damned fools, for instance, would they have tried to leave Detina in the first place?" Before Rollant could even try to find an answer for that, the mage went on, "I don't feel any power here to speak of, either from the old days or from the Thunderer. It's all just so much moonshine, if you want to know what I think."

Rollant hadn't much wanted to know what he thought. But a major didn't have to worry about a common soldier's opinion, especially if the common soldier was a blond. Off the mage went, leaving Rollant behind scratching his head. "What was all that about?" Smitty asked. He was festooned with water bottles now.

"Fellow says this New Bolt Shrine wasn't really any place worth fighting about," Rollant answered.

"Oh, he does, does he?" Smitty rolled his eyes. "Why am I not surprised, and how many lives have we thrown away going after it?"

"Do you know who that was?" Sergeant Joram asked. Both Rollant and Smitty shook their heads. Joram said, "That was Major Alva, that's who. He's supposed to be as hot as any traitor mage ever hatched—he's the fellow who gave us such good sorcerous cover when we went into Caesar."

"Then he ought to know what he's talking about," Smitty said.

That did make sense. It also made Rollant uncomfortable. Alva said there was no power lingering where the blonds had had a holy place, even after the Thunderer also had a shrine made on the same spot. Shouldn't the gods of either blonds or Detinans have left more of an impress on the world than that? And if they hadn't, what did it mean? Rollant wondered if he wanted to know.

Off to the north, smoke was rising from another battlefield where southrons and traitors clashed. Rollant wondered if that fight was as meaningless as the one in which he'd just taken part. How many men were dying for nothing over there?

"It's not exactly nothing," Smitty said when he complained aloud. "Whether we can make special sorcery here or not, we still needed to take this place if we're going to clear the traitors out of Fort Worthless."

Rollant grunted. "That's true, I suppose. But still—"

"Keep quiet," Sergeant Joram said. "If somebody tells us to go forwards, we go forwards, no ifs, ands, or buts about it. Isn't that right?"

"Yes, Sergeant," Rollant said resignedly. Up on a northern plantation, Joram would have made a terrific serf-driver. If Rollant told him that, though, he might take it for a compliment.

"Well, then," Joram said, as if he'd proved something. Maybe he had—he'd proved he could tell Rollant what to do. But Rollant already knew that. Sometimes, though, a sergeant just needed to thump his chest and bellow, as if he were a bull pawing the ground in a field. Rollant couldn't see the sense there, but he'd seen it was true.

"If this New Bolt shrine isn't worth anything, what do we do now?" Smitty asked—but quietly, so Rollant could hear and Joram couldn't.

"We go forward," Rollant answered. "We keep going forward till the traitors can't stop us any more." So far, he sounded like a sergeant himself. But then he added, "And we hope some of us are still alive when that finally happens." Smitty walked off toward the creek for a couple of paces. Then, reluctantly, he nodded.

General Hesmucet had trouble deciding whether or not he ought to be a happy man. His soldiers had forced their way across Calabash Creek. They'd made Joseph the Gamecock pull out of Whole Mackerel. They'd cleared his men from New Bolt Shrine and Fort Worthless. They'd done a lot of hard fighting in some of the most miserable terrain anywhere in Detina. They'd been victorious almost everywhere—and what did they have to show for it?

Less than I'd like, gods damn it, Hesmucet thought. No matter how harried Joseph the Gamecock's forces had been, his army remained in being, and remained between Hesmucet and Marthasville. Joseph was doing his job. Hesmucet peered west from the swampy wilderness he'd just spent a few weeks overrunning. Joseph the Gamecock, as usual, had more entrenchments waiting for him, some on a little knob called Cedar Hill, others farther west on a heavily wooded slope identified on his map as Commissioner Mountain. It didn't look like much of a mountain to him, but the traitors had some perfectly good artificers who would have studied out the ground and turned it into much more than a molehill.

Rain started falling. It had been raining for most of the month. Hesmucet was sick of it. Rain worked for Joseph the Gamecock and against him. It slowed down his advance. Yes, it slowed the defenders, too, but they didn't care. They weren't trying to go anywhere themselves, only to keep him from getting anywhere. They had a good chance of doing it, too.

"Major Alva!" he called. "Where in the damnation has Major Alva gone and got himself off to?"

"Here I am, sir." In a mage's best style, Alva seemed to appear out of nowhere.

Hesmucet was less impressed than he might have been.

In the rain, he couldn't see very far anyway. He came straight to the point: "Can you make the sun come out again and dry up some of this mud?"

"Sorry, sir, but I don't think so," Major Alva replied.

"Why not?" Hesmucet said irritably. "Last fall, you were able to keep things foggy and misty down around Rising Rock, and that served us well."

"Yes, sir, but it would have been pretty foggy and misty regardless of what I did," the bright young mage said. "Here, I would be changing things, and changing them a lot, because it's usually pretty rainy here this time of year. It's a lot easier to ride the unicorn in the direction he's already going, if you know what I mean."

Hesmucet snarled—wetly. He did see what Major Alva meant, but seeing it wasn't the same as liking it. "All right, then," he said. "What *can* we do to make the traitors' lives miserable?"

"Everyone's life has been miserable lately, seems to me," Alva observed.

That held more truth than Hesmucet cared to admit. "The idea is to make the enemy's lives miserable," he said. "That and to keep him from doing it to us."

"Yes, sir," Major Alva agreed. "I have to tell you, though, sir, fooling with the weather will not get you what you want. This time of year in this part of the kingdom, it *is* going to rain, and any wizard who tells you anything different is either lying on purpose or else a gods-damned fool."

"All right," Hesmucet said. One reason he was glad to have Alva around was that the mage wasn't shy about telling him what was on his mind. Eventually, he supposed, Alva would learn tact, but it wouldn't happen soon. "If you can't dry things out, see if you can come up with some other way to make Joseph the Gamecock sorry we're in the neighborhood."

"Yes, sir." Alva saluted and went away.

Hesmucet started to duck back into his tent. Before he could, a scryer called his name. He turned. "What is it?"

"There's a report from Luxor, sir, on the Great River," the scryer replied. "Sam the Sturgeon has met Ned of the Forest in a battle."

"I'll come," Hesmucet said at once, and hurried to the scryers' tent.

The face looking out of the crystal ball at him belonged to Brigadier Andrew the Smith, not to Brigadier Sam (who'd got his nickname from a pair of protruding eyes and a long, long nose). If Sam the Sturgeon wasn't there to tell the tale in person, Hesmucet judged the news unlikely to be good. And, sure enough, the commander of the garrison at Luxor said, "Things didn't work out as you hoped they would, sir."

"You'd better tell me," Hesmucet said.

"Yes, sir." Andrew the Smith was a solid officer. "Brigadier Sam set out moving west through the southern part of Great River Province, sir, and he let his unicorn-riders get out in front of his footsoldiers. Ned of the Forest hit him near a little place called Three Dee Crossroads and defeated him in detail—smashed his army to hells and gone, if you want to know the truth."

"Gods damn it!" Hesmucet burst out. "Sam the Sturgeon must have had three times as many men as Ned."

"Yes, sir," Brigadier Andrew said again. "But he didn't get 'em into the fight, and Ned did. What's left of Sam's army—and it's only bits and pieces—just came stumbling back into Luxor this morning. He was afraid Ned was hot on his heels, too."

"To the hells with what he was afraid of," Hesmucet growled. "I sent him out to keep Ned too busy to strike our supply line. Fat lot of good Sam does, holed up in Luxor. Ned can collect men at his leisure and strike the glideway path whenever he pleases."

"I'm afraid you're right, sir," Andrew said mournfully.

"That man Ned is a demon," Hesmucet said. "There can't be peace by the Great River till Ned of the Forest is dead."

"As may be, sir," the commandant at Luxor replied. "But the son of a bitch is still here now, and in a position to make a lot of trouble."

"We have to keep him too busy to hit the supply line," Hesmucet said. "If Sam the Sturgeon couldn't do the job, someone else will have to. Right this minute, Brigadier, looks like that someone else is you."

"Yes, sir," Andrew the Smith said—he didn't shrink from

the idea, which made Hesmucet happy. "I'll do my best, sir. Ned will probably think he could take on anybody this side of the gods right about now, and that may make him careless. But whether it does or whether it doesn't, you're right—we have to keep him away from your glideway line."

"Good man," Hesmucet told him. "If we had more like you, we'd be in better shape."

"Thank you kindly, sir," Brigadier Andrew replied. "What we could really use is a couple of officers like Ned of the Forest."

Few southrons would have said that. It was true—Hesmucet felt down in his belly how true it was—but few would have had the nerve to say it. "When the gods made Ned, they shattered the mold afterwards," Hesmucet said, which unfortunately also seemed to be true. "I'm glad we have you on our side, Brigadier. I know you'll give the son of a bitch all he wants, and then some more besides."

"I told you once, I'll do my best. I meant it," Andrew said.

"Good." Hesmucet turned and nodded to his scryer. The man broke the mystical attunement between the two crystal balls. The one in front of Hesmucet became no more than an inert sphere of glass; Andrew the Smith's image vanished from it. Hesmucet gave himself the luxury of cursing for a minute or so, but then got up to leave the scryers' tent.

"What will you do now, sir?" the scryer asked him.

It wasn't really any of the man's business. Still, Hesmucet judged him unlikely to go over to the traitors with the answer. He probably wouldn't even gossip; by the nature of their work, scryers had to be discreet. And the truth wasn't all that complicated, anyhow. "I'm going to keep right on hammering away at Joseph the Gamecock, that's what," Hesmucet said. "As long as Andrew or somebody keeps Ned of the Forest busy, Joseph hasn't got enough unicorn-riders attached to his own army to harm the glideway coming up here from Rising Rock, especially when I keep squeezing and prodding his army. So that's what I'm going to do. You hit something long enough and hard enough and sooner or later it'll break."

"All right, sir. That sounds like it makes sense." The scryer was a lieutenant by courtesy, as most mages were officers by courtesy. Having officer's rank let him order common soldiers around, which was often convenient. What he knew about sound strategy, however, would likely have fit inside a thimble without straining things. But he was a freeborn Detinan, and reckoned his opinion as good as anyone else's, including that of the general commanding.

"I'm so glad you approve." Hesmucet intended it for sarcasm. The scryer took it as a compliment. He beamed at Hesmucet as the commanding general left the tent.

Once back in his own pavilion, Hesmucet summoned Doubting George, Fighting Joseph, and James the Bird's Eye. He told his wing commanders what had happened to the luckless Sam the Sturgeon. "He had Ned outnumbered three to one, and he lost the fornicating battle?" Fighting Joseph burst out, his always ruddy face darkening further with anger. "That's disgraceful, nothing else but."

"It certainly is, and who would know better?" Doubting George murmured.

A considerable silence followed. At Viziersville, in the west, Fighting Joseph's men had outnumbered those of Duke Edward of Arlington somewhere close to three to one, but Duke Edward's Army of Southern Parthenia had won a resounding victory over the southrons nonetheless. Fighting Joseph turned red all over again, this time perhaps from embarrassment—although, from all Hesmucet had seen, he seemed nearly immune to that emotion.

At last, James the Bird's Eye broke the silence with a sensible question: "What do we do now, sir?"

Hesmucet gave him the same sort of answer he'd given the scryer: "We'll try to keep Ned busy over by the Great River, and we'll keep Joseph's unicorn-riders close to home so they can't go after the glideway."

James gravely considered that. In due course, he nodded. "Makes sense to me, sir," he said. "We've come a long way doing what we've been doing. If we keep doing it and hit hard, we ought to end up in Marthasville before too long."

"We'd better," Lieutenant General George said. "There are grumblings down south about how long this fight is taking and how many men we're spending to make it. I have friends who send me the news bulletins. I'm sure the rest of you have friends like that, too. What I'm not so sure of is whether they're really friends."

"Bloodsucking ghouls is what they are," Fighting Joseph said. "They haven't the ballocks to fight themselves, and so they pass their time by making the men who do fight doubt themselves."

"It's more complicated than that, I fear," Doubting George said.

Fighting Joseph, by his expression, plainly didn't believe it for a moment. Hesmucet did. He knew how weary the south was of the war against false King Geoffrey, and of its cost in both silver and blood. Victory would make that cost seem worthwhile. As long as the north held Marthasville, as long as Joseph the Gamecock's army remained intact and in the field, the south saw no victory. If the farmers and burghers got sick of sending their sons and husbands and brothers off to die for what they saw as no good purpose, King Avram would have to recognize his rebellious cousin as his fellow sovereign. Hesmucet aimed to do everything he could to keep that from happening.

"Let's take a crack at Cedar Hill, then," he said. "Once we drive the traitors away from it, we'll be in position to move against Commissioner Mountain."

"Good enough," James the Bird's Eye said. Now Fighting Joseph agreed without hesitation. Whatever else you could say about the man, he wasn't shy about going into a fight.

The only one showing any doubts was George. "It had better be good enough," he said. "We'll just have to do our best to make it good enough."

When morning came, Hesmucet assembled his force and moved it west. He expected Joseph the Gamecock's men to have solid entrenchments on the forward slopes of Cedar Hill, and so they did. In spite of a pounding from his siege engines, their lines held firm. Both sides got less use not only from engines but also from crossbows than they would have in better weather; an awful lot of bowstrings were wet. Hesmucet's men slogged on, cleaning out one trench after another.

Toward midday, Hesmucet glanced up to one of the higher crags of Cedar Hill. There looking down at him—there looking down at his whole host—stood half a dozen northern officers in blue. They observed the men moving against them with the detachment of so many instructors at the military collegium at Annasville.

Rage ripped through Hesmucet. Unlike those cool, detached traitors, he took war personally. He spotted Brigadier Brannan, Doubting George's commander of siege engines, who'd just wrestled some of his catapults forward. "Brannan!" he called, and pointed up toward the knot of northerners. "Can you smash a couple of those bastards for me?"

Brigadier Brannan studied the enemy officers. "A long shot, especially uphill," he said, "but I've got a chance. Want me to try?"

"Yes, by the Thunderer's balls!" Hesmucet exclaimed.

"All right." Brannan called orders to his crew. They tightened the skeins and set a thirty-pound stone in the trough. Brannan himself squeezed the trigger. The catapult bucked and jerked and clacked. Away flew the round stone, almost faster than the eye could follow it.

"Look out!" Joseph the Gamecock shouted as the southrons' catapult sent a stone flying toward the knot of officers he headed. Spry for a man of his years, he wasted not a heartbeat taking his own advice: he dove behind a boulder. Someone else dove on top of him. Other northerners scattered in all directions.

Joseph listened for the thud of the stone slamming into muddy dirt. Even skipping along the ground, it could be deadly dangerous. He'd heard of a foolish sergeant who'd tried to stop a rolling catapult ball with his foot—and lost the foot as a result.

The stone smacked down, alarmingly close to Joseph the Gamecock. But the sound it made wasn't the heavy thud of rock hitting mud. It was a wetter noise, a solid smack that made the general commanding the Army of Franklin wince and curse. The southrons had aimed that stone too well. Someone in his retinue had gone down under it.

"Let me up, gods damn it," Joseph growled to whoever

had landed on him. When the officer didn't move fast enough to suit him, Joseph lashed out with an elbow. That did the trick.

Scrambling to his feet, Joseph looked around. There stood Roast-Beef William, and there were a couple of junior officers, also upright and unscathed. But Leonidas the Priest sprawled on the ground, and plainly would never get up again. He still twitched, but that was only because his body hadn't yet realized he was dead. When a thirty-pound flying stone hit a man square in the chest, he was unlikely to get up again. Blood soaked into the red dirt, reddening it further. Leonidas' blood was even redder than the crimson vestments he wore.

His twitching stopped. Joseph peered down toward the southrons and their engine, wondering if they were going to send another stone his way. But they seemed satisfied to have scattered his companions and him. He wondered if they knew they'd hit anyone.

"By the gods," Roast-Beef William said, staring at the smashed corpse of his fellow wing commander.

"Yes, by the gods," Joseph the Gamecock agreed. "The Lion God will have himself a new servant, up there on the mountain beyond the sky." *And may Leonidas serve his favorite god better than he ever served King Geoffrey and me.*

Another officer said, "I think, sir, we can withdraw from this spot without fear of dishonor."

Joseph hadn't thought about that. But he recognized truth when he heard it. "Yes, we'd better," he agreed, "or else they may decide to send us another present. Somebody grab poor Leonidas' legs and haul him off. He deserves to go on a proper pyre."

They retreated farther up Cedar Hill. The southrons down below seemed satisfied with the results of their one shot. Leonidas the Priest's body left a trail of blood as junior officers dragged him along. Joseph the Gamecock never stopped being amazed at how much blood a man's body held.

"What do we do now, sir?" Roast-Beef William asked.

"We do what we have to do, Lieutenant General," Joseph

answered. "We appoint a new wing commander and we go on. Leonidas was a brave and pious man, but we have to go on without him." Leonidas had also been an idiot who didn't like taking orders, but Joseph the Gamecock didn't dwell on that, not aloud. When a man died, you looked for the good he'd had in him. If, with the hierophant of the Lion God, you had to look a bit harder than you might with someone else . . . *Stop that,* Joseph the Gamecock told himself.

The southrons kept pounding away at Cedar Hill. Roast-Beef William said, "I'm afraid we're going to have to fall back to Commissioner Mountain, sir."

"I'm afraid you're right," Joseph said. "If General Hesmucet cares to launch a frontal attack against us there, he's welcome to try it for all of me."

"You don't want to make things too easy for him, though," Roast-Beef William protested.

"Oh, no," Joseph agreed. "I don't intend to do anything of the sort. But this position can be turned. I'd like to see Hesmucet try to turn our lines along Commissioner Mountain and Snouts Stream." Even as he spoke, rain began to fall. He smiled; to him right now, rain was a friend. "I'd especially like to see Hesmucet try one of his outflanking moves in this muck."

His surviving wing commander nodded. "If he did, we'd be on his flank like a tiger on an ox."

William had missed a point: the rain hindered Joseph's movements no less than those of the southrons. But even Joseph the Gamecock, who picked nits as naturally as he breathed, didn't correct him. He didn't need to attack. He needed nothing more than to hold on, and to hold Hesmucet out of Marthasville. As long as he succeeded in doing that, he was living up to the responsibility with which King Geoffrey had entrusted him.

Not that Geoffrey will thank me for it, he thought. *Geoffrey never thanks me for anything. No—that's not true. He'd thank me if I dried up and blew away. But he was desperate enough to put me here, and now he has to make the best of it.*

He knew Geoffrey wasn't happy that he'd had to yield so much of southern Peachtree Province. On the other hand,

Duke Edward of Arlington and the Army of Southern Parthenia had yielded just about all of southern Parthenia to Marshal Bart. Bart was a lot closer to Nonesuch—and to King Geoffrey—than Hesmucet was to Marthasville.

"To whom will you give command of Leonidas' wing?" Roast-Beef William asked.

There was a question to make even a moody man like Joseph the Gamecock stop brooding. But for piety and courage, Leonidas the Priest had been singularly, even plurally, lacking in the military virtues. If his wing acquired a commanding officer who knew what he was doing . . . Joseph didn't smile. That would have been disrespectful to the dead, especially with Leonidas still unburned and with his spirit, therefore, still free and vengeful. Whether he smiled or not, though, he was far from brokenhearted.

"I think I shall appoint Brigadier Alexander—not James of Broadpath's engines chief, who's back in Parthenia now, but the man they call the Steward," he said. "He's a solid fellow."

"Old Straight? I should say so!" William nodded vigorous approval. "Solid as the day is long. Brave, industrious, knows what he's doing."

"It will make a pleasant change, won't it?" Joseph said. That was unkind to the memory of the hierophant of the Lion God, but not too much so.

William added, "I'm sure Lieutenant General Bell will also think well of the choice."

"It's not his to make. It's not his to approve of," Joseph said testily. Day by day, he grew less happy with Bell. The man carped and complained about everything, yet was reluctant to strike when ordered to do so. *It must be the pain*, Joseph thought. *He's only a shell of the man he used to be. Too bad, because I could use that man. The one I have . . .*

As the officers came back up Cedar Hill, Joseph told off some ordinary soldiers he saw to take charge of Leonidas' body. Then he and his comrades went off to his headquarters. He sent a runner to summon Alexander the Steward, and another to give Bell word of Leonidas the Priest's untimely demise. With a little luck, the new wing commander would prove less recalcitrant than Leonidas had been. *He could hardly prove more recalcitrant,* Joseph thought.

The runner he'd sent to Bell returned. "The lieutenant general's compliments, sir," the fellow said, "and he asks if having a new wing commander means we're more likely to advance against the enemy."

"We would be more likely to advance against the enemy," Joseph the Gamecock said icily, "if Lieutenant General Bell were in the habit of following orders."

"Uh, shall I take that message back to him, sir?" the runner asked.

"No, never mind," Joseph said. "He either knows it already or is unlikely to believe it from my lips."

Before long, another man approached him: not a soldier this time, but a fellow in maroon velvet tunic and pantaloons of civilian cut who wore on his head a hat that put Joseph the Gamecock in mind of an inverted chamber pot. Bowing, the newcomer said, "Your Grace, I have the honor to represent Duke Brown, who is of course King Geoffrey's satrap for Peachtree Province."

"Of course," Joseph replied. His opinion of the provincial satrap was indeed brown; he gave the duke far higher marks for mouth than for brains. Wondering what had caused Brown to send out this chap, he inquired, "And what does his Grace think I can do for him?"

His tone suggested that, whatever it might be, Duke Brown was undoubtedly laboring under a delusion. The man with the maroon pantaloons and ugly hat gave no sign of noticing that tone. He said, "The satrap sent me here to remonstrate with you."

"To remonstrate with me? Why?" Joseph asked. "What have I done to him?" *What have I done to set off the gods-damned fool now?*

"Sir, he feels he must protest your excessive utilization of the province's glideway carpets," Duke Brown's man replied. "Your constant traffic in this part of the province is having a most deleterious effect on civilian travel in Peachtree Province."

"You *are* joking," Joseph the Gamecock said.

"By no means, your Grace," the study in maroon said.

"The satrap has received numerous complaints from nobles and commoners alike as to the adverse impact on their travel requirements the continued requisitioning of carpets for your forces has caused, and feels he must respond to the citizenry."

"I see," Joseph said.

The civilian beamed. "I knew you would be reasonable, sir. Ah . . . what is that you are writing?"

"A pass to take you through my lines, so you can bring Duke Brown's complaints directly to General Hesmucet. Since he is the true cause of my excessive use of the glideways, he is the one who should hear about the satrap's concerns. He has the name of a reasonable man. I am sure, when he hears he is bothering civilians, he will turn around and march back down to the south."

"You mock me, sir," Duke Brown's man said indignantly. "You mock my principal as well. This shall not go unnoticed."

"And I shall not lose a moment's sleep over it," Joseph the Gamecock said. "I have some small hope of coping with the enemy. But when the idiots alleged to be on my own side commence to move against me, I find myself helpless to resist them."

"How dare you use such a word, sir?" the civilian said. "How *dare* you?"

"I dare because I am a soldier, and it is my duty to dare," Joseph replied. "That is more than the satrap can say."

"You will go too far, if you have not already," the man in maroon said, biting the words off between his teeth. "And, speaking of soldiers, I will have you know that Count Thraxton has come to Marthasville, and is examining your conduct of this campaign very closely—very closely indeed."

"By all the gods, I'm delighted to hear that—just delighted," Joseph said. "Thraxton the Braggart's the reason the Army of Franklin was in the fix I found it in—and now King Geoffrey sends him up here to sit in judgment on me? Not a chance he'll be prejudiced, is there? Not half."

"Your Grace, I don't know what you want me to say." The man in maroon sounded worried—*not out of any concern for me*, Joseph judged, *but because he fears he'll end up in trouble with the satrap. Well, too fornicating bad for him.*

"Go tell Duke Brown that I am going to use the glideways as much as I need to, so I can defend his province for him whether he wants me to or not," Joseph the Gamecock snapped. "And if by any chance you should happen to see the ever so illustrious Count Thraxton, thank him for me for the lovely predicament he left me in. And now he looks over my campaign? Gods protect me from my friends!"

Had the fellow in maroon velvet lingered another moment, Joseph would have sped him on his way with a good, solid kick in the fundament. He might have realized that, for he withdrew precipitately even without the added impetus of the commanding general's boot. Joseph's stomach twinged. *Hearing Thraxton the Braggart is around makes me as dyspeptic as he is.*

Thraxton had brains. He also had a complete inability to get along with anyone else (a trait Joseph shared) or to make anyone follow his lead (which was not one of Joseph's difficulties). The only exception to the general rule was that Thraxton had somehow formed an intimate friendship with King Geoffrey, a friendship that endured through thick and thin—and, given Thraxton's other talents, or lack of same, there'd been much more thin than thick.

He has Geoffrey's ear. He will drip poison into it. Joseph was as sure of that as he was of tomorrow's sunrise. He shrugged. He couldn't do anything about it. All he could do was hold the line of Commissioner Mountain and Snouts Stream as long as possible. The more southrons who died trying to pry him out of his position, the better the chance that the south would sicken of the war and make King Avram quit it or face upheaval at home.

Lieutenant General Bell would attack, the general commanding the Army of Franklin thought. He tossed his head like a man bothered by gnats. Duke Edward of Arlington, when angry, would twist so he seemed to be trying to bite his own ear. Joseph's gesture wasn't far removed from that. *Bell would do any number of stupid things if only he had the chance. My job, not least, is to make sure he doesn't get it.*

Count Joseph sighed. *But how am I supposed to manage that?* He saw no clear answer. He'd seen few clear answers since the days when the northern provinces first broke away from Detina. He kept fighting nonetheless.

V

Once again, your Majesty, our forces have been ordered to make an inglorious retreat, Lieutenant General Bell wrote in yet another of his secret letters to King Geoffrey. *Once again, we have taken heavy losses trying to hold a position that could not be held, this time including that heroic and pious soldier, Leonidas the Priest. Once again, the spirits of the men suffer because they always fall back and are never permitted to advance against the foe. How long, your Majesty, can this go on?*

Bell examined that, wondering if it was too strong. He decided to leave it in. The king needed to know what was going on up here. *If I don't tell him the truth, who will?* Bell thought.

"Commissioner Mountain," he muttered under his breath. Who would have imagined General Hesmucet could have pushed the Army of Franklin back so far so fast? *Who would have imagined Joseph the Gamecock would fall back so far so fast?* Bell thought. That was what it came down to. "Disgraceful," Bell said, again quietly. He wished he could shout.

Reaching for the bottle of laudanum he always carried,

he yanked out the cork and drank. Then he sat in his folding chair and waited for relief. He needed ever larger draughts to get it, and got less no matter how much he took.

If he looked back over his shoulder, he could practically see Marthasville. Camp rumor said Count Thraxton had come there to take a long look at the way Joseph the Gamecock was fighting the southrons. Bell didn't like the rumor. He was the one who was supposed to be informing King Geoffrey of how things were going. He had no great use for Thraxton the Braggart; the man had made a hash of the fighting by Rising Rock. Bell had been flat on his back then, still recovering from the amputation of his leg. He remembered the jouncing agony he'd gone through in the retreat from Proselytizers' Rise up into Peachtree Province. Thraxton had botched the battle, no two ways about it.

But Thraxton was also Geoffrey's friend. If the king decided to remove Joseph from his command, would he give that command back to Thraxton? Bell shook his leonine head. "That would be madness," he rumbled. "Every man jack and every officer in this army knows of Thraxton's blunders. The command should go elsewhere."

He knew exactly where the command should go. He'd left hints in his letters to King Geoffrey. *Maybe I should stop hinting and come right out and speak my mind,* he thought. *After all, the safety of the kingdom depends on it.*

Voices outside his pavilion—voices, and then one of his sentries stuck his head inside and said, "Sir, General Joseph is here to see you."

"Joseph? Here to see me?" Even with the gentle cloud of laudanum between himself and the world, Lieutenant General Bell knew his superior must not spy the letter to King Geoffrey. He swept it out of sight beneath some other papers, then nodded. "I am always pleased to see him." That was a lie, of course, but a politic lie.

When Joseph the Gamecock ducked his way through the tent flap, he looked more pleased with himself and with the world as a whole than was his wont. "Let the southrons come," he said. "Yes, by the gods, *let* them come! They'll bloody their noses on our line, and they can't outflank it."

"You have said this before, your Grace," Bell replied. "You have also proved mistaken before."

"Not this time," Joseph said. "As long as the rains keep coming, General Hesmucet will have a devils of a time moving men and supplies for them, and we've got solid sets of entrenchments running twenty miles north up Snouts Stream. I don't think they can do it."

"And when shall we attack them?" Bell inquired.

Joseph the Gamecock gave him a sour look. "I am in no hurry to make such an effort—and, if you will recall, the last time I tried to persuade you to send your whole wing forward, you broke out in a case of jimjams."

"The enemy had engines on our flank. To advance would have been to give him a perfect chance to massacre us," Bell insisted.

"You are the only one who ever saw those engines—and that includes the southrons," Joseph said.

"I was there. You were not. Had you been there, you would have seen them, too. But you do not seem to consider your place to be at the fore."

They'd called each other cowards now. They both glared, in perfect mutual loathing. Joseph the Gamecock said, "I have been glad to discover you will at least fight on the defensive."

"Sir, I find your manner offensive," Bell replied.

"I had hoped to find yours offensive, but no such luck," Joseph said. "Still, so long as we fight hard here, the southrons will get no closer to Marthasville. And *that* is the point of the exercise."

"That may be one point of the exercise, sir, but it's not the only point," Bell said. "The other thing we have to do is drive the southrons from our land, drive them back where they belong—and send them off with their tails between their legs, so they'll know better than to trouble us again."

"Good luck if you should ever be in the position to try, Lieutenant General," Joseph the Gamecock said. "I don't think it can be done now, not with things as they are. If some miracle-worker were to appear with crossbows that would shoot twice as far and ten times as fast as the usual weapons, we might whip King Avram's men back to their kennel, but what are the odds of that? Without it, we have to try to make the foe sicken of the war. That's my view, at any rate."

"I know, sir," Bell said sourly. "You never tire of stating it."

"That's because—although you may find it hard to believe— I have officers who don't want to hear it," Joseph the Gamecock replied. "I'm certain you of all people find that incredible."

"Heh," Bell said, unwilling to show Joseph he had the slightest idea what the general commanding was talking about now.

"You are holding an important part of this line, Lieutenant General," Joseph told him. "I expect you to do just that: to hold, I mean. If a breakthrough occurs on the stretch of line where you command, you will find that I do not take the matter lightly. You have already failed more often than you should. Shall I comment further, or do I make myself plain?"

"Libelously so, sir," Bell said.

Joseph the Gamecock clicked his tongue between his teeth. "Libel must be committed to writing, as anyone of your temperament should have learned by now. Slander is oral. And you must always remember that proof of truth is the best defense against either. Good day, Lieutenant General." He left Bell's pavilion seeming even more pleased with himself than he had been when he came in.

Bell muttered something decidedly slanderous. By Joseph's standards, he'd done a good deal of libeling, too. He cared not a fig for Joseph's standards; the only ones that mattered to him were his own. Taking the letter he'd been working on from its place of concealment, he finished it, sealed it, and sent it off to Nonesuch in the same clandestine way as he'd despatched the others.

Sooner or later, King Geoffrey will have to listen, he thought. *Gods grant it won't be too late.*

He wished he were in command of the Army of Franklin. He would get it moving south again. How could Geoffrey hope to establish a kingdom when the southrons sat on half the land he claimed? The Army of Franklin hadn't seen the province of Franklin for months. *If I were in charge, I'd head straight for Ramblerton and set the province free.*

For now, though, Bell had to fight under another man's orders. And Joseph had warned him he was being watched. Bell didn't think King Geoffrey would acquiesce in his dismissal, but didn't care to take the chance, especially not with Thraxton the Braggart close at hand. Nothing unfortunate would or could happen while Thraxton was on watch.

Grudgingly, Bell admitted to himself that, for a defensive position, the one anchored by Commissioner Mountain and Snouts Stream was solid. The southrons would have a hells of a time breaking through it. But Joseph had already abandoned other strong defensive positions. Bell didn't dwell on the fact that he and poor Leonidas had talked Joseph into abandoning the one by Fat Mama. He seldom dwelt on the past, unless it was to his advantage.

After another gulp of laudanum, Bell seized his crutches and levered himself to his foot. Even with the drug, working a crutch under his left arm hurt like broken glass, like fire, like knives. The healers swore the festering in his stump had burned itself out, but he could still feel that not everything was right in there. He doubted it ever would be.

For that matter, he could still feel his whole right leg, though the part of it he still owned stopped not much farther down than his prong hung. Sometimes it was just there, as real as flesh till he tried to put weight on it. Sometimes the part that was missing hurt even worse than the part that remained. Those were the bad times, for even laudanum had trouble dulling the phantom pain. The healers said there was no cure for that but time. He'd even asked the mages if there were any spells to exorcise the ghosts of absent body parts. To his disappointment, they'd told him no.

Not enough one-legged wizards, he thought as he made his slow way out of the pavilion. *If a few more sorcerers had lost limbs, they would have made sure there were better measures against these phantoms.* But no such luck. He had to endure.

"I am a soldier," he said, as if someone had doubted it. Enduring was part of what soldiers did. He hadn't expected it to be the most important part of what he did. Life was full of surprises, some pleasant, some emphatically otherwise.

Even getting out through the tent flap wasn't so easy as it might have been. Ducking didn't involve just the head; it involved the whole body. And when the whole body was supported on one foot and on two crutches that wouldn't bend no matter what . . . Bell counted each separate escape from the tent as a minor victory.

Getting out in the fresh air did little to refresh him: it was as hot and muggy outside as it had been within. Gray clouds came rolling in from off the Western Ocean—more rain on the way. He took advantage of the lull to peer east toward the southrons' encampments. Hesmucet was an aggressive commander. He pushed his men up as close to their foes as they could get. It felt as if he were about to order an all-out assault along the whole line.

Lieutenant General Bell nodded in grave approval. *If I commanded the Army of Franklin, that's how I would lead it: like a fighting man, like a tiger ready to spring. Go straight at the enemy and knock him down.*

Of course, if General Hesmucet came straight at Commissioner Mountain, he might accomplish nothing more than to knock himself down. Would he realize that? Bell didn't know. His own instinct was always to test, to probe, to attack. After all, the foe *might* give way.

"Sir?" someone said at his elbow. He turned his head, the only part of him that would turn readily. There stood Major Zibeon. His aide-de-camp asked, "What did Joseph the Gamecock want, sir?"

"Nothing of any consequence, Major," Bell answered. "He warned me to stay alert against any possible attack from the southrons."

"They'd be fools if they tried it," Zibeon said. He had a hard face. When he smiled, the smile was hard, too, hard and predatory. "Here's hoping they're fools."

"Yes, here's hoping," Bell said, and wondered if he meant it. If the southrons did assail Commissioner Mountain, he couldn't see them succeeding, either. Did he want Joseph the Gamecock winning a victory? For the kingdom's sake, he supposed he did. For his own . . .

Even if Joseph wins here, having him lead the Army of Franklin can't be good for the kingdom, Bell thought. *This army would be much better off with a soldier who's not afraid to use if for some* real *fighting—a soldier like, well, like me, for instance.*

Major Zibeon said, "I believe, sir, we've got about as fine a defensive position here as I've ever seen. Gods damn me to the hells if I can see how the southrons will be able to go through us or around us."

That was about the last thing Lieutenant General Bell wanted to hear. He looked down his long, thin nose at the aide-de-camp. "Really, Major?" he said. "Do you think Commissioner Mountain is as sure to hold as Proselytizers' Rise was?"

Zibeon started to answer him, then turned red. Proselytizers' Rise, of course, had fallen to the southrons. If it hadn't fallen, General Hesmucet's army wouldn't have been able to move so deeply into Peachtree Province. Everyone had declared the northern position there was impregnable. Bell couldn't say anything about that from firsthand knowledge, not when the healers had had him in their grip then.

At last, Zibeon said, "It wasn't the position that went awry there, sir. It was the sorcery."

"And who's to say something won't go wrong here as well?" Bell returned. "My view is, you cannot rely on a position to save you. You have to rely on the soldiers manning the position."

"Yes, sir," his aide-de-camp said. "And aren't our northern men the bravest in the world?"

"They were," Bell replied. "They were, before they spent weeks scurrying from one set of entrenchments to the next, never daring to face the enemy out in the open. Now, Major, who knows?" Zibeon pondered that, then shrugged. *I haven't convinced him,* Bell thought. But he'd convinced himself. That was all that really mattered.

Rollant looked at the traitors' field works on Commissioner Mountain with all the enthusiasm of a man with a toothache looking at a trip to the puller. "Are they really going to send us up there?" he asked.

"Why not?" Smitty said blithely. "We took Proselytizers' Rise, so they must think we can do anything."

They'd both been part of the mad climb to the top of Proselytizers' Rise. They'd been part of a smashing victory there. For the life of him, Rollant couldn't figure out how they'd done it. He had trouble seeing how they could hope to do it again, too.

"Remember when all the northerners in the world came at us near the River of Death while we were up on Merkle's Hill?" he said. "We threw 'em back, and we didn't have anything like what the traitors have waiting for us."

Sergeant Joram said, "That will be enough of that. If we're ordered to advance, we will advance, and that's all there is to it. You've got no business trying to demoralize Smitty here."

"Don't worry about it, Sergeant," Smitty said. "I didn't have any morals to speak of before Rollant started talking at me."

"If I want *your* foolishness, be sure I'll ask for it," Joram said. He made a good sergeant: he growled as nastily at Detinans as he did at blonds. And if his superiors gave an order, he would see that everybody he led obeyed it—*even if it does get every last one of us killed,* Rollant thought.

He asked, "Sergeant, *are* we going to try and drive them off those hills?"

"*I* don't know," Joram said irritably. "Nobody's given me any special orders yet, that's all I can tell you. And I don't think Lieutenant Griff knows anything, either. . . . Gods damn it, Smitty, not one single, solitary, fornicating word."

"I didn't say anything, Sergeant," Smitty protested. He looked as innocent as a heavenly messenger. If Rollant hadn't been marching beside him for a couple of years, the pose might have convinced him. As things were, he let out a snicker that almost turned into a guffaw.

But all the guffawing stopped not long afterwards, when Colonel Nahath assembled the regiment and said, "Men, we are going to go up against Commissioner Mountain tomorrow morning—not just us, mind you, but most of Doubting George's army. We're going to go up against it, and we're going to take it."

"Lion God's claws!" somebody shouted. "Has Hesmucet lost his whole mind?"

Had a serf in Palmetto Province yelled anything like that about a Detinan—*any* Detinan, not just a general—he would have been sorry as long as he lived, which probably wouldn't have been long. Rollant had escaped from serfdom a long time before, but what Detinans reckoned liberty still looked like license to him a lot of the time.

The regimental commander didn't even get upset. He just shook his head and said, "No. The idea is, Joseph the Gamecock has to think this stretch of the line is too strong to be taken. He won't have that many men covering it. And because he won't, we'll swarm up the side of the mountain and gods-damned well take it away from him."

"Maybe we will," Smitty said out of the side of his mouth. "Maybe a lot of us'll come down the mountain on our backs, too."

That also struck Rollant as pretty likely. He had no say in such things, though. All he could do was fight hard and hope the men set over him didn't make too many idiotic mistakes. So far, at least, General Hesmucet hadn't. But if he did, Rollant couldn't even retreat till all his comrades were falling back, too. He wasn't just fighting as himself. He was fighting as a blond before ordinary Detinans, and couldn't afford to look like a coward.

He didn't sleep much that evening. He'd had too long a look at the position Doubting George's army would assail when the sun came up. He knew he would much sooner have defended that position. But he was going to have to attack it, and could only trust in the gods that things wouldn't prove so bad as they seemed.

When the regiment assembled the next morning, Smitty handed him a scrap of paper. "Pin this on my back, will you?"

Other pairs of men were going through the same ritual. Rollant grimaced. "You think it'll be that bad?" he asked.

"Don't know," Smitty answered. "But this way, if I fall up there, my name and where I live'll be on my body. My folks can find out what happened to me and make the offerings to take me on to the next world. If I get real lucky, they may even ship my carcass home so my old man can light the pyre."

"That's the kind of luck I could do without," Rollant said. But then, after a moment's thought, he added, "Have you got any more paper?"

"Sure do," Smitty said. Before long, Rollant had his name and street pinned to the back of his gray tunic, too.

"Have faith, men," Lieutenant Griff said. "Have faith, and victory will be ours." His voice broke a couple of times, but he was very young. He had some paper pinned to his uniform, too. *How much faith has he got?* Rollant wondered.

Every catapult under Doubting George's command started bucking and hurling then. Stones and firepots rained down on the traitors' field works. Repeating crossbows sent streams of darts at the northerners, making them keep their heads down. Horns blared all along the southrons' line.

"Forward!" Griff shouted. Brandishing his sword, he went forward himself. He might—he did—sometimes lack for sense, but he'd shown plenty of courage since taking over the company for Captain Cephas.

"Forward!" Sergeant Joram echoed. Rollant wondered if the underofficer had the brains to be afraid. He did himself, and he was.

Up the slopes of Commissioner Mountain ran the men from the wing Lieutenant General George commanded. Rollant shouted, "King Avram and freedom!" as he had in every fight. The words still rang true. Whether they could help him win a victory here was another question.

In spite of the battering the southron engines had given their trenches, the traitors were still full of fight. Heads appeared in the entrenchments. Soldiers in blue started shooting at the advancing southrons. The northerners had catapults of their own on Commissioner Mountain. They started tearing holes in the southrons' ranks. Had Doubting George really believed the enemy wouldn't have enough men to defend this part of their line? If he had, he should have done a little more doubting.

"We aren't going to make it," Rollant said to Smitty as they drew within a hundred yards of the traitors' works. Men were going down as if scythed. If Hesmucet felt like feeding his whole army into this sausage machine, Joseph the Gamecocks's defenders might kill every man in it.

Smitty didn't argue with him, which convinced him he was right—Smitty always thought the regiment could do more than it really could. All the farmer's son said now was, "Well, we've got to keep trying a little longer."

Echoing that, Lieutenant Griff shouted, "Forward!" again. He *was* brave. Rollant suspected he was a little bit crazy, too, to push the advance here.

A few feet away, the company standard-bearer took a crossbow quarrel in the chest. He stood there swaying for a moment, then crumpled to the ground. The banner, gold dragon on red, fell, too.

Rollant grabbed the staff before the silk of the flag could touch the ground and be deviled. If that wasn't madness, and not a little of it, he couldn't imagine what was. Standard-bearers were always targets. A standard-bearer charging straight at massed crossbows? A *blond* standard-bearer charging straight at massed crossbows? *It's a good thing I've got my name on the back of my uniform*, he thought.

But he went forward even so, holding the company banner high. And he shouted a new war cry, one to which he'd never before felt entitled: "Detina!" If he couldn't shout the kingdom's name while carrying its flag, when could he?

Crossbow bolts hissed past him, some so close he could feel the breeze of their passage on his cheeks. But he wasn't afraid. He didn't know why, but he wasn't. He felt exalted—not as if they couldn't hurt him, but as if it wouldn't matter if they did. And if that wasn't madness, he couldn't imagine what would be.

That mood of glorious indifference lasted till he came within perhaps twenty yards of the enemy's entrenchments. What broke it wasn't a bolt tearing into his flesh, but rather a hand tugging on his arm and a desperate voice crying, "Back, Rollant! We're falling back!"

Rollant looked around like a man awakening from a fever. Sure enough, the southrons had done everything flesh and blood could do. They were streaming east down the forward slope of Commissioner Mountain, bringing their wounded with them, leaving their dead behind.

"Come on!" Smitty said urgently. "They'll kill both of us if you wait around here."

Exaltation drained out of Rollant like wine from a cracked cup. The dregs left behind were exhaustion and terror. He turned away from the enemy's trenches and stumbled back toward the encampments from which they'd set out. The only thing he remembered to do was hold up the flag.

By some accident or miracle, no quarrels pierced him or Smitty before they got out of range. But when Rollant reached up to tug at his hat, he discovered one hole through the brim and one through the crown that hadn't been there before. *If I were a couple of inches taller . . .* He didn't want to finish that thought.

"They aren't chasing us," he remarked when he and Smitty had got back among their fellows.

"Why should they chase us?" Smitty answered. "They've whipped us. All they want to do is hold us back, and we sure aren't going forward now."

That was a self-evident truth. "Gods, I could use something wet," Rollant said. He noticed the banner he was carrying had several new holes in it, too. *None in me, though,* he thought. *Some god or another was watching out. None in me.*

Sergeant Joram handed Rollant a flask. He took a big swig, thinking it held water, and almost choked to death on a mouthful of potent spirits. The stuff seared its way down to his belly. As he wheezed, Joram set a hand on his shoulder, something the sergeant had never done before. "You did good," Joram said.

With a shrug, Rollant answered, "I hardly even knew what I was doing."

"You've always fought well enough," Joram said. "But up there on the mountain . . . up there you fought like—like a Detinan."

Plainly, he knew no higher praise. Rollant wasn't delighted with the way he'd put the praise he gave, but didn't care to quarrel about it. "Thanks," he said, and took another, smaller, swig from the flask. This time, he was ready for the flames in his throat.

Lieutenant Griff came up to him. "Will you carry the standard again?" he asked.

"A standard-bearer shouldn't be a common soldier," Rollant answered. "Will you make me a corporal?"

He waited for Griff to get angry. But the company commander only nodded. "That's business," he said. "Doing business is Detinan, too. I'll go to Colonel Nahath with it. Bargain?"

If Rollant weren't a blond, Griff would have promoted him on the spot. He was sure of that. But few blonds ever got any chance at all for promotion. He nodded and saluted. "Yes, sir. Bargain."

Lieutenant General George looked at the reports his brigade commanders had brought him. Turning to his adjutant, he shook his head and said, "We lost a gods-awful lot of men up there, and what did it get us? Not bloody much."

"Bloody is the word, sir," Colonel Andy agreed. "Close to three thousand soldiers with holes in them, and we didn't hurt the traitors nearly as much."

"That's the rub, gods damn it," Doubting George said. "We can afford more losses than they can, because our army's twice the size of theirs. But we can't afford *a lot* more losses than theirs, not if we don't shift 'em an inch. And we didn't."

"I know, sir," Andy said. *How could you help knowing?* George thought. *We're still where we were when we tried to take Commissioner Mountain, not somewhere on the other side of it. If we'd taken it, Joseph would have had to retreat again, and the northerners would have lost the plain behind it, and Hiltonia and Ephesus to boot.* Colonel Andy went on, "But General Hesmucet thought it was worth a try."

There was no answer to that, none that would have kept George properly subordinate. He shifted his ground instead: "Since it didn't work, we have to figure out what to do next."

"The rain's stopped," Andy said. "That's something."

And so it was. Moving men and catapults and victuals when the roads turned into mud-bottomed creeks was just this side of impossible. Doubting George knew that was another reason Hesmucet had struck here: he'd already had men and supplies in place. But, unfortunately, so had Joseph the Gamecock.

"What can we do?" Doubting George wasn't really asking his adjutant; he was thinking aloud. "Did I hear rightly that we got a foothold on the western bank of Snouts Stream?"

"I believe so, sir," Andy answered.

"We'll have to hang on to that," George said. "We'll have to hang on to that for dear life, as a matter of fact. If we can do with it, then the attack on Commissioner Mountain may turn out to have been worth something after all."

"Here's hoping." Colonel Andy didn't sound as if he believed it.

George set a hand on his shoulder. "Don't fret yourself, Colonel," he advised. "You've got to remember, things could be worse. I'd much rather be here than down on Merkle's Hill with all the traitors in the world roaring for our blood. That wasn't so very long ago, you know." He laughed.

"What's funny, sir?" his adjutant asked.

"Nothing, not really," Lieutenant General George answered. Andy sent him a wounded look, but he didn't explain. He didn't think anyone else would find it funny, anyhow. How could he tell Andy he'd managed to talk himself out of his own doubts?

The sun beat down on him. He took off his hat and fanned himself with it, doing his best to fight the muggy summer heat of Peachtree Province. He'd always thought Parthenia had vile summer weather—and, as a matter of fact, it did. But Peachtree Province was worse.

What there was of the breeze came out of the west. When George inhaled, he wrinkled his nose. He knew what that stench came from: unburned southron bodies, still lying in front of the works on Commissioner Mountain they hadn't been able to take. "If the enemy won't make them a pyre," he said, "the least they could do would be to get them under the ground."

"Bury them, the way the blonds used to do with their dead before we taught 'em better?" Colonel Andy's lip curled with distaste. "I don't know about that, sir. Do you really think the gods would accept it?"

"Better than leaving dead men on the field to bloat and stink, wouldn't you say?" Doubting George asked.

Again, his adjutant remained unconvinced. "Burying's unnatural. Fire purifies the soul."

"I—" George stopped and coughed. If he said he doubted that, he would find himself in a theological argument with Andy. He had neither the time nor the energy for any such thing. Besides, in the general run of things, he didn't doubt it. If he fell in battle, he wanted to be burned. But even burial struck him as preferable to being ignored by everyone save the carrion birds.

Andy looked toward the south. "Here comes General Hesmucet, sir."

Hesmucet reined his unicorn to a halt. As Doubting George stiffened to attention, he reflected that the general commanding rode more like a tradesman than a noble. Then he laughed at himself again. That was true, but it would have counted against Hesmucet much more heavily in the blood-conscious north than in the south, where what a man could do mattered more than who his grandfather was. *This is the side you chose,* George thought. *Make the best of it.*

After descending from the unicorn and tying it to a tree, Hesmucet said, "If the weather holds, we'll be able to do some more against the bastards."

"That's true, sir," George agreed. "Do we have a bridge-head on the west bank of Snouts Stream? I've heard it, but I want to make sure it's so before I go out and celebrate."

"It's so," Hesmucet answered. "Now we have to figure out how to make the most of it—and how to keep the traitors from wrecking it before we can."

"The more we press them, the likelier they are to break," George observed. "If we can slip some unicorn-riders over to the far side of that stream and turn them loose, that might give Joseph something new to think about."

"Well, so it might," the commanding general allowed. He called for a runner, then told him, "Fetch Marble Bill here. If we're going to talk about unicorn-riders, we might as well have their commander listening."

He probably would have come up with that for himself, Doubting George thought. *He's a solid general.* No matter how he tried to hide it, even from himself, not being in command hurt.

Brigadier William—more commonly Marble Bill, because of a pale complexion and a nearly expressionless face—was not a brilliant commander of unicorn-riders. The traitors had a couple of those: Jeb the Beauty, who served Duke Edward of Arlington so well in Parthenia, and grim Ned of the Forest here in the east. But Marble Bill was a competent commander of unicorn-riders. After some of the unfortunate officers who'd led southron unicorns into battle, competence was not to be despised.

Hesmucet said, "Doubting George here had himself a notion." He didn't try to take credit for it himself, as a lot of high-ranking officers might have done. After spelling it out for Marble Bill, he asked, "What do you think? Can we do it?"

"I don't know for certain." The brigadier's voice gave away no more than his face did. After a moment, he went on, "Finding out might be worthwhile, though. I probably ought to take my riders across Snouts Stream by night, to keep the enemy from knowing they're there till they start moving."

Definitely competent, George thought. Hesmucet said, "I'll have Major Alva lay down a confusion spell for you, if you like."

To George's surprise, Marble Bill shook his head. "No, thanks," he said. "The traitors will be looking for magecraft, I expect. Even if they can't pierce it, knowing it's there will put them on the alert."

Very definitely competent, Doubting George thought. He asked, "Can you move a couple of regiments over tonight?"

"Yes, sir," was all Marble Bill said in reply to that. A lot of officers—both General Guildenstern and Fighting Joseph leaped into George's mind—were given to boasting and bluster. Hearing one give a simple, matter-of-fact answer was refreshing. As if thinking of Fighting Joseph were enough to conjure him up, he strolled over and nodded casually to Hesmucet and George in turn.

"Then do it," Hesmucet said with the air of a man coming to a decision. He turned to George and to Fighting Joseph.

"I'll want more soldiers from both of you to help build up the bridgehead."

"You'll have them," George said, imitating Marble Bill's brevity.

Fighting Joseph, by contrast, struck a pose. "My brave men are always at your service, sir, and at the service of the kingdom," he declared.

He meant it. George was sure he meant it. As far as Fighting Joseph was concerned, he selflessly served Detina. As far as any outsider was concerned, Fighting Joseph worried first about himself, and grabbing more power and glory for himself, and about everything else afterwards . . . long afterwards. It seemed painfully obvious to everyone who served with him and tried to command him.

"I'm so glad to hear it," Hesmucet replied now.

"Tell me what to do, and I shall do it." Fighting Joseph struck another pose. George fought down a strong urge to retch.

"All right," Hesmucet said. "This is what you'll do, then— you'll move in support of Lieutenant General George's men and—"

"You want me to do what?" Fighting Joseph demanded indignantly. His ruddy face got ruddier, till it almost reached the high color of Roast-Beef William's. "You want me to move in subordination to another wing commander?"

"Lieutenant General George has more men, and more men in the vicinity, than you do." Hesmucet spoke in reasonable tones. "To me, that means he should be the one with the main responsibility and you the one with the secondary responsibility."

Fighting Joseph rolled his eyes up to the heavens. "By the Thunderer's shaggy beard, how many more such insults must I endure?"

"I don't see that you've endured any," George told him. "If our positions were reversed, I'd certainly subordinate myself to you."

"No one understands me," Fighting Joseph groaned, as if he were an avant-garde artist—or perhaps a six-year-old in a temper. He stormed away from his fellow generals. George wondered if spanking his backside would do any good. Unfortunately, he had his doubts.

General Hesmucet sighed. "He *is* brave," he said, and he might have been reminding himself as well as the officers with him. "He *is* brave," he repeated, "but he's also gods-damned difficult. One of these days . . ." He kicked up some dirt with his right boot, as if kicking the obstreperous Joseph out of the army.

But, as Doubting George knew, Hesmucet couldn't simply dismiss Fighting Joseph. Joseph's seniority entitled him to high rank *somewhere*: if not here, then somewhere farther west. Hesmucet might not want him here, but King Avram didn't want him anywhere closer to Georgetown. In that contest, Hesmucet was bound to lose.

The general commanding sighed again. "You gentlemen know what I want from you now. George, if Fighting Joseph positively disobeys my command, I want to hear about it."

"Yes, sir," George said. If Fighting Joseph gave Hesmucet enough spikes to crucify him, the general commanding would, no doubt, shed nary a tear. George himself wasn't enamored of working alongside Fighting Joseph, and wouldn't have been brokenhearted to see him go, either.

"Brigadier William," Hesmucet said, and Marble Bill stiffened to attention. Hesmucet went on, "Remember, if we can get your unicorn-riders either through the traitors' line at Snouts Stream or around the end of it, Joseph the Gamecock will have to pull back. That will give us Hiltonia, and Ephesus, too."

Saluting, Marble Bill said, "You know I'll do everything I can, sir."

"Good." Hesmucet nodded. "Up till now, from what the prisoners say, our friend Joseph the Gamecock has kept morale up in the Army of Franklin by making his retreats out to be strategy: he tells his men he's luring us deeper and deeper into Peachtree to destroy us. If he loses Hiltonia, if there's only the Hoocheecoochee River between us and Marthasville, that story will start wearing thin."

"I understand what you want of me, sir," Marble Bill said. Hesmucet looked to Doubting George, too, and doubtless would have looked to Fighting Joseph were he still there. Doubting George nodded.

"All right then," Hesmucet said. "Dismissed." He got back onto his unicorn and rode away.

George told Colonel Andy, "Draft orders to set our regiments in motion, as General Hesmucet requires."

"Yes, sir," his adjutant replied. "Ah, sir, is Fighting Joseph really going to support us?" He looked around to make sure no one but George was in earshot before adding, "My guess is, he'll support us like a commercial traveler skipping out on a farmer's daughter after he's put a baby in her belly."

"Heh," George said. "Don't I wish you were wrong?" A field-grade officer approached him. George nodded a greeting. "Hello, Colonel Nahath. What can I do for you today?" He had a warm regard for the regimental commander. Back in the desperate fighting by the River of Death, Nahath's New Eboracers had fought back to back when the traitors tried a flank attack on Merkle's Hill that came much too close to working.

"I have a question for you, Lieutenant General," Nahath replied. "You have a name for being a fair man, so I'm particularly interested in what you have to say."

"Well, you've flattered me and you've intrigued me," Doubting George said. "Now you'd better ask your question, don't you think?"

"Yes, sir," Nahath said. "I have a man in my regiment—in Lieutenant Griff's company—who, up on Commissioner Mountain, took the company standard when the standard-bearer was hit, who brought it forward through everything the traitors could shoot at him, and who was the last man to leave the field. My question is, should I promote him to corporal?"

"Lion God's claws, Colonel, if you promoted him to lieutenant you'd get no argument from me," George said. "Why do you even feel you need to ask?"

"He's a blond, sir," Nahath replied. "Fellow named Rollant, escaped serf from Palmetto Province."

"Oh." George kicked at the mud under his right boot. Every so often, his being a northerner by birth would up and bite him. That a blond might do such a thing had never crossed his mind. He plucked at his beard as he thought.

At last, he asked, "If you did promote him, would the men obey him?"

"I don't know, sir," Colonel Nahath said. "That would be one of the things I'd have to find out. I know I don't need your permission, precisely: there are other blond underofficers, though not a great many. But I did want your view on the matter before I acted."

"I appreciate that." Doubting George plucked at his beard again. At last, with a sigh, he said, "Promote him, Colonel. See what happens. If he does the job, well and good. If not . . . he deserves the chance to fail, wouldn't you say? I rather think he will, but he does deserve a chance."

"Deserves the chance to fail," Nahath echoed. "That's well put, sir. All right, then. I'll do it, and we'll see how it goes."

"Seems only fair," George said. "After all, it's not as if he's an officer, or anything of the sort."

"There *is* a blond officer, you know," Nahath said. Doubting George and Colonel Andy both exclaimed in astonishment, but the New Eboracer nodded. "By the gods, gentlemen, there is: he's a major among the healers in the west."

"What *will* the kingdom be like if King Avram turns blonds into Detinans?" Colonel Andy asked.

"It will be different," George said. "It will be very different. Of that, there can be no doubt. But I will say this, and of it there can also be no doubt: Detina will be one kingdom. And that is how the gods intended it to be, and to remain." His adjutant and Colonel Nahath both nodded.

Colonel Florizel said, "A great pity Leonidas the Priest got killed. We were lucky to have a wing commander on such good terms with the gods."

"If you say so, sir," Captain Gremio replied. He wouldn't argue with the leader of his regiment, but his own view of the situation was that a wing commander with an actual functioning brain would be a pleasant novelty. Piety, to him, went only so far as a military virtue.

Florizel gave what was probably intended for an indulgent chuckle. "Ah, you barristers," he said. "A lot of freethinkers among you."

"I believe in the gods, your Excellency," Gremio protested. "There are days, I admit, when I have trouble believing the gods believe in me."

As soon as the words were out of his mouth, he knew he should have left them unsaid. The first sentence was fine. Not even Florizel could complain about that. The second . . . No, he should have thought it and kept his mouth shut. "The gods believe," the regimental commander said firmly. "And they have ways of showing people exactly what they believe." He eyed Gremio, as if to say the gods were likely to believe he'd made a jackass of himself.

At the moment, he believed that, too. Muttering excuses under his breath, he walked down the trench line, in theory to see how the men of his company were positioned but in fact to get away from Colonel Florizel. After he'd made good his escape, he started really doing what he'd pretended to do when he left. Florizel's regiment had the bad luck to be holding the stretch of line where the southrons had forced their way across Snouts Stream. That meant his men, along with everyone else in the regiment, had to stay especially alert, lest the enemy come swarming at them in great numbers.

Cautiously, Gremio stuck his head up above the parapet and peered east toward the southrons' bridgehead. A hundred yards away, a southron officer's head popped up above *his* parapet at the same time. Each man saw the motion from the other. Both men ducked. A moment later, feeling foolish, Gremio looked up again. So did the southron. Gremio waved: he despised southrons in general, but had nothing against specific southrons in particular. After a brief hesitation, the enemy officer waved back.

He must feel the same about me as I feel about him, Gremio thought. It was an odd notion. More often than not, southrons were simply the enemy to him. How could they be human beings? They were fighting him and everything he held dear. Every once in a while, in spite of everything, one of them insisted on reminding Gremio of his humanity.

In the end, though, how much did that matter? Not a great deal. *If he comes at me, I'm going to try to kill him regardless of what I think about him.* Battlefield reality could be very simple.

A little farther east, behind the southrons' entrenchments, they'd thrown a couple of bridges across Snouts Stream. Gremio didn't like that at all. It meant Hesmucet's men could reinforce their bridgehead whenever they pleased. He wondered where Joseph the Gamecock would find reinforcements in case the northerners needed more men in a hurry. He didn't know. He hoped Joseph did.

"Anything unusual, sir?" Sergeant Thisbe asked him.

"Nothing much," he answered. "A southron and I were playing peekaboo with each other for a little bit, you might say."

"Peekaboo?" Thisbe echoed.

Gremio mimed sticking his head up, looking, ducking down, and then looking again. The sergeant laughed. "Peekaboo," Gremio repeated. "That bastard in gray was doing just the same thing."

"All right." But Thisbe's smile slipped. "Do you think we can throw the southrons back across the stream?"

"No," Gremio said bluntly. "We've tried a couple of times, and paid the price for it. The ball's in their court now. We're just going to have to hold them back as best we can. We ought to be able to do that."

"Oh, too bad," Thisbe said. "I thought the same thing myself, and I was hoping you would tell me I was wrong."

"I wish I could," Gremio answered. He had the feeling that Colonel Florizel still believed they could throw the southrons back. That worried him; if the colonel, or those above him, tried to act on that belief, a lot of good northern men were going to end up dead—and, worse yet, dead for no good purpose. Gremio himself, he knew, might easily end up among their number. He disapproved of that idea with all his orderly soul. He was, to some degree, willing to die for his kingdom, but only if his death would actually do the kingdom some good. Dying in a fight foredoomed from the start struck him as wasteful.

Thisbe said, "I wish the southrons hadn't got this bridgehead."

"So do I," Gremio replied. "We were all so pleased when

we threw them back from Commissioner Mountain. And we should have been—that thrust would have killed us had it gone home. But this bridgehead . . ." He scowled. "It's like an ulcer, or a wound that festers instead of getting better. We can die from this, too, even if it takes longer."

"That's how my father died," Thisbe said quietly. "He laid his leg open with an axe, and it never healed up the right way no matter how the healers and the mages tried to fix it. The flesh just melted off him, and after a while he couldn't live any more."

"Things like that happen," Gremio agreed. "My mother and father are well, gods be praised, or they were last time I heard from them, but I know you can't count on anything. If I didn't know that beforehand, this gods-damned war would have taught me plenty."

"Yes, sir," Thisbe said. "If I were the southron general, I'd either try to find a way through with those men already on this side of Snouts Stream, or else I'd use them to keep us busy here while I did my mischief somewhere else."

"Sergeant, you *ought* to be an officer," Gremio said with unfeigned admiration. "That's as neat a summing-up as I could do in a lawcourt, and how much do you want to bet that the people set over us haven't got their thoughts together half so straight?"

"I don't know anything about that," Thisbe replied. "What I do know is, I don't want to be an officer." He wagged a finger at Gremio. "I really and truly mean that, sir. You've got a 'let's promote somebody to lieutenant' look in your eye, and I won't take the post even if you try to give it to me."

Gremio could hardly help believing Thisbe's sincerity. "But why?" he asked, perplexed. "The company would be better for it. You know as well as I do that there's a lieutenant's slot open. You could do the job. You could do it better than anyone I can think of."

"I don't want it," Thisbe declared. "I've got enough things to worry about being a sergeant. Being a lieutenant would just complicate my life to the hells and gone. All I ever wanted to do was be a soldier. You're not hardly a soldier when you're an officer—no offense to you, sir."

What he said held some truth. Officers worried more about paperwork even than sergeants, while common soldiers didn't have to worry about it at all (a good thing, too, since so many of them lacked their letters). But Thisbe capably handled the paperwork he had. More shouldn't faze him. Something else lay behind his refusal, but Gremio couldn't see what. He tried wheedling: "You'd make more money."

"I don't care." Now the sergeant was visibly getting angry. "I don't want it, sir, and that's flat."

"All right. All right." Gremio made a placating gesture. One thing years in the lawcourts had taught him was when to back off. For whatever reasons, Thisbe really didn't want to become an officer. That puzzled Gremio, who was always in the habit of grabbing for whatever came his way. However puzzled he was, though, he could see he wouldn't change the sergeant's mind.

Later that day, as he'd feared, the southrons started bringing more men—some footsoldiers, others unicorn-riders like the ones who'd come in under cover of darkness the night before—into their bridgehead on the west bank of Snouts Stream. They also started bringing catapults over the bridges spanning the stream. Colonel Florizel ordered the regiment up to full alert. The other regiments in Alexander the Steward's wing also put more men up on the shooting steps of their trenches.

"Can we do anything more than that, sir?" Gremio asked Florizel. By *we* he didn't mean the regiment, but the Army of Franklin as a whole. "Can we bring more men up to this part of the line? Can we bring more engines here? The gods-damned southrons will pound us flat unless we can hit back."

He waited for Colonel Florizel to get angry. He'd long since seen the regimental commander would have preferred a different sort of man as company commander: a noble, a serfholder, all the things Gremio wasn't and wished he were. But Florizel sighed and said, "I've been screaming for that, Captain. It's done no good. We're stretched as thin as can be. To strengthen this stretch means weakening ourselves somewhere else. We have nothing to spare."

"The southrons do," Gremio said.

"I know," Florizel replied.

Then the war is lost, Gremio thought. *If they can stretch us till we break and stay unbroken themselves, the war is lost beyond repair.* He didn't want to dwell on that. In fact, he refused to dwell on it. He said, "We'd better weaken ourselves *somewhere* else, sir, or they're going to tear a hole right through this stretch of line."

"I'm not going to argue with you, because I think you're right," Colonel Florizel said, which did little to make Gremio feel any better.

But reinforcements *did* come in, pulled from the far north. That meant Hesmucet's line began to overlap that of Joseph the Gamecock, but it couldn't be helped. A rupture here and Joseph's line would be shattered. Gremio could see that. The southrons could see it. And, for something of a wonder, so could Joseph the Gamecock himself.

The storm broke a couple of days later. It wasn't a real storm like the ones that had done so much to delay the southrons before and after the battle of Commissioner Mountain: the weather, while hot and muggy as usual, was also bright and clear. The engines Hesmucet's men had brought forward started pounding the northern line. Stones thudded home. Firepots burst, spilling gouts of flame into the entrenchments. Men shrieked when those flames bit. Repeating crossbows sent streams of quarrels skimming low above the trenches' parapets.

Despite the storm of missiles, Gremio shouted, "Up! Up and fight! If we stay hidden, the southrons will just walk right over us."

"Listen to the captain," Sergeant Thisbe said. "He knows what he's talking about."

Not least because Gremio and Thisbe wasted no time getting up on the shooting steps themselves, their men followed them. *And if I'd stayed down in the trench, they would have skulked, too,* Gremio thought. *This business of commanding is a curious one indeed.*

Bowstrings twanged. Bolts whizzed toward the oncoming southrons. Some of the men in gray fell. Others shot back. Gremio drew his sword and brandished it. *Much good that will do,* he thought, but did it anyhow. A crossbow quarrel clanged off the blade. He felt the impact all the way up his arm to his shoulder.

One of the northerners' repeating crossbows began hosing darts at the southrons rushing across open ground. Men went down like grain before the scythe. But others, brave even if they did serve King Avram, kept coming. Some of them, shouting Avram's name and, "Freedom!" leaped down into the trenches to try to force their way through and past King Geoffrey's soldiers.

In that close combat, Captain Gremio's sword was good for something. The blade, nicked where the bolt had hit, soon had blood on it. Men strained and cursed and smote and screamed and bled and died. And, because the fight was province against province, sometimes brother against brother, each side understood every word its enemies said.

When the southrons started crying, "Fall back!" Captain Gremio not only understood but grinned in something reasonably like triumph. "Yes, you'd better fall back!" he yelled. "Provincial prerogative forever!"

"By the Thunderer's beard, sir, we stopped them," said Sergeant Thisbe, who wore no beard of his own.

"They didn't bring enough men forward," Gremio agreed. "I rather thought they would make a better fight of it."

Thisbe panted. He had a cut above one eye and another on his arm, but neither seemed in the least serious. "I'm not sorry they didn't, sir, and that's the truth." After a moment, he added, "You handled that sword of yours mighty well."

"Thank you," Gremio said. He wasn't used to such praise, and didn't think he deserved it—which didn't stop him from enjoying it when it came.

Out in the open land between the northerners' trenches and those of the foe, a southron let out a shriek— somebody'd shot him when he went out to pick up a wounded comrade. Other southrons shouted, "Shame!" and, "No fair!" Men making pickup, like men answering calls of nature, were usually reckoned improper targets.

"Life isn't fair," Thisbe said.

"Of course not," Gremio answered. "If it were, the southrons' army wouldn't be twice the size of ours." *And no one would need barristers, either,* he thought. But he didn't say that aloud.

King Geoffrey's men celebrated their victory at the enemy bridgehead till the late afternoon. That was when word came of the breakthrough the southron unicorn-riders had made at the far northern end of the line Joseph the Gamecock had been defending. Victory or no victory, Gremio's company, along with the rest of the northerners, abandoned the trenches they'd just held and retreated to the north once more.

Joseph the Gamecock had the nerve to be proud of himself. Of all the disgrace and embarrassment attached to the retreat from Commissioner Mountain, that galled Lieutenant General Bell more than anything else. As they rode north, Joseph turned to him and said, "We haven't left them anything they can use, not a single, solitary thing. One of the cleanest escapes ever, if I do say so myself."

"Huzzah," Bell said sourly. "How many more retreats can we make before we go clean past Marthasville?"

That got home. Joseph flushed and scowled. He said, "I still intend to hold Marthasville. Holding Marthasville is the point of this campaign."

"Really?" Bell raised an eyebrow. "I hadn't noticed that it had any point at all, except perhaps giving ground. In the name of the gods, when do we get to fight back instead of running away?"

"Lieutenant General, you are grossly insubordinate," Joseph the Gamecock snapped.

"If I am, sir"—Bell larded the commanding general's title of respect with as much scorn as he could pack into it— "I'd say it's about time somebody was. Now we've gone and lost Hiltonia and Ephesus, too, and how are we going to hold the line of the Hoocheecoochee River against the southrons? We have to hold it, wouldn't you say, seeing as it's the last line in front of Marthasville?"

He'd hoped to whip Joseph into a greater anger than that which already gripped him. Maybe the general commanding would do something unforgivable. Considering how little faith King Geoffrey had in Joseph the Gamecock, it might not take much.

But Joseph, instead of igniting, smiled a smile so superior, it made Lieutenant General Bell's own temper kindle. "How will we hold the line of the Hoocheecoochee?" Joseph echoed. "I'll tell you how: with some of the finest field works ever made, that's how. I've had serfs digging for weeks. If you'd been paying attention, even a little, I daresay you might have found out. But that would be too much to hope for, wouldn't it?"

Bell glared blackly. And he had a comeback ready: "Field works, is it? How many lines of field works have the southrons already turned? I've lost track of just how many, but there isn't one they haven't turned. I know that for a fact."

"Sooner or later, they may push us back over the river," Joseph the Gamecock allowed. "But we also have good positions on the other side."

"How lucky for us," Bell said, acid in his voice. "And what happens when the southrons flank us out of those, too?"

Joseph the Gamecock exhaled in exasperation. "They won't, by the gods. We *can* hold the line of the Hoocheecoochee, and we will." He didn't wait for Bell's next contradiction, but spurred his unicorn forward and away.

Although Lieutenant General Bell could have ridden in pursuit of the commanding general, he didn't. For one thing, riding fast hurt even more than riding at a regular pace. For another, Joseph knew his opinions quite well enough already. And, for a third, Bell didn't want to give too much away. If Joseph the Gamecock got a little more suspicious of him . . .

Well, how much difference would it make? How much was left to save here in Peachtree Province? Did the northerners have enough of an army here *to* save it? *Of course we do,* Bell thought, *provided we have a man in charge who's not afraid to use it.*

When the army started filing into the trenches covering the approaches to the Hoocheecoochee and the bridges over it, Bell discovered, to his surprise and not a little to his dismay, that Joseph the Gamecock had known whereof he spoke. The field fortifications in front of the river *were* formidable, and wouldn't be easy to force. Marthasville and the vital glideway routes east that ran through it remained protected.

But for how much longer? Bell wondered. *What will go wrong? Something always has. We've been retreating for two months now. We can't fall back much farther, because we've nowhere to fall back to.*

While he scowled and fumed, Major Zibeon found him a farmhouse behind the line in which he could make his headquarters. His aide-de-camp said, "Sorry it isn't anything fancier, sir."

"Don't worry about it," Bell answered. "Help me down from this beast, if you'd be so kind." His head buzzed with laudanum; riding *was* hard on him. Zibeon undid the ties that kept him on the unicorn and steadied him while he positioned his crutches. "Thank you kindly," Bell said, though the pain of the crutch in his left armpit was hardly less than he'd known while riding. Plant, swing forward; plant, swing forward. He made his way into the farmhouse.

The farmer had already fled north, for which Bell was duly grateful; he didn't feel like having to be sociable. A couple of serfs' huts stood by the main house. Maybe the fellow who'd lived here had been a petty baronet, or maybe he'd just been a yeoman who'd come into the land to which the serfs were attached. The huts stood dark and empty now, with no naked blond children playing around them. The serfs had fled, too, though odds were they hadn't fled north.

"Is everything to your liking, sir?" Major Zibeon asked after he went inside.

"If everything were to my liking, Major, we'd be fighting a good many miles south of this place," Bell answered. His aide-de-camp grunted and gave him a reproachful look. He relented: "Seeing as we are here, this house will do well enough."

"Thank you, sir," Zibeon said. "That is what I had in mind—as I think you knew well enough."

Few men were bold enough to reproach Lieutenant General Bell to his face. Joseph the Gamecock did it, but that hardly counted. Zibeon had the nerve to speak his mind.

Because he did, Bell treated him with more respect than he would have otherwise. "Well, maybe I did," he admitted.

From up in the trenches, someone shouted, "Here comes the head of the southron army, out of the hills we just left."

"We should never have left them," Bell muttered, more to himself than to anybody else. Then, grudgingly, he spoke aloud: "I'd better go out and have a look, don't you think, Major?"

"Might be a good idea, sir," his aide-de-camp replied. Zibeon softened that; Bell could tell. What it meant in plain Detinan was, *You'd have to be an idiot if you didn't.* Bell made his slow, painful way out of the farmhouse once more and, shading his eyes with the palm of his hand, peered south.

Sure enough, the reddish dust hanging in the air above the hills was the sign of an army on the march. Through the dust came sparkles of sunlight on spearpoints and metal-shod unicorn horns. Bell wished for more rain, which would have laid the dust and slowed the southrons' movements. Now, though, the sun blazed down on the Army of Franklin as fiercely as if the Sun God were angry at the north.

How can we win, if even the gods turn against us? Bell thought. But he shook his big, leonine head. The gods surely fought for King Geoffrey. How could it be otherwise, when they'd subjected and bound the blonds' gods just as the Detinans themselves had subjected the natives of this land and bound them to the soil?

Pointing, Major Zibeon said, "Looks like the stinking southrons are going into line of battle."

"They always tap at our lines, thinking we'll run," Bell said. "It's because we *do* run when Joseph the Gamecock tells us to. They take us for cowards, may they suffer in the seven hells for all eternity."

"We'll make a few of them suffer now, unless I'm wrong," Zibeon said. "They can't hope to shift us when we're in earthworks and they're not."

"Earthworks make men cowards," Bell declared. He was far from the only general on either side to sing that song, but sang it louder and more stridently than most. "If this were my army, we would come out and fight. We wouldn't shelter behind walls of mud, the way we do now."

Up came the southrons. They shot a few bolts at the men in the trenches. Joseph the Gamecock's men shot back. A few southrons fell. The rest drew back. They wouldn't press home attacks against earthworks, either. *Cowards*, Bell thought. *Nothing but cowards.*

Major Zibeon's thoughts were going down a different glideway line. He asked, "How are we going to keep the southrons from reaching the Hoocheecoochee at a point beyond our lines? If they manage that, we're in trouble."

There, for once, Bell felt some sympathy with Joseph the Gamecock. "Patrols of unicorn-riders," he answered. He approved of such patrols. They were aggressive, and anything aggressive met with his approval.

But Zibeon said, "Patrols of unicorn-riders are all very well, sir, but gods damn me if I think Brigadier Spinner's the right man to lead our mounted men. I wish we had Ned of the Forest here."

"Everyone wishes for Ned of the Forest," Bell told him. "There's only one of the man, though, and he's over by the Great River. Spinner is capable enough."

"The southrons can afford to get by with men who are capable enough," his aide-de-camp said. "They have room to make their mistakes good. If we make a mistake, they'll land on us with both feet. What we need is a genuine, for-true genius of an officer leading unicorn-riders. We only had two in all the north: Jeb the Beauty, who was over in Parthenia—"

"And who, I hear, got killed not long ago," Bell broke in with a sigh. "It's a hard war, and it's not getting any easier."

"Jeb the Beauty, who's dead," Zibeon agreed, "and Ned of the Forest. We need him here, at the point of decision, not off running a sideshow in the east."

"He and Count Thraxton had a row, as I recall. That's what got him transferred," Bell said. "I don't know all the details; that wasn't long after I turned lopsided." He waggled his stump a little, even though it hurt. If he could laugh at his own mutilations, no one else would have the nerve to laugh at them.

Zibeon's bushy eyebrows climbed almost to his hairline. "A row? You might just say so, sir. If what people say is true, Ned came out and said he would challenge Thraxton, except he didn't suppose Thraxton was enough of a man to accept it."

From what Bell had seen before his wound by the River of Death, Count Thraxton, whatever else one said about him, was a proud and touchy fellow. His own eyebrows rose. "And the count let that go by without taking the challenge *and* without punishing Ned of the Forest?"

"He did indeed," Zibeon said solemnly. "I have seen Ned of the Forest in a temper, sir. He's not a man anyone at all would care to take lightly."

Zibeon was a pretty hard case himself, and not easily impressed. If he found Ned formidable, formidable Ned was. Even so . . . "How could Count Thraxton possibly live down the disgrace?"

"What disgrace, sir?" the aide-de-camp replied. "Thraxton is King Geoffrey's friend, as you must know. When was the last time you heard of a king's friend who disgraced himself to the point of making people notice?"

That bit of cynicism made Bell's face twist with pain which, for once, wasn't physical. Zibeon had the right of it there, sure enough. *If Geoffrey decides Joseph the Gamecock must go—no, when he decides it, for he surely will— won't he replace him with his friend? And if he does, what becomes of me?*

He began to regret his own letters. Yes, he'd had weakening Joseph's position in mind. But he hadn't intended to strengthen anyone's but his own. Could he serve under Count Thraxton if the warrior mage returned to command? Everyone, not just Ned of the Forest, had trouble serving under Thraxton the Braggart.

Can I write letters of a different tone? Bell wondered. After a moment's thought, he shook his head. *Too late now, gods damn it.*

All he could do now was fight as well as he could and hope Joseph the Gamecock wouldn't suffer some irremediable disaster while Count Thraxton was down here on his watching brief. He would have fought hard anyhow, for his pride's sake, and for his kingdom's sake, too. So he told himself, at any rate. But now he also had solid personal reasons.

Zibeon said, "Maybe this will work out all right, sir. We do have a good position to defend."

"So we do," Bell said. He couldn't afford to malign Joseph, he realized, not even to his aide-de-camp, not for the time being.

"Of course, I have to hope we'll get the chance to defend it," Major Zibeon added.

"How not?" Bell asked in real, obvious perplexity.

"Outflanking. We *were* talking about this, sir." Zibeon spoke with what sounded like exaggerated patience.

"My gods-damned shoulder is hurting again," Bell mumbled. And it always did. But he was such a straight-ahead fighter, he'd already forgotten Hesmucet didn't have to be. He took a big swig of laudanum. "There. I'll think better now," he declared. Zibeon said not a word.

VI

Captain Gremio was no general. Gremio hadn't been a soldier at all before the war, or a domain-holding noble—the closest peacetime equivalent—either. But, like so many others, he'd had plenty of experience since the fighting began in Karlsburg harbor more than three years before.

He said, "These are splendid works, and I hope Hesmucet tries to storm them. He'd bloody his southron nose, the way he did at Commissioner Mountain."

"Yes, sir," Sergeant Thisbe said. "But even though he lost on the mountain, he got that little bridgehead over Snouts Stream, and look at how much trouble he caused with it."

Had Hesmucet not got that bridgehead, the Army of Franklin might well have still been defending the line of the mountain and the stream. Gremio gave Thisbe a half mocking bow. "Very neat, Sergeant," he said. "You agree with me in your first two words, then proceed to show I'm wrong. Very neat indeed."

Thisbe turned red. "I'm sorry, sir. I didn't mean to do that."

"Don't apologize," Gremio told him. "You got me fair and

169

square. I wish I could do so well in front of the judges
a lot of the time."

"Now you're joking with me, sir," Thisbe said. "I don't
much care for that." He was, as so often, almost painfully
serious.

"No such thing. I meant every word of it." Gremio raised
his hand above his head, pointing to the mountain beyond
the sky, as he would have in a lawcourt. "By the Thunderer,
I swear it."

"All right." Thisbe looked back over his shoulder. "Are
we supposed to make a stand with our backs to a river?
If the southrons do beat us here, it would go hard for us."

"I suppose that's true," Gremio said. "But do you really
think Hesmucet can storm us out of this position?"

The sergeant considered. "You're probably right, sir. You
usually are, from everything I've seen."

Now Gremio felt himself blushing. "That's kind of you,
Sergeant—kinder than I deserve, I shouldn't wonder."

"No, sir," Thisbe said. "If ever there's somebody who
knows what's what, you're the one."

"If I knew what was what, would I be *here*?" Gremio
asked with a wry laugh.

That made Thisbe laugh, too, but, as usual, his answer
was thoughtful: "I suppose it depends on how important
you think this is for the kingdom."

*If we don't win here, or at least keep the southrons from
winning, Geoffrey won't have a kingdom,* Gremio thought.
Since he didn't feel like voicing words of ill omen aloud,
he replied, "When we were coming down out of the hill
country towards the Hoocheecoochee, I could see Marthasville." He craned his neck. "Can't quite do it now, but
I know the place is there. Maybe that makes this pretty
important business after all."

"I think so, too, sir," Thisbe agreed.

"What sort of spirits are the men in?" Gremio asked.
"You've got stripes on your sleeves, not epaulets on your
shoulders. That puts you closer to an ordinary man than
I could ever . . . Are you all right, Sergeant?"

Thisbe had suffered a coughing fit, and went even redder
in the face than he had before. "I'm sorry, sir," he wheezed

when he could speak at all. "I swallowed wrong then, and almost choked. Most ways, I'd say, you're closer to an ordinary man than I could ever be." Before Gremio could argue with that, Thisbe went on, "I think your ordinary soldier dislikes a sergeant more than an officer, in the same sort of way that a serf is liable to dislike an overseer more than a liege lord. The sergeant is the one who makes sure he does what he's told, after all."

"Mm, I shouldn't wonder if there was something to that," Gremio allowed. "All right, Sergeant, you've made your point." He put on a severe look. "As I've said, I do wish you'd let me offer your name for promotion."

"No, thank you, sir." As usual on this subject, Thisbe's voice held not an ounce of doubt. "I'd sooner just be what I am. I'd *much* sooner just be what I am."

"I bow to your wishes." Gremio suited action to word. The sergeant smiled and began a motion in return, but arrested it before it was well begun—not quite an answering bow, but something on that order. Gremio said, "It's plain that, once upon a time, you were a fine gentleman."

"I was not!" Thisbe said hotly. "Never once! The very idea!"

He sounded so irate, Gremio didn't ask any of the questions he might have otherwise. King Geoffrey's army held more than a few nobles fighting as common soldiers, either from sheer love of adventure or because they'd disgraced themselves and couldn't claim the rank that should have gone with their station. It had occurred to Gremio that his sergeant might be such a man. If he was, though, he didn't intend to admit it.

And now he went off in what Gremio couldn't help but recognized as a huff. The company commander kicked at the brick-red mud in the bottom of the trench. Even though he had the right to make such comments to Thisbe, he wished he hadn't done it. He didn't want the sergeant angry at him. *The company won't run smoothly if he is*, Gremio told himself. But there was more to it than that. He didn't want Thisbe angry at him because he liked and respected him, and wanted him to be as much of a friend as their different ranks would permit.

"By the gods, if I ever found a woman who suited me as well as Thisbe does, I'd marry her on the spot," he muttered.

Getting married, though, didn't stay on his mind for long. For one thing, he knew of no women—except perhaps a few loose ones—within miles. For another, a troop of southron unicorn-riders trotted past the Army of Franklin's entrenchments right on the edge of catapult range. A few engineers let fly at them. Most of the stones and firepots went wide, but one smashed a rider and his unicorn like a boot descending on a cockroach.

After that, the southrons did a better job of keeping their distance. But they had accomplished their purpose. Gremio saw that clearly. By reminding the northern commanders they were there, they kept Joseph the Gamecock and Brigadier Spinner from loosing the northern riders to harry the enemy supply line. It was long, stretching all the way back to Rising Rock, and it was tenuous, but none of that mattered if the northerners couldn't mount a serious attack on it. And, by all the signs, they couldn't.

Gremio sighed. More and more these days, the war was coming down to demonstrations of what the north couldn't do. That was no way to win it. *We're right, though,* he thought. A moment later, he laughed at himself. A man in the lawcourts might be right, too. How much good did that do him if the judges ruled he was wrong? None whatsoever, as Gremio knew too well. Like any barrister, he always thought he was right. Everyone once in a while, some idiot panel of judges had a different—and no doubt erroneous—opinion.

Brigadier Alexander, the new wing commander, came marching through the trenches. Gremio approved of that. Leonidas the Priest had been a brave and pious man, but hadn't much concerned himself with his soldiers' mundane, day-to-day needs and concerns—or perhaps he simply hadn't cared to get his fancy vestments dirty. Alexander strode up to Gremio, who stiffened to attention and saluted.

"As you were, Captain," the senior officer said. Gremio saw how he'd come to be called Old Straight—he was tall and lean and very erect. And, when he spoke, his words were straightforward, too: "How, in your view, can we best beat back the stinking southrons? What can we do that we aren't doing now?"

"Having twice as many men in the trenches wouldn't hurt, sir," Gremio replied.

"So it wouldn't," Brigadier Alexander agreed. "Ask for the moon, as long as you're making wishes. What can we do that we can do, if you take my meaning?"

He meant the question seriously. Gremio could see as much. He gave back a serious answer: "Sir, holding them out of Marthasville is about as big a victory as we can hope for, wouldn't you say?"

He waited, wondering if he'd misjudged Alexander. Some officers would have taken that—would have taken anything less than a call for an immediate counterattack on General Hesmucet and a march south toward the Franklin line—as defeatism. But Old Straight nodded and said, "You see things clearly, don't you?"

Relieved, Gremio said, "I do my best, sir."

"If we all do our best, Captain, we have some hope of coming out of this campaign with whole skins," Brigadier Alexander said. "If we don't, well, things won't look so good. This is Colonel Florizel's regiment, is it not?"

Gremio nodded. "Yes, sir."

"You men have put up a good record," Alexander said. "If all the company-grade officers here are up to your level, Captain, I can see why. And I'll tell the same to your colonel. Your name is . . . ?"

"Gremio, sir."

"Very well. Carry on, Captain Gremio." The wing commander swept on down the line, now and then pausing to pull his boots out of mud thicker than usual. Gremio doubted he would have that problem himself, not for a while. He would be walking on air for the rest of the day.

And he'd won respect from his men that he hadn't had before. If Brigadier Alexander approved of him and would say so out loud, who were common soldiers to disagree? They obeyed him more promptly than he'd ever seen them do before. He'd enjoy it while it lasted, for he didn't think it would last long.

It did suffice to bring Colonel Florizel over to him. The regimental commander asked, "How did you get Brigadier Alexander to say such fine things about you?" Florizel sounded half suspicious, half jealous. Alexander, evidently, hadn't said any fine things about *him*.

Deadpan, Gremio answered, "I told him I'd learned everything I know about fighting from you, sir."

That actually did hold some truth. Florizel would never become a brigadier himself. He was no great tactician, nor, to be just, did he claim to be one. But he was brave, and he knew how to make his men like him and fight bravely for him. There were plenty of worse regimental commanders in the Army of Franklin, and some worse men in charge of brigades, too.

And, like a lot of men, he was no more immune to flattery than flies were to honey. He coughed and scuffed his boots in the mud and murmured, "Well, Captain, that was a mighty kind thing to say. Mighty kind indeed."

Oh, dear, Gremio thought. *He took that literally, didn't he?* The best thing he could find to do was change the subject, and so he did: "The new wing commander worries that we won't be able to drive the southrons back."

Brigadier Alexander had done more than worry. He'd been at least as gloomy about the campaign as Gremio was himself. But Florizel was and always had been an optimist. Saying something that didn't suggest total victory lay right around the corner took nerve.

"He'll fight hard," Florizel said now, and with that Gremio could not disagree. The colonel went on, "As long as we're still on this side of the Hoocheecoochee, things aren't too bad. We've still got us and the river between the southrons and Marthasville, and we've got to keep them out of there."

"Er—yes." Gremio did his best to keep from showing how astonished he was. If the ever-hopeful Florizel couldn't paint any brighter picture than that, the Army of Franklin was in less than the best of shape.

Florizel set a hand on his shoulder. "The gods may yet decide to smile on us, even if the loss of Leonidas was a heavy blow. We should all try to deserve well of them, to show them we deserve to be the ones they choose in this fierce and remorseless struggle. I think we can do that. I pray we can."

"May it be so." Gremio hoped the gods would favor the north, too. In his glummer moments, he feared nothing short of that would suffice to save Geoffrey's kingdom from Avram's onslaught. The southrons might have been a python, squeezing the life out of the north an inch at a time.

"These *are* very strong works," Florizel said. "The enemy will have a hells of a time trying to go through us."

"Yes, sir," Gremio agreed. "What worries me, though, is whether he can go around us instead. That would be just as bad."

"I suppose it might, but I don't think it will happen," Florizel said. "Brigadier Spinner's patrols ride up and down the Hoocheecoochee."

"I wish we had Ned of the Forest here," Gremio said, not for the first time.

"He's a ruffian, a man of no breeding," Earl Florizel said.

A man of no breeding himself, Gremio replied, "He's also the best commander of unicorn-riders King Geoffrey has who's still breathing. Which carries the greater weight?"

Florizel seriously thought that over. At last, reluctantly, he nodded. "Ned is a very fine man on the back of a unicorn—which makes him no less of a ruffian, be it noted."

"Yes, sir," Gremio said dutifully. "Still, I'm glad he's on our side."

"So am I, although I still wish we didn't have to resort to such tools," the regimental commander said.

"It's a war, sir," Gremio said. "If it weren't for the fighting, we'd all be doing something else." Florizel also nodded at that, but he didn't look happy about it. To a Detinan noble, war was the normal state of affairs, peace the aberration. The world didn't really work that way, but nobles were trained to think it did. *They have other things wrong with them, too*, Gremio thought.

From the hills above the valley of the Hoocheecoochee River, General Hesmucet could look down on Joseph the Gamecock's army and spy out everything the enemy did even as he did it. Hesmucet relished that. The northerners had looked down on his lines from their position atop Commissioner Mountain, and he was sure that had cost him men.

When Joseph halted the bulk of his army on the eastern bank of the Hoocheecoochee, Hesmucet had been surprised. Only a very bold general or a very foolhardy one was likely to offer battle with his back to a sizable stream. Examining the works the northerners occupied, however, convinced Hesmucet that Joseph was neither the one nor the other. He had sound defenses there.

Earlier in the campaign, Hesmucet might have tried to bull his way past those defenses, in the hope of breaking through and wrecking the traitors' army. But he'd tried that at Commissioner Mountain, and it hadn't worked. That made him hesitate now. So did the strength of the entrenchments in which the northerners sheltered.

Joseph's men held a line about six miles long. Hesmucet began sending detachments of Marble Bill's unicorn-riders out beyond their lines, in the hope of getting down to the river and forcing a crossing. *If my men get over the Hoocheecoochee, Joseph will have to retreat in a hurry,* he thought hungrily. *Then he's mine.*

But the enemy commander could see that as well as he could. Blue-uniformed unicorn-riders were numerous and fierce. Marble Bill's men came back again and again without ever reaching the banks of the Hoocheecoochee.

"Anyone would think they had some idea of what we've got in mind," Lieutenant General George said when Hesmucet cursed about the unicorn-riders' misfortunes.

"D'you think so?" Fighting Joseph asked. Hesmucet winced. Doubting George had been sardonic. Fighting Joseph meant it. Time and again, Hesmucet had seen that courage and brains too often had only a nodding acquaintance.

"It is a possibility, you know," George said. "Some folk do seek to study what the foe might be up to. That often saves you from nasty surprises, or so they say."

"Not a bad notion." By the way Fighting Joseph spoke, the said notion plainly was entering his handsome head for the first time. By his record, that struck Hesmucet as all too likely.

"We'll keep moving, that's all," he said. "As long as we *are* moving, something good may happen. If we pull into a shell, the way turtles do, we'll never get anywhere, and that's as plain as the nose on my face."

"Even as plain as the nose on mine," said Doubting George, who owned one of formidable proportions.

"The gods help those who help themselves," Fighting Joseph agreed. Hesmucet wished he wouldn't have done so with a cliché, and then wished for all the gold in the Golden Province far to the east while he was at it.

"Maybe," James the Bird's Eye said, "we could give ourselves a better chance of reaching the river with magic." For a southron to rely on wizardry was out of the ordinary in this war, but Major Alva was no ordinary southron mage.

"Not a bad notion," Hesmucet agreed. "I will take that up with our sorcerers." By that, he meant he would take it up with Major Alva, and all the wing commanders understood as much. The rest of the mages in the army, from Colonel Phineas on down, came close to matching the youngster only if all their efforts were added together. Looking from one officer to another, Hesmucet asked, "Anything else? Anyone think we have a real chance of going through Joseph the Gamecock's position instead of around it?"

Nobody said anything, not even Fighting Joseph, who was much given to overcoming obstacles by charging straight at them and smashing them flat with his hard head. Hesmucet didn't know whether to be relieved at the show of good sense or sorry he didn't get the chance to squelch his annoying subordinate.

With a small shrug, he said, "Dismissed." As the generals trooped away, he called for a runner and told him, "Fetch me Major Alva. Don't just tell him I want him and then leave. Bring him back here yourself."

"Yes, sir." The soldier grinned; he'd been one of Hesmucet's runners for some little while now. "If I don't bring him, he's liable to forget to come at all, isn't he? He'll just stand there thinking fancy thoughts."

"He doesn't know a whole lot about subordination,"

Hesmucet agreed wryly. *Alva knows even less about sub-ordination than Fighting Joseph does,* he thought. *Fighting Joseph understands what he's supposed to do; he just doesn't do it. To Alva, the whole idea is bizarre.* That thought led to another: *if he's not the ultimate free Detinan, who in the seven hells is?*

Off went the runner. He returned in due course, Alva in tow. The mage did remember to salute when he came up to Hesmucet, and seemed proud of himself for remembering. "You wanted me, uh, sir?" he said.

"That's right," the commanding general answered. He gave Alva more leeway than he did to any other soldier in the army. Alva had earned more than any other soldier had. Hesmucet went on, "Can you work out some sort of masking spell that will let Marble Bill's unicorn-riders get down to the Hoocheecoochee without the traitors' finding out about it till too late?"

Major Alva gave him a bright smile. "Funny you should ask me that, sir. Marble Bill asked the very same thing a couple of days ago."

"Did he? Well, good for him," Hesmucet said. That was more initiative than the commander of unicorn-riders usually showed.

"Yes, sir, he did. I gave him a cantrip I thought would serve." Alva's smile slipped. "It didn't. The northerners had a counterspell that sniffed it out, and beat back his column of riders."

"Ah. Too bad," Hesmucet said. "Well, they have good wizards of their own, and keeping us off the Hoocheecoochee is very important to them."

"Their wizards are *strong*, but they aren't all that *good*," Alva said. "There's a difference." If there was, Hesmucet couldn't see it. Alva added, "What's so important about the river, anyway?"

"By the gods!" Hesmucet muttered. His pet mage lived in a world so abstract, things of real value meant nothing to him. Gently, the general commanding explained: "It's the last big barrier in front of Marthasville, Major. If we can get across, Joseph the Gamecock will have a hells of a time keeping us out of the city."

"Oh. All right." The sorcerer nodded. He wasn't stupid—on the contrary—but was as narrowly focused as a good burning glass. "I suppose that means you'll want me to try another masking spell, then."

"I did have that in mind, yes." Hesmucet nodded, too. "Or anything else that will get us over the Hoocheecoochee—I'm not fussy about how it happens."

Alva's face tightened into the mask of concentration Hesmucet had come to know well. Alva sometimes stayed like that, hardly moving, hardly even seeming to breathe, for a couple of hours at a stretch. This time, though, he came out almost at once, to ask, "You will not want this to be a showy spell, am I right?"

"Showy?" Hesmucet frowned. "How do you mean?"

"A showy spell is something the other side notices," Alva answered. "You'll want them to notice nothing at all till the knife goes into their back? Not to have the slightest idea they're being diddled?"

"Isn't that how every single masking spell under the sun works?" Hesmucet asked.

"Oh, no . . . sir." Major Alva sounded shocked. He launched into a technical disquisition in which Hesmucet found himself following perhaps one word in three. He did gather that some masking spells were like lamps shone in the enemy's eyes, while others hung an opaque curtain between the foe and what he wished to see and still others sought to be transparent. He also gathered that the last sort was the hardest to bring off. *It would be,* he thought.

"You have it right," he told Alva when the mage finally ran down. "I don't want the traitors to have any idea what's going on till it's too late for them to do one fornicating thing about it."

"I'll see what I can come up with, sir." Like a groundhog slipping back into hibernation, Alva returned to his trance of study.

There were other ways besides the sorcerous to keep the northerners from finding out what Hesmucet had in mind. He didn't entrench up close to the traitors' positions, but placed pickets well in front of his own lines. The enemy wouldn't be able to see how many soldiers he had in place

and how many he was using for his casts up and down
the Hoocheecoochee, or how ready his army was to move
in a hurry if somehow he managed to find a crossing.

Joseph the Gamecock has to be worried, he thought. *He
knows the Hoocheecoochee is his last strong line as well
as I do.* Feints toward the river both north and south kept
false King Geoffrey's unicorn-riders galloping this way and
that. They couldn't afford to assume that any move *was*
a feint, not here they couldn't. They had to take each one
seriously.

Hesmucet won approval from one source whose opinion
he valued—Doubting George said, "This is all very fine
work, sir. The wider we stretch the traitors, the sooner
they'll break."

"Glad you agree, Lieutenant General," Hesmucet told him.
"And glad we're working together as well as we are."

"So am I, sir," George replied. "Only one who'd laugh
if we pulled opposite ways, though, is Geoffrey."

"There is that." Hesmucet's laugh held little real mirth.
"Not that such considerations have stopped a good many
other officers from wrangling with one another."

"True enough, true enough. We're a band of brothers, is
what we are—and brothers fight like cats and dogs."

"Don't we just?" Hesmucet eyed his second-in-command.
"If you were in Joseph the Gamecock's boots, what would
you do?"

"About what he's doing," George said. "I don't know what
else he could do, not with an army barely half the size
of ours. He's managed to make a nuisance of himself, hasn't
he?"

"Yes." Hesmucet admitted what he could hardly deny.
"Gods damn it, though, we *need* Marthasville. King Avram
needs it. The whole kingdom needs it, to show we're winning the war."

"We go forward," Doubting George said. "One lurch at
a time, we do go forward. And Marshal Bart has Duke
Edward of Arlington and the Army of Southern Parthenia
pushed a lot farther north in Parthenia than they really want
to be."

"So he does," Hesmucet said, "though the latest, I hear,

is that Earl Early the Jubilant has managed to get loose and come south for an attack on Georgetown."

"D'you think he can take the place?" George asked.

"I doubt it," Hesmucet answered, and his wing commander smiled. Hesmucet went on, "Have you *seen* the works around Georgetown, Lieutenant General? They make the ones Joseph the Gamecock has thrown up here look like sand castles by comparison. King Avram set his artificers to work as soon as the war against Geoffrey began, and I don't believe they've slowed down from that day to this."

"No doubt you're right, sir, but if all the soldiers are up in Parthenia with Marshal Bart . . ." Doubting George's voice trailed away. "The best fortress in the world isn't worth a counterfeit copper without some men inside it."

"Avram can fill the forts up with clerks from all the Georgetown offices and hold off Earl Early till Marshal Bart has time to bring some real fighting men down from his own lines," Hesmucet said. "With those works, even clerks with crossbows would do for a little while."

"Here's hoping it doesn't come to that," George said, and then, thoughtfully, "I wonder what sort of works Joseph the Gamecock has waiting for us outside of Marthasville itself."

"We'll find out, I hope." Hesmucet smiled a wolfish smile. "And, once we cross the Hoocheecoochee, all the glideways to the east, to Dothan and the Great River, fall into our hands, even if we can't break into the city yet."

"That's true. I hadn't thought of it quite so, but that's true," George said. "And false King Geoffrey won't be very happy about it, either."

Hesmucet clasped both hands to his breast in false and exaggerated sympathy. George laughed out loud. "Too bad. My heart's just breaking," Hesmucet said in syrupy tones.

George laughed again, louder and harder. "If we do cross the Hoocheecoochee," he said, "poor Geoffrey's going to have kittens."

"So he will," Hesmucet agreed. "I told you once: what Geoffrey calls a kingdom is nothing but two armies and a lot of wind and air. Once we get over the river, we'll show all of Detina how empty the north is."

"May it be so. I think it *will* be so," George said.

"We'll make it so," Hesmucet said. "Once we're over the river, Joseph the Gamecock won't be able to keep us from making it so."

"Only trouble is, we're not over the river yet," George said.

"I think Alva can let us get men down to it even if we can't manage any other way," Hesmucet replied. "And once we reach it, we'll cross it. Our artificers can throw a bridge over it in a hurry. Then"—he grinned—"we see what happens next."

"Corporal Rollant!" Lieutenant Griff called.

"Yes, sir!" Rollant said proudly. He was sure he felt better about being promoted to the lowest grade of underofficer than Bart did about rising from general to marshal. For a blond to get stripes on his sleeve in King Avram's army, to gain the privilege of giving orders to free Detinans . . .

"Take up the standard, Corporal!" Griff said.

"Yes, sir!" Rollant repeated, even more proudly than before. The company's flag and its heavy pole seemed to weigh nothing at all as he lifted them from their stand. The soldiers saluted the standard as if worshiping a god. *And so they are,* he realized. *This flag means Detina to them, and they reverence the kingdom as much as the Lion God or the Thunderer.*

His mouth quirked up in what wasn't really a grin, no matter what it looked like. *They certainly wouldn't risk their lives to free blonds from their—from our—bondage to the land,* he thought. Avram hadn't much wanted to fight the northerners over serfdom. He'd chosen war only when Geoffrey tried to set up his own kingdom in the north.

Horns blared. "Form up!" Lieutenant Griff screamed. The company he led hurried to obey. Rollant started to go to his own place, next to Smitty and Sergeant Joram. He'd taken that place ever since accepting King Avram's silver on enlisting. But it wasn't his any more. Now he belonged at the van of the company, so he could use the standard to signal which way the men should go.

The honor was not unmixed. For one thing, standard-bearers, by the nature of their job, made prominent targets. If the last fellow who carried the flag hadn't got shot on Commissioner Mountain, Rollant wouldn't have had it now. And, for another, he felt eyes on him as he took his place alongside Griff and the company trumpeter. Not all of his comrades were happy to see a blond promoted above them. *Too bad,* Rollant thought. *If they'd wanted to save the standard, one of them could have done it himself.*

Voice cracking as it often did, Lieutenant Griff said, "Men, our company—and Colonel Nahath's regiment as a whole—have the distinction of probing up towards the Hoochee-coochee. This is a privilege granted only a few regiments of footsoldiers. The unicorn-riders are doing much more of it. But Lieutenant General George knows what we can do. He's seen us fight. By the gods, he's fought alongside us, on Merkle's Hill by the River of Death. We'll show him we deserve this chance he's giving us, won't we?"

"Yes, sir!" the men roared.

Rollant shouted as loud as anybody else. He had to, for appearance's sake. But that didn't mean he was excited about getting the chance to try to approach the Hoochee-coochee. He knew what Lieutenant Griff *meant,* no matter what the young officer actually *said.* What Griff meant was, *What we're going to try probably won't work, but it does have a fair chance of getting a lot of us killed.*

He looked toward Smitty. The farmer's son caught his glance, shrugged ever so slightly, and raised an eyebrow, as if to say, *What can you do?* Smitty had been through a lot. He had no more trouble uncovering Griff's hidden meaning than Rollant did.

Once Griff stood aside, Colonel Nahath harangued the whole regiment. His speech was smoother and more polished than Griff's, but amounted to the same thing. Rollant felt like shrugging, too, but couldn't, not standing out there in front of everybody. Nahath had got his orders, and was having to make the best of them. Rollant hoped there was a best to be made.

After the regimental commander stepped back, the horns blared again. "Forward!" Lieutenant Griff shouted, along with all the other men in charge of companies. Forward his own company went. Forward Rollant went at his head.

The day was hot and muggy. At this season of the year, any day in the north of Detina was likely to be hot and muggy. Flies buzzed and bit. With the flagstaff in his hands, Rollant couldn't slap them away so readily as he had had before. His new rank and station had some difficulties he hadn't thought about.

With so much heat and moisture, something close to a jungle grew down toward the southern bank of the Hoocheecoochee. Only a few roads ran through the undergrowth. Hoofprints and unicorn turds warned that the traitors patrolled them regularly. Rollant wouldn't have wanted to meet unicorn-riders in such cramped surroundings.

A squirrel chittered in the branches overhead, scolding the marching soldiers. A jewelbird, glittering green with a ruby head, buzzed around Rollant and then flew off toward the north. The standard-bearer turned to Lieutenant Griff and said, "Sir, where I come from, we'd reckon that was good luck."

"We haven't got that superstition in New Eborac," Griff said. Rollant bristled; he didn't think of it as a superstition. But then Griff softened the comment: "We haven't got that many jewelbirds, either. Too far south, and the winters are too cold."

"I know." Rollant nodded. "I miss 'em." He didn't miss many things about Palmetto Province. Jewelbirds, though, had never done him any harm. "Back around the serfs' huts, some people would hang a bowl of molasses and water up at the top of a pole to get them to come and feed there."

"What for?" Griff asked. "To catch them?"

"No, sir!" Rollant heard the shock in his own voice. "Catch a jewelbird? That'd be about the worst kind of bad luck there is. We just liked to have 'em around, on account of they're pretty. We couldn't have much that was pretty, but I never heard of a liege lord who minded us drawing jewelbirds to our huts—didn't cost anything, except for the little bit of molasses."

Griff tramped on for a while. Rollant wondered if he'd talked too much or too openly. Smitty wouldn't have minded his remarks. Neither would Sergeant Joram. But then the company commander said, "When you first got to New Eborac, Corporal, you must have felt as if you'd fallen into some whole new world. The biggest city in Detina can't be anything like an estate outside Karlsburg."

That was far and away the most perceptive comment Rollant had ever heard Lieutenant Griff make. "You're right, sir," the escaped serf said. "Are you ever right! When I first came down south, I thought I would go clean out of my mind. So many people, and all of 'em packed together like olives in a jar . . . But I got used to it. And do you know what the best part was?"

"I know what it would have been for me," Griff replied. "What was it for you?"

"Nobody could tell me what to do," Rollant said at once. "I was on my own. I'd starve if I didn't work hard. Things weren't easy, especially at first, but I was working for myself, not for my gods-damned liege lord. When somebody gave me silver, I got to keep all of it. That's pretty fine."

Again, Griff marched on for several silent steps. Again, Rollant wondered if he'd gone too far. But the young lieutenant said, "No wonder you've got stripes on your tunic sleeve and our flag in your hands. You sound just like any other free Detinan."

I am just like any other free Detinan, Rollant thought. But that was true only in certain ways. One way it was untrue was in the eyes of a great many free Detinans, from south as well as north. Rollant would have guessed Griff to be among that number, but he seemed to be mistaken there.

On trudged the regiment. "Where are the traitors?" Rollant wondered. "I'd have thought they'd've pitched into us by now."

Lieutenant Griff's leer might have come from Smitty. "Do you really want them around, Corporal?"

"Want them? Hells, no, sir. But what you want and what you get are two different beasts." Any serf learned that in a hurry, generally about as fast as he learned to walk or talk. Soldiers got the same lesson, but at an older age.

"I wish this country would open out a bit," Lieutenant Griff said. "That would help us figure out just where we are. Unless I'm altogether daft, we can't be *too* far from the Hoocheecoochee."

"If it does open out, somebody will see us," Rollant said. "I don't think I want that."

"A point," Griff allowed. "A distinct point. I *do* wish we had better maps, though. They would tell us a good deal about where we are, too."

Now Rollant nodded without reservation. He tremendously admired maps. There was something sorcerous about the way they made paper correspond to landscape. By what he'd overheard army mages saying, there *was* something sorcerous about them: many were made by using the law of similarity, and sorcery between map and landscape could also help guide soldiers.

Something crackled in the undergrowth to the side of the road. Lieutenant Griff snatched out his sword. "What in the hells was that?" he said, his voice breaking like a youth's.

"An animal—I hope." Rollant took a couple of sidling steps away from the company commander. Griff carried a sword, but he wasn't practiced with it. Southron officers, unlike their counterparts in the traitors' armies, for the most part weren't nobles who'd learned swordplay from birth. They carried their weapons as much for show as for fighting—some (though not Griff) also bore crossbows, with which they were actually dangerous.

"It had better be an animal," Griff said, still brandishing the blade in a way that made Rollant nervous. "If it's a gods-damned northern son of a bitch, he'll bring every traitor in the world down on us."

Rollant wished he could have argued with that, but the lieutenant was obviously right. The standard-bearer's head swiveled this way and that. An ambush could do gruesome things to the company, to the whole regiment. *And I don't even need a SHOOT ME! sign,* Rollant thought. *I'm carrying the flag. Of course they'll try to shoot me.*

He wondered whether getting promoted in exchange for making himself such a prominent target was as good a bargain as he'd thought at the time. Yes, becoming a corporal was a great honor for a blond. But could he enjoy the honor with a crossbow quarrel through his brisket? Not likely.

No yells of alarm rang out from the company ahead, nor roaring cries from northern soldiers. No bowstrings thrummed, no triggers clicked. No one yelled false King Geoffrey's name or shouted, "Provincial prerogative forever!" Except for chirping birds and scolding squirrels, the woods remained quiet. The only sounds of men were those of footfalls on dirt.

Lieutenant Griff sheathed his sword once more. "Must have been a beast after all," he said with no small relief.

"Yes, sir." Rollant sounded relieved, too, not least because he no longer ran the risk of being spitted on that long, sharp blade. A crossbowman's shortsword hung on his own left hip. He was no swordsman, either. He'd fought a real swordsman—fought his own liege lord, Baron Ormerod, in fact—in the skirmishes before the battle by the River of Death. He counted himself lucky to have escaped with his life.

A commotion came from up ahead, and a confused babble of voices. It didn't sound like trouble, but Griff got out his sword again. The sense of the cry tore back through the regiment. What people were yelling was, "The river! The river!"

"The river!" Rollant took up the cry, too. "The river!" He surged north. He wanted to see the Hoocheecoochee with his own eyes.

There it was: slow-flowing, brown, perhaps a furlong wide, or a little more. Was it too far south to have crocodiles in it? Rollant didn't know. He also didn't stick a foot into the water, not wanting to find out the hard way.

"How do we get across?" Smitty asked; he'd pushed up with Rollant. "Some of us could swim it, I suppose—if there's nothing in there waiting to get fed, I mean."

"I was just thinking the same thing," Rollant answered. "I don't know. I don't think so, but I don't know for certain."

"Wouldn't want to find out by getting munched," Smitty said.

Colonel Nahath had some very definite ideas on what to do now that they'd got down to the Hoocheecoochee. He sent a runner off to the southeast to let Doubting George know he'd done it, and then issued a series of crisp commands: "Form a defensive perimeter, men. We're at the river. We're going to hold the crossing. Dig in. Set up your trenches and breastworks. If the traitors want us, they'll have to pay for us."

"Shouldn't we try to cross the river, sir?" somebody asked.

"We will—as soon as the artificers throw a bridge over it," the regimental commander said. "That's what they're for. And when they do"—he rubbed his hands together in anticipation—"when they do, boys, it's my considered opinion that we've got Joseph the Gamecock and the Army of Franklin good and cornholed. What do you think of that?"

Rollant whooped and cheered and held the company standard in the crook of his elbow so he could clap his hands. The soldiers were making enough noise to draw every traitor for half a mile around, but no northerners seemed close enough to hear. Nahath sent off another messenger, in case something happened to the first.

Dirt flew as Rollant dug and dug. Inside of an hour, a formidable defensive position took shape all around him. "Let 'em come now," somebody said. Rollant shook his head. He wanted reinforcements to get here first. He wasn't afraid of fighting, but he wanted to do it on his army's best terms if he possibly could.

Hammers thudded on planks. Piledrivers drove treetrunks into the muddy bottom of the Hoocheecoochee River. Doubting George watched the bridge snake toward the northern bank. Only a few yards to go now . . . and the northerners still didn't seem to realize the southron army was about to cross.

Turning to Colonel Nahath, George said, "Your regiment's just taken a long step toward winning this war for us."

"Good," the man from New Eborac said. "Anybody wants to know what I think, this gods-damned war's already gone on too long and cost too much. The sooner we get it over and done with, the better off everybody will be."

"Can't argue with a single word of that, Colonel, and I don't intend to try," George said. He peered toward the north bank of the river. "I wish those engineers would hurry. How long can our luck hold?" Back at General Hesmucet's headquarters, clever Major Alva was probably gnashing his teeth right now. The southrons had found a way to go over the Hoocheecoochee even without his masking spell.

No sooner were the words out of George's mouth than an artificer came pelting back across the bridge and said, "Sir, it's finished. Would you like to be the first man to cross to the far bank?"

Doubting George would have liked nothing better. But the northern courtesy with which he'd been raised made him shake his head. "Colonel Nahath deserves the honor," he replied. "Without him, it wouldn't be possible."

"Thank you, sir," Nahath said. "You're a gentleman."

"Go on," George said with a smile more or less sincere. "Go on, and be quick, before I change my mind."

"I wouldn't blame you if you did," Colonel Nahath said, but that didn't stop him from hurrying across the bridge, his bootheels thudding on the planks. As soon as he got to the end of the timbers, he leaped high in the air and came down with both feet on the ground on the north bank of the Hoocheecoochee. He turned and waved to Doubting George.

After waving back, the lieutenant general hurried across the bridge himself. He'd given Nahath the privilege of going first, but that didn't mean he despised going second. The ground under his feet on the far bank of the river felt no different from that on the side he'd just left. It felt no different, but it was, and he knew it.

So did Nahath. "Let's push on toward Marthasville, sir," he said.

"We will." With a grin, George added, "Or did you mean just the two of us?"

"I'm ready." Nahath grinned, too. By the way his narrow face had to twist to accommodate the expression, it didn't alight there very often. He waved toward the city. "Doesn't look like there's anybody in the way right now to stop us."

He was right about that, but only for a little while. "Some

of those sons of bitches in blue would turn up—they always do. So we'll have to bring some company along, that's all." Doubting George waved once more, this time back toward the southern bank of the Hoocheecoochee. Colonel Nahath's regiment of men from New Eborac had earned the right to cross first, but a great many other regiments were lined up behind them now. Once this force got over the river, Joseph the Gamecock would have a hells of a time throwing it back.

On came the New Eborac regiment, each company with its standard fluttering at its head. One of the standard-bearers made George blink. He turned to Nahath. "Excuse me, Colonel, but did I just see a blond carrying a flag?"

"Yes, sir, you did," Nahath answered. "That's Corporal Rollant, who earned the spot for himself on Commissioner Mountain. You may remember, I brought the question of promoting him to you before I went ahead with it. You said he deserved the chance to fail, but he hasn't failed yet."

With his memory jogged, Doubting George nodded. "I do recall now, thanks. He still makes a strange sight, though."

"This war has shown us a great many strange sights, sir," Colonel Nahath said. "I think we'd better get used to it, because the kingdom won't get any *less* strange in the peace that's coming."

"You're likely right, Colonel." George shook his head. "No, as a matter of fact, you're certainly right. But I'm a northern man myself, you know, and I have to tell you that some things strike me as *very* strange the first time I see them."

"You asked if Rollant was a good fighting man, a good soldier," Nahath replied. "I told you he was, and I meant it. He hasn't had much trouble since he got promoted—less than I expected. If he were an ordinary Detinan instead of a blond, he'd surely be a sergeant by now, and he might well be an officer."

Contemplating the blond corporal was quite enough for Doubting George at the moment. Being a conservative had led him to radicalism, a step he hadn't planned on tak-ing. Blonds freed from the land, blonds promoted to underofficer, blonds who might eventually get promoted further still . . .

As he did whenever such notions disturbed him, he thought, *I'd sooner have that than the Kingdom of Detina torn to pieces*. It was true. Were it anything but true, he would have been fighting for Geoffrey, not Avram. But sometimes, as now, it was also cold, cold comfort.

He left a solid garrison to protect the bridge, then ordered the rest of his force forward toward Marthasville. As long as he was *doing*, he didn't have to brood. And the chief city of Peachtree Province lay only a few miles away. George knew the northerners had a ring of forts around Marthasville, and entrenchments between those forts, but how many men did they have to put into the entrenchments? As long as the Army of Franklin remained on the east bank of the curving Hoocheecoochee, not many.

His army didn't meet its first traitors in arms till it had been marching for most of an hour. Then a couple of unicorn-riders rode right up to the head of his column—and were promptly captured. They were indignant about it. When their captors brought them before Doubting George, one of them demanded, "What are you sons of bitches doing here? You're supposed to be on the other side of the river."

"Life is full of surprises," George said.

"It isn't fair," the second unicorn-rider said. "We wouldn't've come right on up to you gods-damned bastards if we'd known you were southrons. You ought to let us go."

"I'm sure you'd do the same for a couple of our men," George said. The northern unicorn-riders didn't have the crust to claim they would and to make that convincing. George gestured to the men in charge of them. "Take them away and send them south."

"Yes, sir," the grinning guards said. They led their glum prisoners back toward the new bridge across the Hoocheecoochee.

An hour or so after that, real fighting began. Geoffrey's men turned out to have more than a couple of unicorn-riders in the neighborhood. A squadron galloped through the fields that ran by the road on which the southrons were marching. They shot at the men in gray and then galloped off out of range. Some of Doubting George's men shot back.

One enemy rider tumbled off his mount, while a couple of footsoldiers in gray howled when quarrels struck them.

Another couple of squadrons of blue-clad men on unicorns got in front of the marching column and tried to stop it by sheer brute force. They had a battery of engines with them, and flung darts at the southrons from a range longer than that from which George's men could shoot back at them. They were very brave—a lot of northern soldiers were—but it didn't do them much good. George ordered his leading regiments to shift from column into line. They swept forward. The ends of their line lapped around the unicorn-riders on either side. The northerners had to retreat in a hurry to keep from being surrounded. They tried to set up for another stand half a mile farther north, but the southrons made them fall back again before they'd shot more than a couple of darts.

By the time the sun set, George's force was almost half-way to Marthasville. He had a solidly garrisoned supply line leading back to the bridge over the Hoocheecoochee, and ordered his men to entrench around the camp they made. Once that was done, he told his scryer, "Now put me through to General Hesmucet."

"Yes, sir," the scryer said, and got out his crystal ball. George had already sent a runner back to the commanding general, but hadn't spoken with him till now.

Before long, Hesmucet's face appeared in the crystal ball. "Congratulations, Lieutenant General!" he said heartily. "You've stolen a march on Joseph the Gamecock—and you've stolen one on Major Alva, too."

"That did occur to me, yes," George said with a smile. "How's he taking it?"

"He's disappointed," Hesmucet answered. "He was shaping what would have been a really magnificent masking spell, and now we don't need it. He'll just have to learn to live with it—part of growing up, you might say."

"Yes, sir." Doubting George hadn't thought Hesmucet would be angry with him for moving before the planned moment, but was glad to be proved right. Hesmucet put success above method, as any good soldier did. George said, "We're over the last barrier in front of Marthasville now."

"So we are," the general commanding agreed. "And it will be interesting to see what Joseph the Gamecock does about it."

"He can't very well stay on that side of the river," George said. "If he does, we take the city *and* we smash up his army."

"We're liable to do all that even if he pulls back," Hesmucet replied. "You've put him in a very nasty position, very nasty indeed. Congratulations, Lieutenant General."

"Thank you, sir," George said. "I was wondering what in the hells I would do if I were Joseph the Gamecock. By all the gods, I've got no good answers. I'd sure rather be where I am than where he is."

"Don't blame you a bit," Hesmucet said. "But he's kept his force in being. He can still hurt you—he can still hurt all of us—if he gets the chance. We can't afford to be careless, not now."

"Not ever," Doubting George said.

"No, not ever." Hesmucet leaned forward, so that he seemed about to step out of the crystal ball and sit down beside George. "Can I tell you a little secret?"

"Sir, you're the one who's in charge here," George answered. "Only you know whether you can or not—or maybe I ought to say, whether you should or not."

"Well, I'm going to, gods damn it." Hesmucet bared his teeth in a fierce grin. "I'm glad you're the one who found the way over the Hoocheecoochee, and not, say, Fighting Joseph."

"I can't imagine why, sir," George said, deadpan. Both officers laughed. Doubting George had no trouble imagining how puffed-up and full of himself Fighting Joseph would have been had he got across the river ahead of every other southron officer. He would have started agitating for command over the whole force, and would have slandered General Hesmucet, Lieutenant General George, and Brigadier James the Bird's Eye to anyone who would listen. To make sure people listened, Fighting Joseph would have pounded a drum and played a trumpet, too.

"What are your plans for tomorrow?" Hesmucet asked.

"Sir, unless you order me to do something else, I'm going

to push on toward Marthasville," George replied. "The deeper into Joseph the Gamecock's rear I get, the harder the time he'll have doing anything about me."

"That's good," Hesmucet said. "That's very good. It's just what I'd do in your spot." He grinned. It made him look surprisingly boyish. "And if that doesn't prove it's good, I don't know what would. Anything else?"

"No, sir," Doubting George said.

"All right, then." General Hesmucet nodded to someone George couldn't see: his scryer, for the crystal ball suddenly became just a ball of glass. George got up, stretched, and nodded. He knew what he was supposed to do, he knew what he had to do, and he thought he could do it. For a soldier, that was a good feeling.

But George didn't have such a good feeling the next morning. The northerners still had no footsoldiers on this side of the Hoocheecoochee to oppose his army's progress, but enough unicorn-riders were in the neighborhood to make real nuisances of themselves. They swarmed round the southron footsoldiers like the blond nomads on the steppes far to the east of the Great River, now and then darting in to shoot flurries of crossbow quarrels at them.

Disciplined volleys from his men knocked a good many traitors out of the saddle, and knocked over a good many unicorns as well. The white beasts were beautiful; seeing them fall and hearing them scream as they were wounded made George wince, hardened veteran though he was. But the northerners knew they had to slow his men, and they did.

By that time, a scryer with a crystal ball or a swift-riding messenger had surely got word back to Joseph the Gamecock that the southrons were over the Hoocheecoochee and threatening, as they'd threatened so many times farther south, to finish the job of outflanking him, cutting him off from Marthasville, and destroying him. It hadn't happened yet. *This time, though* . . . Doubting George thought. *This time, we just may manage it.*

"Keep pelting those unicorn-riders with your bolts," he called to his men. "If we can get ahead of the traitors . . ."

But Brigadier Spinner's unicorn-riders understood what he

wanted as well as he did himself. Spinner wasn't Ned of the Forest. A man fighting him didn't always have to look out for an unexpected stroke from a startling direction. What false King Geoffrey's commander of unicorn-riders did here was unsubtle and obvious. That didn't make it ineffective.

Every time George's men had to stop and fight made him fume and curse. "Gods damn it," he growled, "they're liable to get away again."

Joseph the Gamecock couldn't have been more disgusted if he'd been pickled in bile. He'd known the southrons would sooner or later find a way around his position on the east bank of the Hoocheecoochee. But the report that Doubting George had crossed the river still infuriated him, for he hadn't expected it to happen nearly as soon as this.

For a couple of hours after the first word came in that his right flank had been turned, he'd done his best to believe it was a mistake, a scout seeing what he feared he would see regardless of whether or not it was really there. But no such luck. Men in gray really had crossed the river, and he would have to respond or see the Army of Franklin smashed between hammer and anvil.

Men in blue fell back to the western bank of the river, marching over the foot bridges his miles of field fortifications had protected. Glideway carpets transported siege engines and other essentials over yet another bridge. The retreat went as smoothly as such things could. *Why not? Joseph* thought bitterly. *We've had practice falling back.*

When the last man and the last glideway carpet had come over the river, Joseph turned to his mages and spoke in harsh tones: "All right, gods damn it, now make sure the southrons can't follow hard on our heels."

"Yes, sir," the mages chorused, and began to incant. The bridge over which the glideway carpets had passed was the first to feel their sorcery. Flames licked along the timbers supporting it. With a rending crash, it fell into the Hoocheecoochee. The spell made the timbers keep burning till they were altogether consumed, even though they were wet.

The foot bridges went next. Their timbers burned as

thoroughly as had those of the glideway bridge. Those timbers rested on stone piers. The magic shook the piers back to their constituent stones and scattered those along the bottom of the river.

"That seems to have worked well enough," Joseph said grudgingly.

"Yes, sir," one of the mages replied. "The enemy won't be able to use the bridges, and he'll be hard pressed to get across the river at all."

"He's already across the river, gods damn him," Joseph the Gamecock snapped. "Do you think we'd be doing this if he weren't?"

"What I meant, sir, was—"

Joseph cut off the mage (if he'd had sword in hand, he might have used that, too). "I don't care what you meant. Why didn't any of you wonderful wizards warn me this was about to happen?"

"We aren't infallible, sir," the sorcerer said stiffly.

"Really? I never would have noticed," Joseph the Gamecock said. The wizard winced and turned away.

Mounting his unicorn, Joseph rode up toward the head of the Army of Franklin. A few men snarled at him as he went by. He didn't blame them. They were free Detinans speaking their mind. Had he been in their place, he would have snarled at the commanding general, too.

Another unicorn came up alongside of his after he reached the front of the column. He made himself turn his head. When he saw who'd joined him, he breathed a silent sigh of relief: it was Roast-Beef William, not Lieutenant General Bell. Instead of carping at him for retreating again, William only asked, "What are we going to do now, sir?"

"What we've been doing all along: try to hold the southrons out of Marthasville," Joseph answered. "*What* hasn't change. *Why* hasn't changed. *How* . . ." He cursed under his breath. "*How* just got harder."

"Yes, sir," Roast-Beef William said. "The Hoocheecoochee was the last real line we had defending the city."

"I haven't given up hope," Joseph said stubbornly. "I don't intend to, either. Marthasville has a solid set of forts around it, and there's high ground north of Goober Creek.

The southrons will have to cross the creek before they attack the city. When they do, I intend to hit them in the flank. It'll be the first decent chance I've had to attack since Fat Mama, and I don't intend to let Bell take this one away from me."

Roast-Beef William stroked his beard. "A bold plan, sir— no doubt of that. But have we got enough men to put garrisons into the forts around Marthasville and to attack the southrons at the same time? They outnumber us badly as things are."

"You needn't remind me of *that*," Joseph the Gamecock said bitterly. "I think the southrons sow dragons' teeth and reap soldiers, the way the Mad Cuss did in the legend. But I don't intend to use the Army of Franklin to hold the forts."

"What then, sir?" William asked, raising bushy eyebrows. "Shall we sow dragons' teeth of our own, or make unicorn-riders of ghosts and shadows?"

"Satrap Brown commands a militia," Joseph said. "The son of a bitch doesn't like me any too bloody well, and I mislike him, too, but I still have the power to impress those men directly into King Geoffrey's service. They've spent the whole stinking war looking precious in their pretty uniforms and scratching their backsides. Now it's time to find out if they can fight even a little bit."

Roast-Beef William looked dubious. He looked so very dubious, he might have practiced the expression in front of a glass. "I'd hate to put them into the line against Hesmucet's men. The southrons are good soldiers, gods damn them, and they're veterans. They'd go through raw militiamen like a good dose of castor oil."

"I don't intend to put them into the line, only into the forts around Marthasville," Joseph the Gamecock answered. "If I'm going to offer the southrons any kind of resistance at all, Lieutenant General, somebody besides my soldiers has to fill those places."

"Yes, sir." Roast-Beef William still didn't sound convinced. That worried Joseph. William, after all, was the man who'd written the tactical manual both sides used in this war. If he didn't think well of Joseph's plan, it was likely flawed.

Almost pleading, Joseph said, "I've got to try *something*. If I don't, the southrons will just walk into Marthasville. We can't have that."

"No, we can't," William agreed. "Who would have thought, three years ago, that things could grow so desperate?"

Anyone with an ounce of sense might have, Joseph thought. *We knew from the start how badly the southrons outweigh us. But we were wild to hold on to our provincial prerogatives, and so we didn't stop to count the cost when we followed Geoffrey and rebelled against King Avram. We're counting the cost now, though.*

With every stride his unicorn took, Marthasville grew nearer. It wasn't a great city, not compared to New Eborac in the south or to Old Capet here in the north. But Joseph had been in the field a long time, in the field or in small towns. Marthasville's hostels and shops and temples made it look very grand indeed, a center of civilization in the middle of nowhere.

He'd seen too much nowhere lately. He was sick of it. He was sick of the whole war. Had someone given him the chance to go off and sit on the sidelines—promising, of course, that everything would go well in his absence—he would gladly have taken it. The trouble was, no one could make promises like that. Joseph had been trained as a soldier. As long as his kingdom needed him, his sword remained at its service.

And if that doesn't make me a loyal northern man, gods only know what would. I've had nothing but insults and disrespect from King Geoffrey. They're all I'll ever get, as long as he is king. But I'll put up with them for my kingdom and for my province. If I were a private man, though, I'd cut the liver out of that gods-damned son of a bitch.

As often happened, a good dose of lese majesty made him feel better. He looked back over his shoulder at the men he commanded. They knew things weren't going any too well. No one but an idiot could think that seeing the southrons on this side of the Hoocheecoochee was good news. Still, they seemed in good enough spirits. If he needed fighting from them, he would get all he needed. *And if I had as many of them as Hesmucet has southrons, this would be a different war.*

But that reflection wasn't what made Joseph the Game-cock look straight ahead once more. It also wasn't what made him urge his unicorn up to a slightly faster pace. Along with all his marching men, he'd spied Lieutenant General Bell, tied onto his unicorn, coming up at a trot. Short of making his own mount gallop, Joseph couldn't escape Bell.

"Well, your Grace," his wing commander rumbled, "what are we going to do now? This skedaddle is a disgrace, nothing else but. A disgrace, I say."

"Would you sooner have stood your ground with the enemy behind us as well as in front?" Joseph the Game-cock demanded. "Nobody would have got back to Marthasville in that case."

"They should never have got over the river in the first place," Bell declared.

"I quite agree," Joseph said.

Bell blinked. "Well, then . . ." His voice trailed off.

"Unfortunately," Joseph the Gamecock said, "we have to deal with what did happen, not with what should have happened. We should have attacked the stinking southrons outside of Fat Mama, but one of our wing commanders saw ghosts in the bushes and got a cold foot, and so the attack did not go in."

"Now see here, sir—" Bell began, he being the wing commander in question.

"Oh, shut up," Joseph told him. "When we go into position behind Goober Creek and when I see what we can do against Hesmucet, I may decide I want to listen to you again. Till then, no."

"What we can do against Hesmucet?" Bell jeered. "You won't do anything but retreat. By the gods, sir, it's all you ever do."

Joseph the Gamecock set a hand on the hilt of his sword. "Gentlemen, please!" Roast-Beef William said, edging his unicorn between Joseph's and Bell's. "When we quarrel, who gains? King Avram, no one else."

"There is some truth in what you say, Lieutenant General," Joseph said. "Some—but not enough."

"Not enough, indeed," Bell said. "We need a *man* in

charge of this army, not someone who takes to his heels whenever the enemy comes near."

They both started reaching for weapons again. "You were the one who wouldn't go forward when I needed you!" Joseph shouted.

"Gentlemen!" Roast-Beef William said again. "I really must insist that you remember we are all on the same side."

"If certain people would act like it—" Joseph the Gamecock said.

"Yes, indeed, if only they would," Lieutenant General Bell broke in. They glared at each other.

"We must all serve the north," William said. "We can settle our differences once victory is ours. Until then, we have to work together."

"I serve the north, by the gods," Joseph said. "In fact, I daresay my service to the north is more pure, more disinterested, than that of any other man in the army. The kingdom always comes first for me, not least because I—" He broke off. *Because I despise the king* might be true—in fact, certainly was true—but would gain him no points in this argument. "Because I was one of the first men out of Detina's old army and into this new one," he finished lamely.

"We need a fighter at the head of our force, a true battler," Bell said. "Then we'd show the southrons what our army can do."

"And if this army gets that kind of battler"—Joseph the Gamecock looked hard at Bell—"what the southrons will show him is that they have too many men and too many engines to be driven off as easily as he thinks."

"How would you know?" Bell retorted. "You've only gone backwards. You don't know what we can do if we can go forwards."

"Yes, I do," Joseph said. "We can throw the war away. If you go forward against a host bigger than your own, that's what you do."

"Duke Edward of Arlington would not agree," Bell sniffed.

"I know Duke Edward, sir. We have our differences, but I will say that Duke Edward is a friend of mine." Joseph the Gamecock fixed his unruly wing commander with a steady, scornful stare. "And I will also say one other thing: you, Lieutenant General, are no Duke Edward."

That got home. Bell quailed and went red under his swarthy skin. Using his good arm, he jerked his unicorn's head away and rode off at something not far from a gallop. Joseph watched him go with considerable satisfaction. Roast-Beef William looked less happy. "That won't do us any good, sir," he said.

"By the Lion God's fangs, it did *me* a lot of good," Joseph said. "I'm entitled to vent my spleen now and again, too." He set a hand on his abdomen. He wasn't quite sure whereabouts in there his spleen resided, but he was sure it had been well and truly vented.

Somewhere not far ahead lay Goober Creek. If he could get the satrap to use his militiamen in the forts around Marthasville, that would free up the whole Army of Franklin to strike at the invaders. Hesmucet had come a long way. He'd had a lot of men killed or wounded, and was using a lot of them to guard the glideway line back to Rising Rock that kept his army fed and supplied. *I can do him quite an injury*, Joseph the Gamecock thought. *I can, and, by the gods, I will.*

VII

Having crossed the Hoocheecoochee, Rollant had hoped for a sudden, triumphant descent on Marthasville. He'd pictured southrons marching through the city in a grand and glorious procession, as they'd done in Rising Rock at the end of the previous summer. But what he'd pictured didn't happen. The traitors' army remained between that of General Hesmucet and Marthasville. Whenever the southrons sent scouts to probe at the enemy's defenses, they got a warm reception.

"We ought to be doing more," he told Smitty one morning as the two of them heated tea over a campfire.

"Nothing I can do about it—I'm just an ordinary fellow, ordinary as they come," Smitty answered. "But now that you're a high and mighty corporal, you could probably stroll right up to Doubting George or General Hesmucet and tell 'em what's on your mind. They'd hop to it, I bet."

"It's a good thing I already know you're a chucklehead," Rollant said. "If I didn't, I'd figure you were trying to get me into trouble."

"You're a blond," Smitty said. "How much more trouble do you need?—and is that water boiling yet?"

Rollant looked into the saucepan he was holding over the flames. "Not quite," he said, and then, "You know, there's a lot of people I'd want to belt, if they went on and on about how I'm a blond."

"Sorry, your Corporalship, sir," Smitty said, his mocking style, as often happened, making it hard for Rollant to tell how serious he was. "I take it all back. You're right—having yellow hair's no trouble at all for you."

"Gods damn it, I didn't mean *that*." Rollant wondered if he'd ever had a day in his whole life go by where being a blond wasn't a trouble in one way or another. He didn't think so. "What I was trying to say was, you mostly don't give me trouble on account of what I am. If *you* talk about it, I don't mind so much."

"Oh." Smitty thought that over, then grinned. "You say the sweetest things, darling." He blew Rollant a kiss. "But I bet you tell them to all the Detinans."

That left Rollant's cheeks hotter than the water, which had begun to boil. He took the saucepan away from the flames and poured its contents first into Smitty's mug and then into his own. Both had ground tea leaves and sugar waiting for the hot water. Stirring the tea gave Rollant an excuse not to do anything else for the next minute or two. At last, he asked, "How did you get to be such a nuisance?"

"I work hard at it," Smitty said, not without pride. "Just ask my father and my mother and my two older sisters and my older brother. If my other older brother was still alive, you could ask him, too." He held up a hasty hand. "I didn't have anything to do with him dying, though. It was the coughing fever."

Rollant gallantly tried to get back to talking about what *he* wanted to talk about: "We ought to push the traitors harder. If they go all the way back into Marthasville, we ought to lay siege to 'em. If they don't, we ought to make 'em stand and fight instead of sneaking away again."

"Didn't your mama ever rap you on the knuckles for being an impatient little brat?" Smitty said. "We're just now getting the whole army, not just part of Doubting George's Wing, over the Hoocheecoochee. Joseph the Gamecock wrecked all the bridges. We've especially got to get one for glideway carpets across the river. Once that happens, I expect we may fight a bit."

"I suppose so," Rollant said. "But the more time we spend getting ready, the more time the traitors have to dig more trenches of their own. Whenever we come at the ones they've dug in, they make us pay for it." He also ground his teeth when he thought of blond serfs doing the digging for the northern soldiers.

"That's part of the game," Smitty answered. "The idea is to get around the bastards' flanks and hit 'em where they aren't dug in, or else to make them try to hit us when we *are* dug in instead."

"It would be nice," Rollant said wistfully. "It doesn't seem to happen very often, though, does it?" He swigged at his tea. It would have been better with some spirits poured into it, but pried his eyes open even as things were.

Sergeant Joram happened to be walking by. He glowered down at Rollant. "Are you suggesting, Corporal, that the traitors have better officers than we do?"

Would he ask me a question like that if I weren't a blond? Such thoughts were never far from Rollant's mind. He looked up at Joram and nodded. "Sometimes, Sergeant. Otherwise, we would've licked 'em already, don't you suppose? And sometimes we're better than they are." *But not often enough, gods damn it.*

He waited for Joram to burst like a flung firepot and spill flames everywhere. But the sergeant only grunted and kept walking. Smitty whistled. "You got away with it," he said. "And I know why."

"It's not because Joram loves blonds any too well," Rollant said.

"No, of course not," Smitty agreed, as if the idea that anyone—anyone Detinan, that is—could love blonds too well was too ridiculous to contemplate . . . and so it probably was. The farmer's son went on, "You got away with it on account of you're a corporal now. If an ordinary soldier— me, for instance—said something like that, old Joram'd run over him like a herd of unicorns."

On account of you're a corporal now. All his life, Rollant had been on the outside looking in as far as status was

concerned. Being born blond would do that in the Kingdom of Detina. Joining King Avram's army hadn't improved
things much. A blond who was also a common soldier was
at the bottom of two different hierarchies.

But now he was off the bottom of one of them. He had
stripes on his sleeve. He was the only blond in the whole
regiment who did. Had Joram given him the same courtesy
he would have given a Detinan corporal, a corporal whose
skin was respectably swarthy, whose hair was respectably
black?

"By the gods, maybe he did," Rollant said softly.

"No maybes about it," Smitty declared. "You're a corporal,
so you've got it easy. You get to tell people to cut firewood and fill canteens. You don't have to do it yourself.
And you don't get the heat people like me do. You'd have
to really make a botch of things to get chewed out."

"Maybe," Rollant said. But he wasn't entirely convinced.
If he made a mistake, he suspected—no, he was as sure
as made no difference—he would lose his rank and become
a common soldier again faster than a Detinan committing
the same blunder.

"Standard-bearer!" Lieutenant Griff called. "Get the flag!
We're going to move out in a few minutes."

"Coming, sir!" Rollant scrambled to his feet, poured the
last of the tea down his throat, and hurried over to the
company's banner. He saluted it and put a pinch of earth
at the base of the staff as he picked it up. It wasn't quite
an object of veneration in its own right, but it wasn't far
removed from being one. Who could tell for certain, after
all, what was divine and what wasn't?

Having gone through the ritual, he took hold of the flag.
Carrying it made him feel stronger and braver than he really
was. Of course, carrying it also made him a target. Were
that not true, he wouldn't have gained the job. *Since that's
the way things work, I'd better be as strong and brave as
I can.*

Colonel Nahath's regiment—and several others—started
moving north a few minutes later. The traitors had fled back
of Goober Creek, a miserable little stream about halfway
between the Hoocheecoochee River and Marthasville itself.

Joseph the Gamecock's men also had unicorn-riders and raiders afoot still loose in the region between the Hoochee-coochee and Goober Creek. They would snipe at General Hesmucet's men whenever they got a chance. The southrons' column advanced with scouts on both wings.

Rollant knew that was so, but couldn't have proved it himself. He couldn't see the front of the column or the rear, and he couldn't see very far off to the sides. That was partly because Nahath's regiment was in the middle of the long file of men in gray and partly because of the choking clouds of red dust the men in front of him had already kicked up. The dust got in his eyes. It got in his nose and made him sneeze. It got in his mouth, leaving his teeth and tongue coated in grit. It turned his tunic and pantaloons a color halfway between rust and blood. It turned his skin the same shade, except where rills of sweat ran through and showed what color he was supposed to be.

Lieutenant Griff looked as much like a man made of red dust as did Rollant. When he spat, his spittle was brick-red. He was sweating even harder than Rollant, but was pretty red under the sweat, too. "Lion God's tail tuft, it's hot," he said. "How does anybody stand this horrible weather year after year?"

"Sir, when I first came down to New Eborac from Palmetto Province, I thought I'd freeze to death every winter," Rollant answered. "It's all what you're used to, I expect." He'd done harder work than marching in hotter, stickier weather than this; Karlsburg took a back seat to nobody for dreadful summers.

"Gods-damned bugs." Griff slapped at himself, but did nothing except raise a puff of dust from his tunic. "This is a horrible place."

"Looks like pretty good farming country to me, sir, you don't mind my saying so." Rollant had had to learn how to contradict Detinans. As a serf in Palmetto Province, he never would have dared do any such thing. As a carpenter in New Eborac City, he had to. If he didn't, everyone would have cheated him unmercifully.

Even in the army, a good many Detinans didn't want to hear a blond telling them they were wrong. Griff took it pretty well. He said, "You'd have to have a leather hide and iron muscles to do a proper job of working it."

"Maybe." Rollant hid a grimace. His blond ancestors hadn't known about iron; they'd used the softer bronze instead. Detinan swords and armor and iron-headed quarrels, along with Detinan unicorns and Detinan magecraft, had cast down the blond kingdoms of the north. Even now, some blonds had a superstitious reverence for iron. Rollant didn't, not in the top part of his mind, but he still knew what the strong metal had done to his folk.

Just then, lightning smote from a clear blue sky, striking the head of the column. Distant screams came back to Rollant's ears. Lieutenant Griff cursed. "They're playing the Thunderer's game," he growled. "And where were our mages? Asleep, or else with their thumbs up their arses."

Northern wizards still had the edge on their southron counterparts, although King Avram's sorcerers were at last gaining. The northerners had always had a need for man-killing magic: they had to hold their serfs in subjection. Southron mages helped manufactories make more. That didn't prepare them to meet lightnings.

Another crash of thunder, as if the Detinan god were indeed pounding mortals here below. More screams rose from the southrons, these louder and closer. *If the traitors strike us again*, Rollant thought nervously, *the next bolt would hit right about . . . here.* He looked up toward the heavens, but saw only sun and sky. Mages made lightning from nothing.

Just putting one foot in front of the other and marching on wasn't easy. Rollant made himself do it, and made himself hold the standard extra high. "Well done, Corporal!" Lieutenant Griff called. "They can't make us afraid if we don't let them."

Rollant *was* afraid. If Griff wasn't, Rollant thought something had to be wrong with him. *I'm not showing it*, he thought. *Maybe he's just not showing it, either.* Men lived behind masks. No one wanted to admit he was a coward, even to himself. And so soldiers who would sooner have run away went into battle without a murmur.

When the next lightning bolt crashed down, Rollant did

flinch. He couldn't help himself. He noticed Lieutenant Griff drawing into himself, too, which helped make him feel better. This bolt didn't land in the roadway and on the southron soldiers; it came down wide to the right, and raised a great cloud of dust and fountain of earth in a roadside field.

"Well, well," Griff said with a certain sardonic glee. "The mages on our side really aren't all asleep. Who would have thought it?"

More thunderbolts smote the advancing column. Almost all of them, after the first pair, missed. But one or two more did strike home. The southrons who weren't killed outright cried their misery to the uncaring sky. Healers ran over to them to do what they could. The trouble, as Rollant knew only too well, was that healers couldn't do very much. A wounded man was only a little more likely to die without treatment as he was after the healers got their hands on him.

Rollant wished he hadn't thought of that. He wished he hadn't had to think of that. Then he marched past some of the men one of those first two levinbolts had struck. The smell of charred meat was thick in the air. Had that been meat of a different sort, his mouth might have watered. As things were, his stomach heaved. He had to fight a lonely battle to keep from puking.

Not all the men the sorcerous lightning had struck were dead. A healer gave a dreadfully burned fellow laudanum. Killing pain healers could do, even if they also often killed patients.

Not far ahead lay Marthasville. Rollant couldn't see it now, not with all the dust in the air, but he *had* seen it, and it remained distinct in his mind's eye even if invisible to those of his body. He knew what it meant: a real victory over the traitors, a burning brand tossed onto the funeral pyre of their hopes. *Let us into Marthasville,* he thought, *and how can the north call itself a kingdom?*

But the southrons weren't there yet. They'd crossed the Hoocheecoochee, the last great natural barrier before the city. Still, Joseph the Gamecock's army remained in front of them and, as Rollant had seen, remained full of fight. Nothing in this war had come easy up till now. Rollant didn't suppose anything would be easy from here on out, either.

Lieutenant General George said, "Well, sir, things may be starting to run our way at last." He spoke with some bemusement; there had been more than a few times when he'd wondered if he would ever be able to say such a thing.

Hesmucet nodded. "The lovely thing about finally being over the Hoocheecoochee is that we don't even have to attack Marthasville to make King Geoffrey pitch a fit."

"I hadn't thought about that when we set out on this campaign, but it's true," Doubting George admitted.

"Well, nobody could see just how things would go when we set out," Hesmucet said generously. "But here we are, and we can cause the northerners almost as much trouble by cutting off their glideway traffic toward the east as we can by taking Marthasville away from them. And if they shift men to try to stop us, how can they keep on covering the city?"

"To the hells with me if I know." Doubting George clapped his hands. "Congratulations, sir. You've wrapped up the whole campaign and tied a fancy ribbon around it."

Hesmucet laughed. "Wouldn't it be fine if things were as easy in the field as they are when we talk about them? I could wish that were so, but I know well enough that it isn't."

"I'm glad to hear it," George said, and meant every word. "Generals who build castles in the air commonly have them knocked down around their ears. That's what happened to Guildenstern by the River of Death: he was so sure the northerners were running away from us, he didn't take the precautions he should have on the off chance he was wrong."

"I don't envy his fate," Hesmucet said.

"Who would?" George replied. "Going out to the steppes to fight the blond savages is hard duty any time, but it's ten times as hard when we've got ourselves a real war here."

When the real war here was over, a lot of men with

brevet ranks of brigadier and even lieutenant general would
go back to being captains. They'd go back to chasing flea-
bitten blond savages, too. Most of the time, that was what
the Detinan army did. George's own permanent rank was
brigadier. He wouldn't have to spend endless years trotting
across the steppe on unicornback. He'd done plenty of that
before this war. He wouldn't be sorry not to do it again,
though sitting behind a desk in Georgetown and drafting
reports no one would ever read also struck him as imperfectly attractive.

Hesmucet's thoughts had gone along a different glideway.
"If you ask me," he said, "we're going to have to kill off
all the blond nomads on the steppe. We're stronger than
they are, we can't do anything useful with them, and they're
too stupid and too stubborn to know when they're beaten.
Once we empty the steppe of them, we can fill the land
with good Detinan farmers who'll do something useful with
it."

With a smile, Doubting George said, "You're solving all
the kingdom's problems this morning, aren't you, sir?"

"Gods damn it, that's what a commanding general is *for*,"
Hesmucet declared. To George's relief, he was also smiling.
A commanding general who took such boasts seriously was
a disaster waiting to happen, as the unhappy Guildenstern
could attest. Hesmucet went on, "I'll want you to move your
wing north and east, Lieutenant General, to put it in
position to harry the glideway lines leading east."

"Yes, sir," George said. "Shall I set them in motion right
away, or do I have some time to prepare first?"

"You have a few days," Hesmucet replied. "I'm still getting
all my ducks in a row now that everybody's on this side
of the Hoocheecoochee. I don't want anything to go wrong
on account of my carelessness."

General Guildenstern would *never* have said anything like
that. "If you worry about it, sir, it's not likely to happen,"
Doubting George said. "Tell me when you need me to be
ready to move, and I will be."

"I know," Hesmucet said. "I can rely on you." He nodded,
touched a forefinger to the front brim of his gray felt hat in
what wasn't quite a salute, and walked away.

Doubting George stared after him. It wasn't that the commanding general was wrong: George knew he would try to do exactly what Hesmucet required of him. But, in a lot of armies on both sides in this war, that would have been a very strange thing. Plenty of wing commanders were at their superiors' throats, wanting to lead armies themselves. Some of them went so far as to disobey and undercut army commanders, regardless of what that did to campaigns.

Fighting Joseph would undercut Hesmucet in a heartbeat, George thought. *In half a heartbeat. So why not me?* The answer to that was obvious: *because we're winning by doing what we're doing with Hesmucet in command. Fighting Joseph wouldn't care about that. I do.*

He called Colonel Andy and said, "We're going to be moving north and east before long, to cut the glideway links with the eastern part of what Geoffrey calls his kingdom. Draft the necessary orders for the move for my approval."

"Yes, sir," his adjutant said. "So there's not going to be any direct attack on Marthasville, then?"

"Not right away, anyhow," George answered. "General Hesmucet feels we can do the traitors about as much harm by cutting these links as we could by taking the city. I think he's right; Parthenia draws men and food from the east, and Duke Edward's army will suffer because those supplies can't come through."

"I hope that's so, sir," Andy said. "It still seems strange to me, though, to have come all this way to Marthasville and then not to try to take the place."

"Oh, I don't doubt that we will try to take it," Doubting George said. "But we can do this more easily—and, once we've done it, Joseph the Gamecock will have to respond in one way or another. Maybe we'll be able to meet his army outside of its entrenchments. That would give us a better chance of licking it once for all."

"Yes, sir," his adjutant said again. "What shall I make the effective date of these orders? When will we be moving out?"

"I don't know precisely, because General Hesmucet didn't know precisely," George replied. "Do you think we can be ready to move in three days' time?"

"I certainly do, sir," Colonel Andy said.

"All right, then—make that the effective date," George said. "I'm pretty sure we won't have to move sooner, and if we aren't ordered out till later, we can just delay day by day, as necessary."

"Yes, sir," Andy repeated. "That makes good sense."

"I'm sorry, Colonel," George told him. "I'll try not to let it happen again."

Colonel Andy opened his mouth, closed it, and shook his head. He walked off without saying anything. George smiled at his retreating back. He knew his occasional fits of whimsy not only perplexed but also alarmed his adjutant. As befitted an aide, Andy was nothing if not serious. George was serious when he had to be and when he felt like it. There were times when he didn't—and, being a general, he could get away with indulging himself now and again.

Raiders from the northern forces still operated on this side of Goober Creek. Snipers with powerful crossbows—not the quick-cocking kind most footsoldiers carried, but bigger, heavier weapons that used either a crank or a foot pedal to draw the bow, and that shot correspondingly farther than an ordinary crossbow—took a steady toll on his men. And Brigadier Spinner's unicorn-riders did their best to disrupt the flow of supplies from Rising Rock up to General Hesmucet's army.

They didn't have an easy time of it. Hesmucet had assembled what was without a doubt the best set of military artificers Doubting George had ever seen. When Joseph the Gamecock retreated over the Hoocheecoochee River, he'd naturally knocked down all the bridges spanning the stream, including the one that had carried glideway carpets. Counting its approaches, that one was three hundred yards long, and thirty yards high at its highest point over the Hoocheecoochee. Hesmucet's artificers—with some help from Colonel Phineas' sorcerers—had taken four and a half days to re-create the span . . . and all the timber they used was live trees when they started the job.

Against men of such talents, even the most diligent destroyers had their work cut out for them. And the southrons kept Brigadier Spinner's unicorn-riders too busy to let them attack the glideway line up to Rising Rock as diligently as they would have liked. Ned of the Forest might have done better; Doubting George, like every other southron general, had developed a fearful respect for the untutored, almost unlettered northern commander of unicorn-riders. But Ned was off by the Great River, and he was too busy to turn his ferocious attention to that lonely glideway line snaking up from the south.

Contemplating that, George said, "Do you know, Colonel, I'm vain enough to think I can stand up against anybody as a tactician."

"I should hope so, sir," Andy replied. "You've earned the right."

George nodded. "I expect I have. But I will say this as well: General Hesmucet is the best strategist I've ever seen, and I take my hat off to him for it." Taking himself literally, he doffed his gray chapeau.

His adjutant frowned. "How do you mean, sir?"

"He goes on throwing enough distractions at Ned of the Forest over in the east to keep Ned from coming this way and playing merry hells with our glideway," George said. "That's a long reach of thought."

"Well, what if it is?" Colonel Andy said. "I'm sure it would have come to you, too."

"I'm not," Doubting George said, "not by any means." *Maybe that means Marshal Bart did the right thing in making Hesmucet commander here in the east, and not me,* he thought, and grimaced. *What a depressing notion.*

"Sir," Andy said, "just remember this: if it weren't for you, this army wouldn't be here today. This army probably wouldn't be anywhere at all today, because the traitors would have smashed it to pieces by the River of Death."

"Oh, I think the men I was in charge of then had a little something to do with that, too," Doubting George said dryly.

"General Guildenstern was in charge of good men, too, and they ran back towards Rising Rock just as fast as they could go," Andy said.

That wasn't fair. Count Thraxton had ensorceled Guildenstern, so that he gave precisely the wrong order at precisely the wrong time. It was one of the very few times in the whole war that Thraxton the Braggart's sorcery had done what he wanted it to do. Lieutenant General George knew as much. He smiled anyhow. Remembering a colleague's embarrassment went a long way toward cheering him up.

Andy went on, "And this wing of the army has done more hard fighting since we came north than any of the others."

"It is the biggest wing, you know."

"Even so," his adjutant insisted. "And it's the biggest wing because you're the best commander General Hesmucet has."

Doubting George considered the competition. James the Bird's Eye was a comer, no doubt about it, but hadn't had nearly George's experience leading large numbers of men. Fighting Joseph . . . George shook his head. He didn't want to consider Fighting Joseph. *All right, maybe I am the best commander General Hesmucet has,* he thought. *But that doesn't mean I'm better than Hesmucet himself, and that's what I want to be.*

He brought his thoughts back to the essential business of winning the war. Standing outside his pavilion, he could see Marthasville. He could all but reach out and touch Marthasville. "We just have to stretch things out," he murmured.

"Sir?" Colonel Andy said.

"Joseph the Gamecock hasn't got enough men," George said. "If we make him do too many things at once, he won't be able to manage all of them."

"May you finally be right, sir," Andy said. "We've been saying since the start of the campaign that, if we did this, that, or the other thing, Joseph the Gamecock's army would break to pieces like a pot made of clay. We've been saying it and saying it, but it hasn't happened yet."

"Well, well." Lieutenant General George eyed his adjutant in surprise. "And here I'm the fellow with the reputation for doubting. I've earned it, too, I must say. Have you caught the disease from me, my dear Colonel?"

"In this cursed northern heat, a man can catch any disease under the sun," Colonel Andy replied. "The healers mostly don't know how to cure them, either. Why shouldn't I catch doubt along with everything else?"

"I'll tell you why," George replied. "Because this time we really are going to lick the traitors right out of their boots, that's why. One of the things that has made this campaign so hard is that Joseph the Gamecock has always had room to maneuver, room to retreat. He doesn't any more, not if he wants to hold on to Marthasville. All the chances for maneuvering work for us now."

"I told you, sir: may it work out as you say." Colonel Andy still looked glum. "But what do you want to bet that something will keep us from making the move to the northeast that General Hesmucet has ordered from us?"

"I can't imagine what that would be," George said.

"I can't imagine what it would be, either," his adjutant said. "But we've already seen a lot of unimaginable things in this campaign. What are a few more?"

George would have been happier had he had a ready answer for that, but he didn't, and he knew it.

Joseph the Gamecock eyed his wing commanders. "Gentlemen, the thing we need most in all the world right now, it seems to me, is room to maneuver."

"Another fancy way to talk about retreat," Lieutenant General Bell muttered. Joseph didn't think he was supposed to hear, but he did.

Here, though, Bell wasn't the only discontented officer he had. Roast-Beef William clucked and said, "Sir, I don't see how we *can* get room to maneuver without moving away from Marthasville, and holding Marthasville is the point of the exercise."

"We can hold Marthasville with Duke Brown's militiamen," Joseph said. "The satrap's men *are* starting to come into the forts around the city."

"Hesmucet has real soldiers with him," Roast-Beef William said glumly. "They'll go through raw militiamen quick as boiled asparagus."

Feeling about ready to burst from frustration, Joseph rounded on his third and newest wing commander and demanded, "How say you, Brigadier Alexander?"

"I want to strike the enemy a blow, as we all do," Old Straight replied, "but I don't want to uncover Marthasville to do it. My opinion is, we would do best to fight close to the city."

"But staying close to Marthasville with our whole force means the southrons can maneuver as they please, while we're trapped here," Joseph protested. "They can swing all the way around the city and surround us, by the gods."

"And in doing so, they will weaken themselves, and we can attack," Bell said.

"I am looking for the chance to attack," Joseph the Gamecock said. "Holding the city with the militia will give us that chance."

"What does King Geoffrey think of this plan?" William asked.

"It appalls him," Lieutenant General Bell replied.

"How do you know that?" Joseph inquired. Instead of answering, Bell took a swig of laudanum. Joseph the Game-cock went on, "I still think we can bring it off, and I still think it would be good for our strategic position if we did. And so, gentlemen, I want you to be prepared to move north and west of Marthasville whenever I give the order."

"It *is* another retreat!" Bell groaned. "I knew it. By the Thunderer's prong, sir, you're abandoning Marthasville to the tender mercies of Hesmucet and his stinking southrons. I don't care to be a part of any such maneuver. I think it's extremely ill-advised—and that's the best thing I can say about it."

"With all respect, sir," Roast-Beef William told Joseph, "I must say that, in this instance, I agree with Lieutenant General Bell."

He'd never said anything like that before. Hearing it from him infuriated Joseph. Eyes and voice deadly cold, he demanded, "Are you refusing my orders, Lieutenant General? I thought you of all people understood subordination."

"I do, sir. I refuse you nothing," Roast-Beef William said unhappily. "But I do not refuse you my opinion, either. And my opinion is and remains that we would do better to fight around Marthasville."

"Very well," Joseph the Gamecock said. It wasn't very well; it was nowhere close to very well. But Roast-Beef William had indeed spoken respectfully, and it was indeed part of a subordinate's duty to give his superior his unvarnished views. Fuming still, Joseph rounded on Alexander the Steward. "Will you follow me without carping, Brigadier?"

"Certainly, sir, if you require it," Old Straight replied. "I would be lying, though, if I said I liked your plan."

"Well, what else can we do?" Joseph the Gamecock asked, aiming the question as much at malicious fate as at his wing commanders. "If we stay here and let Hesmucet maneuver as he pleases, we are liable to lose not just Marthasville but the whole Army of Franklin."

"We need to attack," Bell insisted.

"You keep saying that, like a parrot trained to do it in the hope of getting a sunflower seed," Joseph said. As Bell glared at him, he went on, "Well, Pretty Poll, I have news for you: when the enemy's army is twice the size of your own, you had better have a gods-damned strong position before you go and bite him on the leg."

"If you don't attack, what point to having an army at all?" Bell asked.

"Have you ever heard of defending?" Joseph the Gamecock said.

"Indeed, sir." Bell nodded. "You have defended Peachtree Province so well, the whole southern half of it no longer needs to be defended at all."

"If you'd thrown the army away, as you always seem to want to do, we wouldn't still hold Marthasville," Joseph said.

"You always think we will lose if we attack," Bell retorted. "If we attack and win, we hurl the southrons back and we go forward."

"True—if," Joseph the Gamecock agreed. "Long odds, though, when we're so outnumbered. That's what you keep refusing to see."

"They're only southrons," Bell said contemptuously. "We can lick as many of them as we need to lick."

"It isn't so," Roast-Beef William said. "I must tell you, Lieutenant General, that *is not* so. They are Detinans, too. We have the advantage over them, perhaps, but not to the degree you imply."

"If it were so," Joseph added, "we could have won this war a long time ago. It lacks a good deal of being won right now, or else I've been living a nightmare for the past three years and more."

"If we have the advantage over them, why are we running away?" Bell asked.

"By the gods, you hardheaded jackass, we are not running away," Joseph the Gamecock ground out. "We're looking for room to maneuver."

"We've been 'looking for room to maneuver' ever since Borders," Bell said. "When you had it, you didn't use it. Now that you haven't got it any more, you want it."

"That is uncalled for," Roast-Beef William said.

"This whole campaign, such as it is, is uncalled for," Lieutenant General Bell said.

"You have obstructed me every step of the way," Joseph said furiously. "If this army is having difficulties, they are at least half—*at least* half, sir—of your making. For you to blame me now is like . . . is like . . . I don't know what it's like, but I know it's vile. If the stone that smashed your leg had smashed your miserable rock of a head in its place, this army would be better off today."

"Sir, that is also uncalled for," William said, and Alexander the Steward nodded.

"I see," Joseph said. "It's fine for him to insult me and revile me, but I'm a wicked monster if I pay him back in the same coin. Ah, yes. Yes, indeed. That makes perfect sense."

Something close to desperation in his voice, Roast-Beef William said, "Quarrels only help the enemy, sir. They can afford them, because they outnumber us. We can afford nothing at all."

Joseph was too angry to be placated so easily. "Oh, of course we can! Just ask *him*." He pointed to Bell. "We can afford to charge right out and attack the southrons, and five minutes later they'll all be skedaddling for the Highlow River just as fast as they can. Won't it be *wonderful?*"

Bell had faced a lot of nasty weapons in this war, but he didn't stand up to sarcasm very well. "That's not what I said," he protested, his voice breaking like a youth's.

"No, eh?" Joseph said. "It must be what you meant, though. Unless we win a victory like that, what's the point of attacking Hesmucet at all?"

"You deliberately twist all my words," Bell said.

"You deliberately twist all my deeds," Joseph the Game-cock answered. Bell started to say something, but Joseph forestalled him: "Get out of my sight. You make me sick."

"Sir—" Alexander the Steward began.

But Joseph had no patience for Old Straight, either. "And you," he said. "King Geoffrey gave me this command to save his kingdom. By the Thunderer's brass balls, I'm going to do it, too—as long as nobody gets in my way. I am sick to death of people telling me what I can do and what I can't. I command here, and my orders shall be obeyed, or I'll know the reason why. Have you got that?"

"Yes, sir," Brigadier Alexander said. "You would sooner do it your way than do it right, if I understand you correctly."

Maybe he'd thought he would shame Joseph the Game-cock. Maybe he would have, too, at another time. Not now. Now, Joseph just nodded. "That's exactly right, Brigadier. I'm going to do it my way, and I'll take my chances. You are dismissed." He nodded to Roast-Beef William. "You, too."

He could get rid of his wing commanders, but that didn't bring him the satisfaction he craved. He'd hardly got back to the house he was using for a headquarters before a sentry stuck his head in to say, "Sir, Count Thraxton has ridden down from Marthasville. He'd speak to you, if you would."

"Count Thraxton?" Joseph said. "What does *he* want?"

"I'm sure I don't know, sir," the sentry answered. "Will you see him, or shall I send him away?"

"I'll see him." Joseph had no more desire to see Thraxton than he did some demon from one of the seven hells. As a matter of fact, there had been times during the war when he'd wondered if the Braggart *was* a demon from one of the seven hells. But he couldn't send the man away, not when Thraxton served as King Geoffrey's eyes and ears in Peachtree Province.

"Count Thraxton!" the sentry announced in a loud voice, holding open the farmhouse door.

"Your Grace," Joseph the Gamecock murmured, bowing to the general who'd commanded the Army of Franklin before him.

"*Your* Grace," Thraxton the Braggart replied, returning the bow. Thraxton was tall and lean and sallow, with a face as mournful as a bloodhound's though much bonier. A grizzled beard covered hollow cheeks; sad eyes peered out from beneath a bramble patch of eyebrows. If he'd ever been happy in all his days, he hadn't bothered telling his face about it.

Joseph waved him to a chair. "Sit down, your Grace, please." He didn't like having Thraxton looming over him like a bad omen. The Braggart folded up, one section at a time, as he sat. Joseph stayed on his feet, pacing back and forth as he asked, "What can I do for you today, General?"

"I have come to tell you, sir, that King Geoffrey is not pleased with your plan to man the forts around Marthasville with Satrap Brown's militiamen and to move the Army of Franklin away from the city," Thraxton replied.

"I'm sorry to hear that," Joseph the Gamecock said. "Why does he object to it?"

"His Majesty's view, if I may speak frankly . . ." Thraxton waited for Joseph to nod. Joseph refused to give him the satisfaction. Thraxton coughed a couple of times—wet, almost consumptive coughs—and went on, "His Majesty is concerned that you intend to retreat away from Marthasville, and to leave the place undefended against the southrons. That is insupportable, both politically and militarily."

"In the first place, he's wrong, and, in the second place, he's wrong," Joseph said. "If I put my own men in the forts, how can I possibly hope to attack the southrons? With my own force and nothing more, I can defend but I can't hope to attack."

"King Geoffrey is less certain of this than you are," Thraxton declared.

"Well, bully for him," Joseph said acidly. "I'm here, and he's over in bloody Nonesuch. Which of us is likely to know better what this army is good for and what it isn't, do you suppose?"

"His Majesty has other sources of information besides yourself." Thraxton's tone was opaque, oracular.

Someone's been telling tales out of school, was what the Braggart had to mean. As soon as the words were out of Thraxton's mouth, Joseph the Gamecock could make a pretty good guess who that someone was, too. "Gods damn Lieutenant General Bell to the nastiest hell there is," he growled.

"I don't know what you're talking about," Count Thraxton said, which was a lie, and a lie made all the more annoying because it was so obvious.

"Oh, I'll just bet you don't," Joseph said.

Thraxton's narrow shoulders went up and down in a shrug. He had to be dead to shame—he didn't even care if he got caught out. "It's beside the point, in any case," he said. "Here *is* the point: will you take his Majesty's advice on how to defend Marthasville, or will you not?"

"Did he set me over the Army of Franklin, or is he in command of it himself?" Joseph asked.

"You command the army," Thraxton the Braggart answered, and a twist of his thin lips showed how much he wished he still commanded it himself. "You command the army, but Geoffrey rules the kingdom."

"Fine," Joseph the Gamecock said. "Let him rule the kingdom, then, and I promise not to tell him how to do it—so long as he doesn't tell me how to command the army. Seems a fair enough bargain to me."

Count Thraxton's lips got even thinner and even paler. Joseph hadn't thought they could. "I doubt King Geoffrey will care for the joke, your Grace," Thraxton said in frigid tones.

"I wasn't joking," Joseph said.

"What a pity," Count Thraxton replied.

Lieutenant General Bell had just taken a long, grateful gulp of laudanum when his aide-de-camp stuck his head into his farmhouse headquarters. Bell was anything but glad to see Major Zibeon. He'd gone too long without the drug since his quarrel with Joseph the Gamecock; his nerves were jangling, not only from the agony of his wounds but from craving for the potent tonic that salved him. His voice had a bark in it as he demanded, "What now?"

"Sir, Count Thraxton would speak with you," Zibeon replied.

"Thraxton?" Bell said, and the junior officer nodded. Part of Bell wished he'd waited a little longer to take the laudanum. If he was going to talk with King Geoffrey's friend—to say nothing of the king's snoop here in Peachtree Province—he should have had wits as clear as he could make them. But no help for that now. Clear wits or not, he had to see Thraxton. "Send him in."

"Good day, Lieutenant General," Thraxton said, his tone and expression suggesting that all good days were no more than figments of other men's imaginations. "I have just come from speaking with Count Joseph." His voice got even chillier, no mean feat.

"Good day, your Grace," Bell said. "Is he ever going to use this army of ours, or is he just going to keep running with it?"

"Ah." Thraxton leaned forward markedly. "So you would fight the southrons, then, if the Army of Franklin were in your hands?"

"I sure would, sir." Bell's wits were clear enough to leave him with no doubts on that score. "We could whip those sons of bitches, if the men only had the chance to do it."

"You think so, do you?" Thraxton said.

"Sir, I'm sure of it," Bell replied.

"This is what I had hoped to hear from Joseph the Gamecock," Thraxton the Braggart said. "It is what King Geoffrey has been hoping to hear from Joseph through this whole campaign. He has not heard it. I did not hear it. That being so, I am authorized to remove Count Joseph from his command here."

"And?" Bell could say no more than that, and even the one word came out as a breathy whisper.

"And," Thraxton continued sourly, "to offer the said command to you, Lieutenant General, should you prove willing to accept it."

For a moment, Bell thought the laudanum had taken effect all at once, instead of gradually as it usually did. Then he realized joy could bring a feeling as intense as distillate of poppy juice. "Your Grace," he said, "you and his Majesty honor me far beyond my deserts."

"We had better not," Count Thraxton answered. "The kingdom needs you to go forward and beat the southrons. We cannot afford delay—we have had altogether too much of delay—and we cannot afford defeat."

"You may rely on me and on my brave men, sir," Bell said.

"I do, Lieutenant General. The kingdom does," Thraxton the Braggart replied. "It is late in the day, I know, to make this change, but King Geoffrey decided it must be made. He sends you his wishes for good fortune, and for a fresh start in driving the noxious foe from our soil."

When he said *fresh start*, he hesitated as if the words tasted bad. And, when he said them, Bell saw why he himself had the command and Thraxton did not. Thraxton had already failed with the Army of Franklin. He'd proved he did not have good fortune. Maybe Bell would show he did.

"For the kingdom, sir, I will go forward," Bell declared. "Have you yet told Joseph the Gamecock he is removed?"

Thraxton shook his head. "I have not. I wanted to be certain you would accept the command before announcing the change."

"I am glad to accept, proud to accept," Bell said. "Truly, this is a great day." He could feel the laudanum now as it worked its familiar magic, building a wall between his mind and spirits and the ravaged body that had to serve them. But, even though the laudanum usually dulled his feelings as well as his feeling, joy still blazed in his heart: an enormous bonfire of delight.

"May it be so." Count Thraxton didn't sound as if he believed it. He didn't sound as if he believed anything. *He's old and worn out,* Bell thought. *King Geoffrey is right to leave him on the sidelines.* The Braggart went on, "Now that you have accepted your new post, shall we give Count Joseph the news?"

A certain gloating anticipation suffused his voice. *He doesn't like Joseph the Gamecock, either,* Bell realized.

Nobody likes Joseph the Gamecock. King Geoffrey surely doesn't. But then, nobody save King Geoffrey liked Count Thraxton, either.

"Yes, let's." Bell hitched his slow way out of the farmhouse. Thraxton held the door wide for him. "Thanks," Bell said.

"My pleasure," Thraxton replied, though his voice suggested that whatever he knew of pleasure came by hearsay.

"Major Zibeon!" Bell called. When his aide-de-camp appeared, he said, "Fetch my unicorn, if you'd be so kind. I have a call to pay on Joseph the Gamecock."

Zibeon's eyebrows rose. "Is it *that* kind of call, sir?"

"It is indeed *that* kind of call," Bell answered jubilantly. "By the gods, Major, the southrons have seen the backs of the Army of Franklin for the last time."

"Congratulations, sir," his aide-de-camp said. "May everything turn out as well as we hope."

"A worthy prayer," Bell said. "May the gods hear it."

Zibeon hurried away. He returned in short order with Bell's unicorn. Even with laudanum coursing through Bell, mounting was a painful business. Having his aide-de-camp strap him to the beast so he could stay in the saddle was also a humiliation of sorts. But Count Thraxton said, "Your courage does you credit," and Lieutenant General Bell felt better.

Dismounting from the unicorn in front of Joseph the Gamecock's headquarters was harder than getting aboard had been, but Bell managed. Before he and Count Thraxton could go in, Count Joseph came out. He was half a head shorter than either of the men coming to call on him, but in such a transport of fury that he seemed to tower over them. "You son of a bitch. You *son* of a bitch bastard," he snarled at Thraxton. "Gods damn you to the hells and gone, you're here to take my job away, aren't you?"

"Your Grace, King Geoffrey has authorized me to relieve you of command of the Army of Franklin," Thraxton replied. "After discussing the matter with him at length, I am utilizing that authorization."

"Who's in command?" Joseph asked. "You? Gods help the kingdom if that's so. You won one battle your whole stinking career, and you futtered that one away afterwards."

Count Thraxton's sallow face darkened with anger. "Your successor will be Lieutenant General Bell here."

Joseph the Gamecock pointed a finger at Bell. "I know what you're going to do. I know just what you're going to do. You're going to take this army and throw it right at the southrons."

"It's about time someone got some use out of it, wouldn't you say?" Bell returned. "The men will enjoy going forward instead of back."

"I know the other thing you're going to do, too," Joseph said. "You're going to throw this army away. You can't lick Hesmucet by slugging toe to toe with him. You haven't got the men for it."

"If I don't come out and fight, Marthasville will fall," Bell said. "The kingdom can't have that. And the kingdom won't have it, either. I can drive the southrons back, and I will do it."

Thraxton the Braggart nodded approval. "This is the spirit on account of which King Geoffrey chose the brilliant Bell as your successor, your Grace," he told Joseph.

"If he wants spirits, let him go to a tavern," Joseph the Gamecock snapped.

"Shall I give you a formal written order to turn command of this army over to Lieutenant General Bell?" Thraxton asked.

"Don't bother wasting the time. You've told me. I believe you," Joseph said. "Gods help our kingdom—but if the gods were paying any attention to us, they wouldn't have let that idiot of a Geoffrey put this idiot of a Bell in charge of what's been a perfectly good army up till now."

In spite of the laudanum coursing through him, Bell glared at Joseph. "Now see here, sir—"

"Oh, shut up," Joseph told him. "You can't help being an idiot. You're a brave man, and you think that's all there is to being a general. You make a first-rate brigade commander, because then someone with a working brain points you at the enemy and turns you loose. Of course you try to smash everything that's right in front of you. But for maneuver and coordination and sniffing out what the foe intends?" He shook his head. "You haven't a clue and you haven't a prayer."

"You are dismissed from this encampment, General," Bell said through clenched teeth. "If I see you around my army after today, I will kill you on sight."

Joseph the Gamecock bowed. "Always the man of simple—and simpleminded—solutions. You need not fear. Believe me, I want to stay around here no more than you want me in these parts. Do you suppose I *want* to stay close by while you take the army I built back up after Thraxton here ruined it and go out and wreck it again? I'm going up to Dicon, to wait and see if Geoffrey ever decides he needs to pull me off the shelf again." He turned his back and strode into the farmhouse, slamming the door behind him.

"Graceless lout," Count Thraxton muttered.

"He's retreating again, that's all." Bell looked around at the great expanses of tents. "So this is *my* army now, is it?"

"It is indeed," Thraxton replied. "If I may make a suggestion, your first order of business should be naming a wing commander to take your own place."

Bell didn't want anyone making suggestions now that the Army of Franklin belonged to him. But he had to admit that Thraxton's made sense. After a little thought—*he* would be giving the orders now, so who obeyed them didn't matter so much to him—he said, "Brigadier Benjamin should do the job well enough."

"There are a couple of officers by that name in this army," Count Thraxton remarked. "Which of them did you have in mind?"

"Benjamin the Heated Ham, folks call him, on account of what a bad actor he was in the plays at the military collegium at Annasville," Bell answered. "He's served under me through this whole campaign, and done right well. Do you know him?"

"I do." Thraxton's face froze. Always doleful, he now looked as if his entire family were being massacred in front of his eyes. "The gentleman in question and I . . . have been known to disagree."

Since Thraxton the Braggart had been known to disagree with everyone who'd ever had anything to do with him—with the sole, and vital, exception of King Geoffrey—Bell didn't take that too much to heart. "I'll make the appointment anyhow, I think," he said. "He's brave and he's steady and he'll follow orders."

"You are the commander. You must have the subordinates who suit you." Now Thraxton looked as if his wife were being ravished before getting the *coup de grâce*. But he didn't say no, and that was all that really mattered to Bell. Bowing, the Braggart went on, "Now that we have effected the change, I shall withdraw. You know what his Majesty expects of you. Gods grant that you deliver it."

"Thank you, sir," Bell said. He dipped his head instead of bowing; on two crutches and one leg, the latter was too awkward and painful to contemplate. As Count Thraxton mounted his unicorn, Bell looked around and called, "Runners!"

"Sir!" They hurried up and saluted as they came to attention before him.

"You!" He pointed at one: "Fetch me Roast-Beef William. And you!" He pointed to a second: "Get me Alexander the Steward. And you!" This to a third: "Order Benjamin the Heated Ham to report here at once."

"Yes, sir!" The three men he'd chosen saluted again and hurried away. When he called, they came; when he pointed, they went. The power was as heady as laudanum.

Once his wing commanders had all come to the headquarters formerly belonging to Joseph the Gamecock, Bell spoke without preamble: "Gentlemen, King Geoffrey has removed Count Joseph from command over the Army of Franklin and set me in his place."

"Congratulations, sir," Roast-Beef William said. He was a reliable old war unicorn, and would serve well under whoever commanded him.

"Congratulations indeed," Alexander the Steward echoed. Old Straight was reliable, too; however much Bell disliked Joseph, he'd picked a fine replacement for the late, unlucky Leonidas the Priest.

"As my first act in command," Bell went on, "I am pleased to appoint Brigadier Benjamin here to take my place as wing commander."

"Thank you very much, sir," Benjamin murmured. "I'll do my best to live up to your bold example." He still had a tendency to overact. Since he was flattering Bell, the new commander of the Army of Franklin didn't take it amiss.

As if on cue, Roast-Beef William asked, "And what will your *second* act in command be, sir?"

Bell gave a one-word answer: "Attack!"

General Hesmucet eyed the northern prisoner, a thin, dirty man in ragged blue tunic and pantaloons. "This had better be the truth from you," he growled. "If you're lying, you'll end up wishing for the seven hells before you go to 'em."

"So help me gods," the prisoner said. "It's like I told that other southron bastard—Joseph the Gamecock's out and Bell's in, sure as I'm standing here."

"Well, well." Hesmucet whistled softly. "That's big news, if it's true." He turned to the southrons who had charge of the prisoner. "Keep him by himself. Hang on to him. If he turns out to be telling the truth, we'll let him loose. If he's lying . . ." He slashed his thumb across his throat.

"Yes, sir," the guards chorused. One of them gave the prisoner a shove. "Come on, you. You heard the general."

Later that day, a man who still favored King Avram and a united Detina sneaked out of Marthasville and past the traitors' lines. He not only brought the same news as the prisoner but had a paper to prove it. Hesmucet read Joseph the Gamecock's farewell order to the Army of Franklin and that of Lieutenant General Bell on assuming command.

"Well, well," Hesmucet said again, and nodded to his spy. "Thanks very much. This is worth a good deal to me."

The man eyed him. "I thought you'd be more excited about the news."

"Who, me? No, I don't get very excited," Hesmucet answered—a great, thumping lie if ever there was one. But he didn't want to discourage the northerner from bringing more news, either, if he got it. "I'll pay you twenty—in silver." That made the fellow's eyes glow—real money was in short supply in King Geoffrey's dominions, which were trying to get by with printed paper . . . and were watching prices soar up and up as a result. Hesmucet scribbled a note on a scrap of paper. "Take this to the paymaster, and he'll see to it."

"Thank you kindly, sir." Courtly as most northerners, the

spy bowed before going on his way. Hesmucet touched a
forefinger to the brim of his hat in reply.

Calling for runners, he ordered them to summon his wing
commanders to his headquarters. When they got there, he
waved the paper at them and said, "Geoffrey's sacked
Joseph the Gamecock and put Bell in his place."

"I doubted even Geoffrey would be such a fool," Lieutenant General George said.

Fighting Joseph beamed at the prospect of no longer
moving against his namesake. "Now maybe the traitors won't
scuttle from one line of trenches to the next," he said. "I
want to come to grips with them."

*The last time you came to grips with them, it was at
Viziersville, and Duke Edward tore you to pieces,* Hesmucet
thought. He glanced toward his youngest wing commander.
"You were at Annasville with Bell, weren't you, Brigadier?"

"Yes, sir," James the Bird's Eye replied. "I think Fighting Joseph's right this time." That made Fighting Joseph
preen, as Hesmucet had known it would. James went on,
"Bell is courageous in the extreme. No one could ever doubt
that."

"If he weren't," Doubting George said, "he wouldn't keep
leaving pieces of himself on one battlefield or another."

"Er—yes." James coughed, then went on, "He's also as
bold as you please, bold to the point of rashness."

Hesmucet grunted. "That matches what I've heard about
the man myself. So what do you think it means that false
King Geoffrey's removed Joseph the Gamecock and put Bell
in charge of the traitors' army?"

"A fight." The three wing commanders might have been
singing in a chorus.

"I agree," Hesmucet said. "Joseph sparred with us and
held us off and stalled as best he could, and we've made
it up to Marthasville anyhow. Unless I miss my guess altogether, Geoffrey thinks Bell can drive us away."

"Proves he's a fool," George said.

"We need to warn all our brigade commanders to be
ready for anything the traitors may throw at us," Hesmucet
said.

Fighting Joseph struck a pose. "We can lick them. For

the sake of the army, for the sake of the kingdom, we shall lick them."

"Of course we'll lick them," Hesmucet said. "If Bell thinks he can dislodge us, he's foolish or desperate or both. But he has a better chance if he catches us by surprise, and so the warnings will go out." He gave his unruly wing commander a hard stare. "I trust you don't object?"

"Oh, no, sir. You go right ahead." Fighting Joseph's invincible self-regard armored him against sarcasm.

"Anything else, gentlemen?" General Hesmucet asked. No one said anything. Hesmucet nodded. "All right, then. You're dismissed—and do spread the word to your brigade commanders. Brigadier James, please stay a bit, if you'd be so kind."

"Certainly, sir," James the Bird's Eye replied. "What have you got in mind?"

"Let's take a look at the map, and I'll show you," Hesmucet answered. He drew his sword to point at the large map spread out on a table. "You're already on our left wing, farther north and farther west than any of our other formations."

"Yes, sir." James grinned. "I like to be at the edge of things—the cutting edge of things, you might say." He set a hand on the hilt of his own sword.

Hesmucet smiled, too. "I know. That's why I've used your wing so often to flank the traitors out of their positions. I want you to make what's more or less another flanking move, over to your left again, so that you seize the glideway coming into Marthasville from Julia. Do you think you can do it?"

"I expect I can, sir," the young wing commander answered. "Only problem I see with the move is that it's liable to open a gap between my men and Fighting Joseph's. Do we want to do that when the northerners have a new commander who's going to be looking for a chance to attack?"

"Hells, yes, we do," Hesmucet answered without the least hesitation. "The faster Bell comes out of his trenches and fights, if that's what he intends to do, the happier I'll be. I'll give him bait, if he's fool enough to take it."

"Ah." James the Bird's Eye nodded. "Fair enough, sir."

He eyed the map again, then said, "There is one other drawback to this, you know."

"Oh, certainly. I see it, too," Hesmucet said. "He can concentrate his men wherever he does decide to attack, which makes him stronger there than we are."

"Yes, sir. That's what I meant," James said.

"Thought so," Hesmucet said. "But the other side of that coin is, he's weakening himself along every other part of his line. And he won't be the only one doing the attacking. We'll keep him busy, I promise you."

"Good, sir. I expected as much." James the Bird's Eye grinned, which made him look even younger than he really was. He was tall and handsome and brave, too. Hesmucet, not far past forty himself, felt positively decrepit when he considered his dashing wing commander. "Whatever they do, sir, we'll deal with them," James promised.

"That's what we're here for," Hesmucet said. "They had their chance after the battle by the River of Death. They had it, and they bungled it. Now it's our turn—and, by the gods, I don't think they can stop us."

After James the Bird's Eye had left, Hesmucet went out of his headquarters and stared north toward Marthasville. He could see the city clearly. He could also see the traitors' lines that still, despite everything, held his men away from the town at which they'd aimed for so long. How much more could Bell stretch his smaller army? He would have to do *something* to counter James the Bird's Eye's next outflanking move.

James expected Bell to attack. And James knew him better than any other southron general—or, at least, better than any other under Hesmucet's command. Everyone else agreed with the young wing commander, too. "Come ahead," Hesmucet murmured eagerly. "You come right on ahead." If Bell obliged him, he wouldn't complain. No, he wouldn't complain at all.

He snapped his fingers and called for a runner. *Wouldn't do to make a stupid mistake like that,* he thought. *Don't want to let the traitors have an easier time than they ought to.*

When the runner returned, he brought Colonel Phineas,

puffing, in his wake. Phineas saluted. "Reporting as ordered, sir," the army's senior mage said. He took off his hat and used it to fan his round, bald head.

"Good to see you, Colonel," Hesmucet said. "I've just got word that Joseph the Gamecock has been replaced by Lieutenant General Bell at the head of the Army of Franklin."

"By the gods!" Phineas exclaimed. "Are you certain, sir?"

"It's in a Marthasville paper. I can't be much more certain than that," Hesmucet answered. *If I had really good mages working for me, they would have let me know before I found out from a prisoner or a spy,* he thought. Perhaps that was unfair; the northerners' wizards would have been doing everything they could to keep news from leaking out. But only Alva could have hoped to penetrate whatever deceptions they were spreading, and Alva hadn't thought to look.

Phineas said, "This will probably change the way the campaign is going. Doesn't Bell have a name for being a more, ah, aggressive fighter than Joseph?"

"That's exactly why I called you here, Colonel," Hesmucet said, pleased to see even so much wit from Phineas. "Everyone's best guess is that there will be an enemy attack, and soon. I suspect the traitors will try to hit us with their magecraft as well as with their soldiers."

"That does seem very likely, yes, sir," Phineas agreed.

"I want you to have all your mages on alert, too, to be ready to beat back such assaults," Hesmucet said. "I have confidence in our crossbowmen and pikemen and unicornriders. And I have confidence in the wizards with us."

Sourly, Colonel Phineas said, "You have confidence in Major Alva, you mean. The rest of us are just here to watch him."

That was, in large measure, true. Even so, Hesmucet shook his head. Phineas and the other southron wizards did have *some* use, and disheartening them would make that less true. The commanding general said, "Major Alva will be busy, but so will the rest of you."

"To fetch and carry for him." Yes, Phineas was sour, all right.

Hesmucet shook his head. "By no means, Colonel. Major Alva is best at striking back against the traitors. The rest of you will keep them from striking at us. He is sword, you are shield. We need both."

"Hmm." Phineas considered that. "Very well, sir. You may rest assured that all of us—and I mean *all*—will do everything in our power for the kingdom."

"Thank you," Hesmucet said. Phineas' feathers remained ruffled, but perhaps not so much now. Hesmucet waved toward the north. "We can see Marthasville from where we stand. We had better not let it slip through our fingers now."

"I could hardly disagree with that, sir." Phineas bowed stiffly. "We shall give you what you require, to the best of our ability."

"Can't ask for more than that." Hesmucet clapped the tubby wizard on the shoulder. "Let all the men who share your art learn what I want of them."

"Yes, sir," Phineas said. "We'll do everything we can, sir."

"I know that. I've known that all along." Hesmucet clapped the mage on the back again, hard enough to stagger him this time. *Without Alva, it wouldn't be enough,* Hesmucet thought. *When we didn't have Alva, the traitors' wizards always got the drop on us. Well, no more, by the gods.*

Phineas made more promises that he and his sorcerous colleagues might or might not prove able to live up to. Hesmucet made more polite protestations that he didn't really mean. At last, with what seemed like relief, Phineas decamped. With what Hesmucet knew to be relief, he watched the wizard waddle away.

He looked toward Marthasville once more. *One thing at a time,* he thought. *Let James the Bird's Eye get a solid stranglehold on the glideway line to Julia. Then I'll send Doubting George over Goober Creek. If we can lick the northerners there, we ought to be able to bring our engines up close enough to start flinging stones and firepots into Marthasville itself.*

He didn't want the fight for the city to come down to a siege. He wanted to storm in and take the place away from the Army of Franklin. He was by nature almost as much an attacker as Lieutenant General Bell over on the other side, and Joseph the Gamecock's delaying campaign had left him badly frustrated. But what he wanted most of all was Marthasville. How he got it didn't really matter. If he had to starve the traitors into yielding, he would do that.

He wasn't sorry to see Joseph the Gamecock go. Joseph had been like one skilled swordsman holding off two as he retreated down a long, narrow corridor. He hadn't let them get past him, not even once; to do so would have been fatal. Now Bell would try to come *up* the corridor against the same two swordsmen, or so everyone assumed.

"Let him come," Hesmucet murmured again. He wasn't a particularly pious man, nor one to send up prayers to the gods at any excuse. The gods, he'd always reckoned, would do as they pleased, and let people pick up the pieces as best they could. This time, though, the general commanding doffed his hat and looked up to the mountain beyond the sky. "Please, Thunderer; please, Lion God. Let him come."

He got no immediate answer to his petition. He'd expected none. No Detinan had seen a heavenly choir in years. Even so, looking north once more, he doubted he would have long to wait before finding out whether the gods were listening.

VIII

Colonel Florizel was almost beside himself with excitement. "Now we get to hit back!" the regimental commander burbled. "Now we get to drive the gods-damned southrons out of our kingdom once for all!"

"Well, your Excellency, we certainly get to try," Captain Gremio answered.

"Bell is a man who knows what fighting's all about," Florizel said. "We'll hit the southrons a lick the likes of which the world has never seen the likes of." He was fond of that phrase; Gremio had heard it before from him. He'd never figured out what, if anything, it meant.

He did know he was worried. "They still have more men than we do, sir. We hurt them more when we made them come at us. It won't be so easy when we go at them, I'm afraid."

"If you're afraid, Captain, you may stay behind," Florizel snapped. "I'll send you back to Karlsburg, if you like, the way King Geoffrey sent Joseph the Gamecock down to Dicon. Joseph was afraid to face the southrons—that's as plain as the nose on my face."

Gremio's ears felt on fire. "Sir, you ought to know I'm

not afraid to advance. I've always gone forward as boldly as anyone, and who can say that I haven't?"

"Very well," Earl Florizel said. "I cannot deny that." By the way he sounded, he wished he could. "But I am going to keep my eye on you, young fellow, you may rest assured of that. A man who grumbles too much is not likely to have his heart in the fighting."

"You'll see, sir," Gremio said grimly. If Florizel was going to watch everything he did, he would have to fight as if his life didn't matter at all to him. And, fighting that way, he was much more likely to lose it. He knew that too well.

"We—our regiment, and Brigadier Alexander's whole wing—have the honor of holding the left," Florizel said. "As the southrons come north over Goober Creek, we're going to drive them back into the stream. You'll have the chance to make good on what you say, Captain. Dismissed."

Fuming, Gremio saluted and walked off. He sat down on a boulder, took out a whetstone, and began honing his sword. He wanted the edge as sharp as he could make it. Every little bit helped.

"Is the attack on, sir?" Sergeant Thisbe asked.

That made Gremio look up. "Oh, yes. It's on," he answered. "We get to swarm out of our trenches and drive the southrons back. So says Colonel Florizel, which means it should be easy, don't you think?"

"I don't know, sir," Thisbe said. "We'd better try *something*, though, don't you suppose, before the southrons surround Marthasville altogether?"

That had no good answer. Gremio wished it did. He said, "We'll do the best we can, that's all. Let's get the men formed up, shall we? I want this company to make everyone who watches it proud."

"We'll do that, sir," Thisbe promised. "How can we help it, when we've got you leading us?"

Gremio's ears got as hot as they had when Florizel scorned him, but for an altogether different reason. Before he could find anything to say, the regimental trumpeters blew *assembly*. He knew what he had to say then, and so did Sergeant Thisbe. They had the company in place before any of the others had formed ranks.

Colonel Florizel didn't look impressed. Florizel, Gremio was convinced, wouldn't look impressed at anything this side of his heroic death. His hand dropped to the hilt of that newly sharpened sword. He might have to oblige the colonel. When the rest of the regiment had assembled, Florizel struck a pose and said, "Boys, with Bell leading us, we're going to chase the gods-damned southrons all the way back to Franklin. Isn't that right?"

"Yes!" The deep, fierce roar stunned Gremio's ears. The men were ready to go forward; that was plain. Whether they could . . . Everyone would find out soon enough.

"We're going to catch the bastards crossing Goober Creek," Florizel went on. "Old Straight's wing—that's ours—and Roast-Beef William's wing'll hit 'em together. And, by the gods, we're going to break 'em! Wait for the brigade's trumpeters to blow, then go forward and don't slow down for anything. Have you got that?"

"Yes!" the men roared again.

"That's all I've got to say, then," Florizel said, and stood down. It wasn't a speech that would have done much in the lawcourts. In the field, it was first-rate. The soldiers cheered and waved their crossbows in the air. Gremio dutifully cheered, too. He drew his sword and waved it. Sunlight glittered off the edge.

A few minutes later, trumpets blew *advance!* "Forward!" Gremio shouted. "We'll lick them!" He didn't know if they could. He *was* sure they would give it a hells of a try.

"Out of the trenches!" one of his men said cheerfully as they swarmed up the sandbagged steps that led to the open country between the lines outside Marthasville and Goober Creek. Gremio waved his sword again, urging his soldiers on. He wasn't so happy to have left the fieldworks himself, but he had his orders and he had to obey them.

Looking to the right, he saw the assembled warriors from Brigadier Alexander's wing and that of Roast-Beef William all advancing together. So many men in blue tunics and pantaloons storming toward the enemy at the same time did go a long way towards inspiriting him. How could King Avram's men hope to throw them back?

When he looked ahead, he got a piece of his answer. The

southrons were already well over Goober Creek and coming north toward Marthasville. Through the dust their advance raised, he saw rank on rank of soldiers in gray. His comrades might have the spirits. The southrons, as usual, had the numbers.

But those numbers might not do them so much good this time. Several rills ran south from Marthasville into Goober Creek. The valleys they'd carved in the red land wouldn't be easy to cross. If one group of southrons got in trouble, their comrades to the right and left wouldn't easily be able to reinforce them. Maybe Lieutenant General Bell hadn't picked too bad a time to advance after all.

"Let's let them hear us!" Gremio shouted. His men loosed the roaring northern battle cry that might have come straight from the throat of the Lion God himself. That cry was often worth brigades in battle. The southrons owned no real answer for it, nor had they ever.

"King Avram!" the enemy yelled. "Freedom!" Some few of the southron soldiers had yellow hair and beards: escaped serfs, most of them. Gremio hated to see blonds in gray uniforms—hated it not only because it argued against everything the north held dear but also because those escaped serfs fought with special ferocity, knowing they were likelier to die on the field than be taken prisoner.

Men from both sides raised crossbows to their shoulders and started shooting. As so often happened, they opened the exchange of missiles before coming into range. Bolts thudded into the ground in front of Gremio and his company. But then the first northern man howled when a quarrel pierced him, and the first southron crumpled as if all his bones had turned to water.

Before long, men on both sides fell like autumn leaves as southrons and northerners volleyed away at one another. Men reloaded as fast as they could, as if one more bolt in the air would slay the last enemy in front of them and let their side storm forward. But, for every southron who toppled, another strode forward to take his place and start shooting at Gremio and his comrades.

Lightning smashed down out of a clear sky. He hoped it would clear the southrons in front of him. But the bolts hit ground where no enemy soldiers stood, or else smote Goober Creek and raised clouds of muddy steam. Gremio cursed. After more than three years of war, the southrons were at last becoming able to match the mages on his own side.

"Onward!" Colonel Florizel yelled, brandishing his own blade. He looked around to see what his captains—and, most especially, Captain Gremio—were doing.

"Onward!" Gremio cried, louder still. He ran toward the southrons. *This is a good way to get killed,* he thought. But his men came after him. *This is a good way to get all of us killed.*

A quarrel hummed past his ear and struck a man behind him with an unmistakable meaty thunk. The fellow didn't even cry out. He must have died while hardly knowing what had happened to him. There were worse ways to go. Gremio had seen too many of them.

And then, quite suddenly, it wasn't a fight of crossbow quarrels any more. It was pikes and shortswords and men cursing and shouting—and screaming as they were hurt, too. Gremio beat aside the gleaming iron head of a pike. Before the fellow who carried the heavy spear could draw back for a second thrust, Gremio leaped forward and lunged. His point pierced flesh.

The pikeman howled, staring down and seeing steel inside him stabbing, stabbing. Gremio yanked back the blade. The point was bloody. That wound, he knew, was likely deep enough to kill, if not by making the southron bleed out then from the festering sure to follow. But the fellow wasn't dead yet, and wouldn't die right away. He managed another thrust at Gremio, who had to skip back smartly to keep from being spitted. Only then did the southron's knees slowly buckle.

"Forward!" Gremio shouted. "We'll push the bastards into Goober Creek!" He did his best to roar as if the Lion God were speaking through his body.

Ferocity—perhaps desperation wasn't too strong a word— propelled the northerners into and then through their foes. Some southrons fell back toward the creek. Others simply fell, and would not rise again. For a few heady minutes,

Gremio thought his comrades might indeed throw the enemy back into the stream and work a great slaughter on him there.

But the southrons had too many men. Those who ran away rallied when they met fresh, unpanicked troopers coming up from the south. And the reinforcements poured a couple of withering volleys of bolts into the oncoming northerners. A good many of King Geoffrey's men had slung or thrown aside their crossbows to fight with shortswords instead. They couldn't match the southrons quarrel for quarrel, as they had before.

"Forward!" Gremio cried yet again, and rushed toward the new and dreadfully steady southron line. The enemy might— likely would—kill him, but Colonel Florizel couldn't complain he was a coward. *The things we do for pride,* he thought sourly, brandishing blood-bedaubed blade.

He looked back over his shoulder. His men kept on following, such of them as remained on their feet. Sergeant Thisbe trotted along only a few paces behind him. Gremio didn't know whether to be proud about that or sad. *You're not just getting yourself killed for no purpose, but all the best men in the company.*

"Shoot!" a southron officer yelled. Another volley tore into the men in blue. Gremio heard the shrieks behind him. He looked back again. What seemed like half the men who had still been on their feet were down.

Sergeant Thisbe waved urgently. "Sir, we can't do it," he called.

"We've got to try," Gremio answered, which meant, *I'm going to die before I retreat without orders.* That was very likely a kind of madness of its own, but it was a madness most men on a battlefield shared. Without such a madness, anyone put in danger of his life would simply run away, and how could kings and generals hope to fight their wars like that?

But, before shouting, "Forward!" again, Gremio looked around for Colonel Florizel. If the regimental commander had already fallen, Gremio got some of his discretion back. He knew what he would do with it, too, for Thisbe was right: the attackers lacked the numbers to go any farther forward.

Florizel waved a sword bloodier than Gremio's. Whatever the earl's flaws, cowardice was not among them. "Good fighting!" he bawled.

"If you say so, your Excellency," Gremio answered.

Then Florizel scowled, not at him but at the southrons. "Gods damn it, I don't think we can shift them," the regimental commander said.

The attack had jolted the southrons, but no more. "What are your orders, sir?" he called to Florizel.

A man of sense, seeing no hope the attack could succeed, would have ordered his men back. Earl Florizel said, "Let's give it one more try, on the off chance I might be wrong." He waved his sword again. "I hate to pull back from such a fine fray."

That stuck Gremio as madness, but what point to saying so? What he did say was the only thing that would have satisfied the colonel: "Forward!" Forward he went, with such men as were still able to go with him.

Two more deadly volleys from the southrons broke the charge before it came to hand to hand. Gremio looked for Florizel, wondering if one of those crossbow quarrels had stretched him dead in the dirt. Somehow, the regimental commander still stood, but only a forlorn corporal's guard stood with him.

"Sir, they won't leave a one of us alive if we stay here much longer," Sergeant Thisbe said urgently.

"If Florizel orders me to die here, then die here I shall," Gremio answered. Thisbe was more practical than that, as sergeants had a way of being. If he stayed, it was only because Gremio did: another species of madness, without a doubt.

At last, even Florizel saw it was hopeless. He ordered the men back toward the works from which they'd erupted. Those who could, obeyed.

Lieutenant General Bell scowled at his wing commanders. Roast-Beef William and Alexander the Steward gave back the exhausted stares of men who had seen too much fighting that day. Bell didn't care how battle-weary they looked. He cared about nothing except the results of that fight.

"You failed me," he growled. "Your men failed me."

"Sir, we did everything we could," Brigadier Alexander said.

"That's the truth—the whole truth and nothing but," Roast-Beef William agreed. "The southrons were there in numbers too great for us to move them. We tried. We did everything we could, everything we knew how to do."

"You failed me," Bell repeated. "Your men have turned craven, on account of cowering too long in trenches. They didn't, they wouldn't, push the attack with the spirit required to destroy the enemy."

"Sir, that is not true," William said. "They fought as bravely as any men could fight—look how many dead and wounded we left on the field."

"If they had fought bravely enough, we would have won," Bell said. "We should have won. We didn't win. What have you got to say for yourselves?"

"Sir, if you're going to attack an army that's bigger than your own, you've got to know the odds aren't on your side," Old Straight said.

"But I had to attack. King Geoffrey insisted on it. That's why Joseph the Gamecock isn't commanding any more," Bell said. The misfortune that had befallen his army couldn't possibly have been his fault. "The soldiers just didn't put enough into it. Otherwise, they would have won."

"Do you want to throw away the whole army, then?" William asked.

"No! I want to drive back the southrons. We have to drive back the southrons," Bell said. "If we don't, they can cut the glideways to Marthasville one by one till they hold the town in the palm of their hand."

"They're already doing it," Brigadier Alexander said. "That move to extend their left flank means they're sitting on the glideway path to Julia. We'll get no more supplies from the west."

"Then we have to drive them back," Bell declared. "It's as simple as that."

"Saying it's as simple as that," Roast-Beef William remarked. "Doing something about it won't be so easy, I'm afraid. When you sent us south against Doubting George, you didn't leave

Benjamin the Heated Ham very many men. He may be able to hold back James the Bird's Eye—but, on the other hand, he may not. He surely hasn't got the numbers he needs to attack."

Bell took the laudanum bottle from his tunic pocket and raised it to his lips. Maybe the drug would shield him from things he didn't care to contemplate. Resentment in his voice, he said, "Hesmucet has no trouble attacking wherever *he* pleases."

Patiently, William answered, "Hesmucet has more men than we do, sir. It's in the nature of things that he can do a good deal we can't."

Brigadier Alexander added, "The one thing wrong with attacks is that they're expensive even when they succeed— and a lot more expensive when they fail."

"Gods damn it, I didn't send you out there to fail," Bell said. He studied the map. "We have to strike a blow against their left. We have to. That will free up the glideway line, and we're holding Marthasville on account of those lines."

"An attack would be splendid, if we had the men to do it," Roast-Beef William said. "But whence will you conjure them up, sir?"

"If we can't do what we'd like to do, we'll do what we have to do," Bell replied. "You pull your men out of the fieldworks south of town, Lieutenant General. March them north and west through Marthasville till they outflank the end of the southrons' line, which is—which has to be— unguarded, up in the air. Attack at dawn, roll them up, and send them back in the direction from which they came."

"As easy as that, sir?" William said tonelessly.

"As easy as that," Bell agreed, taking no notice of the way the wing commander sounded. "It will be a famous victory."

"Sir," William said, "my men fought their hearts out today. The ones who aren't hurt are weary to the bone. Send them marching all through the night and you won't get the best from them come morning."

"I certainly will, because I have to," Bell replied. "The kingdom requires it. Are you telling me it can't be done?

Do you want me to have to tell King Geoffrey it couldn't be done?"

"No-o-o," Roast-Beef William said, drawing the word out as long as he could. "I don't say it *can't* be done. But I do say the odds are steep against it."

"It must be done," Bell said. "I order you to try it. Once we hit the southrons in the flank, they're bound to fold up. And Brigadier Benjamin will give you all the support he possibly can."

"What am I supposed to be doing during all this?" Alexander the Steward asked.

"Hold the southrons away from Marthasville if Doubting George tries to come up from the south," Bell answered. "In those trenches, you can do that."

"I *hope* I can do that," Old Straight replied. "I don't have a whole lot of men left myself, you know, what with one thing and another."

"We all have to do everything we can." Bell's gaze swung back toward Roast-Beef William. "Sunrise. Hit them hard. Roll them up. The kingdom is counting on it."

The veteran wing commander let out a long, sad sigh. At last, after waiting much too long for proper subordination, he nodded. "Yes, sir," he said, somehow contriving to make obedience sound like reproof.

"We'll beat them," Bell said. "We've got to."

"We'll do our best," Roast-Beef William said. "And now, sir, if you'll excuse me . . ." He sketched a salute to Bell and left the headquarters.

Alexander the Steward said, "If I'm going to hold the south-facing fortifications with the men of my wing alone, sir, I'd better get back there and spread them out as best I can." He too gave Bell a salute and departed.

And that left the new commanding general for the Army of Franklin alone in the farmhouse with nothing but the haze of laudanum between him and the knowledge that his first attack had failed. He'd hoped to throw the southrons back into Goober Creek. Instead, his own men were back in the fieldworks from which they'd set out so boldly that morning—those who could come back to the works, at any rate. The knowledge of his failure hurt even more than his ruined arm and his missing leg, and the drug did less to ease that pain.

"We have to beat them," Bell repeated. No one was there to hear him now, or to contradict him. It felt as if saying it were plenty to make it so. He laughed bitterly. If only battles were so easy!

He drank more laudanum to help him sleep. Even so, he woke up in the middle of the night. At first, he thought the noise he heard was rain pounding on the roof. He wouldn't have minded that; it would have made moving harder for Hesmucet and the southrons. But what he heard wasn't the patter of rain. It was the patter of feet: Roast-Beef William's men tramping past by moonlight, to take their positions for the morning's attack against James the Bird's Eye and the southrons' left.

Good old William, Bell thought drowsily. *He may not think I'm right—he doesn't think I'm right—but he'll follow orders anyway, and follow them as well as he knows how. I wish all my officers were so reliable.* He fell back to sleep with a smile on his face.

Even before sunrise, the distant racket of battle woke him: bowstrings snapping, firepots bursting, men screaming and cursing for all they were worth. That racket was the sweetest music Bell knew. When he cursed, it was in frustration because his wounds no longer let him take the field. He'd never felt more like a man than when risking his life and taking those of his foes. His injuries had robbed him of that forever.

Those injuries clamored for his notice, too. He reached out with his good hand and grabbed the laudanum bottle, which sat on a table next to his bed. Yanking the cork with his teeth, he swigged. Before long, the fire in his shoulder and in his stump would ease.

Even before it did, though, someone pounded on the farmhouse door. "Just a minute," Bell shouted. Getting out of bed wasn't easy. He had to position his crutches and then lever himself upright. He didn't bother putting on his one boot, but hitched across the dirt floor on the crutches and his bare foot. He unlatched the door and eyed the runner waiting there. "Well?" he demanded.

"We're driving 'em, sir," the runner told him. "We're driving 'em like hells, pushing 'em back like nobody's business."

"Ah," Bell said. That felt as good as the laudanum now beginning to glide through his veins. "Give me the details."

"Haven't got a whole lot of 'em, sir," the soldier answered. "I expect you'll hear more later on. But I know for a fact there's places where we're shooting at the gods-damned southrons from the front and the back at the same time."

"That's good," Bell said, which would do for an understatement till a bigger one came along. "That's very good. If we can drive them to destruction, the entire campaign looks different."

"Hope so, sir," the runner said. "Plenty of good fighting—I'll tell you that." He saluted and hurried away.

Bell wished he were at the head of the wing attacking the southrons, not Roast-Beef William. Nothing made him feel more truly alive than roaring like a lion and flinging himself at the enemy. When his sword bit . . . Feeling steel pierce foe's flesh had a satisfaction even feeling his own lance pierce a woman's flesh couldn't match. He muttered a curse under his breath. With all the laudanum he drank, his lance didn't stand and charge the way it had before he got hurt, either.

That made him remember that attackers as well as defenders *could* get hurt. He forgot that whenever he could. Attacks went in. If they went in properly, they carried everything before them. So he'd made himself believe. It had always—well, almost always—worked for Duke Edward of Arlington and the Army of Southern Parthenia. It had worked for Earl James of Broadpath here in the east at the River of Death. It had worked there even if that fight cost Bell his leg.

That it had worked in those places and for those commanders because the said generals picked their spots and timing with care never entered Bell's mind. To him, such things were of scant importance. Coming to grips with the southrons and hammering them—that was what really mattered.

His hand fell to the hilt of his sword. He cursed again.

For him nowadays, it was—it had to be—a purely ceremonial weapon. He still wanted to kill southrons, but anything that moved faster than a tortoise was safe from him. He couldn't even duel if his honor was affronted. Who would fight a cripple?

Another messenger galloped up on unicornback. The man dismounted and hurried to the farmhouse. "We're still pushing 'em hard, sir," he said when Bell opened the door for him. "Gods-damned sons of bitches are digging like moles, though. Every time we drive 'em another furlong or two, bastards run up another set of earthworks and make us charge 'em. They're usually good for a couple volleys before we reach 'em and clear 'em out, too. Makes the job expensive, but we're doing it."

"Of course we are," Bell said heartily. "We'll lick them right out of their boots. Once we do that, we can count the cost."

Joseph the Gamecock, that old cheeseparer, had counted the cost before he tried to buy his battles, and so he'd never spent the men winning them would have taken. Bell didn't care if he bankrupted himself winning the first. Everything after that would just have to take care of itself.

"Keep hitting them," he told the messenger. "That's the order. We've got to keep hitting them, no matter what."

"Yes, sir," the fellow said, and went back to his unicorn at the run. Clods of rust-colored dirt flew up from under the white beast's hooves as it galloped away.

All Lieutenant General Bell could do was wait for messengers to bring him news of what was happening to the northwest. If Roast-Beef William didn't throw the southrons back from the glideway leading to Julia . . . Bell shook his head. He wouldn't think about that. He refused to think about that.

As morning wore away and afternoon came on, the news the messengers brought was less and less anything Bell wanted to hear. The southrons had stiffened. "We're hitting 'em with everything we got, sir," one man said, "but we ain't got enough. Maybe if we wasn't so worn from marching all night to get to where we needed to be at so as we could hit 'em at all . . . But there's a lot of them bastards, and they don't want to move."

"But they have to!" Bell exclaimed, as if he could push the southrons off the glideway with his one good arm.

With a mournful shrug, the messenger went his way. Bell stared off to the northwest. Men marching and countermarching had raised a great cloud of dust, by which he could tell where the fighting was taking place, but not, try as he would, how it was going. He drummed the fingers of his good hand against his crutch and waited for another messenger to bring more news.

Before long, one did. Even as he rode up, he shouted in excitement: "Lieutenant General Bell! Lieutenant General Bell!"

"What is it?" Bell barked. "What's the word?"

"We've killed James the Bird's Eye, sir," the messenger exclaimed. "The southrons' wing commander's dead as shoe leather, gods damn the son of a bitch to the seven hells!"

"What?" General Hesmucet stared at the messenger in dismay. "James the Bird's Eye dead? I don't believe it!"

"I'm afraid it's true, sir," the southron unicorn-rider said. "Gods damn those traitor sons of bitches to the seven hells, but they shot him right off his unicorn while he was riding toward the thick of the fighting."

"That sounds like him. That sounds just like him, in fact." Hesmucet shook his head in dull wonder. "But dead? That's dreadful! He can't even be thirty-five. He's . . . he was . . . strong and brave and handsome, and everybody likes—liked—him. He was a noble man, and I'm sure King Avram would have made him a nobleman had he lived. What are the gods thinking of, to let him die so young?"

"I'm afraid I don't know how to answer that, sir," the messenger replied.

Hesmucet didn't know how to answer it, either. He knew what Major Alva would have said: that the gods paid much less attention to earthly affairs than people were in the habit of thinking. Hesmucet didn't like to hear such things. But when an officer who had everything to live for stopped a crossbow quarrel, he couldn't help wondering whether Alva had a point.

The rider pointed back towards a unicorn-drawn ambulance coming down from the northwest. "Sir, I don't know for a fact, but I believe that's his body in there."

Seeing the ambulance made hope rise in Hesmucet. "Maybe he's not dead. Maybe he's only wounded," the commanding general said. The messenger shook his head, but Hesmucet shouted for a healer.

As soon as the ambulance stopped, a couple of men removed James the Bird's Eye's body from it. One look told Hesmucet the young wing commander would never rise again. Hesmucet had seen enough corpses the past three years and more to have no doubt when he saw another. The healer stooped beside James, then looked up at the general commanding. "Through the heart, sir, I'm afraid," he said. "It would have been over very fast, if that's any consolation."

"Not fornicating much," Hesmucet snapped. And then, as he had to, he thought about the battle still unfolding. "Who's in command now on the left?" he demanded of the messenger.

"Baron Logan the Black, sir," the man replied. "We're holding pretty well—you don't need to worry about that."

Hesmucet only grunted. Baron Logan had turned out to make a pretty good soldier, but Hesmucet didn't like the idea of having him as a wing commander. He wasn't a professional warrior, but a noble from King Avram's home province who'd got himself a brigadiership in exchange for loudly and publicly backing the king and recruiting soldiers. The southron army, in Hesmucet's view, had too many officers like that. He couldn't do anything about it right this minute, but he intended to when he could.

Another messenger came galloping up. "Baron Logan's compliments, sir, and he wants you to know the traitors are stopped. He expects to start driving them back any time now."

"That's good news," Hesmucet said, and meant it. "Give him my compliments in return, and tell him the northerners deserve every single thing that happens to them."

"Yes, sir." The messenger didn't even waste time saluting. He set spurs to his unicorn. The beast snorted angrily as he forced its head around and urged it back to a full gallop to deliver Hesmucet's reply.

The commanding general called for a messenger of his own. When the man came up to him, he said, "Give my regards to Lieutenant General George and ask him if it's possible, with the traitors so heavily engaged in the northwest, for him to go straight through their defenses to the south of Marthasville and into the city. Give me that back, so I'm sure you have it straight."

After repeating the message, the runner hurried away. When he returned, he said, "Lieutenant General George says he's already probed the line south of Marthasville, sir. He says it's too strong to break through like that."

"All right." Hesmucet wondered if it was really all right, and how hard Doubting George really had poked at Bell's line there. George was as stalwart a warrior as the gods had made when fighting on the defensive, but, to Hesmucet's way of thinking, lacked the push, the drive, of a good attacker.

That's why Marshal Bart made me commander here in the east, he thought. *I've come this far. Another few miles and I'll have done a big part of what he wanted of me.* He scowled in the direction of Marthasville. The traitors had hung on to the place altogether too long, as far as he was concerned.

It didn't fall that day. By the time the sun set, James the Bird's Eye's men—no, Logan the Black's now—had indeed driven Bell's blue-clad warriors back into the lines from which they'd started their attack. A messenger said, "The enemy must have lost twice as many men as we did, too."

"He threw away a lot of soldiers, then," Hesmucet said musingly. "Add those in with all the men he lost yesterday, and with his having fewer than we do to begin with, and how many has he got left?"

"I'm sorry, sir, but I couldn't begin to tell you," the messenger replied.

"Never mind," the general commanding told him. "I didn't expect you to know. But I wonder if my wing commanders do."

With the fighting having died down, he summoned Doubting George, Logan the Black, and (with a mental sigh) Fighting Joseph to his headquarters to talk things over. Logan proved to be younger than he'd remembered—hardly older than James the Bird's Eye, in fact—with a ruddy face, fierce eyes, and a piratical black mustache.

"Yes, sir. They hurt us," he said frankly. "We didn't really expect another strong sally, not when they were thrown back with loss yesterday. It was worrisome out there for a while, when they came close to turning our flank. But we were steady, and we made them pay for coming out of their works."

"So you've already reported, your Excellency," Hesmucet replied. "I'm glad to learn you did so well."

Doubting George said, "Taking it all in all, they must have left a third of their men on the field the last two days. And they didn't have that many to begin with."

He might not have been aggressive enough to suit Hesmucet, but he'd done sums in his head, too. And the answer he reached wasn't far different from the one that had formed in the commanding general's mind. Hesmucet said, "It's only a matter of time now."

"I think you're right, sir," George said, nodding. "Now we can push to the east of Marthasville or to the west, go up north of the place on either side just as we choose, and Bell won't be able to stop us. The most he can do with what he has left, as I see it, is sit tight and stand siege."

"If he does that, he's mine, and so is his whole fornicating army," Hesmucet said. "I'll take it clean off the board, the same as Marshal Bart took Camphorville on the Great River and its defending host last year."

"I don't believe Bell will do that," Logan the Black said. "He's a swinger, a puncher. He'll keep trying to hit us for as long as he can."

"Good," Hesmucet said. "The more he wastes his force, the sooner he won't be able to strike with it at all. I always worried about Joseph the Gamecock. He held his men in. If I'd made a mistake against him, he kept the wherewithal to make me pay for it. But Bell? Bell's thrown away as many good men the past two days as Joseph did during the whole campaign from Borders all the way up to here."

His subordinates nodded. Not even Fighting Joseph could disagree with that. George said, "Bell's a first-rate man to command a brigade. Point him at the foe, turn him loose, and he'll hit hard. But put him in command of an army? Of an army trying to hold off a bigger army? I don't know what false King Geoffrey was drinking when he thought of that, but I hope they serve him more of it."

Logan the Black nodded. "Well said. Our foes' mistakes go a long way toward making this an easy fight for us."

"They can't afford to make mistakes, not any more," Doubting George agreed. "We have the luxury of greater strength, which lets us make our errors good." He dipped his head to Hesmucet. "Not that we've made many on this campaign."

"For which I thank you," Hesmucet replied. If George said a thing like that, he had to mean it, which made the compliment doubly pleasing. Hesmucet went on, "Now there is one other bit of business that wants doing. Brigadier Logan, I am grateful for how well you fought James' wing, but I do not intend that you keep command of it."

"And why not, if I fought it well?" Logan demanded. He was a proud man, and he *had* done his duty and more than his duty. Hesmucet would have to handle him carefully.

He said, "My main reason, Brigadier, is that you are not a professional. Meaning you no disrespect, but I find it easier to deal with men who have been through Annasville, as I have."

"Plenty of them, on both sides of this war, have proved themselves to be idiots," Logan said tartly.

"True enough, your Excellency, but you could also say the same for officers who haven't been through the military collegium," Hesmucet replied. "I am pleased to have you as a brigade or division commander. As a wing commander . . . I'm sorry, Brigadier, but no, not permanently."

However proud he was, Logan took it like a man. "It's your army, General. You *will* have your way here. If you think I'm going to tell you I'm happy about it, you're mistaken. And now, sir, if you'll excuse me . . ." Saluting, he spun on his heel and strode out of the headquarters.

"You did the right thing, sir," Fighting Joseph said. Approval from him was the last thing Hesmucet wanted. Striking a pose, Fighting Joseph went on, "Now you can consolidate your forces. An army of only two wings—led by your two senior commanders—would surely be more efficient than one of three."

And it would double the size of the force you command, which is what you've got in mind, Hesmucet thought. Aloud, he said, "I find myself reasonably satisfied with the command arrangements as they exist at present."

"Do you indeed, sir? Do you indeed?" From Fighting Joseph's tone, Hesmucet might have expressed a fondness for scratching his backside in public or eating with his fingers. More scornfully still, Fighting Joseph said, "And who could possibly replace James the Bird's Eye?" *Who but me?* he all but shouted.

"If you must know, I had in mind Brigadier Oliver," Hesmucet replied.

Now Fighting Joseph frankly stared. "Oliver? You must be joking . . . sir. I hope you're joking. Oliver the blond-lover? Oliver the gods-drunk? Oliver with his right arm gone? Lion God's twitching tail, it'd be like putting a cross between Bell and Leonidas the Priest in charge of a wing."

"No." Hesmucet shook his head. "Oliver's pious, but he knows soldiering as well as he knows the gods. And he's not brash and rash, the way Bell is. He thinks before he moves."

"I agree," Doubting George said. "Before the war, I thought Oliver was a horrible windbag, and I wished he would quit blathering on about loosing the blonds from the soil. But that is King Avram's policy now, so we all needs must follow it. And Brigadier Oliver is a more than capable soldier, as the commanding general said."

"Giving that wing to such an untried man—and a junior untried man—is an outrage when senior officers are available," Fighting Joseph insisted. "Not only an outrage, but also a gross injustice."

"I'm sorry, General, but I don't agree," Hesmucet said. "Brigadier Oliver *will* have that wing."

"Disgraceful." Fighting Joseph drew himself up to his full height, which was perhaps an inch less than Hesmucet's. In a voice like thunder, he said, "If that is your final decision, I cannot abide the insult, and must offer my resignation from King Avram's service and from this, his host."

Without a doubt, he thought Hesmucet would find him indispensable and would knuckle under to that threat. Without a doubt, he had never so badly misjudged a situation—which, with Viziersville on his record, was saying a great deal. Hesmucet had all he could do not to chortle with glee. "Lieutenant General George, you are my witness," he said. "Fighting Joseph has tendered his resignation."

"Yes, sir," Doubting George agreed. "I heard him do it."

"And you shall also be my witness that I accept the said resignation, effective immediately," Hesmucet went on.

"Yes, sir," George repeated. "I will so testify, at need."

Fighting Joseph first looked as if he didn't believe his ears, then as if he didn't want to. "How—how dare you?" he spluttered. "How do you think you can manage this army without me?"

"I expect I'll manage," Hesmucet answered. "And, since you've resigned, it's not your concern anyway. A good evening to you, General. I trust you will make a splendid success of yourself in civilian life."

Still looking as if he'd been hit in the head with a rock, Fighting Joseph, having fought for the last time, stumbled out of Hesmucet's headquarters. Hesmucet found a jar of spirits and poured a mug for himself and one for Doubting George. Though he'd lost James the Bird's Eye, his men had held Bell's, and he was rid of Fighting Joseph. He wondered which of those would prove the bigger victory.

"Bell had his chance," Lieutenant General George told his brigadiers. "He had it, and he couldn't do anything with it. Now it's *our* turn, by the gods, and we'll see how well he likes that."

"That's right," Absalom the Bear rumbled. The big man went on, "The traitors have played games with us for too long. I don't believe they've got the men to play games any more."

"We've got Brigadier Oliver pushing up to our left,"

George said. "Now Hesmucet is going to stretch this wing up toward the right, toward the glideway link with Dothan Province and the one with northern Peachtree Province. Once we've got those in our hands, too, how's Lieutenant General Bell going to feed Marthasville?"

"That's simple, sir," Brigadier Brannan said. Doubting George's commander of siege engines paid close attention to logistics. His handsome face twisted into a thoroughly nasty grin. "He won't. Those bastards will starve, and then we'll clean 'em out."

Absalom shook his head. "No, I don't think that's how it'll happen. When we move against the glideway lines to Dothan and to the north of Peachtree Province, Bell will have to come out against us, to try to knock us away. Then we'll lick him, and what can he do after that? Not fornicating much."

"I think you may be right," Doubting George said. "Bell isn't the sort of man who's going to let himself be shut up in a place and stand siege. What he wants to do is get out there and attack."

"Look how much good it did him these past couple of days," Brannan said. "Of course he'll want to go out and try it again."

George shrugged. "He'll just think he had bad luck, or that his soldiers let him down. Attacking is what he knows how to do. It's all he knows how to do. If you send a carpenter out to try fixing something, of course he's going to hammer nails into it, even if it's a blanket with a rip and not a board at all."

"Let Bell come," Absalom said. "Let him come, and we'll pound nails into him."

"We'll pound nails into the boards of his funeral pyre," Doubting George said. "The beauty of our position now is, we don't have to try to break into Marthasville. We can do the traitors every bit as much harm by stretching out past them. And when we do, they have to come out against us and attack our fieldworks. We don't have to try to break through theirs."

"I like that," Absalom the Bear said. "We've had to go up against too many of their earthworks. It might as well be their turn for a while. And I'll tell you something else: the men will like it, too."

"That's a fact," Brannan agreed. "If you're trying to fix wool or rock or water, a hammer's not the right tool for the job."

"We're the ones with the tools for the job now," George said. "Let's get moving and do it. Some of Brigadier John the Lister's men will fill in on our left as we shift."

Brannan smiled. "Good old Ducky. He's reliable, by the Thunderer's prong."

"That he is." Doubting George didn't doubt it in the slightest. When Fighting Joseph resigned because Hesmucet had named Brigadier Oliver commander of James the Bird's Eye's wing rather than giving it to him, that had given the general commanding one more slot to fill. John the Lister— often called by the nickname Brannan had given him—was a thoroughly capable officer, one who did what needed doing without demanding praise before, during, and afterwards. With him on his flank, George felt much happier than he would have with Fighting Joseph there.

George's wing started sliding around to the right, to the east of Marthasville, the next morning. He'd wondered if Bell would try to strike him a blow at once, but the northern soldiers stayed in their entrenchments. Only a few unicorn-riders in blue dogged the southron troops. Doubting George sent his own unicorn-riders forward and drove them away.

"They're only trying to see what we're up to," Absalom the Bear said. "They can't stop us."

"I know that," Doubting George replied. "I don't care. I don't want them seeing anything, either. It might cause us trouble later on."

As his wing advanced, though, he wondered whether anything would cause the southrons in Peachtree Province trouble ever again. Hesmucet had had the right of it: but for Joseph the Gamecock's army and Duke Edward's over in Parthenia, King Geoffrey had little left with which to hold his kingdom together. And, now that Bell had taken the army once Joseph's and smashed it up, little remained to hold back the men in gray as they advanced.

Oh, every now and then squadrons of unicorn-riders or

Peachtree Province militiamen would skirmish with George's vanguard. Sometimes the northerners would have the numbers to slow down George's men for a little while. But all he had to do was send reinforcements forward and the traitors would melt away. They'd spent a couple of months skillfully contesting every inch of ground from Borders all the way up to Marthasville. This ground to the east of Marthasville was as important as any in all of Peachtree Province, but King Geoffrey had not the men to keep Hesmucet from taking it.

Seeing as much amused Absalom the Bear—as much as anything could amuse Lieutenant General George's grim brigadier. "Geoffrey wanted Bell to get out there and fight," Absalom said. "He got out there and he did it—and now, by the gods, Geoffrey has to wish he'd left Joseph the Gamecock in command."

"I doubt that," George said, which made Absalom chuckle. The wing commander went on, "I don't think false King Geoffrey wants Joseph to have anything to do with anything. The only reason he gave him this command in the first place was that he didn't have anybody else to fix the mess Thraxton the Braggart left behind."

"No doubt you're right, sir," Absalom said. "Now who's going to fix the mess Bell's left behind?"

"I don't think anyone can," George replied. "If he stays in the city, we'll flank him out or starve him out. And if he comes forth again, we'll give him another set of lumps and drive him back. He hasn't got the men to push us, not after he's gone and thrown so many of them away."

"There's always magic," Absalom said.

Doubting George wished the brigadier hadn't said that. Sorcery was the one place where the traitors still enjoyed some advantage over King Avram's forces. But even that edge was shrinking. George said, "By what the northerners have shown on this campaign, we can stand up to whatever they throw at us."

"Here's hoping you're right," Absalom the Bear answered. George nodded.

A unicorn-rider came back from the vanguard, reined in, and waited to be recognized. When Doubting George nodded again, this time toward him, he said, "Sir, we've taken some prisoners. Do you want to help question them?"

"Don't mind if I do," the wing commander replied. "Lead the way."

"Yes, sir." The messenger rode to what looked like the farm of a prosperous yeoman or a small baron. Even before George walked into the farmhouse, he could hear cursing—at the same time highly fluent and slightly mushy. At his raised eyebrows, the messenger explained: "One of the fellows we caught is this militiaman, must be fifty-five, sixty years old. He's got false choppers—or he did, on account of he just broke 'em. That's how come he sounds the way he does."

"I . . . see," George said. "He sounds like the fellow I ought to question, don't you think?"

"Whatever you say, sir," the messenger replied. "If if was up to me, I'd knock him over the head and shut him up for good."

"Oh, I don't know," Doubting George replied. "He sounds like he might be fun to listen to for a while."

He walked into the farmhouse. The northern prisoner gave him a baleful stare and demanded, "Who in the hells"—because of his broken false teeth, it came out as *hellsh*—"are you?"

"I am Lieutenant General George, commander of this wing of King Avram's army," George said gravely. "Do I understand you to be a mite discouraged with the northern cause?"

"Discouraged?" the prisoner shouted. "Discouraged?" He spat on the rammed-earth floor. "*That* for the fornicating northern cause. I curse the northern cause, every fornicating piece of it. I curse King Geoffrey and his ministers and his satraps and public men, clean down to the lowest pothouse politico who advocates his cause. I curse the whole fornicating Army of Franklin, from Joseph the Gamecock and Bell the Bloody Butcher down to the mangiest, most miserable jackass. I curse its downsittings and its uprisings. I curse its movements, marches, battles, and sieges. I curse all its paraphernalia, its catapults and its crossbows. I curse its banners, bugles, and drums. And I curse the whole gods-damned institution of serfdom, which brought about this miserable, fornicating war."

By then, the fellow's guards had tears of laughter running down their cheeks. Doubting George held his face straight, which was one of the hardest things he'd ever done. "You are a man of strong opinions, sir," he remarked.

"I know what's what. I know eggs is eggs. I know pigs is pigs," the prisoner said. "And I know we've got pigs in charge of us. Curse 'em all. Curse 'em, and make bacon of 'em, too."

"Dare I ask your view of my side in this conflict?" George inquired.

"Futter you southrons, too," the northern man said at once. "You bastards are winning the war by magic, and where's the fair fight in that?"

"By magic?" George said in surprise. "Your side is the one credited with the stronger sorcerers."

"Unicorn dung!" the prisoner exclaimed. "Stinks like it, too. Our wizards brag. You ever hear tell of Thraxton the Braggart? We brag, but your buggers really do things. We aren't the ones who keep miles and miles of glideway tunnel in our back pantaloon pockets, way you bastards do."

"Glideway tunnel?" Doubting George had never imagined that as something a wizard might keep handy in a pocket.

But it made perfect sense to the prisoner. "We go after your glideways, how else can you fix 'em so gods-damned fast, without you having tunnel right there ready to go and stick it through a hill? Ought to stick it up Bell's backside, is where it ought to go."

He went back to cursing, this time aiming his venom at the new commander of the Army of Franklin. But he'd been dead serious about the tunnels; Doubting George could tell as much. If only such a thing were possible, it would have been a good idea. When the latest string of blasphemies slowed, George asked, "How did you happen to get caught?"

"I got stuck in the mud, gods damn it," the prisoner answered. He wiped at his forehead with a forearm. That dislodged the wig he was wearing. He didn't realize it had gone awry, and looked even more absurd and bedraggled than he had a moment before.

"Would you say you're representative of the soldiers going into Geoffrey's militia these days?" George asked.

"Why shouldn't I be?" the northern returned. "You see anything wrong with me? You saying there's something wrong with me?" He looked comically indignant.

"No, not at all," Doubting George said soothingly. Eyeing the young, strong guards, he contrasted them to their captive. King Avram's dominions still had plentiful reserves of men. False King Geoffrey, on the other hand, was trying to wring a few last drops of water from a dry fleece.

"What are you southron bastards going to do with me?" the prisoner asked.

"Not much," George told him. "We'll feed you a meal—gods know you look like you could use one—and then we'll ship you south to a prisoners' camp. You'll wait there till you're properly exchanged for a southron your side has captured or till the war ends, whichever comes first."

"Can't be over too soon," the prisoner declared mushily. "I want to get back to my life, is what I want to do."

"Don't we all?" Doubting George said. "If Geoffrey hadn't let Palmetto Province start calling him king—"

"Gods damn Geoffrey! Devils fry him for breakfast and roast him for supper," the prisoner said, and he was off again on another wild string of curses.

George decided he didn't need to hear any more. He hadn't really learned anything from the prisoner, save that the man had a remarkably foul mouth. Or so he thought till he went outside and considered the matter for a little while. True, the fellow with the broken false teeth and the wig askew hadn't told him anything about where the northern armies were, how many men they had, or what they intended to do. But did that mean he'd told him nothing?

After a little more thought, Doubting George shook his head. That a scrawny old man had been hauled into the militia at all said something about the straits the north was in. That he hated the man who called himself his king and the commanders set over him said something, too. And if Grand Duke Geoffrey could have heard what it said, he would have shivered, no matter how oppressively hot the weather in Nonesuch was at this season of the year.

"He *will* hear," George murmured to himself. "We'll *make* him hear, and I doubt it will take very long."

Roast-Beef William was not a happy man. His wing had fought its heart out, trying to push the southrons back into Goober Creek. Then the weary men had marched all night before trying to dislodge Hesmucet's left from the glideway line leading to Julia. They hadn't quite managed either feat, but the number of dead and wounded they'd left on the field told how hard they'd tried.

It told Roast-Beef William, at any rate. He couldn't see that the soldiers' effort and suffering meant that much to Lieutenant General Bell, who was glaring at him like the angry lion he resembled. "I don't care how hard they tried," Bell said furiously. "I care that they failed."

"Sir, if you set out to do the impossible, you shouldn't be surprised when you fall short," William said.

"Impossible? No such thing," Bell declared. "If only your men had pressed their second attack, they would have rolled up the stinking southrons and thrown them back in disorder."

"Sir . . ." Roast-Beef William resisted the impulse to pick up his chair and break it over the commanding general's head. "Sir, we'd fought a battle the day before. We'd marched fifteen miles at night with bad guides to get to where we could deliver that second attack. And then, after the way we fought, you complain because we didn't do enough? For shame, sir! For shame!"

"The plan was good. If the plan was good but didn't succeed, that must be the fault of the men who went to carry it out," Bell said.

Sighing, William said, "Sir, the plan was less good than you think. If you attack soldiers in entrenchments when yours are not, you had better have more men than they do, not fewer. They waited for us to get close, and then they shot us down like partridges. You cannot blame our defeats on the brave soldiers who serve us."

"You're wiser in hindsight than you were in foresight,"

Bell said, "for you didn't protest these orders when I gave them."

That held some truth, more than Roast-Beef William cared to think about. He hadn't opposed Bell's first attack, the one that had failed to push the southrons back over Goober Creek. Casting about for some means to defend himself, he said, "I did warn you the men you sent to attack James the Bird's Eye would be too weary to give their best."

"Oh, what a hero you are!" Bell jeered. In defeat, he was proving as bad-tempered and sarcastic as Joseph the Gamecock or Thraxton the Braggart ever had. Criticizing, it seemed, had proved easier than commanding. Camp rumor said Joseph, before departing, had warned that that would be so. However prickly Joseph was, he'd always known a hawk from a handsaw. Bell . . . Roast-Beef William wasn't so sure about Bell.

He wasn't so sure about himself, either. *Maybe I should have protested harder—protested at least some—when Bell sent us south just after he took command,* he thought mournfully. *No: certainly I should have protested.* He knew why he hadn't. Joseph the Gamecock had been sacked because he wouldn't attack. Bell had been installed because he would. King Geoffrey had wanted attacks against the southrons. How could an officer mindful of that oppose them?

Well, the Army of Franklin, or what was left of it, had found the answer to that. Opposing attacks that failed, that might well have been foredoomed, looked like great wisdom in hindsight. With so many men lost, with the southrons not driven away despite those dreadful losses to the northern force, how were they going to hold on to Marthasville? Roast-Beef William had been a soldier and a teacher of soldiers for a long time. That notwithstanding, he had no idea.

Before he could find a way to put any of that into words, a runner came into the house Bell was using as army head-quarters—the house Joseph had used before being sacked. "Sir—" he began, and then, catching sight of William along with the general commanding, fell silent.

"Say on," Bell told him. "Say your say. Roast-Beef William may be a fool, but he is no traitor to the northern cause."

"Sir . . ." That wasn't the messenger; it was Roast-Beef William himself. But he shook his head. What point in quarreling further? When Bell called him a fool, what he meant was, *He disagrees with me.*

"Yes, sir," the messenger said to Bell. "The news is that the gods-damned southrons are moving against the glideway line running north out of Marthasville, the line to Dicon and the rest of the north of this province. They've already overrun the line to Dothan. They're marching on Jonestown, about fifteen miles north of the city, sir, moving on that line in a long loop from out of the east."

"That's the last line into Marthasville we still hold, sir," Roast-Beef William said. "If the southrons seize it, we're as near surrounded as makes no difference."

"I know that." Bell spoke in an abstracted voice, as if from far away. The pupils of his eyes were very small. William had seen that before, when heroic doses of laudanum had had their way with the commanding general.

Another runner dashed in. He stood on no ceremony whatever, saying, "Lieutenant General Bell, sir, the southrons are starting to fling firepots and stones into Marthasville, sir! What are we going to do?"

"They've moved their engines up close enough to reach the town, have they?" Roast-Beef William said. The second runner nodded.

"One thing at a time," Bell said, more to himself than to anyone else. After a moment, he gathered himself and turned to William. "You go with your wing and massacre the southrons by Jonestown. If they're bombarding Marthasville, they can't have sent that many men north. Crush them, hold on to the glideway line leading north, and, as opportunity offers, push east toward the one to Dothan."

"Yes, sir." William saluted. The order struck him as reasonable—more than reasonable, in fact. Holding the glideway lines coming out of Marthasville was the main reason for holding the city itself. Of course, it would have done more good had the Army of Franklin still controlled the lines leading toward Julia and toward Nonesuch. But those were gone, cut by the southrons. No reinforcements or supplies would go to Parthenia along them.

Without the line to Dothan and the one to northern Peachtree Province, though, no reinforcements or—more vital—supplies would get into Marthasville. Hesmucet could sit down and starve the city into submission . . . if he didn't prefer to knock it flat instead.

Bell had the same thought at the same time. "Hesmucet uses us barbarously, to throw stones and fire into a city still full of noncombatants," he said.

"Sir, I would agree," Roast-Beef William replied. "But if he *will* do it, it may work to his advantage, and I see no way for us to *make* him stop it."

"Barbarous," Bell repeated. "Shameless and barbarous." His eyes hardly seemed to have any pupils at all. "I shall drive them away from Marthasville if I see even the smallest chance of doing so."

"Yes, sir," Roast-Beef William said, and then, because he couldn't help himself, "Sir, please do be careful. We've already lost a lot of men. How many more can we afford to throw away?"

"If we triumph, the men are not thrown away." No matter how much laudanum Bell had taken, he still sounded angry. "Joseph the Gamecock *would* not see that, which is why I command."

"If we triumph, yes, sir," William said. "We've hit the southrons two hard blows, and haven't triumphed yet. We need to be able to defend ourselves, too, against the cursed numbers they enjoy."

"This time, we cannot fail. We must not fail," Bell said. "We have to win by the city, and we have to win up by Jonestown. You tend to the second, and I will take care of the first. You may rely on it."

"I do, sir," Roast-Beef William said. "I have to." He strode out of Bell's headquarters before the general commanding could respond to that. Getting out of there also kept him from thinking about how he meant it, which was probably just as well.

Go north to Jonestown. Drive the southrons away from it. Don't let them seize the glideway line to Dicon. Reclaim the one to Dothan. Put like that, it sounded easy. Bell put it no other way. Turning those broad commands into reality was up to Roast-Beef William. So were all the myriad details of putting his wing of the Army of Franklin into motion. Details mattered little—hardly mattered at all—to Bell.

Roast-Beef William found himself unhappier than ever that Joseph the Gamecock was gone. Joseph had cared about details. Joseph had cared so much about leaves and branches and bark, in fact, that he sometimes had trouble remembering there were trees, let alone a forest. To William's way of thinking, that was a lesser failing than barely noticing the forest because one was gazing at the kingdom of which it formed a part.

But no one cared about his way of thinking. King Geoffrey had proved that. *If he decided he had to sack Joseph, why didn't he put me in charge?* William feared he knew the answer. *It's not just that I have no breeding— neither does Bell. But he's a hero—his missing pieces prove it. All I am is a man who can get the job done. And now I have to—again.*

Work with pen and paper saved him a lot of trouble. By the time he called in his brigade commanders, he had at his fingertips the details Lieutenant General Bell hadn't bothered with. He gave them out, crisply and cleanly.

"How many men have the southrons got?" somebody asked.

"That I don't know," Roast-Beef William admitted unhappily. "But I must be of the opinion that their force is not overlarge. How could it be, when they're operating fifteen miles north of Marthasville at the same time as they're keeping the assault against the city in progress?"

No one argued with him. Had the southrons not had a large host, they wouldn't have been able to operate in two such widely separated places at the same time at all. As far as William was concerned, Marthasville itself remained the most important target. This business of Jonestown was bound to be a distraction, a harassment, nothing more. Once he'd dealt with it, he could bring his wing back up to the city, to aid in the defense.

"Any more questions?" he asked. Hearing none, he nodded. "Very well, gentlemen. You know what's required of you. I expect you will all do your duty, and all do it handsomely. Dismissed. We move in the morning."

Some of the soldiers boarded carpets and went north up the glideway. Others moved by road; not enough carpets remained in Marthasville to transport his entire wing. He sent the men who would have to march up to Jonestown off ahead of those who would ride on the carpets: they would travel more slowly, and he wanted his entire force, such as it was, to get there at the same time.

Bell wouldn't think of such a thing, went through his mind as he mounted his own unicorn and rode off at the head of a column of marchers. *If some got there before the rest, he would throw in an attack with what he had and hope the latecomers could support it. No wonder we're in the state we're in.*

Again, he wished the whole army might have been his. The only answer to that was a shrug of his broad shoulders. What he wished didn't matter. What King Geoffrey wished did. So the gods had made it. That was what the priests said, at any rate. Roast-Beef William couldn't help thinking the gods had made some extraordinarily sloppy arrangements for the north.

He peered. He saw no great clouds of smoke rising into the hot, muggy air. Either the southrons hadn't yet got to Jonestown or no one was in the way to slow them down. He hoped for the former and feared the latter.

When he reached Jonestown, he found with some considerable relief that his hope was fulfilled: the southrons weren't there yet. But when he sent scouts eastward, probing toward the glideway that led to Dothan and away toward the Great River, those scouts promptly came back, bloodied. "A whole great plenty of them bastards in gray," was how one of them put it.

Roast-Beef William thought about pushing on regardless. Lieutenant General Bell would have; he was sure of that. *To the hells with Lieutenant General Bell,* he thought. *My orders don't require me to push on this instant, and I don't intend to. If Hesmucet and his wing commanders want me, let them come here and try to get me.*

"Dig in, men," he called. "Let's make sure we have a safe place before we go gallivanting around the landscape."

By the way his soldiers fell to with spade and pick, they were relieved to get an order like that. They knew the value of earthworks, even if the general commanding the Army of Franklin had yet to figure it out. A trooper with several scars said, "Now we got a nest. If we see our chance, we can fly out. Or we can make those other bastards try and break in."

"That's right," Roast-Beef William said. "That's just exactly right. As long as the numbers are anywhere close to even, we can keep the southrons off the glideway line and out of Jonestown."

A tiny alarm bell rang inside his mind. He knew only too well how many men his wing had lost during the fighting south and then west of Marthasville. He didn't know how many the southrons had lost, only that they hadn't suffered proportionately. And he knew they'd had more men to begin with, and enjoyed a steady stream of reinforcements. *I wish I had the wherewithal General Hesmucet does,* he thought enviously. *People would reckon me a great soldier, too.*

But he couldn't have that sort of wherewithal, which he also knew only too well. He had to make a few tired men into the equivalent of a host of fresh ones. Earthworks helped. And, if he saw the chance, he *would* strike out from them, strike toward the glideway line leading east to Dothan and beyond.

Maybe we'll get it back, he thought. *Maybe things will go just right. They have before, every once in a while.* But when a man had to count on it . . . Roast-Beef William grimaced. When a man had to count on it, his kingdom was in trouble.

IX

"**C**orporal Rollant!" Lieutenant Griff called.

"Yes, sir!" Rollant answered, saluting.

"Take up the standard, Corporal, for we're moving out soon," Griff said.

"Yes, sir!" Rollant repeated. After offering the ritual gestures of respect to the company's banner, he lifted the staff from where it had been thrust into the ground the night before. The company—Colonel Nahath's whole regiment— was part of General Hesmucet's great wheeling move against the glideway lines north of Marthasville. Southron soldiers had already overrun the line leading east to Dothan. Southron mages were now busy putting that line out of commission, so that the traitors could get no use from it even if they took it back.

But Rollant didn't think false King Geoffrey's men would be able to do anything of the sort. The northerners hadn't been able to do much to slow down the great wheel. If they couldn't manage that, how would they make the southrons retreat?

"Jonestown coming up," Smitty said around a yawn. He didn't seem ready for another day's march.

"Jonestown!" Rollant snapped his fingers. "That's the name of the place. It went clean out of my head. If we grab that one, too, the traitors won't have any glideways into Marthasville, will they?"

"Nary a one," Smitty agreed. "But I hear tell there are already northerners around the place, so we're going to have to fight our way in."

"That's the truth," Sergeant Joram said. "I've talked with pickets who bumped up against them. They're from Roast-Beef William's wing, but nobody knows how many of 'em are in the town."

"Doesn't matter how many there are," Smitty said cheerfully. "We'll lick 'em."

A year earlier, a boast like that would have struck Rollant as madness. Now, he found himself nodding. He thought they could clean up a whole wing from the Army of Franklin, too.

"Come on, come on, come on!" Lieutenant Griff shouted. "Time to get moving. We can't sit around here all day."

Smitty sighed. "He's right, gods dammit. It'd be nice if we could, though."

"Wouldn't it?" Rollant hurried forward, to take his place at the head of the company. *I'll be the one they shoot at first*, he thought. *That's what standard-bearers are for. That's why they made me a corporal.*

They hadn't gone far before splashing through a little stream that never came up past their knees. Rollant enjoyed the cool water soaking his trousers, but did call out a warning he'd made before: "Check yourselves for leeches, if you know what's good for you." The country wasn't very swampy, but in this part of Detina you never could tell.

And, sure enough, a couple of men made disgusted noises. "Who's got fire?" one of them said. They had learned not just to yank off the bloodsuckers, but to touch them with a glowing coal and make them let go.

Someone had a firesafe, and got a tiny blaze going from the glowing punk he carried in it. The smoldering tip of a twig got rid of the pests. The company pressed on.

"How far to this Jonestown place, sir?" Rollant asked Lieutenant Griff.

"Not far," the young company commander replied. "Four or five miles."

Rollant nodded. "Thanks."

"You're welcome," Griff answered, a courtesy he never would have given Rollant the year before. He walked along for a few paces, then said, "Do you know, Corporal, you're not what I expected?"

He evidently meant it as a compliment. Rollant said, "Thank you, sir."

"You're welcome," Griff said again. "When we gave you your corporal's stripes—Colonel Nahath and I, I mean, and Lieutenant General George, too—we didn't think you would be able to keep them. We expected there would be quarrels, and men refusing to obey you. But that hasn't happened. I wonder why."

"Maybe they see I can do the job, sir," Rollant said. He hadn't imagined they'd talked with Doubting George before deciding they could promote him.

"Maybe." Griff didn't sound convinced. "I see that you're doing it, mind you, but convincing ordinary Detinans of anything they don't feel like believing is like herding tigers."

He was, without a doubt, right about that. No one knew better than blonds how stubborn Detinans could be. Rollant thought for a while, then suggested, "Maybe they see the stripes on my sleeve and not the man wearing the uniform tunic."

"That could be," Griff allowed. "We've come a long way toward turning all our men into real professional soldiers, and one mark of the professional is respect for his underofficers."

"Don't you worry about it, sir," Rollant said. "I'm sure they call me a gods-damned blond son of a bitch whenever my back's turned."

"And what do you think about that?" the lieutenant asked.

Rollant shrugged. "Sir, if you think I never cussed an underofficer, I have to tell you you'd better think again."

"Not many soldiers who never have, I suppose," Griff said,

and then, in an altogether different tone, "Hello! What's this?"

This was men in blue tunics and pantaloons spread thinly across a field: northern pickets. They cried out in alarm as they caught sight of the southrons. Several of them raised crossbows to their shoulders and started shooting. *Thwuck!* One of the bolts, a frighteningly good shot, tore through the silk of the company standard.

"Forward!" Griff shouted. "If they won't go by themselves, we just have to chase them away."

Rollant held the standard on high and waved it back and forth as he advanced. It told the men where the company was supposed to go and lifted their spirits. That was why both southrons and traitors had standard-bearers. Making themselves conspicuous was why both sides had to change standard-bearers so often.

"Avram!" Rollant shouted. "Avram and freedom!" More than most, he knew what freedom meant.

More crossbow bolts whistled past him. Someone behind him let out a shriek. He couldn't even look to see who it was. He could only go forward waving the standard. He ran clumsily, his head down, watching where he put his feet. If he fell from stepping in a hole and the standard went down, his company's spirits would sag no less than if he got shot. He couldn't do much about getting shot. He could, or at least he might, avoid imitating a jackass with the staggers.

The northerners didn't put up much of a fight. In their shoes, being so badly outnumbered, he wouldn't have been ashamed to run away, either. A few of them turned and loosed hasty shots over their shoulders. A couple of those struck home, too. But more traitors fell. Rollant watched dust puff from the back of one running man's blue tunic as a quarrel hit him. The northerner threw his arms wide. His crossbow flew surprisingly far to one side as he let it go. He ran on for a couple of staggering steps, then fell on his face. He was still thrashing feebly when Rollant pounded past him.

Beyond another belt of trees, the enemy had earthworks waiting. The surviving pickets dove into them. More traitors appeared on the shooting steps. They gave Avram's onrushing men a couple of crisp, thoroughly professional volleys. Bell might have spent his men like coppers, but the ones he had left still knew their business.

They knew it so well, in fact, that they knocked the southrons back on their heels and more. Men who had dashed forward suddenly dashed back. "Stand!" Lieutenant Griff shouted, his voice breaking in fury and humiliation. "Stand, gods damn you! You've been through worse!"

He was right—they had. At that particular moment, though, they weren't much inclined to listen to him. Rollant had seen that before, too. They'd come up against the traitors' trenches too soon, too unexpectedly. What they could have taken in stride had they been ready for it caught them by surprise and threw them into panic. And so they fled.

It wasn't Griff's company alone. That made Rollant feel a little better as he too fell back out of crossbow range from the northerners' position. All the southrons who came up against them recoiled the same way. Officers up and down the line screamed, "Stand!" and "Hold fast, you stupid, cowardly sons of bitches!" and other such endearments, and none of them did the least bit of good.

What saved the day, oddly enough, were the traitors themselves. Seeing the southrons taken with panic, they swarmed out of their trenches and pursued, roaring like lions all the while.

"Come on!" Rollant shouted. "We can lick 'em! Now they're up above ground, same as we are!"

He wasn't so vain as to imagine his voice turned the tide by itself. That would have taken a man like Fighting Joseph, now fighting no more. He heard plenty of officers and under-officers and ordinary soldiers shouting the same thing in different words. But his was one of the voices raised.

And, by one of those chances the Thunderer and the Lion God might have understood but no mortal did, the southrons threw off their fear as quickly as it had seized them. They turned around and started plying the northern men with bolts. Pikemen tramped toward the foe in solid ranks. And the traitors, who had been storming forward as if this were the field by the River of Death, hesitated and then abruptly turned to flight themselves.

Now their officers howled in dismay. What had been a bid for revenge against the defeats they'd suffered closer to Marthasville a few days before turned into another disaster now. The northerners had attacked with all their old verve, but hadn't been able to sustain it. And when fear took them, it seized them even harder than it had laid hold of the southrons.

"Stand!" "Hold!" "Shoot back, gods damn you!" the traitors' officers howled. They might as well have told the Hoocheecoochee River to quit flowing. They could give all the orders they liked, but the men in blue paid them no attention. Having decided they couldn't win the fight against the southrons, they seemed to have decided all hope was lost, and stampeded back toward Jonestown.

Whooping with glee, the southrons pursued. Rollant ran right past a lieutenant from the Army of Franklin who was still shouting curses after his departed soldiers. Afterwards, the blond wondered whether his comrades had captured the traitor or simply slain him. He never found out.

So great was the northerners' fear, they made no serious stand in the trench lines their serfs had dug. A few of them paused, turned, and shot and the oncoming southrons, but most simply kept going. Escape was all they had in mind as they pelted back toward the hamlet of Jonestown.

"By the Lion God's sacred eyeteeth," Lieutenant Griff said in dazed tones, "I do believe we may bag them all."

"May it be so, sir," Rollant said. He waved the standard again and again. Cheers answered him. The southrons had no war cry to match the northern roar. That cry put fear in the heart of any man who heard it. But the shouts that burst from the throats of Doubting George's men as they watched the enemy flee before them were ferocious enough for all ordinary use.

When the traitors reached the outskirts of Jonestown, they did manage a rally of sorts. Rollant soon saw why: they were fighting to hold the southrons away from the glideway carpets that were even then carrying men in blue south out of the battle and back toward Marthasville.

"Where are our catapults?" Rollant shouted. Most of the heavy engines, of course, were back by Marthasville, too, knocking the city down around the ears of its inhabitants and defenders. But some lighter ones had come north with the crossbowmen and pikemen. Now they had a target about which the men who served them could usually but dream. Land a few firepots on those fleeing carpets and no small part of the Army of Franklin's strength would go up in smoke.

Those would be men roasting on the carpets, of course. Rollant did his best not to think about that. As long as they were only targets in his mind, he wouldn't have to dwell on what their torment meant. By reckoning him and his kind only serfs, they'd played the identical game for centuries.

When the catapults did arrive, though, they pelted the rear guard in Jonestown, not the departing carpets, most of which were out of range by then. The traitors had engines of their own in the town, and showed no hesitation about bombarding the southrons. After Rollant saw a soldier from his regiment turned to a running, burning, shrieking torch, he stopped worrying about the rights and wrongs of war. He was in it, and beating down the enemy came before everything else.

Doubting George's men didn't quite manage to bag all the traitors. The rear guard fought skillfully and stubbornly, and managed to withdraw south toward Marthasville in good order. They did know their business, no doubt of that. The war would have been much easier were they ignorant.

Somehow, even the partial failure seemed not to matter so much. "We've got the glideway," Rollant said as the sun set in blood ahead of him.

"We didn't finish the traitors' army." That was Smitty, sounding as indignant as if he were Marshal Bart.

"Do you know what?" Rollant said.

Smitty shook his head. "No. What, your Corporalship with all the answers, sir?"

Rollant snorted. "You're impossible. But I'll tell you what anyhow: we're getting to where it doesn't matter whether we did or not. We've got the glideway line—the lines, I should say. The rest will take care of itself."

✧　　　✧　　　✧

Behind Captain Gremio, more firepots crashed into Marthasville. He could hear their hateful bursts. The breeze was out of the west, too, so he could smell the smoke from the burning city. He would have thought that, by this time, nothing much inside Marthasville would burn. He would have thought that, but he would have been wrong. Every day, the southrons started fresh fires.

They weren't just heaving firepots into the city, either. A rending crash told of a great stone striking home. A soldier from his company said, "There goes somebody's house to hells and gone."

The fellow was bound to be right. When one of those heavy stones came down on something, whatever it hit broke. *And if you don't believe me, ask what's left of Leonidas the Priest*, Gremio thought with funeral-pyre humor.

He was tempted to use the joke out loud. Before he could, Colonel Florizel called, "Come on, men. Move up. The attack will go in in a few minutes." He chuckled to himself. " 'Go in' is right, isn't it, when we're trying to take the Sweet One's shrine away from the southrons? May she give them all a dose of the clap." He extended the middle finger of his right hand in the usual Detinan invocation of the goddess of love. A lot of troopers imitated the gesture. So did Gremio.

"Be ready. We have to be strong and fierce in the field." Sergeant Thisbe spoke as if Florizel hadn't. "If we don't lick the southrons here, this army is in a lot of trouble. We can do it."

"That's right," Gremio said. "We can—and we've got to. If we can take away the Sweet One's shrine and the high ground around it, we cut off the wing that's grabbed our glideway lines east to Dothan and up to the northern part of this province. Then we can break the stranglehold they're putting on us and on Marthasville."

His sword was loose in its sheath. He went forward toward the shrine as if sure of victory. In his heart, he was anything but. The Army of Franklin had lost south of Marthasville. It had lost west of Marthasville. What was left of Roast-Beef William's wing had come scurrying back to

Marthasville from Jonestown in the north with its tail between its legs. And now Lieutenant General Bell was ordering this attack east of the city.

Why not? Gremio thought acidulously. *We've failed in the other three directions. I suppose Bell's trying for a clean sweep.* That wasn't fair. Gremio knew as much. He was past caring. He wished Bell had remained a wing commander. He was up to that job. Army commander? On the face of things, that seemed beyond him—as far beyond him as Mount Panamgam, home of the gods, was beyond the sky.

Colonel Florizel still thought the sun god shone on Bell day and night. As far as Florizel was concerned, fighting was all that mattered. Whether you won or lost seemed much less important to him. Gremio had seen too much combat in the lawcourts and on the field to have much sympathy for that point of view.

Pikemen formed up in front of the northern crossbowmen. Horns blared. Along with the rest of the officers in the attack, Gremio shouted, "Forward!" He waved his sword. He wouldn't lead his men anywhere he wouldn't go himself.

"That's the spirit!" Colonel Florizel said, and he brandished his own blade. A moment later, he turned to bawl something at another of his captains. He wasn't keeping a special eye on Gremio any more. *I did my best to get myself killed when we fought by Goober Creek,* Gremio thought. *I didn't quite manage it, but I did persuade Florizel I'm no coward— for a while, anyhow.*

No one had spoken about exactly where in front of the Sweet One's temple the southrons had their lines. Gremio concluded that was because no one knew. He wasn't surprised. The whole war, on both sides, had gone like that, with armies blundering past each other and into each other as if their commanders were blind men. *Maybe they are. It would explain some of the madness I've seen better than anything else I can think of.*

Old Straight's wing didn't blunder past the southrons. It blundered straight into them, discovering where they were by having a volley of crossbow quarrels tear into it at close range. Screams rose from the northerners. But so did their roaring war cry. "Forward!" Gremio shouted. "Now we've found the sons of bitches, so let's go get 'em!"

And, for what seemed like the first time in this campaign, the northerners had magecraft working for them. Thunderbolts crashed down on the southrons' entrenchments. Dragons and other phantasms appeared in the sky. Gremio was a modern, well-educated man. He knew they couldn't hurt him, and so they couldn't. But if an ignorant farmer's son believed the beasts could devour him or flame him, his superstitious belief gave them the power to do just that.

Roaring their throats raw, the northerners swarmed down into the enemy's trenches. A lot of southrons there were already dead or hurt from the magecraft. Some of the ones who remained threw away their crossbows and shortswords and surrendered. But others, stubborn as if they were good northern men, fought on despite long odds.

A crossbow bolt hissed past Gremio's ear as he jumped into the forwardmost trench. His sword spitted the southron who'd shot at him. The man in gray howled and reeled back.

"Keep moving, gods damn you!" Gremio called to his men. "This isn't the fight we need. We've got to get through these trenches and seize the shrine and the high ground around it. If we can't manage that, whatever we do here doesn't matter."

Sometimes the soldiers did need reminding of such things. To a lot of them, as to Florizel, fighting was an end in itself, not a means. That struck Gremio as madness, but he knew it to be true even so.

"Onward!" he yelled again, and looked along the trench to make sure the troopers could go on. Not far away, Sergeant Thisbe battled a southron who had a better idea than most of his fellows about what to do with a shortsword. Gremio ran to Thisbe's aid. The southron cared no more than any other soldier for the notion of fighting two foes at once. He turned and fled.

"Thank you, Captain," Thisbe said.

"You're welcome. I know you'd do the same for me," Gremio answered. "Now we've got to get moving. If we can drive them back from the shrine, we've really done something."

Out of the trenches and east once more pushed the northerners. But they ran into another line of entrenchments only a furlong or so past the one they'd just cleared. Crossing the open ground cost them a lot of good men killed and wounded. This time, too, the lightnings mostly missed when they struck at the southrons' fieldworks. Little by little, the enemy's magic was coming up close to the level of that of King Geoffrey's wizards.

Colonel Florizel pointed with his sword at the trenches ahead. "Charge!" he cried.

If sorcery wouldn't do the job, crossbow quarrels and shortswords and pikes would have to. Still roaring like lions, the northern men surged toward the second line of trenches. They'd enjoyed the defenders' advantage through most of the fights from Borders up to Marthasville. No more. Now the southrons waited for them to come, waited and took a heavy toll while they were in the open.

I can't go back, Gremio thought. *Everyone in the regiment—everyone in the army—will reckon me a coward if I do.* And so he went forward, in spite of the bolts that zipped past him and tugged at the fabric of his baggy pantaloons. All around him, men fell. When he reached the second line of trenches, he leaped down into it with a roar that was more than half a cry of despair.

More fierce fighting in the trenches slowed the northerners' advance. By the time the last southrons were down or fled, Gremio had a cut on his arm and another above his eye. Blood made tears run down his face. He blinked constantly, trying to clear his sight. When he saw how few men he had left, he wished his vision were blurrier, so they would seem to be more.

"Well fought, boys!" Colonel Florizel boomed. "They can't hold us back when we aim to go forward, by the gods."

To Gremio's amazement, the northerners raised a ragged cheer. They were ready to do whatever their officers demanded of them. And if, every now and again, those officers should happen to ask the impossible . . . Gremio knew the answer there. He'd seen it. Sometimes the men would give it to them. Others, they died like flies proving it an impossibility after all.

"Form up! Dress your ranks!" Florizel called when they struggled out of the southrons' second line of fieldworks. The regimental commander waited till the lines were neat enough to suit him, then nodded in fussy satisfaction. "Very good, men. Now—forward!"

Forward they went once more. After another couple of furlongs, though, they came upon a third line of entrenchments. Like the first two, this one was full of southron soldiers. They started volleying away at the northerners as soon as Gremio and his comrades came into range. And they had catapults to support them. Firepots flew through the air, splashing flames over grass—and men.

"We can't take that position, sir," Sergeant Thisbe said urgently. "I don't think we can get into that trench. I'm sure we won't come out again."

Gremio was sure of the same thing. But he was sure of something else, too: "If the colonel orders me forward, Sergeant, forward I shall go. We've got to take the Sweet One's shrine or die trying."

"To the seven hells with the Sweet One," Thisbe said. "She's a stinking, lying bitch. She'll laugh when we die, that's all."

"It can't be helped, Sergeant." Gremio thought Thisbe was right, but he couldn't do anything about it. He looked toward Colonel Florizel. It was up to the regimental commander now.

To his dismay, Florizel was looking at him, too. *Do you want me to say we should go back, sir?* Gremio wondered. *To the hells with me if I will. You won't get the chance to call me craven.*

But Florizel said, "It's no good, is it, Captain?"

"I am at your command, sir," Gremio answered.

Florizel shook his head. "It's no good," he repeated. "Going forward into the teeth of their defenses would be murder, nothing less. Shall I make you do duty as my barrister before the gods?"

"Colonel, I will obey any order you choose to give me," Gremio said, "and I promise you, sir, my men will follow me."

"But it's no good, Captain." The regimental commander

sounded like an old and broken man. "It's no gods-damned good, no good at all. We'd just get ourselves killed, and we wouldn't shift the stinking southrons even an inch."

Gremio had reached the same conclusion. If Florizel could see it, it had to be correct. He said, "Sir, the decision is yours."

Florizel looked at him—looked through him. "I know what you're thinking. You're thinking I'd reckon you a coward if you advised me to fall back." He shook his head. "I've seen you fight. I know better now. You may not be a nobleman, but you've got a pair of ballocks hanging from you."

"For which I thank you." Punctiliously polite, Gremio bowed to his superior officer. That might have saved his life, for a crossbow quarrel whistled by over his head. He shivered a little as he straightened. "I do not believe we have any hope of taking the position in front of us, either. Nor do I see how we can seize the Sweet One's shrine and the surrounding high ground."

"In that case, we'd best save ourselves for the next fight, wouldn't you say?" Florizel asked.

"There surely will be another fight, Colonel," Gremio replied, and then, try as he would, couldn't help letting some acid out: "After all, we've only failed to beat a bigger army four times in a row now. Bell will surely think that's an accident, and send us out to try again."

When Bell assumed command, Colonel Florizel had been ecstatic. *I should have remembered that,* Gremio thought. But Florizel only sighed and shrugged and said, "It hasn't quite worked, has it? Maybe he'll decide it won't work. But even if we don't go after these bastards, they'll come after us, sure as hells." He raised his voice to a full battlefield bellow: "Trumpeters! Blow *retreat!*"

The mournful notes rang out. In their trenches, the southrons raised a cheer. The horn calls of both armies were the same. *And why not?* Gremio thought. *It was all one army not so long ago.*

Florizel's wasn't the only regiment falling back. A couple of units tried last assaults against the southrons' works, which only got more men shot and burned to no purpose.

Then they too withdrew toward the line from which they'd begun.

"Lieutenant General Bell won't be very happy when he gets word of what happened here," Florizel predicted.

"Too bad," Gremio said. "I'm not very happy about it, either." His wounds were minor, but they still stung. With a shrug, he went on, "Of course, nobody cares what I think."

Florizel only growled and scowled and shook his head. He didn't care what anybody thought, not right then. But Sergeant Thisbe said, "That isn't true, sir!"

"Thank you," Gremio said, and felt better about retreating than he had.

Doubting George stood atop the parapet in front of the earthworks the northerners had held between Goober Creek and Marthasville. These days, Bell's army held a line just outside Marthasville's southern outskirts. Lieutenant General George was more than a little amazed the traitors still held the city. Bell was stubborner than he'd thought.

General Hesmucet was making Bell pay for his stubbornness, too. From where George stood, he had a fine view of the southrons' siege engines lobbing destruction into Marthasville. Pillars of smoke rose here and there in the besieged city. Even as he watched, another fire started.

Brigadier Brannan came walking along what had been the traitors' line. The siege-engine specialist looked pleased with himself. He looked even more pleased with the way things were going. "Good morning, sir," he said, beaming at Doubting George. "Now we get to see what our toys can do."

"Well, I thought *we* already had a pretty fair notion of that," George replied. "Now Lieutenant General Bell gets to see what our toys can do, and we'll find out how he likes it."

"Yes, sir. That's more or less what I meant, sir," Brannan said. "Getting besieged can't be much fun when we've got the power to burn the place where he's sheltering down around his ears."

"I wouldn't think so, anyhow," George said. "And it's not even as if Marthasville had a strong central keep. By the gods, the town's only a generation old, and nobody ever bothered building one here."

"No one ever saw the need," Brannan said, no little scorn in his voice for men who hadn't looked far enough ahead. "No one thought there would be a war between the provinces, or that we would come so far if there were."

"A keep wouldn't do Bell much good anyhow," Doubting George observed. "Even if he managed to stay inside it, we'd still squeeze the life out of Marthasville—we'd seize the glideways, and we'd wreck the manufactories."

"That's right, sir." Brigadier Brannan nodded and grinned. "If Bell wants to go out in a blaze of glory, we're giving him the chance." As if to underscore his words, yet another big fire broke out in Marthasville.

"If you were Bell," George said, "what would you do to get yourself out of the mess you'd got yourself into?"

Brannan's grin got wider. "You mean, besides wish like hells Geoffrey'd never, ever, chosen me commander of the Army of Franklin?"

George smiled, too. "Yes, besides that. By now, he's seen he can't force us back from the city. He's tried four times, he's thrown away what has to be the third part of his army, and he hasn't moved us a foot. I expect he's finally drawing the right conclusions from that, eh?"

"A blind man would. By the gods, sir, a *dead* man would," Brannan answered. "Of course, whether *Bell* would remains an open question."

"Naughty, Brigadier—distinctly naughty," George said. "If he can't force us away from here, what *can* he do? I see two possibilities."

"Magic is one," Brannan said.

"Magic is always one, where the northerners are concerned," Doubting George agreed. "The other is turning his unicorn-riders loose and wrecking the glideway line that comes up from Rising Rock and keeps us in food and firepots and such."

"Congratulations, sir," Brigadier Brannan said. George raised a questioning eyebrow. Brannan explained: "I think you've just spelled out the meaning of what they call a theoretical possibility."

"A theoretical possibility is one that *might* happen but *won't*," George said. "Sort of on the order of false King Geoffrey's turning out to be an honest man." Brannan guffawed. George hadn't been joking, or not very much. He nourished a fine, flourishing resentment against King Avram's cousin for confiscating his estates in Parthenia after he chose a united Detina over the call of his province.

Of course, King Avram had confiscated Duke Edward of Arlington's estates when Edward chose Parthenia over a united Detina. But George was on Avram's side, so he didn't fuss about that. Besides, it wasn't *his* land.

But when General Hesmucet summoned his wing commanders for a conference, he wasn't quite so cheerful. "Bell's turned his unicorn-riders loose, gods damn him," he said. "They're going to see how hungry they can make us."

"Well, it could be worse, sir," John the Lister said. "He's still got Brigadier Spinner in charge of his riders, doesn't he?"

"That's right." Hesmucet gestured to his new wing commander. "I know what you're going to say, Ducky—to the seven hells with me if I don't. You're going to say it'd be a lot worse if Ned of the Forest had charge of the traitors' unicorns."

"Yes, sir, that is what I was going to say," John agreed. "Will you tell me I'm wrong?"

"Not for a minute," Hesmucet said. "Not even for half a minute. What I'm going to tell you is, I'm gods-damned glad you've got charge of that wing now, and not Fighting Joseph any more. He's a brave man, and I'd never say anything less as far as that goes, but he's a first-class son of a bitch, too, and he never did bother learning much about the traitors' commanders here in the east."

"By his record, he never bothered learning much about their commanders in the west, either," Doubting George remarked.

"I didn't say that." Hesmucet grinned. "I may have thought it as loud as I could, but, gods damn it to the hells, I didn't say it."

"Sir . . ." That was Brigadier Oliver, the late James the Bird's Eye's successor. "Sir, must you take the names of the gods in vain *quite* so much?"

He was earnest. He was polite, even plaintive. He was properly subordinate. By all the signs, he even succeeded in embarrassing the commanding general. That impressed George, who hadn't been sure such a thing was possible. After coughing a couple of times, Hesmucet said, "Well, Brigadier, I will try to do better. I've had a ready tongue for a lot of years now, though, so I don't promise I'll be perfect, nor anywhere close."

"The gods do admire effort, sir," Brigadier Oliver said, as if the Thunderer, or perhaps the Sweet One, had come down from Mount Panamgam beyond the sky to whisper as much in his ear.

No god had ever come down and whispered in Doubting George's ear. Given a choice, he would have picked the Sweet One for such a duty, but men seldom got such choices, and often got in trouble when they did. Resolutely pushing his mind away from what the love goddess' whispers might be like, he asked, "What are we going to do if Spinner's running loose?"

"What do you expect me to do?" Hesmucet replied. "I'll send Marble Bill out to keep Spinner's riders off our glideway line."

It was indeed the obvious answer. John the Lister pointed out what George hesitated to: "Bill's not the best commander of unicorns ever born."

"No, but neither is Spinner, so it evens out," Hesmucet said.

"A point," Doubting George said after a little thought. "Sure enough, that is a point. The bland fighting the bland, you might say."

"*You* might," Hesmucet said with a groan. "As for me, I feel the same way about such things as Brigadier Oliver feels about taking the name of the gods in vain."

"Sir," Oliver said, "you don't have a religious duty to punish those who make foolish jokes."

"No, eh?" Hesmucet rumbled. "Well, gods . . . bless it, I ought to have such a duty. Every righteous man ought to have such a duty." He glowered at George. "Don't you agree, Lieutenant General?"

"Well, sir, actually, I am more inclined toward mercy,"

George replied. "My notion is, the gods make note of everything they say. I expect they can deal with these matters in their own good time."

"Hmm." Hesmucet gave him a severe look. "Why do I suspect you're saying that because you're the culprit here?"

"I haven't the faintest idea, sir," Doubting George replied—blandly. "I assure you, I'd do the same for anyone else."

"Of course you assure me of that," Hesmucet said. "You assure me of all manner of nonsensical things and gods-damned lies."

He sounded so pugnacious, Brigadier Oliver spoke up again: "Sir, you would be well-advised to show mercy to those who disagree with you, not to revile them."

"No." Where Hesmucet had sounded fierce while teasing George, now he really was. George could tell the difference. Hesmucet pointed north toward Marthasville, saying, "What I aim to do with those who disagree with me—and who disagree with King Avram, gods bless him—is whip them right out of their boots." He walked over and set a hand on Doubting George's shoulder. "And that's why I put up with this son of a bitch in spite of his foolishness. Put him in the field against the traitors and he's a tiger. Next to that, nothing else matters, not even a little bit."

Oliver bowed. He was a fussily precise man, as stern with himself as he was with everyone else. "Very well, sir," he said. "On that, I cannot presume to disagree with you." Turning, he bowed to George as well. "This, I must say, I find strange, for in our days at Annasville I reckoned the distinguished general likelier to fight on the other side than on ours."

George had reckoned Oliver an officious prig. He hadn't been shy about letting the world know what he reckoned, either. He said, "Brigadier, we still disagree about what ought to happen to the serfs in this kingdom. But we agree wholeheartedly that Detina is *a* kingdom, not two or three or six kingdoms, and that outweighs the rest."

"Indeed it does," Oliver said. "Indeed it does. I rejoice that the gods have put a sufficiency of truth into your heart, sir, even if not its very fullest measure, the measure that would make you recognize all of mankind, regardless of outer seeming, as your brethren."

He still preaches too gods-damned much, Doubting George thought. *But he's a pretty fair soldier himself, even so.* Aloud, he said, "I don't want to recognize all of mankind as my brethren. If I did, I'd miss watching pretty girls, and that would be a shame."

Hesmucet chuckled. John the Lister laughed out loud. Oliver clicked his tongue between his teeth and looked pained. *Oh, dear,* George thought. *He doesn't approve of watching pretty girls, either. Well, too bad for him.*

Perhaps finding it a good time to change the subject, John the Lister asked General Hesmucet, "Sir, do I understand correctly that we don't intend to try storming Marthasville?"

"Not right now, anyhow," the commanding general answered. "We might take it—I think we *would* take it, but I also think a direct assault would be expensive, and the mourning boxes in the papers down south are long enough already. Let's see how Bell likes having the place torn down around his ears without his being able to do anything about it."

"Let's see how he likes that after false King Geoffrey charged him to hold the town, too," Doubting George added.

"That did cross my mind, yes," Hesmucet said. "I wouldn't want to have dear Geoffrey screaming at me right now. But then you, Lieutenant General, would know more about such things than I do, wouldn't you?"

"Not much, sir," George replied. "I knew I would serve a united Detina as soon as Palmetto Province pulled out. Geoffrey confiscated my lands as soon as Parthenia went with it and I declined to join him. To the seven hells with him, but only from a distance. It's been years since I last saw him face to face."

"May the next time we see him be when he meets the headsman." Hesmucet took a flask from his belt, yanked out the cork, raised the flask high, and drank. That done, he loudly smacked his lips and passed it to Doubting George.

General Guildenstern had been in the habit of carrying a flask on his belt, too. He'd also been in the habit of getting drunk from it. Bart, now, Bart had sternly stayed dry, for he'd been known to wet himself to the drowning point. George had seen Hesmucet drink, but he'd never seen him anywhere close to drunk. He drank, too, in the same mostly moderate way. He took the flask and swigged sweet fire. "Ahh!" he said, wiping his mouth on his sleeve. "Peachtree Province peach brandy. What could be better?"

"Thank you kindly, sir," John the Lister said when George offered him the flask. He took a pull and gave it to Brigadier Oliver.

The one-armed man shook his head. "No, thank you. I have never drunk spirituous liquors. I do not believe it to be virtuous."

"Why not?" Doubting George asked, genuinely curious. "I can see not drinking on account of you don't want to get drunk, but why not enjoy it if you're a man who can hold it?"

"We are enough like beasts as things stand, sir," Oliver said. "Such drink only brings us closer to them."

"I'm not worried about getting close to the beasts," George said. "What I want to do is get close to Marthasville." He, Hesmucet, and John the Lister all laughed and all swigged again. Brigadier Oliver also laughed, politely, but stuck to water.

Smoke was a stench in Lieutenant General Bell's nostrils. Every firepot that burst and spread new flames in the streets of Marthasville seemed a personal reproach. He went through even more laudanum than he would have on account of his wounds. It didn't do much to blur his sense of guilt, but it did do something.

"Sir?" Major Zibeon said, and then again, louder: "Sir!"

"Eh?" Bell came out of the laudanum haze. "What is it, Major?"

"Sir, there's a delegation of citizens who'd like to speak to you for a few minutes waiting outside," his aide-de-camp replied.

"Citizens?" Bell echoed irritably. "What in the hells do a pack of citizens know? Not bloody much, that's what." Zibeon didn't say anything. He only waited. Bell scowled. "What do they want? Do they want me to surrender to that bastard of a Hesmucet? I won't do it. What would King Geoffrey do to me if I did?"

Geoffrey was much less happy with him now than on naming him commander of the Army of Franklin. *Gods damn it, I did what he wanted,* Bell thought petulantly. *I went out there and I fought. I did all I could. I almost won. Joseph the Gamecock couldn't have done any better. I'm sure of that. Nearly sure.*

Zibeon shook his head. "No, they don't want surrender. But they are looking for some sort of relief, any sort of relief, from the infernal bombardment the southrons are making us take."

"What *would* they have me do?" Bell demanded.

Zibeon's dour face got no lighter. "Sir, I don't know," he answered, shrugging. "To find that out, you'd have to talk to them."

"Oh, very well," Bell said sourly. He wanted to talk to civilians about as much as he wanted to lose his other leg, but sometimes there was no help for a situation. His repeated attacks against Hesmucet's army had shown him that. That he might not have made those attacks never, ever, occurred to him. "Who are these sons of bitches, anyhow?" he asked, not bothering to keep his voice down.

"One is called Jim the Ball, sir; the other is Jim of the Crew," Zibeon replied. "They are both merchants of some considerable wealth."

With a martyred sigh, Bell yielded to necessity. "Very well, Major. You may send them in, and we shall see what sort of wisdom they offer." He rolled his eyes to show how little he expected.

One look told him how Jim the Ball had got his name; the man was nearly spherical, and his tunic and pantaloons contained enough material for a couple of tents. Jim of the Crew, by contrast, was tall and slim and muscular—the crew to which he belonged was probably that of a river galley. He bowed to Bell. Jim the Ball might have done the same, but he was so round, Bell had trouble being sure.

"Good day, gentlemen," Bell said, wishing he were somewhere else—preferably, at the head of a victorious army, halfway down to the border with Franklin. "What can I do for you today?"

"Sir," Jim the Ball said, "the southrons are—destroying

Marthasville—one piece—at a time." He was so very fat, he had to pause and sip air every few words.

"We want you to let them know how barbarous it is to pound a city to pieces with civilians still in it," Jim of the Crew added. He could speak a whole sentence without needing several breaths to finish it.

"Why do you suppose General Hesmucet would pay the least attention to such a plea?" Bell asked.

"Why do you—think he wouldn't?" Jim the Ball replied, again putting a caesura in his sentence.

"You said it for yourself, sir: he is a barbarous man," Bell said.

"What, by the gods, have we got to lose?" Jim of the Crew said. "If we go to him under flag of truce and he sends us away, we're no worse off than we were. But if he says yes, we save what's still standing, anyhow."

Bell plucked at his beard. A letter cost him nothing; these fellows were right about that. And complaining to Hesmucet might make him look better in the eyes of the world. The north could trumpet about Hesmucet's cruelty and iniquity if he kept on pounding Marthasville after being begged to stop. The world outside Detina—the kingdoms on the far side of the Western Ocean—had been trying to pretend the north didn't exist. No one recognized Geoffrey as a sovereign among sovereigns. It was humiliating. It was infuriating. And the north could do not a thing about it.

Pointing at the two merchants, Bell asked, "If I draft this missive, would you be willing to carry it through the lines to Hesmucet?"

They looked at each other, then both nodded. Several of Jim the Ball's chins wobbled at the motion. "Yes, sir," he said.

"We'd be happy to, sir," Jim of the Crew agreed.

"Very well, then," Bell said. "Return here in two days' time, and we shall see what we shall see."

"Yes, sir. Thank you, sir," Jim the Ball said. "We'll be here."

"If we haven't been burned to charcoal, we'll be here," Jim of the Crew added. "If the southrons haven't attacked, we'll be here."

"They won't attack." Bell spoke with great conviction.

"How do you know that?" Jim of the Crew asked, pressing harder on the commander of the Army of Franklin than he had any business doing.

But Bell answered, "How do I know, sir? I'll tell you how: because they're a pack of cowards. If they weren't a pack of cowards, afraid of showing themselves outside of entrenchments, they would already have attacked Marthasville. They wouldn't do what they're doing to its defenseless civilian population."

He thought he'd impressed the two civilians. But, as they were leaving, Jim of the Crew turned to Jim the Ball and said, "If the stinking southrons are such great cowards, how come they whipped us every time we tried to go after 'em around this city?"

"Beats me," Jim the Ball said.

"That's what I said—they've beaten us," Jim of the Crew told him. "They've beaten us like a gods-damned drum. I don't care who's king over us any more, as long as all these fornicating armies go straight to the seven hells and gone."

Lieutenant General Bell almost shouted for his provost guards to arrest Jim of the Crew as a traitor to King Geoffrey. But then he shook his head. Sending the merchant and his chum across the lines to General Hesmucet struck him as a worse punishment. With any luck at all, the southrons would miss their flag of truce and fill them full of crossbow quarrels. *And it couldn't happen to a more deserving pair,* he thought maliciously.

Still, the idea of writing a formal letter of complaint to Hesmucet had an undeniable appeal. "Major Zibeon!" Bell called.

"Sir?" his aide-de-camp said. If he'd heard the scathing remarks from the two civilians, he didn't show it.

"Fetch me pen and paper, if you please."

"Yes, sir," Zibeon replied. "Do you really think General Hesmucet will heed your request, sir?"

"I haven't the faintest idea," Bell said. "But we're no worse off for finding out, are we?"

"No, sir," Major Zibeon admitted.

Even writing came hard for Bell. Most men wrote with one hand and steadied the paper with the other. Bell's left arm was only a dead weight, his left hand useless and inert. He had to put a large stone at the top of the sheet Zibeon found for him. He gnawed at his luxuriant mustache as he groped for words.

Permit me to say, sir, he wrote, *that the unprecedented measures you have taken against this city transcend, in studied and ingenious cruelty, all acts ever brought to my attention in the long and dark history of war. In the names of the gods of humanity, I protest, believing that you will find that you are depriving of their homes and firesides the wives and children of a brave people. This calculated cruelty can only redound to the disgrace of the sovereign whom you serve, and to your own. Give over, while yet you may. I am, General, very respectfully, your obedient servant, Bell, Lieutenant General.*

He signed his name with a flourish and sanded the letter dry. Then he used wax and his signet to seal it. He thought of summoning Jim the Ball and Jim of the Crew to take it at once, but didn't. After Jim of the Crew's gibe, he almost hoped a firepot burst on the merchant's roof.

Before the appointed day, Roast-Beef William came to see him. That left him imperfectly delighted with the world; he would almost rather have seen the two merchants again. But William was a wing commander, and so not easy to ignore. "What can I do for you, Lieutenant General?" Bell asked after the older man had made his bows.

"Well, sir, I was wondering what sort of plan you had for getting us out of the fix we're in," Roast-Beef William replied.

"I have sent forth Brigadier Spinner's unicorn-riders, as you know, to strike against General Hesmucet's supply line," Bell said. That he was reduced to such small strokes galled him.

That even such small strokes hadn't done all he wanted galled him even more. Roast-Beef William knew what Spinner had done, too—and, more important, what he hadn't. "Supplies are still coming through to the enemy," he remarked.

"I know that," Bell said testily. His arm and his leg hurt more than usual; he longed for laudanum. "But what would you have me do? Do you suppose we can make another sally and drive the gods-damned southrons back from Marthasville?"

He leaned forward eagerly, awaiting William's reply. If the wing commander thought another attack might succeed, he would order it. He hadn't lost the desire to hit back at the southrons, only most of the means. If Roast-Beef William reckoned those available . . . But William shook his head. "No, sir. We haven't really got the men to stand siege any more, let alone strike out. That was why I came to see you."

"Say on," Bell said ominously.

"You know as well as I do, sir, that the southrons are extending their lines north of the city towards the west," William said. "If they keep moving, they'll have us altogether surrounded before long. And then, unless we can break through their lines, they won't just have Marthasville. They'll have the Army of Franklin, too."

That was all too likely to be true. Lieutenant General Bell liked it no better for its truth—liked it less, if anything. He scowled at William, who stared stolidly back. "And what would you recommend, then?" he asked in an icy voice.

"If we can't hold the city, sir, don't you think we'd better save the army?" the wing commander said. "We can get away, at need, before Hesmucet finishes his ring around Marthasville. Before, I say, but not afterwards."

"I can't abandon the city," Bell said. "What would King Geoffrey do to me if I lost the city?"

"What would he do to you if you lost the city and the army, too?" Roast-Beef William asked in return.

"I can't pull out yet," Bell said. "I'm, uh, conferring with Hesmucet, trying to get him to keep from burning Marthasville with the civilians still in it."

"*Are* you?" William raised a bushy eyebrow. "I hadn't supposed you cared much about the civilians hereabouts."

Till Jim the Ball and Jim of the Crew came to him, Bell *hadn't* cared much about the local civilians. But, with such indignation as he could muster, he said, "Of course I do. If it weren't for civilians, King Geoffrey wouldn't have a kingdom, now would he?"

"Of course not," Roast-Beef William replied. "I'm not saying you're wrong, sir, only that you surprised me. Do you think there's any chance Hesmucet will listen to you?"

"I don't know," Bell said. "But he will look like the villain he is if he doesn't, so there may be some hope for it."

"Well, there may be something to that," William said. "By the Lion God's twitching tail tuft, I hope there is—for the folk of Marthasville, if for no other reason."

Bell bristled. He knew what that had to mean. "You don't believe we can hold this city," he said in accusing tones.

"I *wish* we could," the wing commander said. "Think so? No. In my view, as I told you, our choice is between losing the city and losing the city and the army—this in spite of anything Hesmucet may say or do in aid of your letter. It may buy us a few days' time, which is all to the good, but it will do no more."

"Joseph the Gamecock was dismissed from command of this army for voicing opinions less gloomy than those," Bell growled.

"Joseph had less reason for pessimism, for he had more men with whom to work," Roast-Beef William replied. He tipped his hat. "Good day, sir." Only after the older man was gone did Bell realize he'd been given the glove. Cursing, he yanked out his bottle of laudanum and took a long swig. After a little while, he felt better.

General Hesmucet swung his head from Jim the Ball to Jim of the Crew and back again. Jim the Ball fascinated him; he didn't think he'd ever seen a fatter man. The two merchants from Marthasville nervously looked back. "Yes, you can give me Bell's letter," he said. "I do respect a flag of truce, gentlemen—I won't eat you." *And if I did decide to order the two of you butchered, Jim the Ball could subsist my whole army for a couple of weeks.*

Jim of the Crew, as it happened, had the letter. He handed it to Hesmucet. "Here you are, sir."

"Thank you kindly." Hesmucet unsealed the letter and flattened it out in his hands. "Ah, good," he said. "Lieutenant General Bell writes in a tolerably large script. I won't have to fish out my spectacles to read this, no indeed. People seem to write smaller every gods-damned year, but not today."

He went through the letter in a hurry, then rolled it up again and set it on the light folding table he was using for a desk. "Is—is there—a reply, sir?" Jim the Ball asked, his speech oddly punctuated by breaths.

"Yes, there is, but I'll give it in writing: properly, it goes to Bell himself, and not to either of you," Hesmucet answered. "I'm going to send you to refresh yourselves while I draft it, if you don't mind." Jim of the Crew simply nodded. Jim the Ball looked eager. Hesmucet shook his head. *The one who needs refreshments least wants them most. Isn't that the way of the world?*

He sat down behind the folding table, got out some paper, and inked a pen. *To Lieutenant General Bell, commanding the Army of Franklin,* he wrote. *General: I have the honor to acknowledge the receipt of your letter of this date, at the hands of Jim the Ball and Jim of the Crew, concerning my army's bombardment of Marthasville. You style my measures "unprecedented," and appeal to the dark history for a parallel, as an act of "studied and ingenious cruelty." It is not unprecedented; nor is it necessary to appeal to the dark history of war, when recent modern examples are so handy. You yourself burned dwelling-houses along your parapet. You defended Marthasville on a line so close to town that every firepot and many crossbow quarrels from our line of investment, that overshot their mark, went into the habitations of women and children. Roast-Beef William did the same at Jonestown. I challenge any fair man to judge which of us has the heart of pity for the families of a "brave people."*

In the name of common-sense, I ask you not to appeal to the just gods in such a sacrilegious manner. You and your faction, in the midst of peace and prosperity, have plunged a kingdom into war—dark and cruel war—you who dared and badgered us to battle, insulted our flag, and seized our arsenals and forts. You made "prisoners of war" of the very garrisons sent to protect your people against wild blond tribes, long before any overt act was committed by the (to you) hated government of King Avram. If we must be enemies, let us be men, and fight it out as we propose to do, and not deal in such hypocritical appeals to gods and humanity. The gods will judge in due time. I am, very respectfully, your obedient servant, Hesmucet, General commanding.

"Well," he muttered as he sealed the letter, "if that doesn't make the son of a bitch have a spasm, gods damn me to the hells if I know what would." He called for a runner and said, "Fetch back those two fellows from Marthasville. I've got their answer ready for 'em."

"Yes, sir." The young soldier in gray hurried off.

When the two northern merchants returned, Jim the Ball was still gnawing on a fried chicken drumstick. Speaking with his mouth full, he said, "Thank you—for the hospitality—you've shown—to a couple of men—from the—other side."

"You're welcome." Hesmucet handed him the letter. "Take this back to Lieutenant General Bell, if you'd be so kind. You'll have an escort to the front, and your flag of truce should get you through to your own side."

"Can you give us the gist of it, in case it gets wet or meets some other accident?" Jim of the Crew asked.

"Certainly," Hesmucet said. "The gist of it is 'no.' But I do write it down much fancier than that."

Jim the Ball tossed aside the bare chicken bone. Jim of the Crew nodded. He seemed to have a good deal more wit than his comrade and namesake. Maybe that was just because he displayed less appetite. A man who gave in to his belly, as Jim the Ball did, often gave the impression, true or false, of lacking any other interests.

When the two merchants had left, Hesmucet read over Bell's letter again. He shook his head in amusement. The man had to be an optimist, to think he would get Hesmucet to change his course. The only way northern commanders had got him to change his course was to beat him on the battlefield, and that hadn't happened very often.

That evening, he showed Doubting George the letter. His second-in-command went through it, then remarked, "He's trying to make you look bad in the eyes of the world, I think."

"I don't care how I look in the eyes of the world."

Hesmucet checked himself. "I don't care how I look in the eyes of the world, so long as I look like the man who just took Marthasville."

"I understand, sir. I agree with you," George replied. "A soldier won't usually worry about the war of words till he sees it's the only war he has the faintest hope of winning."

"That's well put. That's very well put, in fact," Hesmucet said.

"Thank you kindly," Doubting George said. "Bell's thrown away so many soldiers, words are about what he has left. I expect you answered him the way he deserves, sir?"

"I hope so." Hesmucet summarized his own letter.

George nodded. "That's good. That's very good indeed. With any luck at all, he'll have an apoplexy, and then they'll need a new commander." He thought about that, then shook his head. "No, I hope he doesn't have that apoplexy. Let him stay in command. He's done us a lot of good."

"I think so, too," Hesmucet said. "He had to be a fool to try to slug it out with us. He did it anyhow—and proved how foolish it was."

"Only a matter of time now," George said.

Hesmucet nodded, but discontentedly. "We've taken too long already, gods damn it. Down in the south, they want a victory. We need to give them one."

"We're doing all right," George insisted. "Marshal Bart has Duke Edward of Arlington penned up in Pierreville, north of Nonesuch, and we've got Bell pretty well trapped here. They aren't going to get loose and cause trouble, the way they did last year and the year before."

"You know that, and I know that, but do the fat burghers sitting on their backsides down in the south know that?" Hesmucet said. "Nonesuch hasn't fallen, and Marthasville hasn't fallen, either. If those fat burghers get sick of the war, false King Geoffrey may end up a real king after all. We need to take that town in front of us. That will give the whole south a sign we really are winning the war."

"It won't be long," Doubting George said again. "Would Bell have written a letter like that if he didn't feel the pinch?"

"Well, maybe not," Hesmucet said. "I hope he wouldn't, anyway. But I still want Marthasville."

He got his answer from Lieutenant General Bell two days later, again delivered by Jim the Ball and Jim of the Crew. He sent them off to eat, which would, at least, keep Jim the Ball happy. Unsealing the letter, he read, *General: I have the honor to acknowledge the receipt of yours of the day previous. Had you not sought to justify yourself therein, I would have been willing to believe that, while the interests of the King of Detina, in your opinion, compelled you to an act of barbarous cruelty, you regretted the necessity, and we would have dropped the subject; but you have indulged in statements which I feel compelled to notice.*

You are unfortunate in your attempt to find a justification for this act of cruelty, either in the defense of Jonestown, by Roast-Beef William, or of Marthasville, by myself. If there was any fault in either case, it was your own, in not giving notice, especially in the case of Marthasville, of your purpose to bombard the town, which is usual in war among civilized kingdoms. I have too good an opinion, founded both upon observation and experience, of the skill of your catapult men, to credit the insinuation that they for several weeks unintentionally shot too high for my modest field works, and slaughtered women and children by accident and want of skill.

Finally, you came into our country with your army, avowedly for the purpose of subjugating free Detinan men, women, and children, and not only intend to rule over them, but you make blonds your allies, and desire to place over us an inferior race, which we have raised from barbarism to its present position, which is the highest ever attained by that race, in all time. You say, "Let us fight it out like men." To this my reply is—for myself, and I believe for all the true men, aye, and women and children, in my kingdom— we will fight you to the death! Better to die a thousand deaths than submit to live under you or your king or his blond allies! Respectfully, your obedient servant, Bell, Lieutenant General.

Hesmucet read through that again, and then chuckled grimly. "Well, I struck a nerve there, all right, gods damn me if I didn't," he said, and set Bell's letter aside. The northern commander could complain all he chose, but he couldn't stop the southrons from doing what needed doing, and that was what counted.

The commanding general called for a runner. "What do you need sir?" the messenger asked.

"I want you to send an alert to the scryers for the soldiers in the forwardmost entrenchments," Hesmucet answered. "Warn them that the traitors are liable to try to sally against them today. Bell may have lost his temper."

"Yes, sir. I'll pass it along directly," the runner said. "Uh, sir . . . How do you know that, if you don't mind my asking?"

"Why, Lieutenant General Bell told me so, of course," Hesmucet answered, deadpan.

The runner started to accept that, then turned and stared. Hesmucet waved him on. He went away shaking his head. Hesmucet laughed softly. *The things I do to keep my air of mystery,* he thought.

What he did next was summon Major Alva. "What can I do for you?" the young mage asked. Hesmucet folded his arms across his chest and waited. Belatedly, Alva turned red. "Uh, sir," he added.

He still didn't remember to salute. Hesmucet would have been merciless with most men who stayed so ignorant of military courtesy. The license he allowed Major Alva measured how much the mage impressed him. "I want you to do your best to learn if the traitors are planning any great magical stroke against us," Hesmucet said.

"Well, I'll try," Alva answered. Hesmucet's arms remained across his chest. He drummed his fingers on his sleeves. "I'll try, *sir,*" Alva said. "You do understand, though, that their spells may cloak whatever they're up to?"

"Won't that cloaking tell you something in and of itself?" Hesmucet asked.

"It may . . . sir." Little by little, Alva got the idea. "It may, but it may not, too. One of the things wizards do is, they make cloaking spells that don't cloak anything. People who run into those spells have to probe them, because they may be hiding something important."

"I am familiar with the idea of deception, yes," Hesmucet said.

"Oh, good." Major Alva's tone plainly implied that a lot of the officers he dealt with weren't. "When do you want this magecraft performed, sir?"

"Immediately," Hesmucet told him. "Sooner would be nice."

"How could I perform it sooner than immediately?" Alva blinked, then sent Hesmucet an accusing stare. Officers who weren't perfectly literal-minded seemed outside his ken, too.

"Be thankful you're not working for Doubting George," Hesmucet said. "He'd drive you straight around the bend, he would."

"Why is that, sir?" Alva asked.

"Never mind," Hesmucet answered. "If I'm standing here explaining, you can't go to work immediately, and that's what I want you to do."

"Yes, sir," Alva said resignedly. "I can't perform the spells immediately, you know. They will take some time."

"Yes, yes," Hesmucet said. "I do understand that. If it weren't for time, everything would happen at once, and we'd all be very confused."

Major Alva gave him a curious look. But the wizard decided not to ask any questions, which was a wise decision. He did salute on leaving. That was wise, too. And he hurried away, which was also a good idea. When he came back—not quite immediately, but close enough to keep Hesmucet from complaining—he wore a troubled expression. "The masking spells are extraordinarily deep, extraordinarily thick," he complained. "I'm not sure I got through all of them."

"I don't like the sound of that," Hesmucet said. "What are they hiding?"

"I'm not sure," Alva answered. "I'm not sure they're hiding anything. But I'm not sure they're not, either."

"What are we supposed to be doing about that?" Hesmucet asked.

"I don't know, sir," Alva replied. "You're the commanding general."

Hesmucet grunted. After some thought, he said, "All we

can do is go on. If they throw sorcery at us, we'll do our best to throw it back. And we'll lick them any which way. By the gods, we *will*."

X

irepots kept bursting inside Marthasville, spreading destruction farther with each passing day. North of the city, southron soldiers began moving toward the west and south, aiming at completing the ring around it. With all the glideways leading into the place in southron hands, only wagons could bring in victuals through the narrowing gap in the enemy's lines. Roast-Beef William knew all too well that wagons could not keep the Army of Franklin fed, no matter how badly its numbers had shrunk because of the recent string of lost battles.

When he said as much to Bell, the general commanding gave him a cold stare. "If your men had held at Jonestown, Lieutenant General, we would still hold a glideway with which to bring in necessities," Bell said.

"I *am* sorry, sir." Roast-Beef William did his best to hold on to his temper. "With my little force, I was a boy trying to do a man's job. We must have been outnumbered three or four to one. No one could have held against those odds."

"So you say now," Bell snapped. "What it looks like to me is that your soldiers were too afraid to come out of their entrenchments and give the southrons a proper fight."

That did it. "You may criticize me all you please," William said, "but, sooner than criticizing the courage of my men—who are, I remind you, also *your* men—you would do better to look in the mirror. You were the one who sent me north to Jonestown, sure the southrons would have only a small force in the neighborhood. Your judgment there proved as wrong as most of your other judgments since taking command of this army. Sir."

Lieutenant General Bell flushed. "You are insubordinate."

And you are incompetent. But if Roast-Beef William said that, he *would* be insubordinate. A dogged sense of duty kept him from doing anything likely to get him removed from command of his wing, though escape from the Army of Franklin looked more inviting with every passing day. Without false modesty, he was sure whoever replaced him would do worse. He didn't know how much he could help the army in its present agony, but he didn't want to hurt it.

He said, "I told you several days ago that I did not think we could hold Marthasville. Nothing has happened since to make me change my mind. Did your correspondence with General Hesmucet bear any fruit?"

Bell flushed again. "None whatsoever," he growled. "He does not fear the gods. He is blind to shame. He has proved himself a liar of the purest ray serene."

He will not do what I wanted him to do: that was what Bell had to mean. Roast-Beef William had no great trouble making the translation. "That being so, sir, what's now to be done?" he asked.

Bell's head went back and forth, back and forth, like that of a caged animal. "I don't know, gods damn it. I just don't know."

The comparison to a caged animal, unfortunately, was all too apt. "Will you lose Marthasville, sir, or will you lose Marthasville *and* your army?" William inquired. "That's the only choice you have left."

"I can't leave Marthasville," Bell moaned. "I don't dare leave Marthasville. What will King Geoffrey say if I do?"

"What will the king say if you don't?" William returned. "What will he say if you're trapped here with your army?"

"Go away," Bell said. "This is not a choice I have to make on the instant, and I do not intend to."

"Yes, sir," Roast-Beef William replied, polite again. "But don't take too long—there, I beg you on bended knee. If the manacles close around us, I don't think we can break free of them."

"Go away," Bell said again, and William went.

Men marched to and fro through the streets of Marthasville. Roast-Beef William looked on the activity as he would have looked on the thrashings of a man about to die of smallpox: they seemed dramatic, but in fact meant nothing. The man *would* die; the city *would* fall. William didn't know when and he didn't know how, not yet. Of the thing itself he had no doubts whatever.

He rode back to his own headquarters, which he kept as far from that of Lieutenant General Bell as he could. He still hadn't forgiven Bell for sending him up to Jonestown without enough men to do the job required of him. Bell had thought he could not only hold the southrons but drive them back. But Hesmucet's army had proved larger and stronger than Bell imagined.

I was the one who had to pay the price for his mistake, Roast-Beef William thought as he dismounted from his unicorn. *I had to pay for it, and I got blamed for it. Otherwise, he would have had to blame himself, and it's plain he's not very good at that.*

A couple of wizards in long blue robes came out of the house William was using and hurried up the street in the direction from which he'd come. "Where away so fast?" William called after them.

One of the mages condescended to turn around. He answered, "Lieutenant General Bell has summoned us, sir. He aims to strike yet another blow against the gods-damned southrons."

"Does he?" Roast-Beef William said. The wizard nodded, then hustled off down the street. William started to hurl another question after him, then decided not to bother. Here, for once, he completely approved of whatever Bell tried to do. The southrons had too many men, too many engines, to make charging into battle against them a good bet. Bell had needed four stinging defeats to see as much, but Roast-Beef William was glad he finally had. In mage-craft, though, where the balance of power lay wasn't nearly so obvious.

Maybe we'll get some good out of this, William thought. *It would be nice if we got some good somewhere. We haven't seen much lately.*

All he could do was send orders to his men to keep them alert in case the southrons in front of them tried to storm Marthasville. He wasn't sure they could hold back the southrons, but he did intend to try.

"Four lost battles," he grumbled, though no one was listening. Even after he'd been driven out of Jonestown, Bell had struck at the southrons again, this time east of Marthasville. That hadn't worked, either. Roast-Beef William shook his head. Bell seemed to have a hard time learn-ing some lessons.

William braced himself for lightnings and thunderbolts and dragons in the air and all the rest of the extravagant wiz-ardry northern mages had at their disposal. He didn't know whether wizardry could win the day hereabouts. He did know nothing else was likely to, not for King Geoffrey's cause.

When darkness fell at noon the next day, hope surged in Roast-Beef William. When lightnings crackled through the darkness, he sent up prayers to the Lion God and the Thunderer. When the earth trembled beneath his feet, he cried out for joy, certain the sorcerers had found ways to do what Lieutenant General Bell could not.

But the southrons didn't flee their lines in wild disor-der. They didn't flee at all. The lightnings crackled, but few smote. The shaking earth didn't shake their trenches to pieces and entomb the enemy soldiers in them. And the darkness that had fallen at noon lifted by half past one.

When the mages attached to Roast-Beef William's wing returned from the headquarters of the general commanding, they were in a sad state. They all looked thinner than they had on going off to serve Lieutenant General Bell. Their robes were limp and stained with sweat; the sharp reek of fear filled William's nostrils.

"In the name of the gods, what happened?" he demanded.

"We were beaten," one of the wizards replied in a hollow voice. His eyes were wide and staring, as if he'd seen things men were not meant to see. "The southrons beat us at sorcery. What is the the world coming to, when such a disaster can come to pass?"

"I don't know." William was also troubled; if soldiers hadn't beaten back King Avram's armies, and if magic also looked like failing, what remained for the north? *Not much.* The words tolled like mourning bells inside Roast-Beef William's mind. He asked, "What do we do now? What *can* we do now?"

"Sir, I don't know," the mage said. "I haven't any idea. All I know is, I want to go to bed and sleep for a year. If you'll excuse me, sir . . ." He staggered off, not really caring whether William excused him or not.

William knew he should have gone to see Bell again, to plan the next move for the Army of Franklin. He knew, but he couldn't bring himself to do it. He might have been someone hesitating to enter a sickroom that held a loved one who *would* die soon—such images kept cropping up in his mind. Duty called, yes, but sometimes even duty did no good. What could he say now that hadn't already been said? Bell knew what shape the army was in. Would he choose to let it perish? Even if he didn't, how could he hope to save Marthasville?

As far as William could see, none of those questions had answers he cared to contemplate. *What do we do? What can we do? Wait for the death, burn the body, and then try to pick up the pieces.* That was all he saw ahead.

Two days later, the only thing that had changed was that the southrons were several miles closer to drawing their ring around Marthasville. Roast-Beef William had trouble caring even about that. He was sunk in such gloom when Major Zibeon came to his headquarters and said, "Lieutenant General Bell requests your presence at once, sir."

"He does, eh?" Roast-Beef William eyed Bell's aide-de-camp with more than a little curiosity. "What does he need me for in such a tearing hurry?"

"I couldn't presume to say, sir," Zibeon replied.

"No?" William doubted that (and, doubting, wished Doubting George had chosen Geoffrey over Avram). Any aide-de-camp worth his boots had a pretty good idea of what his principal was thinking. "Well, I'll come and find out."

"Thanks," Zibeon said, as if Roast-Beef William were doing him a favor rather than obeying an order. William scratched his head. Bell's dour aide-de-camp rarely wasted politeness on anyone but the commanding general, and sometimes not on him. But Zibeon went on, "Ride with me, if you care to, sir."

"I don't mind if I do." Roast-Beef William gave Zibeon a quizzical look. "Are you feeling all right?"

"No," Zibeon said, and said not another word till they got to Bell's headquarters. Then he unbent enough to add, "You'll see."

What Roast-Beef William saw was that Lieutenant General Bell was smiling. He wondered how much laudanum Bell had had. He would have thought that enough to make Bell happy would also have been enough to stop Bell's heart. But the commanding general said, "Good day, William. I am convinced we finally have the southrons where we want them."

"Sir?" Roast-Beef William said in real astonishment.

Bell nodded. "Just so. They think to trap us here. By the gods, I shan't allow it. We shall break out from this prison in which they seek to contain us and then strike with all our strength at the glideway line—the single glideway line—that keeps them fed and supplied. What can they do when they start to starve? Run back to Franklin with their tails between their legs, that's what."

"That is . . . a most ambitious plan, sir," William said at last.

"But it will work!" Bell said. "Claws of the Lion God, it *will* work. If we can hit them one good lick . . ."

Slowly, Roast-Beef William nodded. Bell wasn't thinking about abandoning Marthasville. He was thinking about attacking the enemy. As long as he thought about the attack, the abandonment wouldn't bother him. Under other circumstances, that would have horrified Roast-Beef William. As things were, it left him more pleased than otherwise. If the Army of Franklin didn't get out of Marthasville, before long it wouldn't be able to get out of Marthasville.

And so, with another nod, William said, "I think you have a good plan there, sir. We should commence without delay."

"See to it, then," Bell said—he wasn't, and never would be, any sort of military administrator. "Draft the necessary orders for my signature."

"Yes, sir," William said resignedly. *I should have expected this*, he thought. "I suppose you'll want to destroy whatever supplies we can't take with us."

"Indeed," Bell said, which meant he hadn't thought of that for himself. "Take care of all the details. That's why I rely on you."

"Yes, sir. Thank you so much, sir." But then Roast-Beef William shook his head. *Don't put his back up. He's doing what needs doing. If too much of the work falls on your shoulders, then it does, that's all.*

"We're going to make Hesmucet wish he never came so far up into Peachtree Province," Bell declared. "He'll rue the day—see if he doesn't."

And the general commanding had some chance of being right. William could see as much, see it very clearly. The odds were still long, but they were better than they would be if the Army of Franklin stayed here in Marthasville and waited for doom to fall on it. "Give me pen and paper, sir," Roast-Beef William said. "I'll get to work on those orders right now."

Lieutenant General Bell laughed. "That's the man I knew I had. The gods-damned southrons will be sorry yet."

"Here's hoping you're right, sir," William said. "Where's that paper? I want to make sure this is done the way it ought to be."

Gremio touched a torch to a pile of crates. As they began to burn, he said, "I wonder what's in these."

"Wait a while and see what they smell like," Sergeant Thisbe suggested.

"No time," Gremio said. "We've got a lot more burning

to do. And do you know what else? It's more fun than I thought it would be."

"Fun? I don't know about that," Thisbe said. "What I do know is, we've got to do this, or else the southrons will march into Marthasville and use everything we couldn't take with us."

"Me, I'm just glad we're getting out of Marthasville," Captain Gremio said. "I thought we'd stay penned up here till the southrons took us." He paused to set another fire.

"Sounds like Lieutenant General Bell's got himself another idea." Thisbe started a new fire, too. He looked at the incendiary madness all around, as Gremio was doing. "Between the southrons and us, there won't be a whole lot of Marthasville left after all this is done."

"Good," Gremio said, which made the sergeant send him a startled look. He explained: "Better we don't leave Hesmucet anything much to get his hands on."

"Something to that, sir, I suppose," Thisbe said, "but it's hard, it's mighty hard, on the people who live here."

To the seven hells with the people who live here, Gremio thought callously. He couldn't see that the folk of Peachtree Province or Satrap Brown had done anywhere near enough to help the Army of Franklin defend this vital town. But he didn't say that out loud; he'd seen that Sergeant Thisbe was more inclined to give people the benefit of the doubt than he was himself unless he was paid to do so.

"Come on, you men!" Colonel Florizel boomed to the regiment as a whole. "If we're going to deny the enemy these goods, let's not shillyshally around. Let's make a fire the foe will remember to the end of his days."

Something like wonder in his voice, Thisbe said, "The colonel's having a good time."

"Well, why not?" said Gremio, who was having a good time himself. "Doesn't this take you back to the days when you were a boy, starting fires and raising hells for the sport of it?"

"I hadn't thought of it like that," Thisbe admitted.

"You're too responsible now, that's why," Gremio said. "You're far and away the best sergeant I've ever known. If you'd let me put you up for a—"

"Sir, I don't want a promotion," Thisbe said firmly, and Gremio had to give it up again.

His long, thin face lit by the hellsish glare of burning supplies, Brigadier Alexander the Steward stalked among the men of his wing. "Hurry it up there!" Old Straight called to the soldiers. "Set the fires and then form up to move out of Marthasville. We've still got a hells of a lot of fighting ahead of us."

Alexander's tone went further to reassure Captain Gremio than any of the orders Lieutenant General Bell had given lately. Those orders, as Florizel had read them out, seemed an odd mixture of defiance and desperation. Gremio had trouble figuring out whom Bell was defying, the enemy or the gods themselves. The cause for the desperation, however, seemed obvious enough.

"Douse torches!" Colonel Florizel shouted. "Form up!"

Instead of dousing his torch, Gremio threw it onto a fire already burning. Sergeant Thisbe's joined it a moment later. Officer and underofficer grinned at each other. Gremio called, "My company—form up!"

"Get moving!" Thisbe echoed. "You know what needs doing. Do it and don't make a fuss about it."

As the sun rose, the Army of Franklin marched out of Marthasville to the northwest, the only gap remaining in the line the southrons were throwing around the city. Gremio didn't know how many men General Hesmucet had close by. That worried him. But the southrons evidently doubted they had enough for a successful attack on Bell's army, for it escaped without incident.

Seeing land that hadn't been fought over was something of a relief. "Pretty good country," Colonel Florizel allowed. "Not so nice as around Karlsburg, back in Palmetto Province, but pretty good even so."

"Yes, sir." Gremio nodded. "But do you see how many of the serfs' huts are standing empty? Most of the blonds have run off to the southrons."

"Gods damn them, and gods damn that wretch of a King Avram," Florizel said. "How are the lords around these parts going to make a crop now?"

"They probably won't," Gremio answered. "But I don't think Hesmucet cares. Do you?"

"Do I care?" Florizel said—whether sardonic or obtuse, Gremio couldn't tell. "Gods-damned right I care. This is my kingdom. Of course I care what happens to it. It's that son of a bitch of a Hesmucet who doesn't care."

"Yes, sir," Gremio said resignedly. He looked back over his shoulder at the great columns of smoke still rising from Marthasville. Either a few soldiers remained behind setting still more fires or the ones already set had spread from abandoned supplies to the city itself. Gremio wondered how hard the southrons would try to put those fires out. Not very, unless he missed his guess.

"Where do you suppose we'll go, sir?" Sergeant Thisbe asked after they'd marched for a while.

"South, I suppose," Gremio replied. "I don't know just when, but I'd think we're going to have to do that. If we strike at Hesmucet's glideway line, maybe his army will starve and break up."

"That would be a splendid victory," Thisbe said.

"So it would." Gremio didn't tell the sergeant he found it unlikely. He found any hope of victory unlikely. Saying as much would have discouraged those who might be more optimistic, though, and so he held back. The men had enough trouble keeping their spirits up as things were.

Well before noon, southron unicorn-riders began dogging the Army of Franklin. They didn't attack; they just hung close. Gremio waited for the aggressive Bell to order his own riders to drive them away. Those orders didn't come. *What does that mean?* he wondered. Did Bell think his unicorn-riders *couldn't* drive back the southrons? Or was he so desperate to get away from Marthasville that he didn't want to waste time fighting? Whichever the answer, Gremio didn't think it boded well for his force.

When he cautiously remarked on that, Florizel said, "I doubt the southrons will bother us much for a little while. They'll be too busy with Marthasville, don't you think?"

Gremio clicked his tongue between his teeth, considering. "You could well be right, sir," he said.

"We've given 'em a present," the regimental commander said. "They'll take it. Why wouldn't they? It's sitting there for 'em, all sweet and juicy as a blond wench with her legs open."

"And losing it hurts us," Gremio added.

Colonel Florizel nodded. "And losing it hurts us," he agreed. "We'd better cut their army off from its supplies, or Geoffrey's badly wounded."

"You . . . don't usually talk like that, sir," Gremio said. *And the last time I talked like that, you came as near as near can be to calling me a coward. I had to try to get myself killed to make you change your mind.*

"I'm not blind," Florizel answered. "I know we needed to hold Marthasville. I know we didn't do it. I'm not stupid, either, no matter what a highfalutin' barrister might think."

"Sir, I've never said anything of the sort," Gremio insisted.

"I know you didn't. I never said you did," Florizel told him. "I said what you were thinking, and I wasn't wrong, was I?"

He used words as precisely as if he were a barrister himself. Gremio said, "I don't know what you're talking about, sir. You've led this regiment well, and I've never thought otherwise." That was the truth, too, even if it wasn't altogether responsive.

"You wouldn't be breathing if you had run your mouth," Florizel replied. Gremio looked for an answer to that, found none, and decided it might have been just as well.

As he'd expected, the Army of Franklin swung back toward the southeast, the direction of the glideway line that kept General Hesmucet and the southrons fed. The Army of Franklin was for the time being making do without a glideway line; the countryside was rich and fertile, and the soldiers had no trouble keeping themselves fed.

Juices sizzled as a fowl—a fowl that had probably belonged to a loyal northern farmer—cooked over a fire. Turning the stick that spitted the bird, Sergeant Thisbe said, "If we can feed ourselves off the country here, why can't the southrons do the same?"

Gremio started to give that a flip answer, but stopped with the words unspoken. "Good question," he said after a pause. "The only thing I can think of is, there are a lot more of them than there are of us. Of course, they also have a proper baggage train, and we don't."

"We burned ours in Marthasville," Thisbe said.

"We can move faster without it." Gremio put the best face on things he could.

"Yes, and we can start starving faster, too." But Thisbe lifted the fowl from the flames. He blew on it, then drew his knife from its sheath and started carving. Handing Gremio a leg, he said, "You fancy the dark meat, don't you?"

"Right now, I fancy anything that'll keep my stomach from bumping up against the notches on my backbone," Gremio answered. He ate the hot flesh, savoring the grease from the skin. Somebody else had a pot full of turnips boiling over another fire. Gremio got a tin plate piled high with them. He ate and ate, then blissfully thumped his belly. "Do you know what, Sergeant?"

"No, sir. What?" Thisbe spoke with his mouth full: he was still demolishing his plateload.

"Those turnips needed *salt*," Gremio declared.

"You're right," Thisbe agreed. "But I'm still better with 'em than I would be without 'em."

"Can't quarrel with that," Gremio said. "Can't quarrel with anything, not any more." He yawned. "Can't do anything much right now except roll over and go to sleep." He wrapped himself in his blanket—much more to hold mosquitoes at bay than to keep him warm—and did just that.

When the army started marching again the next morning, it kept on going southeast. Without a baggage train to delay it, it did move faster than the southron force. General Hesmucet didn't seem much interested in pursuit, anyhow; maybe Marthasville *was* enough to satisfy him. Gremio hoped so. He'd had enough fighting against long odds to suit him for a while—for the next hundred years, come to that.

Bell passed well south of Marthasville on his way east. Gremio knew at once when the Army of Franklin returned to land that had seen war already this campaigning season. How long would the swath of war, the gouge of the Lion God's claws, scar Peachtree Province? If not for generations, he would have been astonished.

He was astonished when Bell passed over the glideway line with no more than a few hasty spells from the sorcerers. "What's the point of that?" he asked anyone who would listen to him. "Even southrons can put things to rights in a hurry."

But Colonel Florizel, for once, had an answer that satisfied him: "I hear we're heading east into Dothan to rest and refit, and then we'll come back and hit the southrons a proper lick."

"Gods know we could use rest and refit," Gremio said, and the regimental commander nodded. Gremio asked, "Will we get any reinforcements? We could use them, too." They could use them to replace the men Lieutenant General Bell had thrown away in one futile attack after another. Gremio saw no point to saying that, but he thought it very loudly.

Florizel only shook his head. "No reinforcements I've heard about, Captain. If we'd had more men handy, don't you suppose they would have come into Marthasville a long time ago?"

"You're probably right," Gremio admitted. "But the southrons keep getting fresh men whenever they need them. It would be nice if we didn't have to depend on the soldiers who started the war."

That was an exaggeration, but not an enormous one. Florizel's answering grimace showed a broken front tooth. That tooth hadn't been broken when the war was new; Gremio would have taken oath on it. Little by little, the fighting wore the men down in all sorts of ways.

Here, though, marching was easy. Hesmucet mounted no real chase of the Army of Franklin. Maybe Marthasville had been his target all along. Or maybe . . . "Maybe he doesn't think we can hurt him any more," Gremio said once the battered army entered the province of Dothan.

"If he doesn't, he'll get himself a nasty surprise," Sergeant Thisbe declared. "We've still got teeth, by the gods."

Gremio nodded. Man for man, northern soldiers remained at least as formidable as their southron counterparts. Teeth, as Thisbe had said. But how strong were the jaws that held those teeth? The more Gremio thought about the state of the Army of Franklin, the closer he came to despair.

✧　　✧　　✧

"Corporal, take up the company standard!" Lieutenant Griff commanded.

"Yes, *sir*!" Rollant said, and he did. Pride swelled in him till he felt about to float away like an inflated pig's bladder. The more he thought about the state of General Hesmucet's army, about how far they'd come and how much they'd done, the more he imagined he *was* on the point of floating away.

That must have shown on his face, for Smitty, grinning, asked him, "You happy, your Corporalship, sir?"

"Oh, just a little," Rollant answered. "Yes, just a little."

"Form up for parade," Griff called to his men. "I don't want anybody missing a step, not a single step, when we go through town today. Marthasville is ours, and fairly won, as General Hesmucet said in his order of the day. And I want those traitor bastards to know we aren't just good enough to lick 'em—we can be fancier than they are, too." Rollant nodded vigorously. He wanted to show up, to show off before, the people who had once bound him to the land. *Treat me like a cow with hands, will you? You'll see!*

Horns blared. Griff started shouting again. Colonel Nahath's order carried farther: "Forward—march!"

Forward Rollant went, holding the gold dragon on red high. The standard fluttered in the breeze. Griff nodded. "That's good. That's very good, Corporal. Let the folk of Marthasville see the kingdom's true flag. They've looked at the reversed banner too long."

Rollant shook the standard to display the dragon better still. He wanted the Detinans in Marthasville to get a good look at it—and at him. He strutted. He swaggered. He displayed the stripes on his left arm as best he could, so the people who'd called themselves liege lords would see what a blond could do when he got the chance.

Marching through Rising Rock the summer before had been enjoyable. Marching through Marthasville . . .

Lieutenant Griff chose that moment to ask him almost the same question Smitty had: "Having a good time, Corporal?"

Rollant looked around. Lining this main street were hundreds, more likely thousands, of glum-looking Detinans: women, children, and men with beards gray or white. The younger men were in false king Geoffrey's army. Every single spectator seemed to be looking straight at him. He knew that was an illusion, but even so . . .

"Sir, I feel about ready to quit this world altogether," he said.

Griff laughed out loud and slapped him on the shoulder. "I don't blame you a bit. It must be pretty fine, getting to spit in these northerners' eyes."

"As a matter of fact, sir, it is." Rollant looked at Griff with more respect than he was in the habit of giving the company commander. Griff was too young for his job, and too weedy besides, but he was plenty brave enough, and every now and then proved he wasn't stupid, either. His remark showed more understanding of the way blonds thought than Rollant would have looked to see from any Detinan, northerner or southron.

And then the band struck up "The Battle Psalm on the Kingdom." Rollant forgot about Griff, as he forgot about everything but that fierce, triumphant music. No one had ever accused him of singing well. No one ever would. But he was loud and enthusiastic. Past that, what really mattered? If the haughty Detinans of Marthasville didn't care for the way he sounded, too bad for them.

Not many blonds were watching the southron soldiers tramp past. Most of them, he guessed, had already fled their liege lords and the land to which they were supposed to be bound. But the few who'd stayed behind were wildly excited now. A pretty woman, seeing Rollant's golden hair and beard, blew him a kiss and twitched her hips in a way that could mean only one thing.

Lieutenant Griff noticed her, too. "You find her once we go into bivouac, Corporal, and you won't sleep alone tonight."

"I've got a wife, sir," Rollant said uncomfortably. He'd been away from Norina a long time now, and missed her—missed any woman—no less than any other man, blond or Detinan, would have done.

"She's a long way off," Griff said.

"I couldn't do that, sir. I wouldn't do that," Rollant said. "If I did that to her, why wouldn't she do it to me?"

Griff gave him a curious look. "I wouldn't have expected you to take your oaths so seriously."

"Why? Because I'm a blond . . . sir?" Rollant could have said a great deal more than that, but not without being insubordinate.

"Well, let me put it like this," Griff answered: "I know plenty of Detinans who don't turn down whatever they can get, and they don't care a curse about whether they're married or not."

"There are people like that," Rollant agreed. Captain Cephas, who'd commanded the company before Griff, had been a man like that. Now he was dead, along with the blond woman who'd been his lover and her blond husband. Rollant didn't care to bring up Cephas. He did say, "The fun they have doesn't usually make up for the trouble they cause. That's what I think, anyhow."

"Maybe you're right," Griff said. "But not everybody thinks about trouble before he thinks about getting it in." He didn't mention Captain Cephas, either, but Rollant would have been surprised if he weren't thinking about him, too.

Rollant took a look at Marthasville itself, not at the Detinans still living in it. "I can see why Bell finally left this place," he said. "Hardly enough left of it to defend."

"Are you sorry?" the company commander asked.

"Sorry? Me? No, sir," Rollant answered. "But I'll tell you something: even with Marthasville all smashed up the way it is, the Detinans are still living a lot better than they ever let their serfs live."

"From what I've seen in the countryside, Corporal, I'd say you're probably right," Griff told him. Rollant blinked again; he wouldn't have bet Griff noticed anything unmilitary in the countryside.

At last, the regiment tramped out of Marthasville. Hereabouts, people reckoned it a big city. Before escaping from his liege lord's estate in Palmetto Province, Rollant would have thought it one, too. After ten years of living in New Eborac . . . He shook his head. As far as he was concerned, Marthasville was nothing but an overgrown town.

"We camp here," Griff told him, pointing to a meadow next to a stand of pines.

"All right, sir," Rollant said. "Any particular place you want me to plant the standard?"

Griff pointed to a tiny swell of ground. "How about right there?" Rollant shrugged; it seemed as good a place as any other. He stabbed the butt end of the flagpole into the brick-red—almost blood-red—dirt. That done, he took up a pinch of earth and sprinkled it at the base of the pole. Griff nodded approval. "You know all the rituals, sure enough."

Even though you're a blond. That had to be lurking behind his words. That lurked behind so many Detinans' thoughts whenever they dealt with blonds. Rollant knew it would keep on lurking in Detinans' thoughts for as long as he lived. Maybe by the time his children were grown, Detinans would be able to accept blonds as people like any others. And maybe they wouldn't, too.

Colonel Nahath came up to the standard and spoke to Griff: "We're going to act as provost guards in Marthasville, keep the men from tearing the place up too much and keep them from squabbling with the locals. I'm sending companies in on rotation. Yours will go in there tonight."

"Yes, sir," Griff said, the only thing a junior officer could say at an order from a senior. "Uh, sir, a question?" When Nahath nodded, Griff asked, "What about Rollant here and the other blonds I've got?"

Nahath plucked at his beard, but not for long. "They're soldiers," he said. "They can do a soldier's job. If they can't do a soldier's job, they shouldn't wear the uniform." He eyed Rollant. "What do you say to that, Corporal?"

"I'll do my best, sir," Rollant answered. "Of course, some of the traitors won't be used to doing what a filthy, stinking blond serf tells them to."

"A point," Colonel Nahath said. "Do you think you can persuade them?"

Rollant's smile was large and predatory. "Sir, I look forward to it."

Nahath and Griff both laughed. The regimental commander said, "Try to leave them breathing once they're persuaded."

"Oh, I suppose so, sir," Rollant said, which made the two Detinan officers laugh again. Rollant asked, "May I pick a partner, sir?"

At the serious question, the colonel and lieutenant looked at each other. "Well, that's probably not a bad notion. You should have someone you can trust at your back," Nahath said. Rollant gave him a grateful nod. At least Nahath recognized he couldn't trust all Detinans at his back.

"Why me?" Smitty asked as they walked back toward Marthasville together. "What did I do to you?"

"Saved my neck a few times," Rollant answered. "Maybe you'll do it again."

"After you hauled me off to go patrolling?" Smitty shook his head. "Not gods-damned likely, pal. I could be asleep right now."

"Thanks, Smitty. You're a true friend." Rollant thought— he was almost sure—the farmer's son from outside New Eborac City was joking. Smitty cracked wise about anything and everything. But a bit of doubt still lingered. Would Smitty have said the same sorts of things had Sergeant Joram plucked him into duty? *Knowing Smitty, he likely would,* Rollant thought, and relaxed a bit.

Marthasville looked bigger when he came into it as part of a two-man patrol and without an army at his back. Torches blazed in front of every surviving business. Eateries and taverns and brothels looked to be thriving, with long lines of men in gray snaking forward in front of the latter. The women inside those places were almost sure to be blonds. Rollant shook his head and did his best not to think about that.

A Detinan in civilian clothes stared at him and Smitty. "You think you're a soldier, butter-hair?" he asked Rollant. His accent proclaimed him a local.

"No," Rollant answered. "I *know* I'm a soldier. I've been through the war, and that's a hells of a lot more than you can say."

Even by the torchlight, he saw the northerner flush. "You ought to be unicornwhipped, talking to your betters like that."

"Get lost, traitor. If you don't get lost, you'll be sorry." That wasn't Rollant; it was Smitty.

The northerner swore at him: "Gods-damned son of a bitch, you're the traitor—a traitor to the Detinan race."

"You'd better get lost," Smitty said, "or we'll run you in."

"I'd like to see you try," the northern man said.

Rollant didn't need a second invitation. He jerked his shortsword from its scabbard. Smitty's came free, too. "Come along, or you'll be sorry," Rollant said. He took a step toward the man from Marthasville.

Not till the fellow's hands writhed in his first pass did Rollant realize he might have made a mistake. Not till his own feet seemed to freeze to the dirt of the street did he realize he might have made a very bad mistake. Laughing, the local said, "If you're going to net a dragon, you had best think on where you'll find a net to hold him."

Smitty seemed stuck, too. He howled curses. Laughing still, the man—the mage—from Marthasville drew a knife and advanced on them. "In King Avram's name, let us go!" Rollant exclaimed.

And he could move again.

The mage hadn't let him go, or Smitty, either. When they did move, the fellow's jaw dropped. He tried his enchantment once more; it did him no good. He tried to flee, but Rollant and Smitty were younger and faster. Rollant brought him down with a ferocious flying tackle. "Cut the bastard's throat," Smitty urged. "He's dangerous."

Rollant shook his head. "We'll hogtie him and give him to the provost marshal," he said. "Practicing magic against us? They'll make him wish we'd cut his throat." He and Smitty bound the northerner hand and foot, threw his knife in the gutter, and hauled him away.

After they'd handed him over to higher authority, Smitty said, "You called on King Avram, and that freed us from the spell."

"I thought the same thing," Rollant said. "What do you suppose it means?"

"It means King Avram, gods bless him, has a powerful name, that's what," Smitty said.

"*That* powerful?" Rollant asked.

"Well, I wouldn't have thought so, either," Smitty said. "But you saw what happened, same as I did. That stinking wizard had us in trouble." Rollant shivered. The wizard had had them in a *lot* of trouble. Smitty went on, "Then you spoke the king's name, and we were all right again. Good thing, too."

"Yes, a very good thing," Rollant agreed. "Now we know King Avram is someone very special indeed." He frowned; that didn't get his meaning across so well as he would have liked. He tried again: "We knew it before, but now we *know* it." His frown got deeper. That still wasn't right.

Or maybe it was. Smitty said, "We know it in our bellies, you mean."

"Yes!" Rollant said gratefully. And, knowing it in his belly, he got through the rest of the patrol without trouble. By then, he wanted a chance to use Avram's name again. As he went back to camp, though, he decided he might have been lucky not to get one.

Jim the Haystack, the burgomaster of Marthasville, stared nervously at General Hesmucet. "You can't mean that," he said.

"Of course I can," Hesmucet said, watching with a certain fascination the ugly wig that probably gave Jim his nickname. "I am in the habit of meaning what I say. I usually do, and this is no exception."

"But you can't burn Marthasville!" Jim the Haystack wailed. That dreadful wig seemed about ready to topple over sideways in his discomfiture. He looked like a man who needed to run to the latrine.

None of that mattered to Hesmucet. "I not only can, sir, I intend to," he said. "I cannot stay here, not while Lieutenant General Bell is running around loose and making a nuisance of himself. If I left the place intact, you traitors would go on getting use from it. I can't have that, not when I've come all the way up from Franklin to take it away from you. And so I'll give it to the fire."

"I know your mind and time are constantly occupied with the duties of your command," Jim the Haystack said, wig nodding above his forehead. "But it might be that you have not considered this subject in all its awful consequences."

"I believe I have," Hesmucet said.

As if he hadn't spoken, the burgomaster went on, "On more reflection, you, I hope, would not make the people of Marthasville an exception to all mankind, for I know of no such instance ever having occurred—surely never in Detina—and what has this *helpless* people done, that they should be driven from their homes, to wander strangers and outcasts, and exiles? I solemnly petition you to reconsider this order, or modify it, and suffer this unfortunate people to remain at home, and enjoy what little means they have."

"Very pretty, sir, but no." Hesmucet shook his head. "I give full credit to your statements of the distress that will be occasioned, and yet shall not revoke my orders."

"In the names of the gods, why?" Jim the Haystack howled.

"Because they were not designed to meet the humanities of the case, but to prepare for future struggles," Hesmucet answered. "We must have peace, not only at Marthasville, but in all Detina. To stop war, we must defeat the traitor armies which are arrayed against the laws and the rightful king."

"He is not the rightful king," Jim the Haystack said. "He is a low-down thief."

"Well, that is your opinion. I have a different one," Hesmucet told him. "Now that war comes home to you, you feel very different. War is cruelty, and you cannot refine it; and those who brought war into our kingdom deserve all the curses and maledictions a people can pour out. But you cannot have peace and a division of our kingdom."

"You have the soldiers here," Jim the Haystack said bitterly, "so you will do as pleases you best. But I still think it is barbarous, truly barbarous, to send the whole of the population of Marthasville off to fend for itself as best it may."

"I believe you. I appreciate that you are sincere, and that burning this town will work a hardship on the people who live here," Hesmucet replied. "But winning the war comes first. I also doubt that, earlier in the war, you lost any sleep or shed a single tear when the armies that follow false King Geoffrey made loyal civilians—men, women, and children—flee them, barefoot and in rags, down in Franklin and Cloviston."

Jim the Haystack looked at him as if he'd suddenly

started speaking gibberish. No, the burgomaster cared for nothing but his own people and his own side. That didn't surprise General Hesmucet, but it did sadden him. Jim only said, "Have you no mercy? Have you no compassion?"

"None, not when there's a war to be won," Hesmucet said. "And that, sir, is about all the time I have to give you. You have made your views very plain. Now let me make one thing very plain to you. If any men of Marthasville attempt to interfere with my soldiers in the performance of their duties, I will show exactly how little mercy I have. If you think being dispossessed works a hardship on your population, opposing me will work a much greater one. Do you understand?"

"Perfectly," the burgomaster replied. "You are saying you not only *are* a barbarian, but are proud to be one." Hesmucet stared at him, unblinking. Jim the Haystack flinched. He said, "I will take your words to the honest citizens of the town I govern."

"Take my words to the sons of bitches, too," Hesmucet said. "I expect they're the ones who really need to hear them. Good day, sir."

Wig still nodding shakily above his brow, Jim the Haystack departed. Once he was gone, Hesmucet allowed himself the luxury of a chuckle. He called for a runner and asked him to summon Doubting George. He was still chuckling when his second-in-command arrived.

"What's so funny, sir?" George asked.

"The arrogance of some of these northern men, who think they can turn me from my course even after their army has lost battle after battle," Hesmucet answered. He explained what the burgomaster of Marthasville had tried to talk him into, or rather, out of, doing.

Doubting George shook his head. "Some people don't understand the way the world is put together," he said sadly. "Of course, you could say the whole north doesn't understand the way the world works. If it did, it never would have tried to leave Detina."

"You're right about that," Hesmucet said. "We're bigger than they are and stronger than they are, and we're beating them down. That burgomaster didn't care what his side's soldiers did farther south, and he never expected to see us come this far north."

"What Geoffrey calls his kingdom has a miserable scrawny body, but a head full of fire," George said. "Plenty of fine officers to lead the men, but they have a hard time keeping them in food and shoes and clothes."

"I like the figure," Hesmucet said. "We southrons, we've had a big, strong body with a head full of rocks. But the north will never be anything but scrawny, no matter how fiery its head gets. And our head can get a little fire of its own."

"Just so," George agreed. "You and Marshal Bart have gone a long way towards proving that. You've whipped the Army of Franklin, and Bart's got the Army of Southern Parthenia penned up north of Nonesuch."

"Only trouble here is, Bell doesn't know he's whipped, gods damn him," Hesmucet said. "He keeps wanting to make trouble."

"People who want to make trouble find themselves in it more often than not," George observed. "I don't think Bell will be different from any of the rest."

"I intend to go after him," Hesmucet said. "He thinks he can give us fits by cutting the glideway link from Rising Rock. I don't think he can do it for long, but even if he does, what difference will it make? His gods-damned army's living off the countryside now. Does he think we can't do the same?"

"If he does, he's a fool," Doubting George said. "Of course, nothing much he's done in this campaign would make me believe he's *not* a fool."

"I'm going ahead with things just as planned," Hesmucet said. "We chase the people out of Marthasville, we burn the place, we leave a garrison behind to hold the ruins and keep the traitors from getting any more glideway carpets through, and then we go after the Army of Franklin."

"Sounds good to me, sir," George said.

The only people to whom it didn't sound good were the inhabitants of Marthasville. Their opinions mattered not at all to General Hesmucet. They cursed and reviled him as his provost guards routed them from their homes. "You may stay if you like," he said cheerfully. "You'll go up in smoke, but you may stay. I won't stop you, but I sure as hells will burn you."

They cursed him harder than ever after that, but not a one of them stayed to burn with the city. He'd expected nothing different.

The stink of smoke still lingered in the air from the time when Bell's men had fired whatever they couldn't bring with them. "I bet the traitors had a roaring good time burning things," Hesmucet told one incendiary. "But we'll have a better one, on account of this whole stinking town goes up now."

Go up Marthasville did. Hesmucet's soldiers spread cooking oil and whale oil all through the city before starting their blazes. That made the fires flare up even hotter and brighter when the men did set them. Hesmucet took off his hat and fanned his face with it, but the heat still made drops of sweat run down his cheeks.

Not far from him, a northern woman cried out in despair: "Traa! I've got to get back to Traa!"

"Oh, shut up, you stupid bitch," said the handsome man with jug-handle ears next to her. "The southrons burned that place weeks ago."

"You go to the hells, Thert the Butler!" the woman said furiously. "I'll build it up again, you see if I don't."

"Frankly, my dear, I don't give a—" Thert answered, and then howled, because she kicked him in the shin.

"Move along, both of you!" a provost guard shouted. "Move along right now." He was a blond. Not only that, Hesmucet saw, he was a corporal. If the northern man noticed that, he wouldn't like it at all. But he seemed more interested in quarreling with the woman than in arguing with the provost guard.

As the flames took hold and spread, the provost guards stopped having to order people to abandon the burning Marthasville. No one could stay in or close to those flames and hope to live. Hesmucet, no coward, had to retreat himself. He watched the fires from a distance of several hundred yards.

Not far from him, an artist sketched the scene. Hesmucet

nodded approval. "You get it down just the way it looks," he said. "I want people to remember this for the next hundred and fifty years."

"That's what I'm doing, sir," the artist said. "Let people see what they get for rebelling against the rightful king."

"Good," Hesmucet said. "People should see such things. They should know what treason costs. If the gods be kind, we'll never have to fight another war like this in all the history of the kingdom."

"That's what I'm hoping for, sir," the artist said. "You've certainly set the scene for me, I will say that."

"No, indeed." Hesmucet shook his head. "The men who followed false King Geoffrey into betrayal set this scene for you. If not for them, Marthasville would still be a thriving northern town."

"Yes, sir." The artist nodded vigorously. "Instead, they've got—this." He held up the sketch so Hesmucet could get a good look at it. The flames from the burning city gave the commanding general plenty of light.

"Good job," he said. "Gods-damned good job. Let it be a warning to those who talk of treason and rebellion. We ought to be fighting out on the eastern steppes, driving back the blond savages who've caused us so much trouble over the years. That's what we ought to be doing, not squabbling amongst ourselves. Geoffrey's treason has cost us years—years, I tell you—in which we could have been bringing this whole great land under Detinan rule."

"Can't turn blonds into serfs any more," the artist said, perhaps incautiously.

But General Hesmucet, in an expansive mood, shrugged instead of snarling. "Those savages wouldn't make good serfs anyway," he said. "They don't bend, the way the blonds in the kingdoms of the northeast did hundreds of years ago. They break instead. They're brave men; I don't deny it— they might almost be Detinans, as far as that goes. But we *will* break them, and sweep them off the land, and use it for our own purposes." He might almost have been talking of breaking so many untamed unicorns.

The artist nodded again and returned to his work. *I'd better do the same,* Hesmucet thought. He shouted for his unicorn. When he'd swung up onto the beast, he rode rapidly up toward the head of his army. Every few hundred yards, the marching men in gray tunics and pantaloons would raise a cheer. Each time they did, Hesmucet took off his hat and waved it. Every cheer made him feel as good as if he'd just had a strong slug of spirits.

"Are we going to lick these stinking northern sons of bitches?" he called to the men as he took his place at the fore.

"Yes, sir!" the soldiers shouted, and raised another cheer.

"Are we going to make them sorry they ever tried to pull out of Detina?"

"*Yes, sir!*" The yells came louder than ever.

"Are we going to make them wish gods-damned Geoffrey's father had pulled out of his mother?"

"Yes, sir!" This time, bawdy laughter mixed with the soldiers' replies.

"All right, then," Hesmucet said. "We are the meanest, toughest bunch of soldiers the Kingdom of Detina has ever seen. We *have* licked the traitors, and we're going to go right *on* licking them, and there isn't one single gods-damned thing they can do about it. And what do you think of that?"

By their yells and whoops, the men liked the idea. Hesmucet liked it, too. But there was one thing the northerners might do, and he knew it. If they did cut the supply line back to Rising Rock and keep it cut, his life would get harder. *Have to make sure they don't keep it cut, then,* he thought, and hoped he could manage that.

Horns blared, all through the camp of the Army of Franklin. "Forward!" Colonel Florizel shouted.

"Forward!" Captain Gremio echoed. Forward the men of his company, Florizel's regiment, and the whole Army of Franklin went, west out of Dothan and back into Peachtree Province once more. Lieutenant General Bell had grit, if nothing else. And a few days to rest and recuperate, a few days away from the hells Marthasville had become, did wonders for the army. By the way they marched, the men once more believed they could lick any number of southrons on the face of the earth.

Gremio wasn't so sure they were right. But now they weren't pinned in the city. Now they could pick where along Hesmucet's tenuous supply line they attacked. The supply line surely had more weaknesses than the army did.

It had better have more weaknesses than the southron army did, Gremio thought. *If it doesn't, we won't be able to hurt it. And if we can't hurt it, we—and Geoffrey's kingdom—are in a lot of trouble.*

Sergeant Thisbe tramped along beside Gremio, never complaining, always competent. Catching the company commander's eye on him, he nodded and said, "We'll give it our best shot, sir."

"I know we will," Gremio answered. "That's what we have to do. Uh, one of the things we have to do," he amended. Remembering one of the other things the Army of Franklin had to do these days, he raised his voice to a shout: "Foragers out to the flanks! Move, move, move!"

Move the men did, many of them with grins on their faces. The Army of Franklin had no formal supply train, not any more. The southrons had closed all the glideway lines into Marthasville, and east of the city those were few and far between. If the army was to survive, it had to live off the countryside. The men had done that plenty of times in enemy-held territory, less often in land nominally ruled by King Geoffrey. But necessity made a stronger law than any of the ones Gremio had argued in the lawcourts. The soldiers took what they needed, and worried not at all about it.

"A good thing this is rich country," Thisbe remarked as the foragers went a-scrounging. "We'd be hungry if it weren't."

"True enough," Gremio said. "Good for us—but it's also good for the southrons. Even if we do cut them off from their base of supply, they may well be able to live off the country, too. I worry about that."

"Do you really think they can forage as well as we can, sir?" Thisbe asked.

Gremio laughed. "I'd have to doubt that," he admitted. "We've got the best collection of thieves left uncrucified running around loose in this army. They'll nab anything that isn't nailed down, and they'll try to pry up the nails if it is. I'm proud of them, by the gods."

"Where exactly are we headed for?" Thisbe said.

With another laugh—a sardonic one this time—Gremio answered, "What, you think they tell me anything?" He raised his voice again, this time to call to Colonel Florizel: "Sir, where are we going?"

"Back to Whole Mackerel, from what I hear," Florizel replied from unicornback. "The southrons have a supply base there. If we take it away from them, we live high on the hog for a while, and they don't."

"Sounds good to me." Gremio imagined plundering a southron supply base. His mouth watered at the thought of it. But food wouldn't be the only thing there. He thought of shoes and pantaloons and medicines and all the other things that kept an army going and that were in sadly short supply in the north.

A farmer wailed as foragers took his livestock. "You bastards are nothing but a pack of brigands!" he wailed. "Might as well have the gods-damned southrons here instead."

"You will be compensated for your loss," Gremio said. He pulled a scrap of paper and a pencil from a pantaloon pocket. "Let me have your name and what was taken from you. I will write you a receipt."

"A receipt? A gods-damned *receipt*?" the farmer shouted. "Who in the hells is going to pay me for whatever's wrote on a stinking *receipt*?" Every use of the word seemed filled with greater scorn.

"King Geoffrey's government will, sir, after the war is won," Gremio answered.

Snatching the paper form his hand, the farmer tore it to shreds and flung those shreds to the breeze. "Bugger King Geoffrey's government with a pine cone!" he cried. "The son-of-a-bitching thing's gonna be as dead as shoe leather when the war's over. Why in the hells didn't I get southrons stealing from me? *Their* receipts'd be worth something later on, I reckon."

"Be careful how you speak," Gremio said coldly. "You tread close to treason."

"Futter you, too, pal," the farmer said. "I talk like a free Detinan, on account of I gods-damned well am one. If you don't like it, too bad. You think we've got a chance of winning against King Avram's bastards? You got to be crazy if you do, and you don't look like no crazy man to me." He stormed off, still cursing.

Captain Gremio stared after him. He didn't think he was a crazy man, and he didn't think it likely King Geoffrey's men could beat King Avram's. After more than three years of war, that seemed a very forlorn hope indeed. *Why go on fighting, then?* he wondered.

He shrugged. The Army of Franklin wasn't beaten yet. As long as Lieutenant General Bell could still strike the encroaching southrons, the northern cause wasn't lost. *We have to keep trying,* Gremio thought. *As long as we keep trying, something good may happen. If we give up, it surely won't.*

Was that reason enough? Gremio shrugged again. He didn't know. He did know some detachments of provost marshals were crucifying deserters. That was another good reason to stay on.

General Hesmucet's men had unicorn-riders patrolling well east of the glideway line. Gremio got only a glimpse of them as they rode off to the west to let the main body of southrons know they'd spotted the Army of Franklin. He sighed. "I wish we could have taken Whole Mackerel by surprise."

"When the southrons came at it, they came at it from out of the east, and now we're doing the same thing," Sergeant Thisbe said. "That's strange."

"I hadn't thought about it like that, but you're right," Gremio said. "One thing: the foraging won't be so good from here on out. The southrons will have been there before us. We'll just have to run them out of the place and take away all the food they've stored up in town."

He made it sound very easy. If fighting the southrons were easy, though, Bell would have done better all through this campaign. Of course, Hesmucet had always had the advantage of numbers. He wouldn't here. Gremio didn't know how big the garrison at Whole Mackerel was, but it couldn't hope to match the whole Army of Franklin. The rest of Hesmucet's army would still be up near Marthasville.

That meant . . . "We'd better move fast," Gremio said. "We have to take the town before they can reinforce it."

"That makes good sense, sir," Sergeant Thisbe agreed.

It might have made good sense to them. It didn't seem to have crossed Bell's mind. He paused to camp for the night about five miles outside of Whole Mackerel. "We ought to keep going," Gremio said discontentedly.

"I'm pleased to see your spirit," Colonel Florizel told him. "Still and all, though, we'll do better going in fresh and well rested."

"True, sir," Gremio said. "But the southrons will have all night to get ready for us, and that won't help our attack."

"You really *are* bolder than you were," Florizel said. "You can't attack by yourself, though."

Gremio didn't think he was any bolder than he'd ever been. He was just quibbling over tactics, as he often did. When he complained because he thought Bell was charging ahead when he shouldn't, Florizel reckoned him a coward. He'd been right then, but it hadn't done any good. Now he thought Bell was hanging back when he ought to go on. That made the regimental commander happier, but it also wouldn't change anything else.

Maybe I ought to keep my mouth shut, Gremio thought. For a Detinan, and especially for a Detinan barrister, that was a very strange notion indeed.

Horns blared before daybreak the next morning, ordering the northern army into line of battle. "We'll do the best we can, and we'll strike the enemy a strong blow for King Geoffrey," Gremio told his men. They raised a cheer.

"And we'll steal all the good food and the crossbow quarrels the stinking southrons have fetched up here to Whole Mackerel from Rising Rock," Sergeant Thisbe added. "We'll eat like nobles, and we'll shoot like we've got repeating crossbows."

The soldiers in blue cheered louder for Thisbe than they had for Gremio. "Well said, Sergeant," Gremio told him. "You got a better rein on what makes them go than I did."

"Thank you very much, sir," Thisbe said. "Trying to put in a little extra, that's all."

"You did splendidly," Gremio said. "You should speak up more often."

Before Thisbe could answer, the horns screamed again, this time ordering the Army of Franklin forward against the southrons' entrenchments in front of Whole Mackerel. *They tried ours and didn't like them very well,* Gremio thought. *Why should we have an easier time with theirs?*

Some of the entrenchments the northerners would be assailing *were* the ones their serfs had dug a few months earlier. Now King Avram's gray-clad soldiers held them. And those men in gray seemed no more inclined to give them up than the Army of Franklin had been earlier in the year.

"Only a piddly little garrison in front of us, boys," Colonel Florizel boomed. "They'll run like rabbits, the gods-damned sons of bitches."

Roaring as if possessed by the Lion God, the northerners swarmed toward the easternmost trenches. Even before they came into range, firepots and stones flew through the air. Repeating crossbows began their harsh *clack-clack-clack.* No, the southrons weren't about to give up and go away.

But Florizel had been right. Yes, the southrons had men in their forward trenches and engines behind them, but they didn't have very many men or very many engines. Lieutenant General Bell's men pelted them with bolts and stones and firepots of their own. Before long, the southrons fell back towards Whole Mackerel, the artificers in charge of their engines hitching those to teams of unicorns and hauling them away to keep them from being captured.

"Forward!" Gremio called. "We've got to keep pushing them, not let them rally. Keep moving!"

When they came to the southrons' second line of trenches, another storm of missiles greeted them. Looking ahead, Gremio saw that the enemy's main lines of defense didn't guard the town of Whole Mackerel itself, but rather the nearby supply depot. Sure enough, they knew what Bell wanted.

Roaring and shouting, the Army of Franklin bore down on those works. Now the southrons had no room for retreat, not unless they wanted to give up what their foes so desperately needed to take. They had to fight.

They had to—and they did. They had a great many more engines in amongst these fieldworks than they'd used farther forward. Stones and firepots and darts took a heavy toll on the northerners. The southrons whooped and cheered to watch their foes fall.

"Keep moving, men!" Gremio shouted again. "Look, there on that parapet—that's got to be their commander. If we can kill him, maybe we'll suck the spirit out of them."

That wasn't sporting. It wasn't chivalrous. A man of noble blood probably never would have said anything so crude. None of that stopped Gremio from thinking he'd had a good idea there. His men did, too. So did the crews of a nearby battery of engines. They started aiming at the black-haired officer waving a sword, too.

A moment later, he clapped a hand to his cheek and tumbled off the parapet. Gremio and everyone close by raised a cheer. "Forward!" he yelled. "*Now* let's see how tough those bastards are!"

He soon found out how tough their commander was. The man reappeared inside of a couple of minutes. He was even easier to spot than he had been before—a bloody bandage covered half his face. Gremio could hear his shouts through the din of battle: "We can whip these bastards! Who the hells do they think they are, coming around to bother honest people? Give 'em a good kick in the arse and throw 'em back!"

And the southrons obeyed. They fought with a stubborn, stolid courage different from the incandescent northern variety but no less effective for that. Some of their outer entrenchments fell to the Army of Franklin, but only after they were filled with dead men wearing tunics and pantaloons both blue and gray. And the northerners didn't come close to overrunning the supply depot, though they fought all day.

Towards evening, Bell ordered a withdrawal. Colonel Florizel put the best face on things he could: "Well, boys, we'll hit 'em another lick tomorrow, and then we'll whip 'em for sure."

"What if the southrons send up reinforcements by then?" Gremio asked.

Florizel started to say something harsh, but checked himself. "No, you were all for forging ahead," he reminded himself. "In that case, Captain, we don't have such an easy time of it. Satisfied?" Gremio nodded, though that wasn't the word he would have used.

XI

Lieutenant General Bell glowered at his scryer. "You're sure you intercepted the southrons' message?"

"As sure as I'm standing here before you, sir," the scryer answered. "They might as well have been talking right into my crystal ball instead of Brigadier Murray the Coarse talking to General Hesmucet. Murray, he said, 'I am short of a cheekbone, and one ear, but am able to whip all hells yet.' And Hesmucet, he answered, 'Hold the fort! I am coming!' He was up near Commissioner Mountain then, sir, so I reckon he could come pretty gods-damned quick."

"To the hells with him," Bell said furiously. He could hear the moans of the wounded in his encampment here. He knew he wouldn't be able to rouse his army to another attack before morning, and also knew morning was all too likely to be too late. Whole Mackerel had held.

Laudanum, he thought, and took a swig. The pain in his ruined arm and missing leg diminished. He could even look at the pain in his spirit with more detachment, which was really why he'd gulped down the drug. But that pain wouldn't die, not altogether. He'd needed a win over the southrons and, yet again, he hadn't got it.

"Anything else, sir?" the scryer asked.

"No," Lieutenant General Bell answered. "Just pick up your crystal ball and get the hells out of here." The scryer did.

Major Zibeon came into Bell's tent a moment later. "You put a flea in his ear," Bell's dour aide-de-camp remarked. "What did he have to say?"

"That the stinking southrons are on their way here," Bell answered. "We've wounded the commander here at Whole Mackerel, but he thinks he can hold out till Hesmucet arrives."

"He's likely right, especially if Hesmucet marches his men through the night," Zibeon said, which was exactly what Bell didn't want to hear. His own description of the words that had passed between Murray the Coarse and Hesmucet made them seem bloodless, businesslike. The scryer's version hadn't been like that. Both southron officers had sounded more than confident. That worried Bell as nothing else had. Zibeon grimaced, then asked, "Can we face the whole southron army?"

"No," Bell answered. "No, gods damn it, we can't." He hated nothing more than admitting that. King Geoffrey had put him in command of the Army of Franklin to whip the southrons and to hold Marthasville. He hadn't managed either. He didn't like having to confront his limits and those of his army.

"What do we do, then, sir?" his aide-de-camp asked.

"We fall back," Bell answered—strange and unnatural words to find in his mouth. They tasted bad, too, but he saw the need for them. "We fall back, and we try to hit that gods-damned glideway line somewhere else."

To his surprise, Major Zibeon nodded. "Not bad, sir," he said judiciously. "Even if we don't wreck it, how much can Hesmucet do if he's chasing us over the landscape where we've already fought? And he'll have to chase us, too, on account of this army is still too big to ignore."

Bell didn't care for the sound of that *still*. Zibeon might as well have said, *This is what's left after you went and made a hash of things*. But he nodded because, tone aside, his aide-de-camp had the essence of his plan down. "That's right, Major. If Hesmucet is such a great hero, let's see him catch us when we don't feel like getting caught."

Zibeon chuckled. "The southrons won't like that."

"Futter the southrons!" Bell exclaimed. "If they think I'm going to dry up and blow away because they squeezed me out of Marthasville, they can think again. They'll have to work to drag us down."

"I think that's good, sir. I think that's very good," Major Zibeon said. "If the gods favor us, we may even be able to sneak back into Marthasville again."

"That would be very fine." Bell started to perk up, but then slumped again. "It *would* be very fine, I mean, but there's not much left of Marthasville any more. Place isn't worth having, not for anybody. And gods damn Hesmucet for that, too, along with everything else."

"They will. I have no doubt of it." Zibeon spoke with great conviction. "But we'd better do something to him in this world, too."

"Draft the order for our move to the south, then," Lieutenant General Bell said. "If he wants us, he'll have to pin us down. And do you know what, Major? I don't think the southrons can do it."

"Yes, sir," his aide-de-camp said. "And no, sir, I don't don't think they can pin us down, either."

When morning came, a red-dust haze in the north warned that the southrons were approaching fast. Grunting and cursing and half blind with pain in spite of a new dose of laudanum, Bell clambered aboard his unicorn. Major Zibeon made him fast to the animal like a man lashing a sack of lentils to an ass' back. And then, just before he was about to lead the army south, he had an idea. Calling the mages together, he asked them, "Can you make the southrons think we've gone east instead?"

They looked at each other: sad-faced men in blue robes, some afoot, others riding asses. The next mage Bell saw aboard a unicorn would be the first. *He* could manage, without one leg and with only one working arm. As for them . . . He shrugged, which also hurt. They *could* work magic—when things went well.

At last, one of them said, "I think we can, sir—for a

while, anyway. Sooner or later, though, they'll realize they've been following a will o' the wisp."

"Buy us as much time as you can," Bell said. The mages nodded mournfully.

Bell did lead the Army of Franklin south then. He kept looking back over his good shoulder to see how close the southrons were getting. Looking back wasn't easy, not when the dust of thousands of marching feet obscured his view. After a while, though, he did spy what looked to be just as much dust rising from the east. He hoped the mages would remember to mask the dust his army was actually making. He almost sent a rider back to remind them to be sure of that, but at the last minute checked himself. Mages had their pride, too.

A unicorn-rider from his own rear guard came trotting up to him. Saluting, the man said, "Sir, looks like the stinking southrons have swung off to the east. They aren't coming right after us, anyways."

"Good," Bell said. *Something* had gone right, then. He made a noise halfway between a sigh and a groan. Not too many things had gone right for the Army of Franklin lately. To be relieved because the enemy's pursuit had been drawn off was . . . *Pitiful* was the word that sprang to mind.

Another rider approached him. He eyed Roast-Beef William with more suspicion than he had the courier. Roast-Beef William hungered for his command, just as he'd hungered for it when Joseph the Gamecock had it. Was William writing letters to King Geoffrey? *He'd better not be,* Bell thought.

"What now?" he growled, his voice rough and edgy.

"I was going to ask you the same question, sir," his wing commander replied. "I understand we can't hope to hold our position with so many southrons coming after us, but where do we go from here?"

"Someplace with good foraging, from which we can strike a blow at the glideway up from Rising Rock, or at a detachment of southrons if they give us the chance," Bell answered. There had been a time when the Army of Franklin could have stood up to the whole southron host—before it lost four expensive battles in a row outside Marthasville. Bell tried not to dwell on that.

"Sooner or later, the whole southron army will come after us," William said.

"Later," Bell told him, and explained what the mages were doing.

Roast-Beef William's big head bobbed up and down. "That's good, sir, but it won't last forever. And the southrons are hard to fool the same way twice."

"We've bought some time now." Bell had never been a man to look to the far future. It would take care of itself. The problem right at hand always seemed more important. Without solving it, he couldn't get to the far future, anyhow.

"Do you think the southrons are after us with their whole force?" William asked.

"Seemed that way, gods damn them," Bell said. "Let them come. They aren't going to accomplish anything that way."

"Not unless they crush us," Roast-Beef William said. But then, almost reluctantly, he nodded again. "We're lighter and quicker than they are, no doubt."

"Even so," Bell said. "Any man who knows me knows I hate retreat to the very marrow of my bones—but there are times when it is needful, and this is one of those times."

"Yes, sir," Roast-Beef William said, and then muttered something under his breath.

"What was that?" Lieutenant General Bell asked sharply.

"Nothing, sir," his wing commander answered. Bell glared at him. William looked back, stolid and innocent. Bell couldn't press any more. What he thought he'd heard was, *That's what Joseph the Gamecock kept saying.*

It wasn't quite insubordination, but it came close. As far as Bell could see, the two cases were as different as chalk and cheese. Retreat seemed Joseph's natural state. He fell back because he dared not face the foe, or so Bell was convinced. He himself, on the other hand, moved away from the southrons only because they so dreadfully outnumbered him. They hadn't outnumbered Joseph to anywhere near the same extent.

Why the southrons now outnumbered the Army of Franklin so much more than they had when Joseph the

Gamecock commanded it was something Bell stubbornly refused to contemplate.

As Bell and the Army of Franklin moved south and east, the general commanding had no trouble telling where General Hesmucet's army had gone earlier in the summer and where the land had not seen the red-hot rake of war. Earthworks and field fortifications scarred the ground where Hesmucet's men had moved. One wheatfield had entrenchments in three sides of a square dug through the middle of it. What the farmer would be able to do about that, Bell couldn't imagine.

Farmhouses were burnt, barns and serfs' huts razed. Of livestock and blonds in the region where Hesmucet's men had gone, Bell saw next to none. Half a mile away from the southrons' path, cows and sheep and unicorns grazed, though he still noted hardly any blonds. "Bastards," he muttered, not knowing himself whether he meant Hesmucet's men or the serfs who fled to them.

A little before noon, one of his wizards came up to him and said, "I'm sorry, sir, but their sorcerers just penetrated our spell of deception."

"Well, gods damn them to the seven hells," Bell said. But it scarcely counted as an outburst; he'd expected that news for a couple of hours. He gave the mage a grudging nod. "You did the best you could."

"Why, thank you, sir!" The man sounded not only relieved but astonished. He must have looked for a firepot to come down on his head.

Bell condescended to explain: "You bought us more time that I thought you would. We've got away clean now."

"Ah." The mage nodded, with luck in wisdom. He gave Bell a salute that would have disgusted any sergeant ever born. "Happy to be of service, sir." He saluted again, even more disreputably than before, and went off to rejoin his comrades in wizardry.

I take it back, Bell thought. *I do know one mage who rides a unicorn—Thraxton the Braggart.* The lines furrowing his brow, for once, had nothing to do with pain. Thraxton was a mighty sorcerer, no doubt about it—and the Army of Franklin would have ended up better off if he'd never cast a single spell, no doubt about that, either. *If a man is an ass, who cares whether he rides a unicorn?*

What would Thraxton have done with the Army of Franklin, had King Geoffrey given it back to him instead of to Bell? Something unfortunate—Bell was sure of that. Again, what he'd done to the Army of Franklin himself never crossed his mind. *The men let me down.* He was sure of it.

We'll smash up the glideway line. We'll cut Hesmucet off from all his supplies, Bell thought. *We'll see how much the soft southrons like living off the land. We'll see how well they fight when they're hungry and short of everything, the way we always are.*

He had visions of Hesmucet's men stumbling across the plains of Peachtree Province with hollow eyes and bony fingers, moaning for a crust of bread. On the other side of the Western Ocean, Great King Kermit's army had all but come to pieces when it had to retreat from Pahzbull in the middle of a hellish winter. That was more than fifty years ago now, but people still told stories about it.

Liking the vision in his own mind, Bell offered it to his aide-de-camp. Major Zibeon chewed it over, then said, "That would be very nice, sir—now which gods are going to supply the Sorbian winter here in Peachtree Province?"

Bell's ears heated. Zibeon had been polite in calling him a fool, but he'd called him a fool nonetheless. "We can still whip them," Bell growled.

"I hope you're right. I even think you're right, sir," Zibeon said. "But I don't see southron soldiers starving in the snow, not hereabouts."

"What precisely do you see, Major?" Bell's tone was certainly cold enough for a Sorbian winter.

"Right now, I see that we've stolen a march on the enemy," Zibeon replied. "I see that we'd better take advantage of it, too." And not even Lieutenant General Bell could argue with him there.

Rollant sprawled down by a campfire with a groan. "I'm sick of marching," he said. "I don't like it even when we're going where we're supposed to. When it turns out we spent the first half of the day going in the wrong gods-damned direction . . . I don't fancy that a bit."

Smitty was every bit as worn as he was, but managed a weary grin. "You go tell that to General Hesmucet, Rollant," he said. "He's bound to listen to you, right? After all, you're not just anybody. You're a corporal."

"And you're an idiot," Rollant said. Smitty gave an extravagant wave of the hand, as if accepting praise far beyond his deserts.

Sergeant Joram tramped past. "Get water, Rollant," he said.

Before Rollant had been promoted, that would have meant his going down to the closest creek with the squad's water bottles. But, now that he was an underofficer, he got to tell other soldiers to go instead. But picked a couple who hadn't had the duty for a little while: "Gleb, you and Josh take care of it."

Josh groaned as he got to his feet, but didn't argue. Gleb said, "I don't want to do it. You had me do it a few days ago."

"Yes, and it's your turn again," Rollant said. "We've been through everybody else in the squad since then. Go on. Get moving."

Gleb shook his head. "Hells of a note when a blond thinks he can tell a real Detinan what to do."

Ice and fire ran through Rollant. He hadn't had much of that trouble—less than he'd expected—till now. Maybe he could head it off here. Tapping the stripes on his sleeve, he said, "It isn't a blond telling you what to do, Gleb. It's a corporal telling you. Now go fill our water bottles."

"No," Gleb said.

"He can put you on report, Gleb," one of the other soldiers said. "Go on."

"He can kiss my arse, that's what he can do, gods-damned yellow-haired son of a bitch," Gleb said, and stayed where he was.

Rollant did think about reporting him. But there was authority, and then there was authority. He sighed. He might have known this day was coming. Lieutenant Griff and Colonel Nahath had expected it sooner. Well, it was here now. He put down his crossbow, unbuckled his sword belt, and laid the shortsword by the bow. "Get up, Gleb," he said.

"My, my," the Detinan said as he got to his feet. He also undid his sword belt. "Think you're hot stuff, don't you, on account of you got yourself promoted? Well, I'll tell you something, blond boy—that doesn't mean a thing to me."

"You talk too much." Rollant's heart thudded in his chest. He didn't know if he could take Gleb. If he couldn't, he doubted he'd ever be able to give another order again. But he surely wouldn't be able to if he let the Detinan get away with disobeying.

He'd hoped Gleb would surge forward without any thought at all. No such luck—the soldier advanced cautiously, eyes wary, arms outstretched. Rollant threw a looping left. Gleb ducked under it and laughed scornfully. He dug a fist into Rollant's ribs. "Oof!" Rollant said, and took a couple of stumbling steps backward.

Gleb laughed. "You're not so fornicating tough, are you? I'm going to like stomping the shit out of you, you bet."

The right Rollant threw was even wilder than the left had been. And it served its purpose: to persuade Gleb Rollant had no real stomach for a standup fight. With a nasty chuckle, Gleb closed on him.

Rollant slid a foot behind the Detinan and pushed, hard. Gleb let out a startled squawk. But, as he was falling, he grabbed Rollant and pulled him down, too. Everything till then had gone just as Rollant planned it. After that, the fight stopped having a plan. It was punch and gouge and kick and knee and elbow. Gleb's teeth snapped shut an inch away from Rollant's ear. He didn't know whether that was because the Detinan was trying to bite him or because he'd just landed a good one to the pit of Gleb's stomach. He couldn't stop and ask, either.

Gleb hit him in the side of the head. He saw stars. But the Detinan howled and clutched at his own right hand. Rollant landed a blizzard of punches and brought his knee up between Gleb's legs. Gleb let out a bubbling shriek. Rollant scrambled to his feet and kicked the Detinan several times. "Had enough?" he got out through bruised lips.

Gleb nodded. Rollant kicked him again, maybe hard enough to break a rib or two, maybe not. He didn't want Gleb thinking he'd almost won and trying for another installment.

Something like that was on Gleb's mind. "Wasn't for your gods-damned hard head—" he mumbled.

That got him another kick. Once more, Rollant didn't know if he'd broken the other man's ribs, but he didn't think he'd missed by much if he hadn't. He stood over Gleb, breathing hard. "Get up," he growled. Gleb stared at him out of one eye; the other was swollen shut. "Get up, you son of a bitch," Rollant repeated. "You're gods-damned well going to get your arse down to the creek and fill our water bottles."

He waited. If Gleb said he couldn't, he'd be even sorrier than he was already. Slowly, the Detinan struggled to his feet and started collecting water bottles. "Yes, Corporal," he said mushily as he headed for the stream with Josh, who'd waited to see what happened. When he spat, he spat red.

So did Rollant. He ran his tongue over his teeth. He didn't think he'd broken any. That was something. He looked at the other soldiers in his squad. Nobody said anything. He gestured. "Go on. Get back to setting up camp. It's finished." They all but fell over one another as they scrambled to obey.

Later that evening, Sergeant Joram came by, looked at Rollant, did a double take, and looked again. "By the gods, what happened to you?"

"Nothing," Rollant answered, as a toddler might after breaking a vase.

Joram snorted. "Nothing, eh? I see *that*. Was it the kind of nothing I'd guess first time out?" Rollant only shrugged, which hurt. The sergeant tried another question: "What happened to the other fellow?"

"Nothing," Rollant said again, but he couldn't help adding, "Maybe a little more nothing than happened to me."

"That a fact?" Joram said. Rollant nodded. That also hurt. Joram grunted. "Well, too bad for him and good for you. He decide he didn't like the color of your hair?"

"I don't know what you're talking about, Sergeant," Rollant said.

Joram made as if to clap him on the shoulder, then thought better of it. "All right," he said. "Sounds like you took care of it, and that's what counts."

When Rollant called for men to put more wood on the fire or for any of the other small chores that needed doing, they kept on springing to obey. *Maybe I should have fights more often.* Then he shook his head, which also hurt. He'd come too close to losing this one. Now, if the gods were kind, he wouldn't have to have any more. *I'd sooner fight the traitors anyhow.*

Once, not long before he lay down and went to sleep, he caught Gleb looking at him. The Detinan's gaze flinched away when Rollant's met it. Gleb, Rollant was happy to see, looked a good deal worse for wear than he did himself. And, by the way Gleb kept nursing that finger, he might really have broken it against Rollant's head. Rollant felt not the least bit sorry for him.

Lieutenant Griff didn't notice either Rollant or Gleb till morning. As Joram had the night before, he gaped at Rollant's battered features. "With whom did you fight, Corporal?" he asked.

"Me, sir? I walked into a tree," Rollant said woodenly.

"You look like you walked into a grinding mill," Griff said, and then shouted, "Company—form up!"

The men obeyed. Griff stalked among them till he came to Gleb. "And what's *your* excuse, soldier?" he demanded, his high, thin voice getting higher with suspicion.

"I fell down, sir," Gleb answered, which was true, though he'd had help from Rollant.

Griff studied him. Now that his bruises had had time to appear, he looked ghastly. *I suppose I do, too,* Rollant thought. Griff said, "If you fall down again, you'll be very sorry. Do you understand me?"

"I'm already sorry, sir," Gleb mumbled.

"You'll be even sorrier. So will anyone else who tries falling down that particular way." Lieutenant Griff was growing up. He made the threat sound much more convincing than he could have when he first took over the company.

Rollant paid his ritual respects to the company standard and took the flagpole from the ground. Leaning the pole against his shoulder meant leaning it against a bruise. *Gods damn you, Gleb,* he thought as the regiment started after the Army of Franklin.

"What do you think of this whole business, Corporal?" Griff asked him.

"Me, sir?" Rollant said. "I think it'd be a good thing if we took the real path the traitors are using, instead of letting their mages trick us again."

"I think so, too, but that isn't what I was talking about," the company commander said. "Don't toy with me. I won't stand for it."

"Sorry, sir," said Rollant, who was anything but sorry. Reluctantly, he went on, "I wish it hadn't happened, that's all. I hope it won't happen again."

"Not likely, not the way Gleb looks," Griff said.

Rollant was moderately—more than moderately—grateful that Lieutenant Griff said nothing about the way he looked himself. He said, "Sir, the only way I would've lost that fight was if he killed me. I couldn't afford to."

Griff nodded. "I understand how you might feel that way."

Did he? Rollant had as many doubts as Doubting George. Griff was a Detinan. How could he knew how desperate a blond might get in a kingdom where everything was stacked against him? Simple—he couldn't. If he thought he could, he was imagining things.

"Still and all, though, Corporal, if you have cases of insubordination, you should bring them before me, just as I would bring them before Colonel Nahath," Griff said.

"Yes, sir," Rollant said resignedly. No, the lieutenant didn't understand. Gleb hadn't been insubordinate because he didn't want to obey a corporal. He'd been insubordinate because he didn't want to obey a blond, which wasn't the same thing at all. The man inside the uniform had been more important than the stripes on the tunic's sleeve. A corporal could appeal to the army's disciplinary mechanism without losing face. A blond . . . Rollant shook his head. He'd had to fight that battle by himself. Now that he'd fought and won it, maybe he wouldn't have to do it again. He'd proved his point, or so he hoped.

Shouts rose from up ahead. Rollant peered through the

dust the men in front of him had kicked up, but he could not see much. "What's going on?" Griff called, along with a good many other officers back in the middle of the army.

The answer took a while to reach Griff. At last, somebody said, "Our unicorn-riders are skirmishing with the traitors up at the front of the force. It's nothing, really."

It couldn't have been anything much, or they would have got orders to deploy from column into line of battle. Rollant was as well pleased to keep marching, even if it was through land where he'd fought earlier in the summer. "Sir," he asked, "what happens if the northerners do wreck our glideway line?"

"Not much," Griff answered. "For one thing, this country is a forager's dream. And, for another, we've got awfully good at repairing whatever damage they can do, and almost as fast as they can do it. So don't worry your head about that."

"All right, sir—I won't," Rollant said. Maybe Griff was patronizing him, saying that, as a blond, he was too ignorant—or perhaps just too stupid—to understand grand strategy. At another time, a time when his bruises didn't hurt so much, he might have been offended. Now he just shrugged. Offended or not, quarreling with his company commander didn't pay.

Before long, horn calls did summon the army to form line of battle. Rollant waved the company standard overhead so his comrades could go into line behind him. *One more chance for the traitors to shoot me,* he thought. But he wore a corporal's stripes and drew a corporal's pay precisely because he gave them that chance whenever his regiment went into action.

Then the horns rang out again, returning the force to column for marching. "That's good," Smitty said. "That's very good. Somebody up there's really clever."

"Could you do better?" Rollant asked.

Brash as any Detinan, Smitty answered, "I couldn't do a hells of a lot worse, could I?" Detinans always thought they could handle anything. Sometimes they were right, sometimes—more often, from everything Rollant had seen—wrong. But they never lacked for confidence.

"I wonder what happened up ahead," Rollant said.

"What do you want to bet they ran away from us?" Smitty said.

"I wouldn't touch that," Rollant said. "I've got better things to do with my silver than giving it to you."

"Since when?" Smitty said. "Name two. It's not even like you sit around throwing dice all night long or spend it on loose women."

"I've got a wife," Rollant said stiffly, as he had to Griff in Marthasville.

"Hasn't stopped a lot of people I know of, from General Guildenstern on down." Smitty chuckled fondly. "He'd screw anything that moved, he would."

"All I want to do is go home again and be with the woman I belong with," Rollant said. In fact, that wasn't quite true. What he wanted to do . . . *But I haven't done it,* he thought, and then, *Gods, I hope this war ends soon.*

Roast-Beef William saluted Lieutenant General Bell. "Reporting as ordered, sir," he said.

Bell returned the salute. His right arm still worked. It was one of the few pieces of him that did. *Including his brain,* William thought sourly. But King Geoffrey had named Bell to command the Army of Franklin, and so William—who prided himself on being known as Old Reliable—was duty-bound to obey him. *No matter how much I want to do something—anything—else.* Bell said. "I am going to use your wing as our rear guard, to hold off the gods-damned southrons as we move south."

"Yes, sir," Roast-Beef William said resignedly. "I hope you bear in mind the pounding we took at Jonestown."

"I do," Bell said. "All parts of the army suffered heavily around Marthasville, as I'm sure you know."

And whose fault is that? William wondered. He thought of Joseph the Gamecock, who'd gone into retirement up in Dicon. What was Joseph saying about Geoffrey and Bell and about the way the army had been handled since his own departure? Nothing good—William was sure of that. Of course, considering everything that had happened since, nothing good deserved to be said.

"You will, I presume, perform the duties required of you?" Bell asked, an edge to his voice.

"Yes, sir," William said. "Of course I will, sir. I hope we don't need to do a whole lot of fighting, though."

Bell sneered. "Haven't got the stomach for it?"

"Haven't got the men for it," Roast-Beef William said. "Sir." He turned on his heel and strode out of the farmhouse Bell was using for his headquarters. *By the gods,* he thought, *for a couple of coppers I'd . . .* He shook his head. Such thoughts about a superior officer would only land him in trouble. *I've got to get away from this army. Enough is enough. Too much, in fact.*

He shook his head again, trying to clear it. *As if I'm not in trouble already. As if the whole army isn't in trouble already. To the hells with me if I know what Bell's doing. Rear guard? Where are we going? What will we do when we get there?* He had no real answers. He didn't think Bell had real answers, either, except letting Hesmucet chase after him for as long as the southron commander would.

The sun was setting, but enough light remained to let Roast-Beef William take a long look to the north. No sign of Hesmucet's force at the moment. Maybe the Army of Franklin could keep on outrunning the southrons, but how much good would that do overall? Not a great deal, as far as William could see.

"Halt!" an alert sentry called. "Advance and be recognized."

"I'm Lieutenant General William," William said, moving slowly to keep from alarming the man and perhaps ending up with a crossbow quarrel between the ribs. "Do you recognize me?"

"Uh, yes, sir," the sentry said. "Sorry, sir."

"Don't be," Roast-Beef William said. "You should stay alert."

"Well, yes, sir," the man said. "But I shouldn't come close to putting a hole in one of our generals, either. That wouldn't be so good."

"If you think I'm going to quarrel with you, soldier, you'd better think again," William said, and the sentry laughed. William wasn't so sure it was funny. For one thing, both sides had lost officers because their own men had shot them.

For another, he couldn't escape the nagging feeling that the Army of Franklin might be improved if a couple of its officers suffered such accidents. Thoughts like that bordered on mutiny. They were not the sort of ideas that should have been going through the mind of a man known as Old Reliable.

Roast-Beef William couldn't drive them out of his head even so. If that wasn't a telling measure of the state to which the Army of Franklin had fallen, he couldn't imagine what would be. *Maybe I should start writing letters. Anywhere would be better than here.*

"Where will we be going now, sir?" the sentry asked.

"South, for the army as a whole," William answered. "My wing will serve as rear guard."

"Can the southrons catch up to us?" The sentry sounded interested and curious, not anxious and afraid.

That only shows he doesn't understand the state we're in, Roast-Beef William thought. As wing commander, he himself understood it altogether too well. *If only King Geoffrey had put me in Joseph the Gamecock's place once he decided he couldn't stand leaving Joseph in command. By all the gods and goddesses, I couldn't have done worse than Bell did.*

But Bell looked like the Lion God and fought like a tiger, always hitting the enemy with everything he had. In Geoffrey's eyes, those attributes counted for more than reliability. *And so I kept right on being a wing commander, and so we lost a third of the army, and we lost Marthasville, and we took a couple of long steps toward losing the war.*

"We'll lick 'em, won't we, sir?" The sentry sounded as if he had no doubt of it.

"We're doing everything we can," William answered. "If we can get astride the glideway line and cut it, the southrons may yet come to grief."

"We'll do it," the sentry said.

And, more than a little to Roast-Beef William's surprise, they *did* do it a couple of days later. A few miles south of Fat Mama, the Army of Franklin swarmed athwart the glideway line. William formed up his men facing north, to hold off Hesmucet's southrons while mages disrupted the delicate spells without which glideway carpets would have done just as well in somebody's parlor.

With no sign of the southrons anywhere close by, Roast-Beef William rode back perhaps a quarter of a mile to watch the wizards at work. The men in blue robes looked as weary as the soldiers guarding them. Almost, Roast-Beef William wished Thraxton the Braggart were back with the army. Almost. It wasn't so much that Thraxton, like Bell, had led the Army of Franklin into disasters. That Thraxton was so gods-damned disagreeable while doing it counted for more. He'd proved that being a powerful mage wasn't the same as being a successful one—proved it over and over, in fact.

The wizards chanted and made their passes and danced back and forth across the glideway line. They looked a lot like a holiday gathering at the Sweet One's shrine. As soon as that thought crossed William's mind, he wished it hadn't. He had to fight the giggles for the rest of the incantation.

A line on the ground—presumably, the one tracing the path of the glideway line—began to glow red. The mages chanted harder than ever, and the glow got brighter and brighter. Before long, William was squinting at it through half-shut eyes. Even then, tears ran down his cheeks till at last he turned away.

With a sound as sharp and fierce as a bursting firepot, the spell ended. The assembled wizards cried out in triumph. Roast-Beef William turned back. The glideway line wasn't glowing any more, but the air still quivered above it, showing the heat the mages had released.

"Well done!" William clapped his hands. "That should hold up the southrons a good long while, wouldn't you say?"

"I hope so," one of the mages answered answered. Roast-Beef William coughed. "Uh—I hope so, sir," the mage amended. "We killed the glideway power dead as shoe leather, sure as hells we did." His colleagues nodded.

"Well, then, the next time Hesmucet's men try to use the line, they'll get a nasty surprise," William said. "Or am I misunderstanding something?"

"No, sir, you're right about that," the wizard said. "Question is, though, how long does it take 'em to repair what we just did?"

"How long would it take *you*?" Roast-Beef William asked.

Before answering, the man in the blue robe and his comrades put their heads together. At last, he said, "We'd probably be held up for a week, easy. We did a proper job here, we did."

"That's not bad," Roast-Beef William said. It was almost as much as he'd hoped for, which, considering the way the war had been going lately, came close to a miracle straight from the gods.

But now the wizard coughed. "Uh, sir, you've got to remember, the southrons are better than we are at this kind of sorcery, same as we're better than they are at battle magic."

Roast-Beef William cursed softly. The fellow was bound to be right. Everything William had seen in the war pointed that way. He said, "All right, then, I'll ask a different question: how long do you think the southrons will need to fix what you just did to the glideway line?"

The sorcerers huddled again. When they broke apart, the fellow who did the talking said, "A couple of days, if we're lucky. A couple of hours, if we're not."

"A couple of days? A couple of *hours*?" Roast-Beef William clapped a hand to his forehead in astonished dismay and disbelief. "And it would stop you for a *week*? I knew we were behind them in that sort of sorcery. Thunderer's prong, though—I never imagined we were so far behind."

"Sorry, sir," the wizard said. "That's how it is."

"In that case . . ." William plucked at his beard. "In that case, let's see what we can do about it."

Being the commander of the rear guard, he was supposed to hang back and resist the southrons anyhow. He posted a regiment in the pine woods near the glideway line with some very specific orders. He stayed behind himself, too; he wasn't willing to order the men to try anything he wouldn't do himself. He told the colonel, "If this doesn't work out the way we want it to, we'll just pull back. I'm not out for us to get stuck with an attack that hasn't got a chance of working."

"No, eh?" the colonel said. "You'd better not tell Bell that, or else he'll throw you out of this gods-damned army."

Roast-Beef William cleared his throat. "I'm going to pretend I didn't hear that."

"Go ahead," the colonel told him. "Won't make any difference one way or the other. You can hear or not. Bell won't." As William had with the mage, he cleared his throat again. The colonel refused to be cowed. He said, "I'm a free Detinan, sir, and I'll gods-damned well say what I please. Somebody ought to, don't you think?"

"You can say it, Colonel," William answered. "You can say it, but that won't do you any good. Lieutenant General Bell *will* command this army, and we've had enough dissension already, don't you think?"

"Oh, hells, yes," the regimental commander said. "We've had all the dissension anybody could need. What we haven't had, though, is a general who knows what the devils he's doing." He shook his head. "No, I take that back. We did have *one*, but King Geoffrey gave him the sack."

He liked Joseph the Gamecock, did he? William thought. *Only proves he didn't know him very well. Hardly anybody who knew Joseph very well liked him.* But that was neither here nor there. Aloud, Roast-Beef William said, "Let's worry about the southrons, shall we, and not about who did what in our own army?"

"Yes, sir," the colonel said. "If everybody thought the way you do, we'd have a lot better chance of whipping those bastards, and that's a fact."

He didn't think that way himself. He'd proved as much, with his own factionalism. He didn't even notice. Roast-Beef William didn't waste time trying to correct him, either. He just made sure the northerners were as well positioned as they could be. After that, he had nothing to do but wait.

The southrons didn't show up till close to noon the next day. By then, the northern officers were having all they could do holding their men in place. The soldiers of the Army of Franklin would fight like wildcats. Sometimes, though, they showed little more discipline than wildcats.

Southron mages wore gray robes. Other than that, by looks there was little to choose between them and their northern opposite numbers. They rode asses, as the northern wizards did. Even at a distance, they had the air of men who weren't always sure what was going on around them. That put Roast-Beef William in mind of northern wizards, too.

They didn't need long to discover where the northerners had wreaked sorcerous havoc on the glideway line. As soon as they found it, they set to work repairing the damage. Watching them, Roast-Beef William believed they wouldn't take long to set it right. They showed a matter-of-fact competence often missing in battle.

They did, that is, till the bad-tempered colonel sent his men roaring forward. Roar they did, as if the Lion God had emerged from those pine woods. The southrons hadn't been such fools as to let their wizards go to work alone— William thought wizards had no business doing *anything* alone—but they'd detailed only a couple of platoons of soldiers to guard them. And a couple of platoons weren't nearly enough.

Volleys of crossbow quarrels knocked over some of the southron defenders and some of the mages. Even from the woods, Roast-Beef William heard the other wizards cry out in alarm and despair. Some turned to flee, which resulted in a couple of them being shot in the back. One, with more presence of mind than his friends, managed to call down two lightning bolts on the northerners before he too fell.

In a few minutes, it was all over. Neither William nor the colonel wanted to linger and face the full wrath of Hesmucet's army. They pulled back to the north with a small, neat victory in hand. The troops were in high spirits. Victories, even small ones, were hard to come by lately.

Roast-Beef William wished he shared their delight. Part of him did, but only a small part. The rest . . . The rest wanted nothing so much as escape from an army where even small victories were hard to come by.

Doubting George shrugged. "Well, sir, what happened was, they snookered us. Nobody expected they'd be laying for our wizards, but they were, and they made us pay."

"Pay too much," General Hesmucet told him. "Much too much."

"We can't bring these things off perfectly all the time." But George knew Hesmucet was right. "I won't let it happen again, sir."

"All right. I can't ask for more than that from you, and I know you mean a promise like that when you make it," the commanding general said. "The next question is, what's Bell got in mind with his peregrinations all over southern Peachtree?"

"Making us go hungry, I'd say," Doubting George replied. "He's been after the glideway like a hungry hound after a beefsteak."

"But *he's* doing well enough without anything you'd call a supply line," Hesmucet burst out. "Is he really so stupid as to think we can't do likewise? By the gods, Lieutenant General, I could march my whole army across Peachtree Province to Veldt by the Western Ocean, and I wouldn't go hungry, and the gods-damned traitors couldn't even slow me down if I set out to do it."

For a moment, George thought he was exaggerating for effect. Then he took another, longer, mental look at the question. Slowly, he nodded. "I do believe you're right, sir."

"I'm sure as can be that I'm right, gods damn it," Hesmucet said with an arrogance that would either land him in serious trouble—as it had General Guildenstern—or make him a great soldier. Either way, it was an arrogance George knew he lacked himself. Hesmucet went on, "As a matter of fact, I've started talking by crystal ball with Marshal Bart and King Avram about doing exactly that."

Doubting George's bushy eyebrows flew up. *Have* you?" Hesmucet had managed to do it without starting rumors flying all through the army—no mean feat. George wondered what sort of dire threats he'd used to keep the scryers quiet. Whatever they were, they'd worked.

"I have indeed," Hesmucet said. "I don't think I'm going to be able to bring Bell to battle. Doesn't look that way, anyhow. He's willing enough to raid and to strike at the glideway line, but he hasn't got the stomach—or the men—for a standup fight any more. We've finally persuaded him of that."

"He never was much of a scholar at Annasville, so I'm not surprised he took too long to learn," George said. "He went a long way toward losing the traitors the war before he finally got the idea."

"That breaks my heart," Hesmucet said.

"I doubt it," George said, and they both laughed.

But Hesmucet soon sobered. "Besides, the only other thing I might do is keep chasing Bell over this ground, and I don't see much point to that, not when we fought over it earlier in the year—and not when I'm unlikely to catch up with him, as I said before."

"I see your point, sir, but I have a question of my own," George said. Hesmucet waved a hand, inviting him to ask it. He did: "If you go marching through Peachtree to the Western Ocean, what will the Army of Franklin do?"

"You mean, without our dogging its tracks?" Hesmucet said, and Doubting George nodded. The commanding general gave a splendid shrug. "Do you know what, Lieutenant General? Frankly, I don't give a damn. I don't think it can hurt King Avram's cause enough to be worth worrying about."

"Suppose it strikes down into Franklin," George said. "Suppose it attacks Ramblerton or goes past the provincial capital down into Cloviston or even as far as the Highlow River."

General Hesmucet shrugged again. "Bell's welcome to try. My opinion—my strong opinion—is that he can't pull it off."

"What's Bart's opinion, sir? Or the king's?"

"They aren't so sure *I* can pull it off," Hesmucet answered. "To the hells with me if I know why not, though. Lion God's fangs, George, except for the Army of Franklin, what do the northerners have in the way of fighting men hereabouts? None to speak of, and you know it as well as I do. But Bart and King Avram aren't out here in the field. They can't see it for themselves, not with their mind's eyes."

He had a point. When Satrap Brown called out the Peachtree militia, he hadn't been able to put very many men in false King Geoffrey's service. Even so . . . "If you do head toward Veldt and the Western Ocean, you're cutting yourself loose from your supply line. No glideway back to Rising Rock any more."

"So what?" Hesmucet retorted. "I keep telling anyone who'll listen, Bell's already living off the countryside. Do you really think we'll starve to death if we march to the Western Ocean?"

"Starve? No sir," George answered. "I just think . . . I think I'd come up with a different plan, sir, is what I think."

"You're a more cautious man than I am," Hesmucet observed. To George's surprise and relief, it seemed only an observation, nothing more—not a slur on his courage, which it easily might have been. The commanding general continued, "Nobody can top you when it comes to making a stand and fighting on the defensive. I've seen that, and I've seen why they call you the Rock in the River of Death. You deserve all the praise you got there. But for going after the enemy and sticking your claws in him . . . There, Lieutenant General, I think I have the edge on you."

"You're probably right, sir," George said in the same dispassionate tones Hesmucet had used. "Between the two of us, we make a pretty fair general, don't we?"

Hesmucet laughed out loud. "Not too bad, by the gods. Not too bad." He scratched his chin. His short, bristly beard rasped under his fingernails. "If I do get leave to strike out for the Western Ocean, I may leave you behind."

Now Doubting George didn't try to hold back his disappointment. "What have I done to deserve something like that?" he demanded.

"I told you: you're a good defensive fighter," Hesmucet replied. "If I go west, I may send you back into Franklin to make sure Bell doesn't run wild down there."

"That's your privilege, of course, as the general commanding," George said woodenly. "I will serve the kingdom as best I can wherever you place me."

"I know you will," Hesmucet said. "That's why I'm thinking of doing it."

"But, gods damn it, I want to be in at the death!" George burst out.

"I know. I know. I do understand that, believe me." Hesmucet sounded sympathetic. But he also sounded unlikely to change his mind. "If I go west, I'll need to leave someone behind I can rely on absolutely. From where I'm sitting now, that's you. It is, if you look at it the right way, a compliment."

"That's what the priest of the Lion God told the courtesan after he shot his seed too soon," Doubting George replied. "*He* may have thought so, but *she* surely didn't."

Chuckling, Hesmucet said, "You've always got a story, don't you?"

"Every now and again, anyhow." If he trotted out the wry jokes, George didn't have to show how sorely he was hurt. He'd never been badly wounded; if he were, he suspected he would use his wit the same way. He wondered how much good it would do. It did less than he wanted here.

"This may all be moonshine, remember," Hesmucet said. "Marshal Bart and the king are less happy about the notion than I am. They may just order me to keep after Bell with my whole army, no matter how useless that looks to me."

"I told you, sir: I *will* do as you require," George said. "I'm not Fighting Joseph, to stomp off in a huff because I don't get my own way. He reminds me of a three-year-old throwing a fit because his mother took away his toy."

"A lot of truth in that, by the gods." Easy and friendly, Hesmucet came over and patted him on the shoulder. "You're a good man, George. You've had some nasty jobs, and not the ones you would have taken if you'd had your druthers, and you've done fine with every gods-damned one of them. And now here's one more, and I'm perfectly confident you'll do fine with it, too." He walked out of George's pavilion, proud and cocky and in command.

Go ahead, George. Here's some more garbage. You're so good at cleaning it up, I know you'll do fine cleaning up this lot, too. That was what Hesmucet meant, and he could say it and Doubting George had to take it, for he was a lordly, exalted general and George only a lowly lieutenant general.

Bart could have picked me to command this army. Knowing that gnawed at George. *He could have, but he didn't. And so Hesmucet gets to march to glory—if he doesn't make a mess of things and let the traitors win glory instead. And what do I get? I get to stay behind and clean up another mess. If there is a mess. Maybe I get to stay behind at Ramblerton and twiddle my thumbs. Wouldn't that be exciting?*

He left the pavilion himself and stared south. Somewhere up ahead there, Bell was flitting ahead like a will o' the wisp, drawing King Avram's army after him, keeping it from doing what it should be doing. Hesmucet was right about that, sure as sure he was. But his being right took away none of the hurt. *I want the glory. I want the people cheering me.*

Over in King Geoffrey's army, people called Roast-Beef William Old Reliable. He hadn't got the job he wanted, either, not when Geoffrey fired Joseph the Gamecock. The Rock in the River of Death? It sounded fancier than Old Reliable, but what did it mean? The same gods-damned thing.

Colonel Andy came up to him. "Sir—" he began.

"What the hells d'*you* want?" Doubting George snarled, taking out his frustrations on his adjutant.

Andy stiffened. A very minor noble—a mere baronet— he had more than minor pride. "Pardon me for existing, sir," he said icily.

"I'll think about it." George's voice remained gruff. But then he relented: "I'm sorry, Colonel. I'm truly sorry. It had nothing to do with you."

"It did not sound that way," Andy observed.

"I know. I *am* sorry," George said, and explained the visit he'd just had from Hesmucet.

"He goes off to have adventures and leaves you behind?" Andy said when he was done. "I don't blame you a bit for being upset, sir." His adjutant was fiercely loyal.

George knew he'd tried his best not to deserve such loyalty. "I do apologize," he said again. "I had no business barking at you."

"Never mind, sir. Never mind," Colonel Andy replied. "Can you do anything to get him to change his mind?"

"I doubt it," Doubting George said. "If I wore his boots, I daresay I'd do the same thing, and leave it up to some other sorry son of a bitch to handle whatever else needed handling. But I'm the sorry son of a bitch in question, and I suppose that's why I barked."

"Terrible. Just terrible." Andy stroked his beard. "Did he tell you what forces you would have?"

"No, but I can make a good guess: whatever he doesn't want and whatever I can scrape up," George answered.

"Terrible. Just terrible," Andy repeated. "We have to keep this from happening."

"Only thing I can think of that would do it would be to beat Bell up here—beat him and take his army off the board altogether," George replied. "I don't believe it's likely, though."

"Why not?" With his plump cheeks and angry expression, Colonel Andy resembled nothing so much as an indignant chipmunk. "We've licked the Army of Franklin whenever it would give us battle."

"*That's* why not," Doubting George replied. "I don't think Bell has any intention of giving us another crack at him. I think he'll keep on running and hope we keep on chasing him."

"Cowardly son of a bitch," his adjutant said with a distinct sniff.

"No, not Bell." George shook his head. "You can call Bell a great many things, but he's no coward. He's finally figured out that one traitor isn't worth two southron men, that's all, and that what the northern bards have to say about it doesn't mean a thing. It took him a lot longer than it should have, but he's got it now."

Andy sniffed again. "He's pretty stupid."

This time, George nodded. "He *is* pretty stupid. Brave and deadly—and stupid. He's like a hawk on somebody's wrist. Point it at prey and it will go out and kill. But ask it to figure things out for itself? No."

"Only Geoffrey did," Andy said.

"Only Geoffrey did," Doubting George agreed. "Of course, Geoffrey is pretty stupid, too, if anyone wants to know what I think. He had a perfectly good general in charge of his army here, and sacked him for no good reason."

"He wanted a general who would go out there and fight," Colonel Andy said.

"Be careful what you want—you may get it," George said. "Before he put his fighting general in there, he still had Marthasville, and the Army of Franklin was still a real army. Now Bell's running around trying to make a pest of himself with what he has left, and there isn't enough left of Marthasville to talk about. Brilliant change of command, wasn't it? Just fornicating brilliant."

Andy smiled. "Somehow, I don't think you're too sorry about that."

"Who, me?" Doubting George said.

Rain poured down out of a leaden sky: surprisingly cold rain that soaked Rollant and the standard he bore and turned the red clay of southern Peachtree Province into red glue. He slogged on, one step after another, pulling each foot out of the mud in turn and then setting it down again. Every so often, he stepped off the road to scrape muck off his boots with some grass or a shrub.

The southron army's asses and unicorns couldn't do that. Not only did they struggle more than the footsoldiers, they also chewed up the road worse. One stretch was almost like soup. "I wish they wouldn't send the beasts and wagons down the same road we use, not in this weather," Rollant grumbled.

"Wish for the moon, while you're at it," Smitty said.

"Thanks, friend. You always know how to make me feel better."

Smitty grinned. Water dripped off the brim of his hat—and off the end of his beaky nose. "Your wish is my command, your Corporalship, sir. As a matter of fact, your command is my command."

"I'd command you to stop your nonsense, but I know better than to waste my breath," Rollant said.

"Only proves you're married, I'd say."

"You know I am." Rollant pointed at Smitty. "And I know you're not. So what do you know about it?"

"Just watching my ma and pa," Smitty answered. "But they've been together thirty years now without killing each other, so I expect they're doing something right."

Rollant had trouble arguing with that. A few minutes later, traffic on the road didn't merely slow; it stalled altogether. "What the hells is going on here?" Rollant demanded irately, and he was far from the only one. As he stood there, the mud tried to suck him down into its cold, wet, slimy maw.

Lieutenant Griff sent a man forward to see if he could discover what had gone wrong. The fellow sensibly trotted along on the grass by the side of the road, not in the roadway itself.

He came back by the same route. "There's wagons up ahead stuck in what looks like a bog, sir," he reported to Griff. "It's so deep, I wouldn't be surprised if there were crocodiles in it."

"Well, why aren't people going around?" Griff asked.

"A lot of 'em are trying to haul out the wagons," the soldier replied. "They aren't having much luck, though."

"What are we supposed to do in the meantime?" Sergeant Joram asked. "Stand here in the mud and drown?" It must have been doing its best to pull him under, too.

Before long, a southron captain who was so muddy he might have been dipped in rust-colored paint ordered Griff's company forward. "You men can lend a hand on the ropes," he said.

That was when Rollant found out what underofficer's rank was really worth. As corporal and standard-bearer, he stood around with Lieutenant Griff and Sergeant Joram and the other men with stripes on their sleeves. The common soldiers sloshed down into the bog—and the messenger had described it accurately—seized the long ropes fastened to the front end of the lead wagon, and pulled like men possessed.

I've still got just as much chance of getting killed as anybody else, he thought. *More chance than most, because I bear the standard. But the rest of a corporal's job looks a lot better than a common soldier's.*

Try as they would, the mud-streaked men in gray couldn't shift the wagon. Then a mage on an ass muddy all the way to the belly rode up. The captain who'd summoned Griff's company recognized him. "That's Colonel Albertus!" he said. "He's called the Great, thought gods know why." He raised his voice: "Colonel Albertus, can you help us, sir?"

Albertus reined in. Most of the time, Rollant judged, he would have been an impressive man, with a long, pointed gray beard; a long, pointed nose; and piercing black eyes.

At the moment, he resembled nothing so much as a drowned billy goat. His voice was deep and resonant: "I shall do what I can."

"Sounds more like a circus mountebank than a proper wizard," Sergeant Joram said behind his hand.

"Well, let's see what he can do," Rollant answered, and the sergeant nodded.

Colonel Albertus fixed the lead wagon with those piercing eyes and began to chant. He made pass after pass, his fingers writhing like so many serpents. The wagon began to twitch and shake. After a moment, it tried to rise, but was held in place by the sucking power of the mud. Albertus paused for a moment to curse, then incanted harder than ever.

"By the gods, maybe the old bastard can bring it off after all," Joram said.

"I hope so," Rollant said.

With a horrible squelching noise, the wagon did pull itself free of the encumbering mud. The weary soldiers who'd been trying to get it out raised a cheer—which cut off abruptly when, instead of stopping just above the bog, the wagon continued to rise till its dripping, mucky wheels were a good ten feet off the ground.

The men on the ropes who'd been closest to the wagon started to rise into the air, too, till they let go and fell back into the mud. Some of them squawked. Some cursed. Some did both at once. Rollant didn't blame those last. Albertus the so-called Great had produced a sorcery more successful than it might have been. And, as with a lot of sorceries, this one, proving more successful than it might have been, was at best useless and at worst a help to the enemy.

"Well, Colonel, what in the hells are you going to do now?" demanded the captain who'd summoned Albertus. *So much for respecting a superior officer,* Rollant thought. But wizards were officers by courtesy, to let them order common soldiers around. Real fighting men, as he'd seen before, disdained them.

Albertus gave the wagon a distinctly wall-eyed stare. The stare he sent the contemptuous captain was something else again. Rollant was glad it wasn't aimed his way; a poisonous snake might have aimed that sort of look at its prey the instant before it struck. "I shall endeavor to repair matters," the mage said in a voice as coldblooded as a serpent.

If he put the captain in fear, that worthy hid it very well. "You can endeavor all you gods-damned well please," he snarled. "You wouldn't have to if you'd done it right the first time."

"And if you splendid soldiers had done everything right the first time, this cursed war would have been over year before last," Colonel Albertus retorted. The captain sputtered and fumed, but he kept quiet, because the wizard had spoken self-evident truth. Albertus' smile didn't show fangs, but it might as well have.

Turning back to the wagon, Albertus began another spell. This one sounded less imperious, more cautious, than the one he'd used before. Its results seemed less dramatic, too. Rollant approved of that; high drama and trouble were intimately associated in his mind. When Colonel Albertus called out a word of power and pointed at the uncannily floating wagon, it seemed more a request than a command.

And the request got results, too, where the earlier command had only caused a new and more spectacular problem. Little by little, the wagon drifted down till its wheels rested on the air a few inches above the mud from which it had been rescued.

Albertus gave the captain of footsoldiers an icy bow. "Now your men should be able to push and pull the wagon to drier ground," he said.

"Go ahead and try it, boys," the captain called. Cautiously, some of the soldiers took hold of the ropes and began to pull. Even more cautiously, others got behind the wagon and pushed. They all let out a cheer when it moved forward far more readily than it had while stuck in the mud.

"Thank you very much, sir," the captain told Colonel Albertus. But he couldn't resist getting in another dig: "Now do you suppose you can get the rest of 'em out of the muck without sending 'em halfway up to Mt. Panamgam?"

The mage aimed a harried look his way. "I shall bend every effort to that purpose."

His efforts could have used a bit more bending. His first

spell with the second wagon failed to get it out of the mud. The captain let out a loud, scornful snort. Colonel Albertus kept on incanting. When at last the wagon did emerge, it rose only two or three feet into the air. The men could push and pull it forward without much trouble.

Albertus' spells went better still on the third and fourth wagons. He'd learned what needed doing by then, and he did it. Those wagons came out on the first try and rose only a foot or so above the surface of the mud. Not even the captain could complain. All he said was, "Appreciate it, Colonel."

"Yes, well, I'm sure you're welcome," Albertus the Great said. He scrambled aboard his ass as if he'd never mounted it before and rode off down the road.

By the time Colonel Nahath's regiment made camp, Rollant felt about ready to drop. His men had a hells of a time starting fires, even though the rain had eased off by then. Wet fuel and wet tinder made things difficult. At last, the squad got a couple of smoky blazes going. "Wish we had a mage along now," Rollant grumbled. "He'd have set us up in a hurry."

"Either that or he'd have burned down half the gods-damned province trying," Smitty said. Rollant nodded. Mages could bungle things, sure enough, and often did.

He sat down on the wet ground. His tunic and pantaloons were already soaked; a little more water made no difference. To his surprise, the trooper named Gleb sat down next to him. Gleb's face still showed the marks of their fight. He supposed his own did, too. Did Gleb want another try? If he did, Rollant was ready to give him one.

But all Gleb said was, "Ask you something, Corporal?"

"You can ask," Rollant said roughly. "I don't promise to answer."

Gleb nodded. "All right. That's fair enough." He still hesitated. Rollant gestured impatiently, as if to say, *Come on*. Words spurted from Gleb in a rush: "How was it you were able to lick me when we tangled?"

To Rollant, the answer to that was plain as the sun in the sky. "How? I didn't dare lose, that's how."

By Gleb's frown, that made less sense to him than it did

to Rollant. Of course, he'd never been a blond. He proved that by continuing, "But how *could* you beat me? I mean, you're, uh, not a proper Detinan, and I am."

As patiently as he could, Rollant said, "You've seen me fight the traitors, haven't you?"

Gleb nodded again. "Well, yes."

"I did that all right, didn't I?" Rollant asked. Gleb nodded once more. In some exasperation, Rollant said, "Those bastards are Detinans, aren't they? If I can fight them, why the hells can't I fight you?"

"I don't know." Gleb's broad shoulders went up and down in a shrug. "They're the enemy. You're supposed to fight them."

Rollant tapped the stripes on his sleeve. "You know I almost had to get myself killed before they'd put these on me, don't you?" This time, Gleb's nod came much more slowly. Rollant persisted: "And you know why, too, don't you? On account of I'm a blond, that's why. You know all about that."

The trooper muttered something. Rollant couldn't make out what it was. *Just as well,* he thought. Then Gleb said, "It wasn't like I thought it would be."

"I'm trying to tell you why, gods damn it," Rollant snapped. "I had to work so hard to get these stripes, I don't want to lose them. If you licked me, I likely would've lost them. And so you would have had to kill me to make me quit. Is that plain enough for you?"

"Oh," Gleb said. Maybe he got it. Maybe he didn't. Rollant didn't much care one way or the other. As long as the Detinan took his orders and gave him no trouble, what Gleb thought didn't matter to him.

He wondered how much Gleb actually did think. Not much, unless he missed his guess. That didn't matter, either, not unless his stupidity endangered the men around him— or it led him to something like picking a fight with a corporal who also happened to be a blond.

But I don't happen to be a blond, Rollant thought. *I am a blond. I happen to be a corporal. That's how Detinans see it, anyway.*

How Detinans saw it, though, didn't matter so much to

him, not any more. Regardless of how even Detinans in King Avram's army with him looked at the world and at him, certain facts no one could deny. Here he sat, wet and miserable, in the middle of an invading army in the middle of Peachtree Province. He wore a gray tunic and pantaloons like everybody else's. He got paid like everybody else, too. And that he'd come here with weapons to hand, ready to kill any Detinans who didn't agree with his comrades and him, went a long way toward proving how much had changed since he was first grudgingly allowed to fight.

After the war, everybody's likely to try to forget blonds did some of the fighting for King Avram, he thought. *That's the sort of thing ordinary Detinans won't want to remember. They can go back to thinking we're "just blonds" if they forget. Well, we can't let that happen.*

"Gleb," he said, "looks like we're a little short on firewood. Chop some more." He waited to see what the soldier would do.

"All right, Corporal," Gleb replied, and went off to obey the order. Slowly, Rollant nodded to himself. Sure as hells, some things had changed.

XII

"What the hells is Bell playing at?" General Hesmucet demanded, going over the reports the scouts brought in about the Army of Franklin's movements. "If he keeps going in this direction, he'll be all the way down to Caesar by the time he's through. That's where this campaign started, near enough."

Doubting George perched on a stool in the farmhouse Hesmucet was using for a headquarters. Hesmucet wondered how many farmhouses he'd used for temporary headquarters since the war began. He couldn't have guessed, not even to the nearest dozen. When the war finally ended, if it ever did, he intended to stay away from farmhouses from then on.

George said, "One thing Bell's doing: he's making you dance to his tune instead of the other way round. You imposed your will on Joseph the Gamecock. You haven't done that with Bell—if you leave Marthasville out of the bargain, of course."

"Oh, of course," Hesmucet said dryly. "No one would want to talk about Marthasville at all. Bell didn't care one way or the other what the devils happened to it."

"That's not what I meant, sir, or not exactly," Doubting George said.

Whatever he'd meant, he had a point, or at least a good part of one. As long as the southrons kept chasing Lieutenant General Bell and the Army of Franklin all over southern Peachtree Province, Hesmucet couldn't do what he really wanted to: make the north regret ever starting a war against King Avram. *If I can march to the Western Ocean, that will prove Geoffrey's king over nothing but air and brags,* he thought. *I can* do *it. I know I can.*

He sighed. "Turning into a hero would be a lot easier if the bastards on the other side cooperated a little more."

"I'm sure you're right, sir," Doubting George replied. "One thing, though: I'm reasonably sure they feel the same way about you."

"That's something," Hesmucet agreed. "It's less than I'd like, but you're right: it is something."

After his second-in-command left, he summoned Major Alva and asked him, "Can you divine what Bell has in mind trying next?"

"I can do my best," the bright young mage said. "How good my best will prove depends on how well Bell is warded and how firm his plans are in his own mind. If he doesn't know what he's going to do, I can't very well pick it out of his brain, now can I? . . . Uh, sir."

"What brain?" Hesmucet said scornfully. "The next sign of having one in actual working order that Bell shows will be the first."

Major Alva smiled. "That's funny, sir. I like it. I like it a lot."

"Glad to amuse you," Hesmucet told him. "Now, can you manage this wizardry?"

"As I say, sir, I can certainly try the requisite spells," Alva replied. "I don't know how much I'll learn from them till I do."

"Get on with it, then," Hesmucet said. "Report back to me after whatever happens, happens."

"Yes, sir." Alva saluted and hurried away.

Only after the mage had gone did Hesmucet realize he hadn't had to correct him on military deportment even once.

Little by little, Alva was learning. If he kept learning, he might eventually turn into a civilized human being, and perhaps even into a tolerable soldier. Hesmucet wouldn't have imagined either one of those as the remotest possibility a few months before.

Alva came back late the following day. "Well?" Hesmucet barked.

"Well, sir, the wards weren't so well established as I thought they might be, and Bell is sure about what he wants to do next," the brash young mage said.

"I'm not surprised they didn't bother warding him," Hesmucet said. "They must have figured no one would want to look into such an empty head." Alva's laugh was deliciously scandalized. The general commanding went on, "All right—you were able to look around inside the emptiness. What did you find?"

"He intends to strike at Caesar, sir," the wizard replied. He hesitated, then risked a question: "Uh, is that good news or bad?"

"Depends," Hesmucet answered. "If we can get there with our whole force before he hits the place, it's good news for us and bad news for him. If we can't, it might be the other way round—and he's ahead of us."

Alva nodded. "Yes, that would seem to make sense. What do we do if we can't get there ahead of him?"

"Tell the garrison commander to fight like a mad bastard till we can come up," Hesmucet said. "Murray the Coarse did it, and he can, too. He's got a good natural position to defend. Joseph the Gamecock used it to good advantage against us. Now it's our turn."

"Can we do it?"

"I aim to find out," Hesmucet answered.

Commanding the southron garrison was a colonel named Clark the Seamster. When Hesmucet got in touch with him by crystal ball, he said, "Your news is no surprise to me, sir. I've just had one of Bell's men come in under flag of truce demanding our surrender. I've seen notes I liked better."

"Oh?" Hesmucet said. "What does it say?"

"Here, I'll read it for you." Colonel Clark paused to set spectacles on his nose, then took a sheet of paper from his breast pocket. "Here we go. *Sir: I demand the immediate and unconditional surrender of the post and garrison under your command and, should this be acceded to, all Detinan officers and men will be paroled in a few days. If the place is carried by assault, no prisoners will be taken.*" He looked up at Hesmucet over the tops of the spectacles. "Perhaps I should remind you, sir, that I have a couple of regiments of blond troops under my command."

"You need to know we're still a couple of days away," Hesmucet said. "What did you tell him?"

"One moment, sir, and I'll read you a copy of my answer." Clark the Seamster found another paper. "Here. I wrote, *Your communication of this date just received*—which is true; I got it less than an hour ago. *In reply, I have to state that I am somewhat surprised at the concluding sentence, to the effect that, if this place is carried by assault, no prisoners will be taken. In my opinion, I can hold this post. If you want it, come and take it.*"

"You told Bell *that?*" Hesmucet said in astonished but delighted disbelief.

"I sure as hells did," Colonel Clark answered. "I can hold the son of a bitch off, and I'm not about to put men under my command in danger of being murdered or seized and sent back to their old liege lords. They'll fight like madmen to keep that from happening, and you can count on it."

"Good for you, Colonel. I admire your spirit. Now I rely on you to make it good." Hesmucet clapped his hands. He didn't share Clark's confidence in the fighting ability of blonds. He remained of the opinion that few of them made good soldiers. But he couldn't help applauding the bravado the garrison commander had shown.

"I'll do my best, sir," Clark said. "I just wonder if the one-legged marvel will even have the nerve to put in a real attack on Caesar. When he tried one at Whole Mackerel, he got his nose bloodied for him."

"Well, actually, Murray the Coarse was the one who came away from that fight with a bloody face, but I take your point," Hesmucet said. "Hang on for two days, no matter what he does to you, and then we'll be there. I swear it by all the gods."

"I'll do it, sir. You can count on me," Clark the Seamster said.

"I do, Colonel." Hesmucet nodded to the scryer. Colonel Clark's image vanished from the crystal ball. Hesmucet left the scryers' tent and shouted for a runner.

"Yes, sir?" one of his bright young men said.

"Go fetch me Marble Bill," Hesmucet snapped.

"Yes, sir!" The runner saluted and hurried off to find the commander of unicorn-riders. He brought him back even sooner than General Hesmucet had hoped. Pride in his voice, he said, "Here you are, sir."

"Thank you." Hesmucet turned to Marble Bill. "Can you get a couple of regiments of riders into Caesar by tomorrow afternoon?"

Marble Bill frowned. "Without resistance from the enemy I could, obviously. It depends on how much we'd have to fight through on the way, so I can't really give you a certain answer."

Hesmucet drummed his fingers on the right thigh of his pantaloons. That wasn't the sort of reply he'd wanted to hear. In a couple of sentences, Marble Bill had shown why he was an indifferent commander of unicorn-riders. Fortunately, Brigadier Spinner on the traitors' side was no better, and Marble Bill seemed the best officer Hesmucet had. But *best* wasn't the same as *good*, and Hesmucet knew that only too well.

"What do you think?" he asked. "Against what you're likely to run into along the way, can you get there?"

"If you give the order, sir, I'll do my best," Marble Bill replied.

That wasn't what Hesmucet wanted to hear, either. He wanted to hear, *Yes, sir!* That failing, he wanted to hear, *If I can't find a way, I'll make a new one. Those gods-damned traitors can't stop me.*

But Marble Bill was what he had to work with. "Go try. Do everything you can," Hesmucet told him.

"Yes, sir," the commander of unicorn-riders answered.

"You'll be doing the trapped garrison an enormous favor if you succeed," Hesmucet said, hoping to build a fire under him.

It didn't work. Marble Bill remained cool. "I told you, sir: I'll do my best." He saluted and took his leave.

Having given his orders, Hesmucet could only wait to see what became of them. He muttered in frustration. Here he was, in command of the greatest army in the east, but every bit as dependent on time to show what lay ahead as any other soldier. He wished it were otherwise, but in his years he'd wished for all sorts of things that hadn't come true.

He got back in touch with Colonel Clark. "They're prodding us, sir," Clark said, "but they aren't putting all their force into it, I don't think. Either that or they've got less force to put than I thought they did."

"Well, if they aren't hitting you with all they've got, what in the hells *are* they doing?" Hesmucet demanded.

Clark the Seamster sent him an exasperated look. "Sir, I can hold Caesar, or else I can throw scouts out all over the landscape. To the hells with me if I see how I can do both at once with the little force I've got here."

"I daresay you're right," Hesmucet admitted, "but I wish you were wrong."

"Will I get help?" Clark asked.

"I've sent out unicorn-riders under Marble Bill," Hesmucet said. "If everything goes well, they'll be there tomorrow. I know I'll have footsoldiers there the day after. I already told you that."

"Yes, sir, you did," Colonel Clark said. "I'm sure the footsoldiers will come. I'll believe the unicorn-riders when I see 'em."

Another man with confidence in Marble Bill, Hesmucet thought. But then, in one way or another, unicorn-riders had been disappointing King Avram's armies ever since the war was new. Why should this campaign prove any different from so many of the earlier ones? *Because I'll scream and fuss till my commanders do it right,* Hesmucet thought. He hadn't quite managed that yet. He'd got to the point where the unicorn-riders—unless they had the misfortune to bump up against Ned of the Forest—didn't go too egregiously wrong too often. But that still wasn't the same as turning them into a weapon to match the one that had done the traitors so much good.

Before long, he found out what that part of the Army of Franklin not attacking Caesar was up to: wrecking more glideway line. Clark the Seamster did have some scouts out, and reported northern mages working as much destructive magic as they could. The news alarmed Hesmucet much less than it would have a couple of months before.

"Let them do what they want," he said. "We'll either repair it or we won't worry about it. We're more or less living off the country now."

He did curse Lieutenant General Bell for pulling him down here to southern Peachtree Province again. His full mind, his full heart, weren't on this pursuit. He had to remind himself to take it seriously. He kept looking away, looking away, looking away toward Veldt and the Western Ocean.

If I can get there, this war is as good as won. Peachtree Province helps feed Parthenia. If I burn my way across this province, Duke Edward and the Army of Southern Parthenia will get pretty hungry pretty fast. It's not just a matter of doing things here—what I do here affects the whole gods-damned war.

Marshal Bart had been the first one to realize that. He'd brought King Avram with him, and Hesmucet as well. The sovereign and his two chief commanders saw the war as a single entity, with all the parts connected. Hesmucet didn't think any northerner looked at it the same way. He was sure false King Geoffrey didn't.

Duke Edward? After a little thought, Hesmucet shook his head. Duke Edward was a brilliant commander, but he fought battles, not campaigns. Being so embattled, he couldn't afford to look at a wider canvas.

Turn me loose, then, Hesmucet thought. *Let me move against the traitors. Let me march through Peachtree Province. I'll peel it right down to the ground, and let's see the north keep fighting after that. They'll remember my name here a hundred years from now. The rest of Detina may not remember so well, but that won't matter, for it will be one Detina.*

Roast-Beef William watched the Army of Franklin's mages destroying the glideway line south of Caesar. He watched unicorn-riders posted around the mages to warn of any sudden southron onslaught. *A good raid,* he thought. *This is what the Army of Franklin has been reduced to. We're raiders now, no more. We couldn't have done worse with me in command. We might have done better.*

He sighed. They hadn't wanted him—neither Thraxton the Braggart nor King Geoffrey. *I'm Old Reliable. I'm good enough to lead a wing, but not an army. They put a hero in to lead the army. And oh, hasn't he done a splendid job? I wonder what he'll try next.*

Bitter? Roast-Beef William asked himself. *Why shouldn't I be bitter? If anybody's earned the right, I'm the man.*

The ironic thing was that, little by little, Lieutenant General Bell had started to learn. William had expected him to throw the whole army at Caesar, but he hadn't. When the southron commanding the garrison cast defiance in his face, he'd skirmished against the soldiers there and then gone after the glideway. He'd got a rude surprise trying to overrun the little force up at Whole Mackerel, and he didn't care to get two such surprises.

If he'd learned that lesson after his first failed attack outside Marthasville, the Army of Franklin might still hold the place. Roast-Beef William sighed. If pigs had wings, everyone would carry umbrellas.

A courier rode up and spoke with one of the unicorn-riders on guard duty. The rider pointed toward William. The courier came over to him at a trot. Reining in, the fellow said, "Lieutenant General Bell's compliments, sir, and you are requested to report to his headquarters immediately."

Bell hasn't been in the habit of giving me compliments lately, even those of ordinary courtesy, William thought. But the man remained in command of the Army of Franklin, or of what was left of it. "I'll come, of course," he said.

His own unicorn was tethered not far away. He swung up into the saddle and followed the courier back to a farmhouse that offered no visible virtues past a roof and four walls. Those modest attributes were not to be despised, not in a countryside that had seen as much fighting as this one.

Dismounting, Roast-Beef William strode into the farmhouse. There sat Lieutenant General Bell, putting away the little bottle of laudanum that let him deal with the pain of his wounds—and that might have robbed him of some of the rather poor wits he owned. No help for that, either, though. William saluted and said, "Reporting as ordered, sir."

"Ah, yes, Lieutenant General." Bell straightened, grimacing as he did so, and returned the salute. "I've just received a despatch from Nonesuch concerning you." He glowered at William from under bushy brows. "You did not tell me you had sent a request to be detached from service to this army."

I've been delighted serving here, Roast-Beef William thought. *It's a rare privilege, taking orders from a man junior to me in time served in rank . . . and watching him butcher what was a fine fighting force.* If he said any of that aloud, he would be screaming before he was through. *At least I have the sense to know as much.* What he did say were two perfectly safe words: "Yes, sir."

"Well, whether you told me or not, your request has been approved," Bell said. "You will be transferred out of the command of the Army of Franklin."

Oh, gods be praised, Roast-Beef William thought. Saying that to the man who held the command in the Army of Franklin could only cause trouble. He didn't want trouble, not when he was escaping. He asked, "Where is my new assignment, sir?" *Anywhere but here! Oh, gods be praised indeed!*

"Here is the order." Bell found a sheet of paper and thrust it at him. "I wish you the best of luck in your new post."

Roast-Beef William took the sheet. "Let me see that, sir, if I may." The script was as ornate as one would expect from the royal chancery. The prose style was ornate, too. William waded through flowery compliments and endless subordinate clauses till he got to the meat. *You are requested and required to repair immediately to the vicinity of Veldt,* the scribe wrote, *there to organize defenses against General Hesmucet's anticipated westward movement. You are to oppose him as far forward as you can, and to continue to oppose him with all resources at your disposal.* William looked up at Bell. "You've read this?"

"Oh, yes," the general commanding replied.

"It says I'm supposed to oppose the southrons with all the resources at my disposal," William said. "When I get to Veldt, what sort of resources will I have at my disposal?"

Lieutenant General Bell started to shrug, winced, and cursed softly under his breath. "I haven't the slightest idea. Whatever garrison's in the citadel there, I suppose, and however many militiamen you can persuade Satrap Brown to turn loose and arm."

That was what Roast-Beef William had been afraid of. "I'm supposed to take up a collection of miserable odds and sods, then, and stop Hesmucet with them?"

"Seems to be what the order says, wouldn't you agree?"

"So it is," William said heavily. "But how in the hells am I supposed to do that when the whole Army of Franklin couldn't manage it?"

"Not my responsibility," Bell said. Roast-Beef William wanted to kick him. He went on, "I'm sure you'll do your best."

"Yes, sir. Of course, sir," William said in a hollow voice. "But what will you and the Army of Franklin be doing in the meantime? You're the best protection Peachtree Province has."

"These past several weeks, I've done my best to drive General Hesmucet mad," Bell replied. "If he's chasing the Army of Franklin all over the landscape, he can't very well march west against you, can he?"

"Well . . . no, sir," William admitted. "But suppose he stops chasing you and goes on his merry way?"

Bell looked mysterious, which inclined Roast-Beef William toward violence against his person once more. Then he said, "I probably shouldn't tell you this, since you're going away, but they do call you Old Reliable, and I think you've earned the name." After that sort of buildup, William expected to be disappointed by whatever he said, but he turned out to have made a mistake there, for Bell declared, "Ned of the Forest is bringing his unicorn-riders west to rejoin the Army of Franklin."

"*Is* he?" William exclaimed. Bell's leonine head solemnly nodded. William said, "That *is* good news, sir. Ned's a fine officer, even if he can be a bit . . . touchy."

"He couldn't get along with Thraxton the Braggart, is what

you mean," Bell said. "Of course, nobody gets along with Thraxton."

You didn't think that when he put you in command here, William thought—which didn't mean Bell was wrong. With a sigh, the departing officer said, "I wish things here would have turned out better."

"So do I," Bell replied. "If anyone is mad enough to believe I *wanted* to leave Marthasville to the tender mercies of the southrons . . . Do you know, Lieutenant General, when they paraded through the city, they had the gods-damned gall to use a blond as one of their standard-bearers—and not just a blond, mind you, but a blond underofficer, of all the impossible things!"

"Blonds in King Avram's army have fought better than Detinans ever imagined they could," Roast-Beef William said. "It's no wonder some officers in this kingdom—in this army—have begun to wonder if we shouldn't put crossbows in their hands and see what they can do for us."

Bell sneered. "I heard about Brigadier Patrick the Cleaver's memorial to King Geoffrey. I couldn't very well keep from hearing about it, when I was flat on my back after I lost my leg. Look what happened to Patrick: he was ordered not to talk about it, and he's been passed over for promotion every time a new command came open. No, thanks, Lieutenant General—I want no part of arming blonds."

"If we can get enough Detinan soldiers, well and good, sir," William said. "If not, and if blonds can fight—shouldn't we get some use out of them, seeing that our enemies do?"

"Arming blonds destroys everything being a Detinan means," Bell said.

"Yes, sir," Roast-Beef William agreed. He had no great love for blonds—except, perhaps, for some of their prettier women. But he couldn't help adding, "Losing the war destroys everything being a Detinan means, too. If arming blonds would keep that from happening *now*, we could worry about everything else *later*."

"I don't think it's a good idea. King Geoffrey doesn't think it's a good idea, either," Bell said. "You may not care about my views, Lieutenant General, but those of the king *will* prevail."

He was right, of course. He was right about Geoffrey's suppression of Patrick the Cleaver's memorial. He was right about Patrick's failure to get promoted. Of course, Patrick the Cleaver probably didn't altogether understand what being a Detinan meant. He wasn't a northerner born, but had crossed the Western Ocean from the Sapphire Isle himself as a young man. To him, blonds might seem like people, not like natural-born serfs.

If a few brigades of well-armed blond crossbowmen and pikemen were waiting for me at Veldt, I'd be a lot happier going there—I could do something against Hesmucet in that case, William thought. But then he frowned. *Or could I? Could I trust them not to shoot me in the back and go over to the southrons?*

"If we did use them, we'd have to promise to treat them like Detinans once they left the army," he mused.

"Cows will fly before we arm blonds," Bell said. "Don't waste your time thinking about it."

And he was bound to be right about that, too. Roast-Beef William saluted. "If you will excuse me, sir? I have a lot to think about before I take over my new command."

"Of course. You're dismissed, Lieutenant General," Bell said. "And I wish you the best of fortune in the west."

"Thank you, sir," William said. "The best fortune I can think of would be for the southrons not to come west at me. If tearing up the glideway line will keep that from happening, I'm all for it."

"I think it will," Bell said. "After all, the Grand Marshal's army was nothing but a starving band of fugitives on the retreat from Pahzbull fifty years ago. They got in, but most of them didn't come out again. I don't see any reason why the same thing can't happen to General Hesmucet and his men."

"Yes, sir," Roast-Beef William said. What went through his mind while he got out the polite words was, *Oh, if I weren't leaving, I'd tell him to his face what an idiot he is. The Sorbian army didn't ruin the Grand Marshal and his host when he marched west. The Sorbian winter did. The Kingdom of Sorb has the worst winters in the world. Peachtree Province has some of the mildest winters in the world. Where are the blizzards to wreck Hesmucet's army? If you have one up your sleeve, you'd better pull it out pretty gods-damned soon.*

"Again, good luck to you, and I hope the southrons stay far away," Bell said.

"Thank you, sir," William replied. "So do I. May I ask you something?" He waited for the general commanding to nod, then put his question: "Now that I'm leaving, are you going to name Patrick the Cleaver wing commander in my place?"

Bell didn't hesitate for a moment. "No. He's a good fighting soldier, and brave as they come, but I don't think he makes a suitable wing commander. Besides, even if I thought he did, even if I proposed it, King Geoffrey would never approve the appointment. We've already talked about the Cleaver's memorial. The king doesn't forget something like that."

He was bound to be right. He didn't have much of a sense for politics in the broader meaning of the word, but a shrewd understanding of the way the king's mind worked went a long way toward making up for the lack. Roast-Beef William also noticed one other irony: Bell's description of Patrick the Cleaver might have been a description of himself. Of course, Bell had been given command of not just a wing but an army. And, having got high command, he'd proceeded to prove he wasn't suitable for it.

Well, that's King Geoffrey's worry now, William thought. *He wanted Bell in command, and he got him, and everything that went with him. I wonder when he'll take Joseph the Gamecock off the shelf again and see if he can repair the damage.*

William left the farmhouse. He swung up into the saddle of his unicorn to ride away from the Army of Franklin. As he booted the beast into motion, he felt as if he were escaping a sinking ship. But he shook his head a moment later. The only way to escape the sinking ship, he feared, would be to flee King Geoffrey's kingdom altogether. The clouds gathering over the north looked very black indeed.

I can't run away, Roast-Beef William thought. *I'm a soldier. My duty is to fight for my king and my kingdom, to fight as long as I can and as hard as I can. I may lose— I likely will lose—but I have to try.* He rode off to the west to do what he could to hold back the building storm.

❖　　❖　　❖

Captain Gremio sipped from a tin cup of what the cooks called tea. He made a horrible face. Even with plenty of honey slopped into it, it was bitter enough to pucker his mouth. "Gods, that's vile," he said.

Sergeant Thisbe, sitting cross-legged on the ground beside him, took a cautious sip of his own. He nodded. "Couldn't be much worse. Whatever roots they're using, they'd better use some different ones the next time. . . . Why are you drinking more of it, sir?"

The company commander put his free hand on the left side of his chest. "Why? Because no matter how foul it tastes, it's making my heart beat faster and my eyes open up, that's why. Maybe the cooks know something after all."

Thisbe took another, more experimental, sip, then nodded again. "I suppose you're right. It's still nasty, though."

"If it wakes me up and gets me going, I don't much care how nasty it is." Gremio drained the cup. "I suppose the blonds drank tea from roots like these all the time back in the old days."

"I'm sorry for them if they did," Thisbe said. "The gods really must have hated them."

"Ha!" Gremio said. "If only you were joking. After all, what did the gods bring them? The gods brought them us, that's what. And, since the gods love us, they must have hated the blonds. Stands to reason, eh?"

"Makes sense to me, sir." Thisbe finished his own cup of tea and then made as if to retch. Gremio laughed, though that really wasn't funny, either. Thisbe asked, "What do we do today?"

"March along aimlessly. Forage as much as we can. Skirmish with the southrons if we happen to bump into them," Gremio answered. "I can't imagine anything more exciting. Can you?"

Thisbe gave back an uncertain smile. "If you don't like what we *are* doing, what do you think we *should* be up to?"

"Defending Marthasville," Gremio said at once. "If we'd kept on trying to defend the place instead of attacking an army twice our size, we might still hold it."

"Well . . . yes, sir," the sergeant said. "But it's a little too late to worry about that now, isn't it?"

"No, indeed," Gremio answered. Thisbe looked puzzled. The company commander explained: "It's *much* too late to worry about that now."

"Er, yes." Thisbe's grin was uncertain, too. Somewhere not far away, a sergeant from another company started shouting at his men, getting them up and ready for another day's march, no matter how aimless. Thisbe also climbed to his feet. "Form up, you lugs!" he shouted. "If you think you're going to be lazy all day, you can gods-damned well think again."

Gremio's bones creaked when he rose. When he walked off behind a bush, his left foot felt cold. Examination showed the sole of his left shoe was staring to separate from the upper. He muttered something nasty under his breath as he buttoned his fly. He couldn't even complain about something like that, not out loud, not when a fair number of the men he led had no shoes at all.

Geese mournfully honked overhead as the Army of Franklin got on the road again. Pointing to them, Gremio said, "I wish I could fly north for the winter, too. Then I wouldn't have to worry about a lot of things."

Thisbe gave him a quizzical look. A couple of soldiers started honking. As such things had a way of doing, the raucous noise spread through the whole company. "What in the damnation is wrong with your men, Captain?" Colonel Florizel demanded.

"Why, nothing, sir," Gremio replied. "They aren't down at all, and they still have plenty of pluck."

"Oh. Good. Glad to hear it," Florizel said vaguely. Thisbe sent Gremio a horrible look. He tipped his hat to the sergeant. Thisbe snorted. *That tea must be rotting my brains,* Gremio thought.

He tramped along the back roads of southern Peachtree Province. When he went through a muddy stretch, he had no doubt that his shoe was starting to come apart. Again, he kept his curses quiet and private.

"Where exactly are we going, sir?" Sergeant Thisbe asked as Gremio squelched along with mud between his toes.

"Good question, Sergeant. Excellent question, in fact," Gremio replied. "At the moment, though, I don't even know where approximately we're going, let alone exactly. This isn't the first time you've exposed my ignorance, either. Shall we consult with Colonel Florizel, or shall we try to retain our touching, simple faith that the general commanding has some idea of what we're doing?"

"Er—whatever you like, sir," Thisbe said.

"In my dreams, Sergeant, but nowhere else," Gremio said. "So"—he bowed—"what is your pleasure?"

"Well . . . never mind, sir," the sergeant answered. "I suppose we'll both find out."

"I suppose we will." Gremio bowed again, as if impersonating a very punctilious nobleman. "Now I do hope you won't ask any awkward questions about what we're going to do when we get there."

Thisbe gave him an odd look. "I wouldn't think of it, sir. Are you feeling all right?"

"But for one sloppy foot and that touching, simple faith I was telling you about, I'm fine, Sergeant, though I do thank you for asking." Gremio bowed yet again.

The look Sergeant Thisbe sent him this time was a good deal more than odd. But, before the sergeant could say anything, horns blared from off to one side. Colonel Florizel bellowed, "Shift from column into line of battle! Move, move, move!"

"Hello!" Gremio exclaimed. "I still don't know where we're going, but now, at least, I've got some idea of what we're doing: we're going to fight." He raised his voice to a shout: "My company, shift from column into line! Move!"

They performed their evolutions with the automatic speed and precision endless hours on the practice field had drilled into them. As they moved, Thisbe asked, "*What* are we going to fight, sir? General Hesmucet's whole army?"

"To the hells with me if I know," Gremio answered. "One more thing we'll find out, I'm sure." If they were going up against Hesmucet's whole army, not many of them would come back from the encounter. He knew as much, as Thisbe was bound to. Neither of them dwelt on it.

Horns blared again. Colonel Florizel shouted, "Forward!"

Did he know what he was advancing against? Gremio was inclined to doubt it. The regimental commander ordered the men forward nonetheless.

When Gremio tramped past a stand of trees that had obscured his view, he discovered the Army of Franklin wasn't the only one that made mistakes. A couple of regiments of soldiers in gray had also formed line of battle, and were trying to scrape up breastworks and dig holes in the ground for themselves. "They must have been coming up from the south to reinforce Caesar," Gremio said.

"Why don't they surrender?" Thisbe said. "They haven't got a chance, not against so many men."

"I don't know," Gremio answered. Then, as he came closer to the embattled foe, he understood: "Oh. They're full of blonds."

"They're going to be full of dead blonds if they don't give up," Thisbe said.

"I don't think they think they *can* surrender," Gremio said. "They may be right, too. I haven't got much stomach for a massacre, but . . ." Plenty of soldiers in the Army of Franklin would—he was sure of that.

"King Avram!" the men in gray shouted. "King Avram and freedom!" No, they showed no sign of wanting to surrender. Some of them started singing "The Battle Psalm of the Kingdom."

How much fighting had they seen? How many men would they kill, could they kill, before they went down to death themselves? They seemed big and strong and ready to fight. Gremio knew perfectly well that the Army of Franklin couldn't afford the losses it would take subduing them. He also knew perfectly well his comrades couldn't walk away from the blonds. He sighed. He hated quandaries like that.

"Be careful," he called to his company. "Those bastards up ahead have nothing to lose. Don't throw yourselves away if you can help it. King Geoffrey needs every single one of us."

They weren't going to listen to him. He could tell at once, by the way they leaned forward, how eager they were to get into this skirmish. Some of them were liege lords themselves. Others aspired to estates with serfs. Blonds who bore

arms against Detinans contradicted everything they held dear
and conjured up pictures of peasant revolts. Now the
northerners had a chance to make the blonds pay, and they
were going to take it.

As usual, soldiers from both sides started shooting too
soon. Coming into crossbow range of each other, though,
didn't take long. Gremio hated the sound of quarrels hum-
ming past his ear. He hated even more the flat, unemphatic
smack they made when they slapped into flesh. And the
sounds that came from a man who'd been shot . . . He hated
those most of all.

Blonds ahead began falling. Gremio wondered how many
of them came from the southron provinces and how many
were runaway serfs. He couldn't very well pause and ask.
All he could do was run toward them waving an officer's
sword that wouldn't do him a bit of good till he got close
enough for them to have a fine chance of killing him, too.
The more he thought about it, the stupider a way to pass
his time this seemed.

However much he wanted to, though, he couldn't go
back. Even if his superiors didn't crucify him for cowardice, he'd never again be able to hold up his head among
men. That mattered to him more than the possibility of
getting shot. Not for the first time, he wondered why it
should.

Beside him, Thisbe said, "It's a good thing they're all
crossbowmen. We couldn't charge them like this if they had
pikemen with them."

"Oh, yes, a very good thing—a bloody wonderful thing,"
Gremio said in tones of something less than complete
enthusiasm.

Sergeant Thisbe's laugh abruptly turned into a yelp of
pain. Instead of running, the underofficer took a couple of
staggering steps and crashed to the ground, clutching at his
left leg.

Gremio skidded to a stop just beyond him. "Go on, sir,"
Thisbe said. "Go on. I'll be all right." He tried to get to
his feet, tried and failed. The left leg of his pantaloons
started to turn red. He began crawling away from the fight
ahead.

"Here, I'll help you." Gremio knelt beside him. "Give me your arm. I'll heave you upright, and you can use your good leg for a little ways. We've got to get you back to the healers, get that wound seen to."

Thisbe waved him away, repeating, "Go on, sir. I'll be all right."

"Sergeant, give me your arm," Gremio said in a voice harsher than he'd ever used with Thisbe. "That is an order."

Thisbe looked as if he wanted to argue further, but then the wound must have twinged again, for he winced and nodded. "Yes, sir."

"That's better." Gremio put the underofficer's arm over his shoulder. "Let me have some help from your good leg if you can, Sergeant." He straightened. Thisbe wasn't a big man. Gremio had less trouble getting him up than he'd expected. "Come on," he said.

"Sir, I don't want to go to the healers," Thisbe said.

"What you want doesn't matter very much right now, Sergeant," Gremio said. "What you need matters, and what you need is healing. I'll get you there, never fear."

"Sir, could you bandage me yourself?" Thisbe asked desperately. "By all the gods, sir, I'll give you anything you like, anything at all, if only you don't take me to the healers."

"Why are you so afraid of them?" Gremio asked. "Is it for the same reason you never wanted to be promoted, no matter how much you deserve it?"

He was talking only to distract Thisbe from his pain, but the underofficer seized on his words and gave him a quick, urgent nod. "Yes, for just the same reason, sir! Don't take me there, I beg you!"

Gremio used his free hand to scratch his head. If ever a man seemed in earnest, Thisbe was the one. "What is this precious reason of yours, sergeant?" the company commander asked.

Something more like fear than pain twisted Thisbe's face. "I can't tell you, sir. I don't dare tell you. I don't dare tell anybody."

What was that supposed to mean? Gremio started to come out and ask the question, then stopped with the words unspoken. He'd had an arm around Thisbe for some little while now, while Thisbe had had one around him. The sergeant didn't usually care to be touched. This time, there'd been no choice. Gremio thought he understood now why Thisbe had fought shy of it before. What he thought was madness, but there were times when madness made more sense than anything else. What he saw, what he heard— he could be wrong about all of that. What he felt? No. Madness or not, he thought it was true.

"Sergeant, I'll look at your wound," he said. "If I think I can just bandage it, I'll do that. If I think it has to go to the healers to save your life, I'll take you there. That's the best I can offer, because I don't—I especially don't— want to lose you."

"I suppose it'll have to do, sir." Despite pain, the underofficer picked up nuance. "Especially?" How much dismay was in that voice?

"Especially," Gremio said firmly. He eased Thisbe down to the ground. "I'm going to look at the wound now. And then, Sergeant, I think you have a lot—a *lot*—of explaining to do."

Thisbe let out a long, long sigh and then nodded. "Yes, sir."

Lieutenant General Bell nodded happily to his aide-de-camp. "By the gods, Major, I know where I'm going again."

"I'm glad to hear it, sir," Major Zibeon answered. "Where *are* you going? Is the Army of Franklin going with you?"

"It certainly is," Bell answered. "The time has come for the Army of Franklin to return to the province from which it takes its name. Franklin has groaned under the southron yoke since the war was young. High time it should be liberated from the hated, hateful foe."

"Er—yes, sir," Zibeon said. "How do you propose to arrange that, sir?"

"How? I'll tell you how. By marching straight to Rambler-ton and taking it away from the enemy, that's how," Bell answered. "We can do it. We're ahead of Hesmucet. What have the southrons got in Franklin? A few piddling garrisons, that's all. Ned of the Forest's riders have driven them mad. When a real army erupts in their midst, they'll run like rabbits."

Major Zibeon didn't say anything. He didn't say anything at all. He looked from one map to another in Bell's farmhouse headquarters, then turned away. He walked out into the cold rain, still without a word. He didn't even shake his head. He simply walked away.

Bell started to call back his dour aide-de-camp. He didn't. He let Zibeon leave. Calling him back would have meant wrangling with him, and Bell had had all the wrangling he could stand for a while. He felt as weary as a man bowed under the burden of twice his years. And his leg—or rather, the phantom still haunting the place where his leg had formerly dwelt—began to burn like fire.

The pain wasn't real. How could it be, when the leg itself was gone a few inches below the hip? But, real or not, it hurt him. Not to put too fine a point on things, it tormented him. Cursing under his breath, he groped for his little bottle of laudanum.

He found it, pulled it from the tunic pocket where it hid—and dropped it. Had his left hand been in working order, he might have caught it. But, as far as movement went, his left hand—his whole left arm—was as much a phantom as his amputated leg. The bottle, the precious laudanum, thumped down on the rammed-earth floor.

Being made of thick glass, it didn't break. Bell cursed in good earnest nonetheless. How the hells was he supposed to recover the drug for which his body screamed? For a whole man, it would have been the work of a moment. But then, a whole man wouldn't have needed the laudanum so desperately as he did himself, and he was anything but whole.

Later, he realized he could have asked one of the young, hale sentries outside the door to retrieve the little bottle. That was later. At the moment, only two thoughts went through his head: *I need the drug* and *I can do it myself, gods damn it*. Mutilated or not, he remained as stubborn in his pursuit of independence as did the northern kingdom Geoffrey ruled.

And so Bell made his slow way over to the iron-framed

cot on which he slept. He eased himself down till he was
sitting on the floor beside it. Propping his crutches carefully against the cot, he stretched out at full length and
began an inchworm's progress toward the laudanum.

In fact, his progress was more like that of an inchworm
which had been stepped on but wasn't quite dead. Crawling
didn't go well, not with one good arm and one leg with
which to work. He tried to roll, but his ruined left shoulder
let out a horrible shriek at the very idea. He ended up
hitching forward again and again while lying on his right
side.

He felt like shouting when his questing fingers closed on
the little bottle. He drew the cork with his teeth and poured
down a long draught—a draught that would have sent him
into oblivion a few months before. But his tolerance was
more than it had been; even such a heroic dose took its
own sweet time bringing him relief.

As always, the laudanum made him feel as if he were
floating on air. But whatever he felt, in truth he remained
on the floor. He had to hitch his way back to the cot in
the same fashion he'd used to get the bottle. Then he pulled
himself up onto the cot with his good arm. The strength
that required was one more thing he didn't think about.
It was just something he had to do, and he did it.

Having done it, he lay there panting for a little while.
Then he made one more urgent effort and sat up.

"Oh, by the gods!" he said. He hadn't been down on
a dirt floor for a while, or thought about what moving
across one on his side and belly would do to his uniform.
It was thoroughly filthy. *I'm probably filthy, too,* he thought.

He brushed at himself. Dust flew from his tunic and
pantaloons in a choking cloud, as if his hand were an army
on the road in a summertime drought. After a while, the
uniform looked . . . less grimy than it had. He used his good
arm and remaining leg to heave himself upright, then stood
swaying till he got the crutches in position under his arms.
That done, he went over to a chest of drawers, found a
rag, and sat down at a table on which stood a pitcher of
water. He wet the rag and daubed at his face. Before long,
the rag, which had been white, turned the red-orange of

the dirt floor. He dared hope that meant his face took on its normal color and appearance.

His hope was tested as soon as one of the sentries came in. The man didn't stare or gape or point or exclaim, so Bell supposed he'd made himself at least tolerably presentable once more. *You went through all that for the drug?* he wondered. But he would have endured worse humiliations for the relief—and the pleasure—laudanum brought him, and he knew it.

"Sir, there's a colonel of unicorn-riders, a fellow named Biffle, outside who'd like to see you," the sentry said.

"Oh, good," Bell said. "Yes, I've been expecting him. Send him in, by all means."

"I'll do it," the sentry said. "Don't you go anywhere, now."

As if I could, Bell thought as the soldier went outside. Colonel Biffle came in a moment later. He was a tall, solidly made man with a high forehead and a long black beard. He wore a uniform so old and faded, it might almost have been southron gray. Saluting, he said, "Good to see you looking so hale, sir."

"Thank you." Bell didn't feel particularly hale, and doubted he ever would again, but he inclined his head at the compliment. Then he asked, "And how is Ned of the Forest?"

"He's very fine, thank you kindly, and about two days' ride east of here with all his riders," replied Colonel Biffle, who was one of the famous northern officer's regimental commanders. "We had ourselves a busy time out in the east by the Great River, so we did."

"Yes, I heard about some of that," Bell said. "You smashed up a southron army twice your size in Great River Province—"

"Three times our size, sir, easy," Biffle said with a reminiscent grin. "Smashed 'em up and made 'em run for Luxor with their tails between their legs. And we raided Luxor our ownselves, and almost nabbed the southron general commanding in his bed, but the son of a bitch managed to sneak away in his nightshirt." He had a rustic northern accent. By all accounts, Ned of the Forest's was thicker still. But

neither Ned's accent nor his unsavory past as a serfcatcher
had kept King Geoffrey from promoting him to lieutenant
general, though he'd begun the war as a common soldier.

Bell nodded. "I heard something about that, yes. And I
heard something more about your raid down into Cloviston—
wasn't there a place called Fort Cushion, on the Great
River?"

"Yes, sir." Colonel Biffle nodded, too, though his face
turned grim. "That was a nasty business. Most of the garrison in the place were blonds. Their officers surrendered
them, and then they started fighting again. Can't have that
sort of thing going on. We didn't leave a whole lot of them
alive."

"I heard bits and pieces about the 'Fort Cushion massacre,' yes—that's what the southron papers call it, you understand," Bell said. "If you ask me, the blonds surely had it
coming. If they try to face their betters with weapons in
their hands, such things *will* happen."

Colonel Biffle visibly relaxed. "Glad you see it that way,
sir. Ned didn't give the order to kill the bastards, but I
can't say he was sorry it happened, either."

"Who could be sorry about getting rid of blonds? We just
smashed a couple of regiments of them ourselves," Bell said,
and then got down to business: "You tell me Ned is two
days away?"

"That's right." Biffle nodded again.

"Excellent, Colonel." Bell felt as happy as anything but
his drugs could make him. "I look forward to his joining
us. We'll show the stinking southrons there's still life in
Geoffrey's men."

"Er—yes, sir." Colonel Biffle coughed a couple of times,
then went on, "Uh, sir, Lieutenant General Ned, he asked
me to ask you, just what have you got in mind once you
put his unicorn-riders together with your army?"

"What have I got in mind?" Bell struck a pose. "I'll tell
you what I've got in mind, by the gods. I aim to lift the
southrons' yoke from Franklin, reconquer Ramblerton, sweep
down into the province of Cloviston—my home province, I'll
have you know—roll on to the Highlow River, and then,
again with the help of the gods, cross the river and attack

the town of Horatii in Highlow Province." *That'll impress him,* Bell thought.

But Biffle remained unimpressed. "No, sir," he said. "Sorry, sir. That's not what Ned of the Forest had in mind— not even a little bit. What he meant was, what do you aim to do about Brigadier Spinner? The two of them, they purely don't get along. Lord Ned swore a great oath he'd never fight alongside Spinner again, on account of Spinner stole his best men after the battle by the River of Death. That was one more of Thraxton the Braggart's nasty little tricks."

Bell grunted. There lay his glorious vision of northern triumph, shot dead by a petty political squabble. Or perhaps not so petty: he remembered rumors that had slid through the Army of Franklin while he was recovering from his amputation. Now, maybe, he could find out if those rumors held any truth. "Tell me," he said, "did Ned of the Forest really challenge Count Thraxton to a duel?"

"He did, sir. By the gods, sir, he did. I was standing closer to him than I am to you right now, and I heard it with my own ears," Biffle answered. "He made the challenge, and Thraxton didn't have the stones to answer it."

"Isn't that interesting?" Lieutenant General Bell murmured. As his maneuvers against Joseph the Gamecock proved, he wasn't above political squabbling himself. Having a weapon to use against Thraxton the Braggart might come in handy. You never could tell.

"I want you to know, sir, Lord Ned, he's dead serious about this business," Colonel Biffle said. "He said, 'Biff, you tell that fellow—if I'm stuck under Spinner, I'll stay down here in Franklin and give the southrons a hard time all by my lonesome.' His very words, sir; Lion God claw me if I lie."

"He would disobey a superior's direct order?" Bell rumbled ominously.

That didn't impress Ned of the Forest's regimental commander, either. "He's disobeyed a whole great pile of them in his time, Ned has," he replied, "and usually he's come off better on account of it."

"I ought to send him packing for dickering with me like this," Bell said. Colonel Biffle only shrugged. Plainly, he didn't care one way or the other. However difficult Ned of the Forest was, Bell knew him to be a genius at handling unicorns. Brigadier Spinner was competent enough, but nobody had ever accused him of genius, and nobody ever would. No matter how grandiose Bell's visions, he also knew he needed all the help he could get to bring them off. He plucked at his beard. "You may tell Lieutenant General Ned that I will place Brigadier Spinner on detached duty harrying General Hesmucet's men here in Peachtree Province. Will that satisfy him?"

"Yes, sir," Biffle said. "I'm sure of it."

"All right," Lieutenant General Bell said. "We'll do it that way, then." It wasn't all right. He had every intention of writing King Geoffrey about it. But, while that would put him on the record and make him feel better, Ned of the Forest was unlikely to get excited about it. Ned did what *he* wanted, not what anyone else wanted. No, Bell didn't like bargaining with subordinates. But no matter what he liked, he couldn't afford to lose this one.

Now that Biffle had got what he—or rather, Ned—wanted, he was all courtesy himself. He gave Bell a smart salute and said, "I'll head back to Lord Ned fast as my unicorn can take me, sir, and we'll see you in a little more than two days' time."

"Good," Bell said. He hardly noticed Colonel Biffle leave the farmhouse. He was looking south with his mind's eye, looking south toward the victory that had eluded him in Peachtree Province, looking south toward glory.

Doubting George was gnawing on some pork ribs when Colonel Andy ducked into his pavilion. George's adjutant looked even more like an irate chipmunk than usual. "Sir," he said, "there's a messenger from General Hesmucet waiting outside. You're ordered to the commanding general's head-quarters at once."

"Well, if I'm ordered, I should probably go, eh?" Doubting George heaved his bulk off the folding chair where he was sitting. "And if it's at once, I probably shouldn't finish dinner first. You're welcome to the rest of the ribs, Colonel. They're mighty good."

"It's not right, sir," Andy said in injured tones.

"What? The ribs?" George said. "You might as well eat 'em. Gods only know when I'll get back."

"No, not the ribs," Colonel Andy snapped. "The ribs have nothing to do with it. The orders General Hesmucet's going to give you—they're not right."

"Well, maybe they are and maybe they aren't," Doubting George replied. "But, right or wrong, they're legal and binding, because he's the commanding general. If I didn't believe in following legal and binding orders, I'd be fighting for King Geoffrey today, wouldn't I? And then you'd want to kill me."

"Never, sir," Andy said stiffly.

"Oh, of course you would—I'd be the enemy," George said. "But I'm not, and I don't intend to be. And so . . . I'm off to General Hesmucet's. Enjoy the ribs." He left before his adjutant could carp any more.

Trouble is, I agree with every word Andy's saying, George thought as he climbed aboard his unicorn. But, whether he agreed or not, he could obey Hesmucet or he could go home. After a moment, he shook his head. He couldn't even go home. Over in Parthenia, the traitors still held the estate they'd confiscated.

Hesmucet's aides and sentries saluted when he rode up to them. When he dismounted, one of them took charge of the unicorn. Another one said, "General Hesmucet will see you right away."

"Well, good," George said agreeably, "because I'm going to see him."

"Hello, George," Hesmucet said when his second-in-command went into the pavilion. The general commanding quivered—he practically glowed—with excitement. George knew what was coming even before he spoke: "I've got it, by the gods! Marshal Bart and King Avram have given me leave to march across Peachtree, tear up everything in the way, and take Veldt."

"Congratulations, sir," Doubting George said. "I trust you'll send me a postcard or two as you go?"

Hesmucet coughed and turned red. "I told you, Lieutenant General, I need someone I can count on in Franklin, to keep Bell from making mischief."

"Yes, you told me that," George said. "Just because you told it to me, though, doesn't mean I have to like it."

"Whom else could I send?" Hesmucet asked him. "After me, you're the next best general we've got here. I am taking what I think is the most important job ahead of us. I'm leaving you what I think is the next most important job. That strikes me as fair."

"Who knows?" Doubting George shrugged. "The groom has the most important job on his wedding day, the best man the second-most. But I'll tell you one thing, sir: the groom has a lot more fun."

"Not necessarily. No, not necessarily, by the gods," Hesmucet said. "Remember, you'll still have Bell to deal with. And so, with any luck at all, we'll both get to screw the traitors." He threw back his head and laughed. "You give me so many of your sly little stories. This time, I got in my own punch line."

"Yes, sir," George said resignedly. He'd known this was going to happen. Now it had, and he had to make the best of it. "What sort of force will you leave me to defend Franklin?"

"Well, for one thing, you'll have all the garrisons already posted through the province," Hesmucet said expansively.

"Oh, happy day," Doubting George replied in a hollow voice. He knew—and Hesmucet surely knew, too—that the garrisons in Franklin were a case where the whole was much less than the sum of its parts. They were enough to hold northern raiders at bay. Against the Army of Franklin . . . George didn't want to think about that. Some of those garrison soldiers hadn't done any real fighting in years. "What else have you got for me? Something, I hope."

"Oh, yes." ·Hesmucet nodded brightly. "I've ordered a good solid division to come west from across the Great River. But they're a little occupied right now, what with Earl Price of Sterling's unicorn raid down into ShowMe."

"Splendid. Nothing plus nothing equals nothing," Doubting George said. "If I'm going to defend Franklin against a real live army, shouldn't I have at least part of a real live army of my own?"

"Oh, I suppose so." By the way Hesmucet sounded, he

didn't really suppose any such thing, but was humoring a willful subordinate. He went on, "I'll give you half of the wing you've been commanding. I intend to take all of Absalom the Bear's men with me."

"What?" George felt on the point of bursting with outrage. "Half? And the worse half, at that?"

"Half," Hesmucet said. "*And* I'll give you Hard-Riding Jimmy and his brigade of unicorn-riders, all of them carrying these fancy new quick-shooting crossbows."

"Hard-Riding Jimmy's still wet behind the ears," George said, which was true: the officer couldn't have been much above twenty-five.

"If you don't want him, I'll be glad to keep him."

"I didn't mean *that*, sir," George said quickly. Yes, Jimmy was young. Yes, he'd been a staff officer till not very long ago. But he'd shown signs of making a good fighting soldier, his riders were very tough . . . and George doubted he'd get any other men if he didn't take Jimmy's.

Hesmucet smiled at him. "I thought you were a good, sensible fellow. So that's all settled, then."

He sounded perfectly happy. *And why shouldn't he?* George thought. He'd settled everything to his own satisfaction. George was the one left with the odds and ends of military meat. He said, "Give me one other thing."

"What's that?" All of a sudden, Hesmucet didn't sound so happy any more.

"Give me John the Lister, too, as my second-in-command."

Sure enough, the idea seemed to affront Hesmucet. He said, "John's a fine officer. I had in mind taking him along with me."

"I'm sure you did," George said. "But you're taking everything you want and leaving me with nothing but dribs and drabs. You say you count on me to keep order in Franklin and make sure Bell doesn't steal the place while I'm not looking. Well, I need somebody I can count on, too. Give me John the Lister, gods damn it."

When had someone last presumed to swear at the general commanding? Not for a while, unless Doubting George missed his guess—probably not since Fighting Joseph decided he was underappreciated and so spectacularly left King

Avram's service. Hesmucet did take it pretty well. He
scowled, but didn't growl when he might well have. And,
in the end, he nodded. "All right, take him. I may not like
it, but you make good sense."

"I thank you, sir," George said. "To the seven hells with
me if I think Brigadier John will thank you—or me. He's
got to be looking forward to marching across Peachtree
himself. But somebody has to stay and do the dirty jobs."
He chuckled. "And besides, misery loves company."

"It may be a dirty job, but it's an important one,"
Hesmucet said. "If Bell comes, he'll come full force, and
you're the best defensive fighter I've got."

"Flattery won't get you far, sir," George said.

"It's not flattery. It's the truth. Standing on the defensive, you're as good as anybody on either side of this gods-
damned war. When it comes to putting in an attack, I'd
choose some other men before you."

"Tell that to the traitors who tried to hold Proselytizers'
Ridge against my men, sir," Doubting George said hotly.

"Well, you have a point—of sorts," Hesmucet said. "But
you got a little help from Thraxton the Braggart, you know."

He was right about that. However much Doubting George
wished to deny it, he couldn't. He did the next best thing,
saying, "You'll find out whether I can manage an attack
or not, by the gods. You wait and see."

"I look forward to doing just that, Lieutenant General.
With any luck at all, we'll both smash up the traitors. And
if we can do that, and if Marshal Bart can keep the Army
of Southern Parthenia bottled up in Pierreville—well, if all
that happens, the war's within shouting distance of being
over."

Doubting George couldn't very well deny that, either, nor
did he want to. Instead of telling Hesmucet to go to the
seven hells, which was what he wanted to do, he gave him
a precise salute. "If you'll excuse me, sir, I'll start getting
ready to move with what you've so generously left me."

Again, Hesmucet refused to take offense. "If thinking I'm
a first-class son of a bitch makes you meaner, Lieutenant
General, then go right ahead, and I hope you get some good
from it."

Muttering, George ducked out of the commanding general's pavilion. Muttering, he mounted his unicorn and rode back to his own headquarters. Muttering still, he dismounted and tied up the beast. Colonel Andy came over to him. "Well, sir?" the adjutant asked.

"Not very well, as a matter of fact," Doubting George replied. "I get half my present command, along with every soldier in every garrison in Franklin—and a division tied up across the Great River. Put them all together, and they add up to . . . not bloody much."

Andy cursed with surprising fluency and passion for a small, round, chubby-cheeked man. "Justice is dead. No, by the gods, justice is murdered. And we both know who killed it," he said.

"It can't be helped," George said. Andy looked at him as if he'd just turned traitor. He still wasn't happy—he was anything but happy—but he went on, "Hesmucet's right: the job needs doing. He chose me to do it, that's all. Someone has to. I've just got to make the best of it."

"For that job, he could have chosen any general," his adjutant declared. "Why did he have to pick you?" He answered his own question: "To keep you from going along with him, that's why."

"I thought that, too," George said. "It made me furious, let me tell you: so furious, I almost drew blade on him. But then I asked him for John the Lister as *my* second-in-command, and I began to understand."

"Which is, sir, more than I can say I do," Colonel Andy sniffed.

"Think on it," Doubting George told him. "I wanted at least one good, solid officer to help me, because I can't be everywhere at once. If he'd left me Absalom, I wouldn't have asked for John, and I wouldn't have made a fuss till I gods-damned well got him."

"I still don't understand a word you're saying," Andy replied.

"Hesmucet did the same thing I did," George explained. "I want John the Lister to back me up. Hesmucet wants someone he's sure he can trust to back him up—and I happen to be the man. It's a compliment, of sorts."

"Of sorts," Andy echoed bitterly. "He marches off toward Veldt, and if that goes well the bards will sing of it for the next hundred years and more. And you go back to Ramblerton, and when has anybody ever won glory by going back instead of forward? For all you know, for all Hesmucet knows, Bell won't try to come south at all. You can march your garrison back and forth, back and forth, through the mud. Happy day!"

That had also occurred to Doubting George. He wished his adjutant hadn't spelled it out quite so plainly. "It's the chance I take. I have to make the best of it. And if Bell doesn't come south, maybe I'll be able to move north after the Army of Franklin myself. Who knows?"

They hashed over possibilities for a while. Little by little, both George and Andy grew resigned, perhaps even mollified. As Andy said, "You kept the Army of Franklin from wrecking us altogether by the River of Death, more than a year ago now. Maybe it's fitting that you be the one to finish it off."

"If I can." Doubting George started to say something more, then pointed. "Someone's riding this way in a hells of a hurry. Wonder who that could be."

"Looks like John the Lister," Andy replied after a brief pause.

"Why so it does," said George, who was anything but surprised. As John reined in, George raised his voice: "Hello, John. What brings you here?"

"You do, you—" With visible effort, John the Lister restrained himself . . . to a degree. "You're the reason I can't go west, gods damn it." He was red with fury all the way to the top of his bald head.

"I am sorry about that, Brigadier. I truly am." George meant it. He spent the next quarter of an hour calming the irate John and explaining exactly why he'd chosen him.

John the Lister was a capable—and, even more to the point, a sensible—man. As George had before him, he listened and, a bit at a time, calmed down. At last, he said, "Well, I still don't love you for it, but I can see why you did it. If Bell does bring his men south—and what other move has he got left?—we'd better be able to stop him. He won't get through us, eh?"

"I doubt he will," Doubting George replied. "By all the gods, John, I doubt it very much."

HYSTERICAL NOTE

Although *Marching Through Peachtree* is purely a work of fiction, with no connection whatsoever to anything that ever happened in the real world (oh, come on, of course it is—it says so right here on the box), my Kindly Editor has for some reason or other prevailed upon me (using no undue force at all: certainly none that would leave a mark) to offer the following reminiscence culled from the annals of our own Civil War.

In May 1864, U.S. General William Tecumseh Sherman marched south and east from Chattanooga, Tennessee, against C.S. General Joseph Johnston's army, which was drawn up in front of Dalton, Georgia, on the railroad leading south towards Atlanta. Sherman tried to trap Johnston by attacking at a gap called the Buzzard Roost to pin him down and at the same time outflanking him and seizing the railroad at Resaca, thirteen miles farther south. This didn't quite work; Johnston executed a skillful retreat and lived to fight another day—many other days, in fact.

It also set the tone for the rest of the campaign down to Atlanta. Johnston bought time by yielding space, while Sherman continually tried to get around his flank and get between his army and the vital railroad and manufacturing center of Atlanta that he was defending. At a place called Kingston, Johnston also discovered that one of his corps commanders, John Bell Hood, who had a reputation for aggressiveness, wouldn't always obey a direct order to attack, even when the situation seemed advantageous. Hood, unbeknownst to Johnston, had a brief of his own: he wanted command of Johnston's army, and Jefferson Davis rather wanted him to have it, for Davis didn't trust Johnston, and feared he would keep right on retreating without fighting, as Davis believed—for the most part unjustly—he'd done in the past.

There were further clashes near Allatoona pass and near Dallas, with both sides learning the value of entrenchments. Johnston had slaves prepare trenches for his men in advance, and when he was forced out of one position he simply fell back to another at least as strong. In front of Marietta, at a place called Pine Mountain, Sherman saw a group of Confederate officers looking down at his men, and ordered his artillery to fire on them; a shell killed Bishop Leonidas Polk, one of Johnston's corps commanders. Sherman soon tried a frontal attack at Kennesaw Mountain—tried it and saw it bloodily repulsed. Sherman began the game of outflanking again, and by doing so forced Johnston out of the position that could not be taken by frontal assault.

Johnston fell back behind the Chattahoochee River, the last major barrier in front of Atlanta. But Sherman's men broke through Johnston's cavalry screen and got two divisions of infantry across the river before the Confederates realized they had done so. The last barrier turned, Johnston had to fall back into Atlanta itself. Johnston understood—certainly better than Davis did—that holding Atlanta was potent politically, especially as the USA had a Presidential election coming up. But when he proposed to hold Atlanta with militia and use his main army as a mobile force to strike at the Federal troops, Davis took counsel with Braxton Bragg (something he was in the habit of doing, and something that went a long way toward losing the war for him), sacked Johnston, and replaced him with Hood.

The one thing Sherman dreaded above all else was having Nathan Bedford Forrest's cavalry turned loose against his long supply line back to Chattanooga. That never quite happened, for Union forces kept Forrest too busy elsewhere to attack it. They were defeated quite consistently—and, at Brice's Crossroads in Mississippi, spectacularly—but even losing, they kept Forrest from doing what he most needed to do . . . and, by then, the Confederacy had little margin for error.

Hood went out and attacked Sherman as ferociously as he could—attack was the one thing he knew how to do. He fought him at Peachtree Creek, on the Decatur road, and at Ezra Church—and, by the time he was done, he'd lost about a third of his army and any hope of holding Atlanta. Sherman's men forced Confederate General Hardee's men off the railroad south of the city at Jonesboro, and on September 1, forced with the choice of losing Atlanta or of losing Atlanta and all that was left of his army, Hood abandoned the city. The war took a long step closer to being won.

Hood then assailed Sherman's railroad lifeline back to Atlanta himself, trying to make the Federal forces starve. He moved as far back up as Resaca, and Sherman followed. Then Sherman decided to forget about both Hood and his own supply line and march east to the sea across Georgia, while Hood, joined at last—and much too late—by Forrest's cavalry—planned to move north against Nashville and, with luck, to the Ohio River. The stage was set for the last major act of the war in the west.